THE

HERO

COMPLEX

THE

HERO

COMPLEX

HELEN COMERFORD

BLOOMSBURY

LONDON OXFORD NEW YORK NEW DELHI SYDNEY

BLOOMSBURY YA
Bloomsbury Publishing Plc
50 Bedford Square, London WC1B 3DP, UK
Bloomsbury Publishing Ireland Limited
29 Earlsfort Terrace, Dublin 2, D02 AY28, Ireland

BLOOMSBURY, BLOOMSBURY YA and the Diana logo
are trademarks of Bloomsbury Publishing Plc

First published in Great Britain in 2025 by Bloomsbury Publishing Plc

A catalogue record for this book is available from the British Library

ISBN: PB: 978-1-5266-6763-2; eBook: 978-1-5266-6765-6;
ePDF: 978-1-5266-6764-9

2 4 6 8 10 9 7 5 3 1

Typeset by RefineCatch Limited, Bungay, Suffolk

Printed and bound in Great Britain by CPI Group (UK) Ltd, Croydon CR0 4YY

MIX
Paper | Supporting
responsible forestry
FSC® C013604

To find out more about our authors and books visit www.bloomsbury.com
and sign up for our newsletters
For product safety related questions contact productsafety@bloomsbury.com

For all the nerds with heroic hearts
(Especially Gareth)

CHAPTER 1

'*There was a time when I could have just been a hero.*
But my past … my past is a pair of shoes I thought I could
wear in.
I have been crushed. Reshaped by loss. Hardened by the
pinch in my soul.
Now, when I see your dark desires, I understand …
Criminals, I see you.
There is no shadow that will hide you, not from me.
I am more than a hero—'

'Joy!' I hiss. 'If you don't stop monologuing, we're going to get
caught.'

'Urgh. Fine.' The dark statue brooding over the quiet high
street morphs back into my best friend as she makes her careful
way over to me. We chose the flat roof of the shoe shop Size
Nines as our lookout, but it's still a long way to the cobbles below.

'That gravel voice is going to damage your vocal cords.' I hold out an arm and steady her as she joins me to sit by the fire exit.

Joy makes her voice even huskier. *'You're no fun tonight, Jenna Ray.'*

'Psssht.' My head thuds gently off the door. I never knew that boredom could make your eyes sting. 'I'm starting to wonder why heroes do this whole hanging-out-on-the-top-of-a-building thing.' I reach into one of the many pockets of the black combat trousers that I bought for our vigilante nights. 'Crisp?'

'I'm pretty sure it's for the silhouette.' Joy takes a handful and winces as the crinkle of the packet echoes through the night. 'We should get stealthier snacks.'

Joy might be developing her tortured vigilante alter ego, but my insides are heavy with the weight of doing nothing. It has been two months since I defeated King Ron with my surprising new power of controlling water. Two months since I announced to the world that I was a hero. Now I've got no idea who I am. The media have started referring to me as *The Jenna Ray Issue*. I am an Issue, not a Love Interest, not an official HPA hero and definitely not normal. That's never going to be an option again. Even though I steer clear of busy places, I am constantly asked if I'm Jenna Ray. I've said no so many times, even my name doesn't feel like mine any more.

At least on these nights with Joy, I can just be a teenage girl, eating crisps on a slightly damp roof, watching another stag party weave across the cobbles. Who knew that after our town survived its prophecy, it would become the must-visit location for stag and hen dos? On our first night as vigilantes we rescued a drunk stag partier who fell into the harbour. Joy distracted his mates, whilst I dived in and pulled the man out by his Babygro.

Although I barely used my powers to rescue the adult baby, we thought that we'd cracked the whole 'how to hero without the HPA' thing. But now we've dedicated a fortnight of our summer to late-night heroism and no one else has needed saving. Not even a cat stuck up a tree. It's becoming painfully clear that the residents of Nine Trees don't wait for the cover of night to carry out nefarious deeds. They watch the news and then go to bed.

'Maybe one of them will fall in the river?' Joy crosses her fingers and leans forward to watch two of the stag party have a play fight on the Harbour Bridge.

'Maybe.' What am I doing waiting here patiently for another drunk person to take a dip? Maybe my hero name should be the Lifeguard. If we went to the city, I could help people, but the registration chip in my wrist flags when I leave Nine Trees. Going to the city in the middle of the night will ring alarm bells, and the British Heroics and Power Authority stopped imploding long enough to make it quite clear that if I use my powers in public, they'll come down on me like the charred remains of the Culture Complex.

Joy sighs heavily as the stag party wander off the bridge and stagger out of sight. 'Fine, Nine Trees. I give up. You are too boring.' She squeezes the crisp in her fist into a fine powder. 'If I could have just punched someone evil. Even shouting something clever at them whilst you blasted them with water would have been enough. I needed something …' The crisp powder drifts into the night as Joy deflates, lowering her head on to her knees.

'Tea? I can crack open the emergency thermos?' Guilt twists in my gut as I scan the area. These vigilante nights were never just about me. All I need is a robbery or a lost child or anything at all to keep Joy distracted from—

'Nick messaged earlier.' Her voice is muffled by her trousers.

'Of course he did.' My lip curls. Nick. He broke my best friend's heart when he ended their relationship and left early for university, and now he won't leave her alone.

'His parents bought him a house. They bought him a *house* in Swansea, Jenna. He's going to stay there forever.'

'Maybe something bad will happen to his new home, like a very specific tidal wave,' I mutter, still scanning the area. 'Or maybe he'll keep having watery mishaps and go into all his lectures looking like he's wet himself …' Something draws my eye to the roof of the pub opposite. 'Joy,' I whisper. 'Can you see anything on that roof?'

There's another shift in the shadows by the Drunken Diviner's chimney, but it could be my imagination. The skin prickles across the back of my neck. This keeps happening: a sense that someone is there, just out of sight. That I'm being watched.

'There's nothing there.' Joy's eyes narrow as she gazes into the darkness. 'At least, I don't think there's anything there …'

A deafening buzz splits the air. My stomach flips and Joy grabs me.

'Skies! Joy, ow!' My phone vibrates again and I peel off her vice grip so I can find it.

'Why isn't that on silent?!' Joy exhales shakily. 'Or, if it's going to make noise, at least choose that tense droney sound all the action films use. Is it Megan?'

It's got to be my sister; she's the only person, apart from Joy, who would message me this late. I'll have to be careful opening her message up here. My best friend knows that Megan is away, but I haven't been able to tell her the real reason why.

Megan, the new Diviner who the HPA are so desperate to find, has been gone for weeks trying to figure out a prophecy. Six terrifying words that came back night after night, until she finally left.

Destroy the EV, destroy the world.

'I have to go north,' she told me, slinging stuff into a ruck-sack. 'I have to figure this out, Jen-bear. The EV, it's in us. It's in everything and if it disappears … I have to go.'

'I can help,' I'd tried, but she'd glared at the HPA chip scar on my wrist and left.

The door of the pub opens to expel another noisy group on to the street as I find my phone. It takes me two goes to unlock it and then … My heart tries to drop and leap at the same time and ends up sort of squeezing.

The messages aren't from Megan. They're from Blaze.

'They're, er … they're from …'

'What does he say?' Joy practically climbs on me trying to see my phone.

Hey Jenna, Just had a run-in with some EV pigeons! It's less fun without you! & the new HPA boss started today, maybe things will finally get sorted. ✌️

Also, you never replied about the combat drills. Are you still running them? I can send you a link for pads and gloves? Oops GTG x

Warmth hums through me as I picture him, soft lips pursed as he types. On the night of the storm, Blaze, the hero, told me he loved me, told me he liked me and told me his name, his real name, Laurie Lin, in that order. I haven't seen him since.

'It's just friendly.' I pass my phone over to Joy, trying to dampen the heat growing in my chest. When I finally see him again, I can't expect things to just pick up from that kiss in the ruins of the Culture Complex. He might not want that any more. 'That is just friendly, right?' I lean into Joy.

'Ow!' She rubs her arm. 'You gave me an electric shock.'

'Another one? Sorry.' I shuffle away, but Joy is already focused back on my fledgling-maybe-probably-not-though romance.

'Ray.' She frowns at me. 'I know you're new to this, but he says that you make facing psychotic birds fun. This is textbook flirting.'

A little bubble of hope grows in my chest. 'Oh, OK ... So, I'll reply?'

'Yes.' Joy nods encouragingly.

'And I'll say ...' This has to be perfect. I bite my lip. 'I'll say *Hey* ...'

'Nice.'

'*Blaze* ...'

'Good ...'

'*You all right?*' I glance at her.

'Mother Earth,' Joy mutters. 'Just give it here.'

'Wait.' I push the bright phone away from our faces.

Three men dressed head to toe in black, with scarves across their faces, slip from shadow to shadow along the high street. It is so obvious they are up to no good that they might as well be carrying a flashing neon BAD GUYS sign.

'Criminals!' Joy shakes my knee. 'It's happening! *Criminals emerging from the darkness, ready to unleash their—*'

'Shhh.' I lean forward to track them.

The biggest man, who could definitely be a rugby player if he wasn't a criminal, motions to the alley next to the pub and all three disappear into it. Joy grips my arm, jabbing her finger at the opening door of the Drunken Diviner. A silver-haired man stumbles out and swerves across the cobbles towards the Harbour Bridge. Joy's fingers sink into my bicep as the three criminals emerge from the shadows to follow him.

One of them pulls out a weapon.

'Mother Earth.' I'm up on my feet and my insides are buzzing. *Finally.* It's finally time to take action. 'We need to help him.'

'Come on.' Joy is already on her way to the rickety staircase.

We dart out on to the high street and stick to the shadows of the shopfronts, following as quietly as we can. Thank the

7

skies we already ate those crisps; a random rustle now and they'd spot us in a heartbeat. The silver-haired man meanders up and on to the bridge, stopping in the middle. He sways there with his hands in his pockets and river mist curling up around his ankles. It's almost as if he's waiting for something.

The criminals crouch by the entrance to the bridge and we duck into a bus stop a few metres behind.

'We need to move fast.' Their leader's whisper reaches our hiding place. 'Shoot first. Ask questions later.'

'They're going to kill him?!' Joy peers out, face set in a determined scowl.

'No.' I nudge her back into the shadows. 'Stay here.'

The mist has already thickened, turning the night a milky grey. The men in black are only just visible as they leap up and rush on to the bridge. A delighted laugh rings out from the silver-haired man and, for some reason, he claps at them before taking a step back and disappearing into the fog.

'Fire!' their leader yells, and shots ring out as the mist swallows them too.

'Stop!' I sprint after them. My hands are out, calling the water, and a powerful wave crashes on to the bridge to surge ahead of me. The flood must take everyone off their feet. Thuds and yells echo back through the fog.

There's a curse ahead and I slow as someone pushes themselves up in front of me. It's the enormous figure of the leader of the criminal gang. He's got his back to me, but he must hear me sloshing to a halt. He spins and steps into the orange glow of the street lamp. Water is running off him and I'm ready to blast him, but my gaze fixes on the three small letters embossed on his black top.

H

P

A

Feck.

The men in black aren't criminals.

They're HPA soldiers.

Did I just stop the HPA from arresting someone?

The big man storms towards me.

'I'm sorry—' I reach out a hand to dry him, but he grabs the front of my jumper with one hand and lifts me off the ground.

'Jenna Ray!' He peels his damp black scarf off his face to reveal a snarl. Any hope that he might not recognise the girl who just flooded the bridge evaporates. 'You are not allowed to use your powers in public.' The street lamp is more than bright enough to see the vein pulsing in his forehead. 'And you just used them against the HPA.'

The other two – soaking wet – soldiers wade through the ankle-high water and strings of seaweed to join us.

'Villain.' The smallest man has a red scar across his face. He spits harbour water out of his mouth as he raises his weapon to point it at me.

'Let her go!' Joy splashes her way towards us. 'Don't point that thing at me!' I can't see them, but the last soldier must be aiming at her. My fingers flex and the water swirling around the men's boots starts to rise. HPA or not, I'm not going to let them hurt Joy.

'All right, everyone, enough.' The silver-haired man marches over, the mist evaporating around him. 'Put her down, Sergeant Cadell.'

He has a heavy German accent, and as tipsy as he looked earlier, he's now completely alert, like swerving across the cobbles was an act. Like nothing here is what I thought it was.

Cadell's knuckles whiten on my jumper and there's a sharp tearing sound from the region of my armpit. Megan's *second date, keeping it casual* jumper won't be able to survive much more of this.

'Cadell.' The silver-haired man stops next to us. 'This seems like a misunderstanding. This young woman and her friend intervened in what looked like an attack. It's what you'd have done in her place, *ja*?'

Cadell grinds his teeth, but he drops me and I step back next to Joy.

'All right?' she murmurs.

'Uh-huh,' I reply.

'Ray.' The silver-haired man pushes past the soldiers, batting their weapons down, and sticks out a hand. 'I'm Tomas. These gentlemen were running an exercise; I was their target.'

I shake his hand. This Tomas might be important enough to order around HPA soldiers, but he smells faintly of beer and Cadell is still glaring at me from behind him. This isn't over. I flooded the harbour bridge. I used my powers against HPA soldiers. It doesn't matter how friendly Tomas seems, I am in a whole world of trouble.

'You hid from them in the pub?' Joy asks.

'It was a long day and an even longer exercise.' Tomas shrugs and offers Joy his hand too. 'Ms Jusic.'

'Yes, hello.' Joy shakes his hand before turning to me to mouth, *What is happening?*

'I think that will do for now, won't it, Sergeant Cadell?' Tomas yawns. 'Congratulations, you and your alpha team finally found me. Let's call in the rest of Squad One and go to our beds.'

'She's under arrest.' Cadell jabs a finger towards me and my heart sinks.

'Really?' Tomas sighs. 'We can call her in tomorrow. It's late. Perhaps you stopped for a nap mid-exercise, but I need my sleep. As do these young women.'

'She's under –' the tendons in Cadell's neck tighten as he spits the words out –'arrest. Cuff her, Corporal Armstrong.' Cadell nods at the man with the scar, who pulls out a pair of handcuffs.

'Fine.' Tomas holds out a hand to stop the corporal. 'Ms Jusic, it's been a pleasure. Go home. Ray, with me.'

'No,' I say at the same time as Joy blurts out, 'You can't take her.'

'She's—' Cadell steps towards us.

'*Ja, ja, ja*, she's under arrest. *We know.*' Tomas steps in front of me and leans in to whisper in my ear. 'It's easier if you come back to base with me. No handcuffs, no drama, nothing to report except a little misunderstanding.'

The desire to blast them all with harbour water, grab Joy and run simmers in my stomach, but how would that end? HPA

11

soldiers hunting me down, surrounding our house, helicopters circling, blowing the leaves off our neighbour's trees. Sydney Jones leaping out from behind a bush to report my dramatic capture to the world.

I clench my jaw. It looks like I'm heading back to the HPA.

CHAPTER 2

After they put a chip in my wrist, the HPA gave me a handbook called *So you've registered your powers, what next?* I wish I'd read past the '*Using your powers in public, and why that's a bad idea*' chapter. It probably has a section on what the HPA do to registered people who break their rules. At least then I'd know if they're going to lock me away under the museum, or even send me to the Castle, like Ron.

My stomach churns as Tomas puts a gentle hand on my shoulder and guides me across the bridge. I know the way and it's far too short. Cross the lapping water of the harbour, descend a stone set of stairs and there's the entrance to the HPA's subterranean base.

'I'll wake your dad up. We'll get you a lawyer!' Joy calls from behind Cadell's hulking figure. 'Don't you hurt her. I've got my camera ready.'

At least with Joy on the case, I can't disappear into the

HPA cells without anyone knowing what happened to me.

The water is mostly gone from the bridge now, but there's still seaweed strewn across the cobbles and I step over a drain that's bubbling in an unsettling way. Why did this all have to happen right next to the HPA? If they'd arrested me in the city, at least I'd have had the terrifying journey along the Wild Road to make a plan. And if I was still coming up empty, I could have leaped out of the car and taken my chances with the squirrels.

I breathe out *two, three, four.*

My forehead is sticky with sweat, but I need to keep calm. Keep breathing.

We reach the stairs and I try to remember the three-things exercise our counsellor gave us in our group session.

Name three things you can see:

The orange street lamps, the top of the stone steps down to the HPA, Cadell in the corner of my eye.

And exhale three times.

It's not helping. I clench and unclench my fists and try the next exercise.

Name three things you can hear:

Footsteps on the stairs. Cadell breathing. My pulse echoing in my ears.

Exhale three times.

I can't let this turn into a panic attack. The last time I had one, it felt like my power was trying to explode out of me.

Three more things I can see:

Security's glass door. The scanning booth. Mia.

'Mia?' I splutter as the glass doors swish open and we all troop in.

Mia lifts their eyebrows at me, glossy lips in a tight line. Their outfit is an unsettlingly conventional green jumpsuit and their black hair is pulled into a simple bun. There are dangly gold earrings that sweep down as far as their collarbone, but this is Mia at their most serious.

Back before Ron was arrested, Mia had usually seemed pleased to see me. They were always busy, running around doing pretty much everything, but they seemed to like me in their own slightly cynical way. Not any more. Now their dark eyes are hard. Maybe it's because I was working with the Villains last time I was here, or because I sent their boss to prison, or because I just attacked the HPA ... Skies, maybe it's all of the above?

'I'll take her from here.' Mia swipes open the door into the base and beckons to me. I hesitate, looking at the exit. This is my last chance to run, before I end up deep within the HPA. Big hands land on my shoulders, turn me and shove me towards the corridor so hard I lose my balance and land heavily on my hands and knees.

'Sergeant Cadell!' Tomas snaps.

Mia helps me back to my feet and turns to the men. 'Tomas, thank you. And Squad One, you're dismissed.'

'But—' Cadell booms from behind me.

'You are dismissed.' Mia's voice is icy. 'This way, Jenna.'

Mia leads me along the concrete corridor and past the windows that look down on the cavernous training studio where Blaze and I first kissed. At least Blaze didn't show up on the bridge.

15

I don't know if he'd have rushed to my rescue or been the one to bring me in. Probably the second, given his 'probation' status that the press have been speculating about. My heart is thrumming in my chest, but it hasn't had to deal with the embarrassment of being arrested by the boy I like, so that's something, I guess.

Halfway up the stairs I realise where we're going. Level -1. This is where the offices are. Where the new boss of the HPA must be. We head along the grey corridors that became so familiar as I went to Ron's office for my lessons in Hero Legacy. Why did I think being a vigilante was a good idea? Heroism always leads me back to Ron's door.

The gold plaque with his name has been removed but as Mia opens it, I still expect to see him standing behind his desk, dressed in an immaculate three-piece suit, shaking his head. *'Well, Miss Ray,'* he'd probably say. *'What have you done now?'* Or he'd reach out a hand and try and kill me again.

But the office is empty.

The wood panelling is gone.

The pop art is gone.

The plush red rug is gone.

Ron is gone.

His decadent space has become another brushed concrete HPA office with harsh lighting. The only souvenir from Ron's time is the dark wood desk at the far end which has been set up with new computer screens. The desk was always the most beautiful thing in here. I'd have kept it too.

'Go on,' Mia says.

My footsteps echo on the concrete as I cross the yawning

distance between the door and the desk. There are a couple of boxes with *office* scrawled on them by the wall, but otherwise there's nothing to give me any clues about this new person who holds my fate in their hands. I finally reach the metal chair in front of the desk and sit with my back rigid. Mia walks past me and I expect them to press a button and summon the terrifying new boss of the HPA from their bed, but instead they sit in Ron's old spot.

'So,' Mia says. 'What exactly did you think you were playing at?'

'You're in charge?' My mouth drops open. Mia is the new head of the HPA?

'Don't you dare smile, Jenna Ray!'

I clench my lips. 'I'm not.'

'You just got yourself arrested on my first day in charge!' Mia throws up their hands. 'What were you thinking?! You know you're not allowed to use your powers in public.'

I try the innocent press look that they taught me.

'Don't even *think* about lying to me.' Mia spins their computer screen so I can see a grainy CCTV feed of the Harbour Bridge, where the drains now look like fountains, gushing water back on to the road. 'You were the top of my list. The first thing I was going to address as the new head of the HPA. You couldn't have given me a day to get settled before pulling something like this?'

'How?' I blurt out, and they raise their eyebrows. 'I mean, how are you in charge?'

'You want to know about the interview process?'

'No, but you were in wardrobe …' I bite my lip. I don't want to annoy them even more than I already have, but Mia nods.

'I was in wardrobe, I was the press secretary, I took care of special projects for Ron like dealing with Love Interests.' They motion to me. 'I was the most senior person left standing after the trial, the unofficial deputy that was in no way involved in Ron's evil plans. This is new and I don't know how long it will last, but they were desperate and I was here, which means the HPA has its first non-binary boss and I have a chance to make this organisation better.'

'This is incredible.' I am smiling now. 'Congratulations.'

A ghost of a grin crosses Mia's face before they purse their lips and cross their arms. 'And now there's a damp mess on the Harbour Bridge that I am going to have to explain tomorrow. What happened?'

Tomas's words resurface. 'It was a misunderstanding. I was passing and I thought someone was being attacked. I couldn't look the other way.' I look at Mia as innocently as I can manage.

'You were just passing.' Mia's tone is flat. 'Dressed like that.'

I shrug. 'I wear black sometimes.'

Their eyes narrow. 'When I started out in wardrobe, I dressed Catalejo. He was a vigilante for several years before the Chilean HPA caught up with him and gave him an ultimatum. Join up or go to jail. He chose the HPA, but when it came to his hero outfit, he insisted on keeping his vigilante look. Clothes are power, and the power he needed was black, comfortable and had pockets.' Mia motions to my trousers.

'Pockets are practical.'

Mia rolls their eyes. 'It's late, Jenna. I want to go to bed, so I'll cut to the chase. You're being issued with an official caution for using your powers in public.'

I sit forward. That doesn't sound like I'm going to be locked away.

'And an official invitation,' Mia continues. 'To join the HPA as the first female hero.'

My skin goes cold, then hot, and my mind goes into free fall.

An invitation to become an official hero.

The HPA cannot be trusted. That's been drummed into me ever since Mum left, but Mia is the boss now. But Ron was the boss before. But Blaze … my heart flutters in my chest. If I join the HPA, we'll be teammates. I'll get to see him every day.

'Will you arrest me if I don't join?' I ask, almost hoping that the choice is taken from me, like Catalejo.

Mia shrugs. 'I think we can look the other way if you pull the occasional drunk out of the harbour by their Babygro.'

My jaw tightens. Mia knows everything. The HPA have been keeping tabs on us this whole time. That would explain the sense that I was being watched.

'If you agree to join the HPA, we'll arrange a press conference, announce you to the world,' Mia continues. 'We'll give you a mentor, a hero outfit and train you up to join Blaze in the field.'

Blaze. Even hearing his name sends a thrill through me, but I take a moment to breathe. Shortly before I got tricked into a lighthouse that was blasted into the sea, my family held an intervention. They said that I made bad decisions where Blaze was involved. I can't do that now. I can't give my life to the HPA just because I'll get to see him and train with him and save people with him and maybe kiss him …

'It will be hard.' Mia steeples their fingers. 'Harder than it has any right to be. Trailblazers need to be more than perfect, trust me on that.' They give me a small smile. 'You'd need to be flawless, but, Jenna, if this works out, who knows what other heroes the HPA will be able to recruit. We could change the face of the HPA forever.'

That's the invitation: Join the broken system to fix the broken system.

'I'd need to be confident that your loyalties lie with us.' Mia locks eyes with me and I know they're talking about the Villains. My bracelet feels heavy on my wrist, but I nod slowly. I'm not agreeing, not yet, but they haven't said that I'd have to cut all ties with my mum and her merry group of anarchists. Maybe, with Mia at the helm, the HPA and the Villains could even find some common ground.

'There's one last thing I need you to be aware of.' Mia looks at the ceiling. 'Love Interests.'

My eyes widen in horror as I picture my first rescue mission with Joy. Was the drunk in the harbour my first official rescue? If joining the HPA means I have to start dating that adult baby, then I am out.

'Love Interests are important for several reasons,' Mia says. 'The media love them, or love to hate them, as you well know. The general, non-powered public feel a sense of security that the hero has chosen one of them to be with and protect. And –' Mia exhales – 'heroes can't be with other heroes.'

I frown, thinking back through the heroes and their relationships. There have been male Love Interests, but Mia's right, there's never been two heroes together.

Like me and Blaze.

My insides knot as the penny finally drops. After all the pressure to become Blaze's Love Interest, Mia is now telling me that I can't be with him.

'But that's stupid!' I blurt out. 'What possible reason—'

'It's International HPA policy.' Mia cuts me off. 'Hero work is too high stakes. You're the front line of defence against the EV. You can't afford the distraction of romance with your teammate. I know that you and Blaze became close during your time as his Love Interest, fake or not, but as two heroes …'

Mia's voice fades into the background as images of Blaze flood my brain: dark hair, kind brown eyes, sweet smile, dimples …

Him rescuing me from the fire.

Arguing with him at BLAZECON.

Saving him from the pigeons.

Kissing him.

'You can either be a hero or a Love Interest. You can't be both.' Mia's eyes shine with sympathy. 'The whole world is watching; the other HPAs, the other heroes, the media. If you join me, Jenna, you join me on a knife-edge. If we want to remake the HPA, there's no space for slip-ups. I'm sorry, Jenna, but a relationship with Blaze would be off the table.'

CHAPTER 3

'Jenna!' Dad leaps up from a bench in the glass foyer of HPA security. He is wearing a coat over his pyjama bottoms and his mouth is thin with worry. Joy jumps up too, still ready for action. Guilt washes through me, followed by a stronger wave of exhaustion. That conversation with Mia was too much for midnight on a Monday.

Mia needs to know whether I'll accept their invitation to join the HPA in time for a press conference, so they've given me until midday to make up my mind. My stomach lurches. I've got twelve hours to decide the shape of the rest of my life.

'Are you all right?' Dad's forehead seems extra lined in the harsh fluorescents and there are creases from his sheets etched into his cheek.

'They said you didn't need a lawyer, but we were heee …' Joy breaks off to yawn. 'Sorry. Here. We were here for you.' She puts her hands on my shoulders. 'Ray, are you OK?'

Missions, mentors, first female hero; Mia's words run through my mind again and excitement tingles across my skin.

I give myself a shake. 'I'm fine. It's OK. They're not arresting me.'

The doors swish open to let us back into the night and Dad puts out an arm to stop me wandering back towards the bridge.

'I've got the car,' he says. 'What happened?'

That makes sense, Dad wouldn't walk across town in his pyjamas. I shake my head, trying to get my thoughts in order as I head into the underground car park. 'I, um, accidentally used my powers in public and the HPA weren't happy.'

'Jenna Louise Ray.' My dad's tone makes me stop and face him. 'You *accidentally* used your powers?'

Skies. I was so terrified about the response of the HPA, I forgot to worry about Dad. His concerned expression is slowly morphing into something a lot closer to anger.

'She saved someone,' Joy jumps in. 'Sort of.'

'They took me to see the boss,' I continue quickly. 'Mia is the new head of the HPA.'

'Mia the driver?!' Joy exclaims.

'And everything else,' Dad adds. 'When the council needs something from the HPA, Mia Kaplan is the one we go to.' He holds up a finger. 'We're still going to discuss exactly why you were out in the town, in the middle of the night, dressed like a commando, using your powers – but what did Mia say? Are you in trouble?'

'They gave me a caution.' I rush off across the car park and lower my voice. 'And Mia asked if I wanted to join the HPA and become a hero and said I should let them know tomorrow.'

'Wait, what?!' Joy's shout echoes around the car park as she hurries after me. **'They finally asked if you wanted to be a hero?!'**

'Absolutely not!' Dad booms after me. *'That is NOT happening and I won't let you get suckered in by that deadline. Tomorrow?! Those immoral pressure sellers—'*

'JENNA, would you slow down?! This is huge. You and Blaze would finally be working together!'

'Blaze is irrelevant! You cannot be lured into an organisation like the HPA by a crush!'

'A crush?!'

'IF I'M A HERO TOO, WE'RE NOT ALLOWED TO BE TOGETHER!'

My strangled shout comes out louder than both of them and I wince. 'Sorry. Can we just go home?'

There's a distant beep as Dad unlocks the car and I veer towards the flash.

'You're not allowed to be with Blaze after they spent all that time shoving you together?' Joy falls into step with me. 'Why?'

'HPA policy.' The words already taste bitter in my mouth. 'I can be a Love Interest or I can be a hero.'

'Because people can't be more than one thing,' Joy mutters. 'What are you going to do?'

'I …' I hesitate. I can feel Dad holding his breath as he listens. I should say that I didn't want to be a part of the HPA when I was a Love Interest and I still feel the same now. I don't trust them. 'I think I'm going to say no,' I say, and I sound like I'm telling the truth.

Dad's fingers tap on the steering wheel non-stop as we drop Joy off and drive back home through the quiet streets. As we pull up to the house, I yawn so dramatically I almost dislocate my jaw. Maybe, if I can make it clear how tired I am, some parental instinct will kick in. He'll send his poor, over-tired offspring to bed and we can postpone the lecture. Dad is still holding his tongue as he opens the door and I yawn again, throwing in a stretch for good measure.

The door clicks shut behind us, which, apparently, is what he was waiting for.

'This is not the right time to make a decision like this.' He makes it to the stairs first and blocks my escape route. Feck. Since running away to my bed isn't an option, I scoot past into the dark kitchen and flick on the kettle.

'Setting the HPA to the side for a moment ...' Dad is hot on my heels. He hits the big light on and I have to stop as I'm temporarily blinded. 'In a little over a month you start your last year of school. You've got your exams to think about, and university, if that's still what you want.'

School. I hide my shudder by ducking into the fridge. I missed the last few weeks of year twelve to attend Ron's trial. Sneaking into my exams was bad, but no one can whisper about you when they're not allowed to talk. If I go back after the summer holidays feeling as uncertain as I do now, I'll end up dissolving into an anxious mess by the end of my first lesson.

'There's no rush,' Dad says as I emerge from the fridge with the milk. He's stationed himself in the doorway, leaning on the frame. 'There are other ways to help people.'

I drift back to the kettle on autopilot. I don't even want any tea. All I want is to sink into my bed and not think about school, or my powers, or the HPA for a few hours. 'Are you suggesting the Villains?'

'No! Although at least your mum would look after you.'

'I'm not joining the Villains.' I keep my back to him as I find a mug. Mum is gone. Megan is gone. I'm not going to leave Dad on his own. 'Tea?'

'Jen-bear, don't go back to the HPA tomorrow. They can take that as your answer. If they sense any weakness in you, they'll pounce. They'll force you into a decision. Just stay away.'

26

'They're people, Dad. Not lions.' The kettle vibrates as I turn to him. 'And I can't just leave Mia hanging. I, um, made a bit of a mess that they have to explain.'

'Then call them. There's no need for you to go anywhere near that base.' His eyes are wide with worry. 'This is *your* life, Jenna. Don't make a decision that you're going to regret.'

'I won't.' The rumble of the kettle intensifies as I hold his gaze.

'Promise me,' Dad says.

Right now, I would promise to do an exclusive interview with Sydney Jones if it meant I got to go to bed. 'I promise I won't make a decision that I'll regret.'

'And that you won't go to the base,' Dad adds.

'I won't go to the base,' I repeat.

The kettle clicks behind me and I blink, breaking the moment.

'I just want you safe, OK?' His voice is so full of quiet worry that my shoulders sag.

'OK.' I barely ever hug Dad these days, but I go to him and am wrapped up in his familiar arms. 'OK,' I murmur again. I am so tired it's all I can do not to sink into a puddle on the floor. I slip out of his arms and into the corridor.

'We're not done talking about this,' he calls as I leg it up the stairs. 'Tomorrow we're going to sit down and think this all through properly.'

'Love you,' I call back.

A moment later, I am finally in bed. My limbs are heavy, my eyes are stinging and I've never been so desperate to get some sleep, but under the warm weight of my duvet, my thoughts have been turned up to eleven.

Mia said missions, mentors, first female hero ...

You've always wanted to help people.

That's why you ran back into the flames.

That's why you took on Ron.

That's why you saved your town.

You were never really a Love Interest, but you told the world you were a hero.

Maybe this is the way back to who you're supposed to be?

After several hours of what may or may not be sleep, my chest is tight, my eyes ache and the only thing that can sort my head out is the sea. That is why it's OK to sneak out of the house whilst Dad's in the shower. I need to feel the salt water on my skin and absorb some energy from the waves, then I'll be ready for part two of *that* conversation. I close the front door as quietly as I can and jog down the sunny street, my swimming gear bouncing off my hip.

Mia and Dad played on a loop in my mind for most of the night and they are still going this morning, firing shots across my brain like it's a battlefield.

Missions ...

There's no rush.

Mentors ...

There's no rush.

First female hero ...

This is your life, Jenna.

I'm halfway into my wetsuit before I register where I am. I don't remember running along the high street or scrambling down the cliffside, but the water of Hidden Beach is now sparkling turquoise in front of me. The sun warms the skin of my face and the low rumble of the waves eases the tension in my shoulders. Even when I'm busy spiralling about my future, Hidden Beach is my happy place.

The silvery layer of my bubble prickles across my skin as I sink gratefully into the cool water and shoot out through the cove. As the calming blue of the deep fills my senses, the battle in my mind finally fades. My eyes still ache, but my chest feels lighter, like the water is taking the weight of my worries. I stop and exhale slowly. I was right, this is what I needed.

My eyes flutter closed and the water holds me safe within it ...

There's no rush.

But potentially idiotic heroism is what you do.
Is time really going to change that?

But Blaze ...

I groan as I wipe the crumbly sleep from my eyes and force them open. BLUE. Everything is blue. I spin, my bubble holding firm. Mother Earth, did I fall asleep under the sea?! A silvery fish flits past my face. Feck. Panic bubbles in my gut. I didn't know I could do this and I don't know how long I've been down here. Did Dad already leave for work? Skies! Has midday come and gone?

A strange vibration hits my bubble and I blink. Something is wrong. There. And again. This must be what woke me up. The bursts reaching me feel like panic. There's nothing under the waves, so I shoot up to the surface, emerging in time to hear a piercing scream coming from the coast.

'Feck.' I scan for EV creatures, ready to hurtle over.

'Again!' A high-pitched yell floats across the water and I see the family in the distant shallows. A child in orange armbands is thrown into the air by her parents and shrieks as she falls into the waves. A moment later the vibrations reach me, but she's already been plucked out of the water by her mum.

The child is fine, that family is fine, but my heart is still racing. I would have shot to their rescue without a second thought. I would have used my powers to save them, even if it meant drawing the attention of the media, the HPA locking me up or another lecture from Dad.

A passing wave lifts me and I catch a glimpse of a tour group up on the cliff edge by the lighthouse. There will be so many other people who will need my help, ones who I would never even know about as a civilian. Joining the HPA is a risk, but isn't that what heroes do? They risk themselves to help others. Dad says there's no rush, but what if someone who I could have saved is hurt? My entire body clenches at the thought.

What if someone I could have saved dies?

That feels like a reason to rush.

My current pushes against me and I hold myself so I have a chance to think this through. But there's nothing left to consider.

I know what I am going to do.

I let my current take me and shoot back towards the land.

Dad is going to kill me.

The distant clock tower chimes midday as I make my way back down the steps to HPA security. Mia is waiting for me, eyes on mine as the doors swish open. Cold air blasts me, raising the hairs on my arms as I stop in front of them, bag of swimming gear over one shoulder and my entire future in the palm of my hand.

And it's inevitable.

It was inevitable from the moment I made columns of water surge into the sky on TV.

I'm breaking another promise to Dad, signing up to join Mum's mortal enemies, and if Megan ever comes back, she'll probably try and burn this base to the ground, but I think this is who I am supposed to be.

Mia raises their eyebrows.

'I'm in,' I say. 'I'll be one of your heroes.'

Mia nods and a relieved smile spreads across their face. 'You had me worried for a second there.'

'But I want to stay in school,' I add quickly. 'With the option to go to university.'

Mia holds up a hand. 'Fine. That's all fine.'

'And I don't want a Love Interest.'

They don't hesitate. 'Also fine.'

I let out a breath I didn't realise I was holding. If I can still live my life, and go to school, and love whoever I want (apart from Blaze) then this is going to work. I might even be able to win Dad over.

'We can sit down, talk logistics and make sure you're happy with everything.' Mia nabs a clipboard off the desk and waggles it at me. 'I had a feeling you'd agree, so I put together a little itinerary.'

'What would you have done if I said no?' I slip my Villain bracelet off and step into the scanner.

Mia shrugs. 'Waited.'

Security finish checking me in and I follow Mia into the base.

'I wanted to give you a taste of being a hero before you signed on the dotted line, so first, there's someone I want you to meet properly.' Mia pushes through the training studio doors. 'Tomas?'

I dump my bag by the wall and head across the bouncy grey mat to where Mia has stopped with their hands on their hips. Tomas, the silver-haired man from last night, is lying across a row of the studio's foldable chairs. Loud snores escape from the white baseball cap he's placed over his face.

Mia sighs. 'Tomas Weber, your mentor.' They clap their hands loudly. 'Tomas!'

He lets out a quiet groan and throws an arm over his ear. After the enormity of what I've just agreed to, this feels surreal. I'd assumed my mentor would be like Ron, strict, charming and awake, but Tomas is evidently a different flavour of hero. I should know who he is and what his power is, but I can't remember him from Hero Education.

'This is on me. I told him to be here, but I didn't specify that I wanted him awake.' Mia claps again. 'Tomas!'

No response.

Mia sighs. 'I had some water put out in case you started training today.' They point at a vat by the wall. 'Would you mind?'

I look from the vat to Tomas and back to Mia. 'You want me to pour water over my new mentor.'

'I'd do it myself, but –' Mia holds up their golden nails – 'these are acrylic.'

'Mother Earth,' I mutter, and pull a tennis-ball-sized sphere out of the vat. I liked Tomas when I met him last night. He seemed to be on my side, as much as someone can be when they're arresting you. This is going to make a bad second impression. 'Tomas?'

He murmurs something and I don't speak German, but I'm pretty sure it's *go away*.

'Do it,' Mia says.

The sphere drops. I cringe. A tennis ball of water is actually quite a lot.

I'd expect anyone splashed awake to lurch up, but Tomas stills.

'Could—' Mia starts.

Tomas's hand shoots out and now I know exactly who he is.

Sturmschmied, the infamous German storm-maker who saved the Port of Hamburg and then got chucked out of a tavern and tried to rip it out of the ground with gale-force winds *on the same day.*

And that is why there's now a tornado heading straight for us.

CHAPTER 4

'Tomas!' Mia shrieks as I drag them out of the tornado's path.

I didn't think wind had a colour, but the swirling vortex is thundercloud grey. It's already my height and getting more powerful with each passing second.

'Mother Earth!' I pull a jet of water from the vat to fire at it, but all it does is make the growing funnel glisten. It follows us across the studio, sucking at my hoody as it wobbles from side to side. One of Mia's black pumps flies off their foot, into the tornado.

'Hey!' Mia yells, and the vortex careers towards us again.

'How do you stop a tornado?!' I pull Mia towards the wall and spy Tomas still stretched out on the chairs. Is he doing this in his sleep?! Blasting the vortex with water didn't work. The only way I can affect this thing is via the person who made it.

The twister changes direction again to head towards us as I pull another lump of water out of the vat and dump it on Tomas.

'Wake up!' I shout.

The tornado stops a few metres from us, its spin slowing. Tomas sits up, lifts the dripping baseball cap off his face, and grins at me. My mouth drops open. He wasn't asleep.

'You did that on purpose?!' I can't keep the shock from my voice.

Tomas lopes over to us, rubbing the water from his face. His tanned skin and blue eyes immediately make me think that he's the type of man my mum would fancy. 'Not bad, Ray, although you do rely on blasting things with water. That won't always work. You know, if you can change the temperature of the water in the tornado, you could stop it?'

I shake my head. Are all of Tomas's lessons going to be this dramatic?

'Get me my shoe back,' Mia hisses through gritted teeth. 'If it's broken, you're replacing it.'

'*Ja*, of course.' Tomas pushes his wet hair off his forehead and directs his hand back at the tornado. '*Schlafen*.' The wind whistling round the tight vortex widens and disperses in all directions, leaving the lights swinging above us and Mia's pump upside down on the mat. Tomas scoops it up and returns to present it to Mia. 'There we go, boss, as good as new.'

Mia scowls and snatches it back.

'I didn't think I would be seeing you today,' Tomas says to me. 'I thought, this girl is too much of a rebel to sign on the dotted line. Evidently, I was mistaken.' He's twinkling at me. I've not met very many people who twinkle, especially older men, but his eyes are lit up, laughing. 'Can you?' He motions to the water in his hair and his damp red sweatshirt.

'Oh, yes.' I lift the water particles off Tomas and send them back to the vat.

'Good.' He looks at Mia. 'This I can work with.'

Mia glares at him for a moment, before facing me. 'Jenna, Tomas will be responsible for your training in all things hero related. Unless I fire him, which is feeling like a distinct possibility.'

Tomas tilts his head at me. 'If you're happy to be trained by me, of course.' He holds out his hand for the second time in less than twenty-four hours.

'Er. Yes. OK.' The twister-related surge of adrenalin hasn't dimmed yet, but I keep my hand steady as I shake his. He just threw a surprise tornado at me, but I think I like this Sturmschmied.

'All right.' Mia's eyes flick to the clock on the wall. 'We're running behind. We need to get Jenna to her hero outfit fitting.'

'Ja, OK.'

'Oh, and I just need to …' Mia clicks their fingers and the studio doors are banging shut behind them before I have fully detangled their last sentence. Excitement zips through me. There's already a hero outfit for me?

'And there goes the boss.' Tomas grins at me. 'I remember my first hero suit. Silver, inbuilt shield, wings so I could ride the wind.' He shakes his head fondly. 'Of course, my hair wasn't grey back then. It would look ridiculous now. Do you know your way to wardrobe? I'll wait for you here.'

I follow his gaze back to the chairs where he had been lying. 'Were you actually asleep when we first came in, um, sir?'

'Tomas,' he says. 'What kind of mentor would be asleep in the middle of the day?'

I raise my eyebrows at him. 'That wasn't a no.'

He grins at me again. 'Off you go then.' He waves in the direction of the door. 'You don't want to upset the wardrobe wizards. I lost my cape that way.'

'Enjoy your nap,' I call on my way out.

My very own hero outfit! This is all happening so fast. Butterflies bounce around my stomach and I almost skip back through the familiar brushed concrete corridors of the base. Blue. That's what colour I want my suit to be. Blue with hints of turquoise, like the sea under a blanket of cloud.

'Jenna Ray.'

Blaze's voice comes from behind me. The gut butterflies detonate like fireworks and my heart leaps into my mouth and I have to stop where I am because I think I've forgotten how to walk.

'Hi, Jenna.' He sounds almost apologetic. He could be beside me, or in front of me, or anywhere he wants by now, but he's waiting for me to turn around.

I breathe out, *two, three, four,* and face him.

Eyes. His brown eyes are bright and they crinkle as he smiles at me.

Suit. His black-and-red hero suit is dusted in something that might be sand or maybe volcanic ash. And I am not looking at the line that tracks his muscles up his arms, or thinking about how it feels to be held by them.

Smile. My eyes find his face again, which is hardly better. He's looking at me like I'm a cold drink on a hot day. Joy is the only emotion I can read in the dent of his dimples.

Mother Earth, has this boy got hotter?!

I swallow my urge to tell him that he's the most beautiful thing I've ever seen. It doesn't matter that my body is fizzing with excitement.

Blaze is a hero.

I am a hero.

I chose being a hero over a potential relationship with Blaze and it had felt like the right thing to do. But now he's more than a few random messages. He's more than a memory of strong arms and stolen kisses. He's right here.

Everything just got a lot more complicated.

I take a step back. 'We're not allowed to be together.' The words rush out of my mouth. 'I agreed to be a hero and the HPA have this policy, so we can't.' I motion between us. 'We can't.' My voice drops to a whisper.

Blaze holds up his hands. 'I know. You were always going to be a hero, Jenna, so I've known …'

'Since the Culture Complex,' I say.

He nods. Suddenly his distance makes sense. He was waiting for me to be invited to the HPA, for me to choose being a hero over him.

'This sucks,' I say. 'Why didn't you say anything?'

Panic flashes across his face. 'I didn't want to assume … I didn't know, after everything that happened …' He gestures frantically between us.

'Oh.' My cheeks are heating now too. 'I didn't know either, if you wanted to …'

'I mean, I would have.' He bites his lip. 'But I knew how it would play out and, honestly, I was just looking forward to seeing you again. I've missed talking to you. It's all been a bit … It's been hard.' Blaze shrugs and for a moment the lost boy who came to see me in the gift shop is back. His messages had been so casual, but his life was turned upside down. He sent his mentor, the man who practically raised him, to prison and it sounds like he's on probation which must mean they haven't figured out how to deal with his stolen powers.

'I've missed you too.' I exhale slowly. I want to wrap him in a hug and protect him from everything. After all this time, do I like him more? Or did I just forget what it felt like to have every atom of my being screaming to get closer to someone? 'And we're allowed to do this, aren't we? Just talk to each other.'

'Of course.' Blaze nods, looking more certain. 'We're going to be working together.'

'Yes.' I nod back, trying to look enthusiastic. 'And that's really exciting.'

'Really exciting.' His voice is strained.

I swallow and glance up at the shiny black orb of a CCTV camera.

'Skies!' My eyes flick back to meet his. 'I wish we could just catch up, but I feel like if I'm too friendly I'm going to set off some kind of intimacy alarm.'

He blinks at me. 'We could move to somewhere less, um, public.'

If no one is watching, maybe I can hug him. Hugs are safe. I hug Joy all the time. 'Let's do that.'

'If I blur us, no one will even see where we've gone.' Blaze nods at the cleaning closet beside him.

Actually, I'm supposed to be at wardrobe. And should we really be sneaking into a cupboard together? And I don't know if I can control myself around you …

'That's a good idea,' I say.

It takes less than a second for him to grab me and blur us into the closet. As he flicks the light on, I realise there's almost no space in here. Several mop handles are poking me in the back, and in front of me, with less than a few centimetres between his body and mine, is Blaze.

'So.' He swallows. 'How have you been?'

My lips are on his before I know what I'm doing and he's kissing me back with a passion that sings through my body. The mops clatter as I pull him even closer. I remember this. I remember how much I needed this: his soft lips, his strong shoulders, his touch that trails fire down my back.

'I missed you.' I pepper kisses down his neck.

'You have no idea.' His hands guide my lips back to his and I am lost in him—

There's a sharp rap on the door. My eyes fly open, and I look past Blaze to find the door open and Tomas leaning on it.

'Where is your protégé, Tomas? She was just coming from down the corridor, Tomas. Do you think she's lost, Tomas?' I see wardrobe were right to be concerned.' My mentor crosses his arms, and my stomach twists itself into a knot.

Blaze spins, so I'm looking at Tomas over his shoulder. 'Sorry, Sturmschmied, sir, we were just catching up.' The backs of his ears have gone red. I think my entire face is probably the same colour.

What am I doing? I told myself I could handle anything if it meant I could save people and I immediately ended up in a cupboard with Blaze?! Tomas is going to tell Mia. I'm going to get fired on my first day. But my insides are still fizzing with need. If Tomas wasn't leaning on that door, there's every chance I'd try and close myself in here with Blaze again.

What is wrong with me?

'Ah, catching up. We called it something different when I was young, and again, please do call me Tomas,' Tomas says. 'You know why there's the rule, *ja*? And why it's zero tolerance?'

Blaze and I both mumble '*yes*'.

'It won't happen again.' I ignore the sweet tingles as I brush Blaze's arm on my way out of the cupboard. I glance at him for help, but he's chewing his lip. 'We just haven't seen each other since everything happened.'

Tomas looks between us and sighs heavily. 'I'll look the other way this time, but only this time. You, boy, go and save someone. And, Ray?'

'Go to wardrobe?'

'We'll go together this time.' Tomas motions in front of him and marches me down the corridor. 'I was dreaming when that radio woke me up. I was on the white sands of Fiji, Bavarian beer in hand. It was perfect and delicious, not real, but delicious ...'

I glance back to see Blaze, still standing there, watching us go. He screws his face up and I do the same. Tomas gave us a pass this time, but if it had been anyone else ... I clench my lips. We both want to be heroes, so it's simple. We'll just never kiss again.

CHAPTER 5

'Now obviously this isn't your final hero suit.' The new blond man in wardrobe steers me in, past the tiered racks of clothing. Blaze's options are still at the top, but the bottom rack that used to have Ron's suits is empty. It's unsettlingly quiet in here without Mia's rock music.

'The updated design came through three hours ago. *Three hours ago*, babe.' He steers me towards the long cutting table. 'Honestly, we should be the ones that wear capes.' He sounds American and hasn't told me his name yet. Something about his rushed manner reminds me of the small woman in Norway who kept calling Blaze, Beige.

Tomas made sure that I was in this man's custody before wandering off, muttering something about finding his phone. I'm still trying to unpack my mentor's reaction. Blaze and I broke the no-romance rule and Tomas was mildly concerned; I can't imagine what would get more of a response from him. He won't tell Mia, but my cheeks are still burning. I should be focused on this fitting, but I can feel the strands of Blaze's hair between my fingers and his lips pressing against mine—

'Jenna Ray.' The Blond snaps his fingers and I blink at him. 'Here's your interim suit. Try it on for me, will you? I'm due in Paris in a few hours.'

'Oh.' I take the silky bundle being thrust in my direction and my brow creases. 'It's pink.'

'There's a changing booth with a mirror just over there.'

As I pull the slinky pink leggings on, my gut twists. The outfit is entirely pink, from the powder-pink skintight leggings with an inbuilt frilly skirt, to the reinforced military bodice with darker pink panels that for some reason leaves my arms bare. I like pink – I wore Megan's berry-coloured hoody today – but how is light pink Lycra practical for a hero who spends most of her time in the water? And what are these frills?! Do they want me to call myself the Jellyfish?

'How are you getting on in there, babe?'

'I …' There are white, heeled, knee-high boots waiting for me under the mirror. White. Heels. My stomach rolls. I don't think I'd be able to make it out of wardrobe in them, let alone go on a mission.

'Nope,' I mutter, and shove my feet back in my trainers. Did Mia design this? Clothes are power, they said that before they zipped me into a perfect Love Interest dress and they said it again last night. Hero suits are Mia's art. I look at myself in the mirror again and try to adjust the bodice where it pinches my waist. They wouldn't do this to me, would they?

'Time is money, Jenna Ray,' the Blond calls.

There's a sour taste in my mouth. I should just take this suit off, but I don't know if I dare make more waves after getting arrested last night and kissing Blaze in a cupboard ten minutes ago.

'Jenna?' Perfect, now Mia is here too. 'Let's see it.'

A bright pink, horrified version of myself stares back from the mirror as I try and smooth down the ruffles of the skirt. I am the first female hero and they want me to look like a doll. There must be more to this outfit than that. I pull on Megan's hoody, zip it up and step out of the cubicle.

Both Mia and the Blond frown.

'Where are the shoes?' The Blond steps forward and unzips my hoody.

I step out of reach and zip it back up again. 'I didn't want to break an ankle on my first day. So, what's the deal with this outfit? What does the skirt do, turn into a shield or something?'

The Blond frowns. 'What does the skirt do? It makes you look adorable. That's the aim.'

'Will any part of this outfit help me on a mission?' I glance at the cubicle. I'm going to wriggle back out of these leggings and we are going to have a discussion about pockets.

'Jenna, wait a second.' Mia puts a hand on the Blond's arm. 'Can I have a quick word?'

Mia takes the Blond towards the door. The boss isn't happy, thank the skies. I can't pick out much from the murmured argument that follows, but the words 'waterproof', 'original

46

design' and 'Shelly Taylor' float back to where I'm eavesdropping.

Mia turns to me with a smile. I smile back, ready for them to say *just kidding, your real suit is over there*.

'This will be fine for now,' they say. My smile freezes. 'Keep your trainers on and your hoody, it's a look. We need to get to the next thing on the itinerary.'

Mia is already striding away, so I take a last longing look at my jeans and follow. *'Fine for now'* must mean this isn't what Mia envisioned either. If it's not my final suit, I guess it won't hurt to keep it on a bit longer. The Blond rolls his eyes as I pass. I hope he's gone when I get back. I'm going to snap the heels off those boots so no one ever tries to make me wear them again.

'What's next on your itinerary?' I fall into Mia's wake as they power walk down the corridor and swipe us on to the lift.

'Now, I know you're not going to like this.' The mirrored walls are a disconcerting mix of Mia's worried gaze and all the shades of pink I'm wearing. 'But you are ready. I know you are, I trained you.'

My mouth tightens into a thin line. It can't be what I think it is. Not yet. Not dressed like this.

'A small press conference to announce you to the world.'

Mother Earth. I clench my fists. I can't do a press conference. It's bad enough I came to the base after promising Dad I wouldn't; how is he going to react to seeing me announced on TV?

The lift pings open and the hubbub from the reporters echoes off the walls of the concrete corridor. It feels like

47

all the doors could slam open and expel a sea of press towards us.

'But I haven't signed anything—' We leave the lift and I wobble into Mia.

'Skies! You just gave me a shock.' They stop, rubbing their arm. 'Jenna, I want to make sure you have everything you need, but this press conference was already arranged to announce me as the new head of the HPA.'

'But, the suit.' I motion at my outfit and get friction burn from the ruffles.

Mia grits their teeth. 'It's a work in progress, but it's vital that we start legitimising you as a hero. We don't get to brand you, like Blaze, because everyone already knows who you are. I'll have to explain what happened on the bridge last night and having you by my side will help it look official. Jenna, this could be huge. The first non-male head and the first non-male hero …' They trail off and look at me with pleading eyes.

If only I had stayed on the roof of Size Nines.

I should tell Mia no, I know I should, but the press is here and I have already agreed that I'm in this thing, and it's Mia …

My shoulders sag. 'All right.'

Mia beams at me. 'You'll have to answer two questions tops.' They set off again, walking so quickly I almost have to jog to keep up. 'This is it. The start of our brand-new HPA. We're going to make a world where anyone can be a hero, Jenna Ray, just you wait and see.'

The flash of cameras when we enter the room is blinding. I fix my gaze on Mia's back, follow them up to a table set up with microphones, and slip into a chair. Once the spots clear from my eyes, I take in the rows of reporters. They're all staring up at us, judging us. My heart thuds so loudly in my ears I barely hear Mia introducing themself as the new head of the HPA.

'… announce that Jenna Ray has officially joined the HPA as our first female hero.' Mia gestures to me with a flourish. 'We've got time for a few questions.'

A reporter launches to her feet. 'Sydney Jones.' The taste of vomit surges into my mouth. *Of course* Sydney Jones is here. 'Mx Kaplan, are you planning to recruit more non-male heroes?'

'After her role in bringing Ron King to justice, Jenna has proved that she has what it takes to be part of the HPA,' Mia replies. 'She is the right person to blaze a trail for others to follow.'

The vomit taste intensifies as all the reporters look my way.

'And Jenna.' Sydney fixes her gaze on me and I lean forward, ready to tell her that being a hero is an honour and I can't wait to get started. 'Footage of you flooding the Harbour Bridge has leaked online. Care to tell us what happened?'

I blink at her and glance at Mia, whose face is set. Did they know about the leak?

'How could you see what happened? It was really misty,' I try. Sydney raises her eyebrows and writes something down.

Mia puts a hand over my microphone. 'Last night Jenna was running a training exercise with her new mentor, Sturmschmied. We wanted to get her started as soon as possible.'

'What of the sources that say Jenna was using her powers illegally?' Sydney fires at us.

'Whoever your source is, they clearly didn't have all the information.' Mia releases my mic. 'We've cleaned up the Harbour Bridge and fixed a long-running drainage issue, so Jenna actually did the town a favour.'

Some reporters chuckle at that, and as Sydney sits back down, the tightness in my chest eases.

Another reporter leaps up. 'Carrie Le Roux, *Take Five Magazine*.'

'Go ahead, Carrie,' Mia says.

'Jenna, your new outfit is the sweetest thing! Did you choose it? Who designed it?'

I bite back *'Well, Carrie, someone dredged my nightmares and found this legging skirt combo'* and manage a tight smile. 'It's a work in progress.'

'We're trialling a few different outfits for Jenna to see what works best with her powers,' Mia cuts in.

'Will we get to vote on which is our favourite?' Carrie asks.

'No.' Mia frowns. 'Jenna and her team will pick an outfit that helps her to save lives.'

Carrie shakes her finger at the ceiling. 'Good thinking. Leave the poll to us.'

There are titters from the more serious journalists, but Carrie sits to write excitedly in her notebook.

'Name?' Sydney Jones is back on her feet.

I know this one. 'Jenna Ray,' I answer confidently.

'What is your hero name?' Sydney says slowly, as if I'm an idiot.

Oops. 'I don't have one.' I bite my lip and look at Mia for help.

'Jenna had a non-traditional route into her role and a name has yet to present itself,' Mia answers.

Another hand is up. 'Ian Collins, *River Times*.' He stands. 'How do you expect to move forwards when you've traded an experienced leader for a little girl in pink ruffles, and the last prophecy from the Diviner has been and gone? Have you found the next Diviner? Or perhaps an epilogue in her book of prophecies? Or are you just making it up as you go along?'

The bottom drops out of my stomach, but Mia's smile doesn't waver. 'Ron King is a criminal. With Jenna, we will create the type of organisation that the next Diviner would be proud to join.'

'Will you restart King Ron's search?' Ian Collins asks.

'No.' Mia shrugs. 'We've closed the hotline for reporting suspected powers and we're not going to tear the country apart looking for the next Diviner. That bloodline might have moved abroad, she could be anywhere—'

Like Scotland. I clasp my hands tight under the table.

'The Diviner will come to us when she is ready,' Mia finishes.

A forest of hands shoot into the air and the thought of Megan seeing this makes my chest tighten. I know what she'd say, because it's the same thing currently running on a loop through my mind.

Jenna, I hope you know what you're doing.

I literally CAN'T with the STATE of this nation.

By Sarah Popkin for H-Mail Online

8403 shares

What is HAPPENING?

First, Blaze, the infant hero, pulled a disinterested girl out of the flames and, I'll hold my hands up, I thought Jenna Ray was beyond dull. Then it turned out she has un-registered POWERS?! Didn't anyone check who Jenna Ray was before they let her become a Love Interest?

I know I keep saying it, but King Ron has been there for us for YEARS. He brought over foreign heroes when The Controller upped and left. He shepherded us through countless prophecies. He fought the EV and protected us, day after day, and, with the help of the ACTUAL VILLAINS (why is no one talking about that???!), Jenna Ray got him sent to THE CASTLE.

Did the liberal wokerati get bored of being safe? Oh, I'm sorry, snowflakes, did King Ron have to make some choices that left a bad taste in your mouth?

And today it's official. We've added a whole new layer to the Jenna Ray Issue and traded King Ron for this teen-ager. The first female hero. Ring the bells, our saviour is here and she is wearing powder pink. Baby's first press conference was full of lefty waffle from new HPA head Mx Mia Kaplan (are we now eradicating men from the HPA entirely?), who doesn't believe in reporting on the powered or searching for the Diviner or little things like NATIONAL SECURITY, apparently.

And Jenna Ray just sat there, chewing her lip like she had something to hide, making me question EVERYTHING that we've been taught about heroes; everything they've done throughout history and everything we've witnessed in our own lifetimes. It's like it's all come to nothing. Blasted away in a plume of dirty water.

If I was a foreign power trying to destabilise the country and steal our Diviner out from under our collective noses, Jenna Ray is how I'd do it. I'm not making any accusations, of course, but it makes you think, doesn't it?

I am going to say it first, I think, and certainly I am going to say it loudest. I DON'T TRUST HER. A Love Interest turned hero. There's never been one before and for good reason. It doesn't matter if she's dressed like a grungy fairy-tale princess and can empty a swimming pool with a flick of her fingers, I NO LONGER FEEL SAFE in my own country.

I did not agree to this trade and I don't think it's going to have a happy ending.

BRING BACK KING RON. #BBKR

CHAPTER 6

The rest of the press conference passes in a stomach-twisting blur and by the time the reporter-related nausea has faded, I'm back in my jeans and sitting in Mia's office. My first real contract is spread across the desk. Mr George had scribbled something on a piece of lined paper for my job at Lighthouse Souvenirs, but Mia talks me through a document with salary, National Insurance and a code of conduct. The section on what happens if I die whilst heroing makes my palms sweat; I didn't realise paperwork could be terrifying.

'Do you want to take this home and get your dad to look over it?' Mia asks.

Dad would shred this document and set fire to the pieces. 'No, it's OK,' I reply.

'All right then.' Mia hands me a pen.

By the end of my three-hour written English exam, it felt like my pen was made of cement. This biro is heavier. On the piece of paper glaring up at me, there's a line with my name printed under it and the date. That's where I sign. That's where I commit. I made my decision and I've already gone in front of the press, so I don't know why I'm hesitating now. Mia's computer beeps as another email arrives and I realise I've been staring at the contract for at least a minute.

'Do you want to take some more time to think things through?' Mia asks.

Their computer beeps again and my pen is on the dotted line, moving across in the squiggly signature that I work-shopped with Joy. A wave of excitement washes over me as I drop the biro. There's no turning back now.

'Welcome to the HPA, Jenna.' Mia smiles. 'Would you like to move on to the base tonight?'

I blink as my excitement morphs into confusion. 'Move on to the base?'

Mia holds my gaze. 'Heroes don't live at home with their parents. We went through the section on accommodation.'

'But I have accommodation.' The floor falls out from under me and the image of Dad sitting alone at our kitchen table stamps itself on to my brain. I can't move on to the base. 'I didn't think it applied to me. I already live in Nine Trees, I thought—'

Another email pings and Mia puts a hand on mine. 'All right, Jenna, take a breath. Today has been a lot. Go home and rest. We'll find time to talk through the transition. You start at 8 a.m. tomorrow. Your first proper day of training!' Mia's voice is enthusiastic, but as another email pings, one of their eyelids twitches.

My head is still swimming as I emerge from the base into the warmth of the late afternoon sun, my copy of the contract heavy in my bag.

Heroes don't live at home with their parents.

I don't want to leave home; that's where my room is, where Dad is and where Megan knows we'll be.

My fingers trail up the damp stone banister to the bridge. Maybe Joy will be at the shop and I can hide in the stock room and debrief with her. She'll tell me that everything is going to be all right, and I need to hear that before I face Dad and tell him I signed something I didn't understand.

It's been raining. I can still feel the moisture in the air as I wander down on to the slick cobbles of the high street. The sun might be breaking through the light grey clouds, but the water around me feels heavy, like someone turned up the pressure.

'Sorry!' A delivery bike hurtles past on the pavement and I jump out of the way, colliding with a street lamp.

As I push myself upright, a blue spark shoots between me and the black pole.

'Ouch!' I rub my arm where the spark hit. 'What?' Faint blue sparks are crackling across the skin of my hand. They're almost invisible in the bright sunshine, but the pins and needles pinch make me certain that I'm not seeing things. My heart thumps extra hard as sparks hop across my other hand too.

'Oh no,' I mutter.

The sparks are new, but I know what this is and every time

this happens, it gets worse. Dancing spots of blue appear in the corners of my eyes, so I yank my sunglasses out of my bag and shove them on.

'*The worst that can happen during an attack is you'll feel uncomfortable. You can live with that.*' That's what the counsellor said at one of our group sessions. So I am acknowledging my feelings. I am breathing out, *two, three, four*. I know the adrenalin will fade and my heart will calm, but now, each time an attack comes, the breathlessness has been swapped for the feeling my power could explode out of me.

My shaking hands tingle as they find the water on the cobbles. It's all I can do not to pull it all towards me.

I breathe out, *two, three*—

There are people passing, peeling off into shops or chatting as they wait for the ice-cream man. All of them are going to notice if the puddles start floating off the ground. All of them are going to see. On my first day as a hero, I broke the no-romance rule, stressed out Mia and now I am going to lose control of my powers in public.

The world spins as I use everything I've got to shove my power back down inside.

I breathe out, *two*—

My power burns at the tips of my fingers and the water shifts below my feet.

They'll see me. They'll film me. Sydney fecking Jones is probably already on her way here.

Shimmering blue floods my vision.

Mother Earth. I can't stop this.

Something sharp pinches my upper arm and the shimmering recedes.

An arm loops around my waist and I'm guided down a shaded alley.

The blue is gone, but my power is still fizzing, trying to break out of me. I sink down to the wet ground with my head in my hands. I don't know who saved me. It must have been Joy, she's done it before, leading me away from the cameras at BLAZECON. Or Blaze, finding me somewhere to hide like he did at Brooke and Red Stripe's wedding. I claw my power back inside and hold it there, like I'm closing an overfull suitcase.

'Stay,' I mutter. 'Please.'

I breathe out, *two, three, four*, and my pulse slows.

This must be what happens to powered people who have panic attacks and it sucks.

'Are you better, Jenna Ray?'

My insides squeeze as I recognise the gentle voice. The last time we saw each other I gave him back his free will, and he leaped off, leaving me to face Ron alone.

'Thank you for releasing my heart.'

I lift my head and take off my sunglasses to find a hooded figure in front of me. Prince #2, the AI robot sidekick who everyone thought had been destroyed but who turned out to be the mysterious Secret Ninja, reprogrammed to carry out Ron's dirty work. I haven't heard anything about him in the months since he escaped. The HPA evidently managed to keep the identity of the Secret Ninja away from the media.

'You were struggling with your powers, Jenna Ray.' He

lowers his hood, and I take a sharp breath. It's like Prince #2 looked up images of humanoid AI on the internet and decided to lean into it. His face is a waxy white, with a surprisingly expressive mouth and familiar grey eyes, but the rest of his skull is polished silver. Maybe he always looked like this under his Secret Ninja costume.

Pain flares again in my upper arm and I rub it, half expecting to find a dart there.

'Apologies. I gave you a small electric shock,' Prince #2 says. 'You didn't seem to have control, but I think that helped.'

'Thank you.' It still stings, but it's better than a full meltdown in the middle of the high street.

'Do you know – know – know …' Prince #2 shudders.

'Are you all right?' My eyes widen as I watch him.

'Do you know what's happening to you?' Prince #2's voice is smooth again.

'It's just a panic attack.' I feel steady enough to grab one of the bins and pull myself up. Before I've realised what I'm doing, I've used my power to dry my jeans. My heart is still racing, but my power has already stabilised. 'I'll be all right now. Where have you been?'

'It's not …' Prince #2's head jerks. 'You should …' It snaps back. 'Help.'

I step hesitantly towards him. 'Do you need help?'

'No, Jenna Ray.' He smiles at me. 'I'm having some minor software issues. Nothing I can't handle.'

'Is that why you are in Nine Trees? Do you need the HPA or someone else … ?' I think he knows I'm talking about Femi, the Villain's technopath, but his grey eyes don't give anything away.

'N – N – No. I do not require assistance. I was passing through. And now you are safe. I should go.' Prince #2 flips his hood back up. 'I'm glad I was able to help you. I want to find a way to help, but I need – need – need …' He shakes his head.

Prince #2, the android who gave so much to so many, is broken and alone. He might not be human, but watching him back away makes my gut twist. Even if he didn't help me with Ron, I should help him now. It's the right thing to do.

'Wait. Please. I can find a way to fix you.'

'Thank you, Jenna Ray.' He turns and walks out of the alley. I follow, but when I reach the busy street, the robot is gone.

The house seems quiet as I make my shaky way up the drive. After the attack, I needed the safety of home and, despite my reluctance to face Dad, touching the front door eases the tension in my chest. My key clicks in the lock and I half expect Dad and Megan to be waiting in the corridor, ready to yell at me like they did after BLAZECON, but no one's there.

'Dad?'

No answer. Guilt curls through my insides. He must have seen the news that I broke my promise to him and officially joined the HPA. I was always going to come home to shouting or silence and I guess I know which one I'm getting. This is history repeating itself. When I agreed to become Blaze's Love Interest, Dad might as well have moved into his office. I didn't see him for days.

'Skies.' I rub my arms to try and get some warmth back into my body as I wander into the kitchen. Being back where I last talked to Dad brings the enormity of today into focus. I wish he was here, shouting at me. At least then I'd know that he's OK.

We'd planned to have risotto tonight, so I start chopping onions in the hope that it grounds me. I am hunting for our garlic crusher when I notice a small black jewellery box on the windowsill. There's no card and I'm pretty sure it wasn't here earlier today. I snap it open. A gold heart charm sits on a plush purple cushion. I've felt like I'm being followed for weeks and now some mystery jewellery appears in my house. Do I have a stalker?

My phone buzzes and I almost take out one of our dining chairs in my rush to get to it. I unlock the screen, hoping for a furious message from Dad or Megan, but it's from an unknown number.

Jen-bear, add the charm to my bracelet. Squeeze for ten seconds if you're in danger. I won't receive replies on this number.

'Mum.' I'm not in danger, so I shouldn't use the charm, but perhaps if I'm fast enough, I can reach her before she ditches the phone. My hand shakes as I type out a response.

I need to talk to you.

Contacting the Villains on my first day as a HPA hero is hardly the action of a perfect trailblazer, but Mum will know how to help Prince #2.

My entire world shrinks to the screen of my phone as I wait for a response, but the typing dots don't appear and eventually I give up and go back to the garlic. I check my phone again after I've added the charm to my bracelet, after I've finished prepping dinner and while I stir the risotto. Mum doesn't reply, Megan doesn't ring to yell at me, Dad doesn't come home and I think about Prince #2 out there, broken and alone, as I eat dinner by myself.

CHAPTER 7

'Jenna Ray?'

The soldier behind the security desk is unacceptably perky. Despite a shower in my deathly quiet house and the walk here in the early morning mist, my limbs are leaden and my eyes haven't fully opened. Basically I feel like death. An 8 a.m. start is too early. Someone needs to explain to Mia how teenagers work.

'Mmm?' I step out of the scanner and retrieve my bracelet, complete with my new heart charm, sliding it under the sleeve of my grey HPA tracksuit top.

'You've got post!' They hold out a white envelope with my name written in a cursive hand.

'Thanks.' I bump backpack first through the doors and head towards the training studio. Stifling a yawn, I rip the envelope open and pull out a letter.

JENNA RAY.

YOU ARE BEING POSSESSED BY THE EV.

IT HAPPENED TO YOU YESTERDAY.

YOU ARE BROKEN.

THE HPA WILL LOCK YOU AWAY IF THEY FIND OUT.

I CAN HELP YOU.

I'M PROBABLY THE ONLY ONE WHO CAN.

R.

R? Who is—

'No!' All traces of tiredness vanish.

This letter is from Ron.

Ron King. Ex-hero. Current prisoner. The man who tried to kill me.

I rush back to security. 'Who left this?'

The soldier jumps, spilling their coffee. 'It was just here when I started my shift. Are you all right?'

'Yep!' I say far too loudly. I spin back through the doors. Mother Earth. I'm not all right; my heart is racing and my face is sticky with sweat. How did Ron get a message into the HPA? He can't have escaped from the Castle, the HPA's impenetrable prison. No one gets in or out of there. I bring up the news on my phone, expecting to see a *MANHUNT FOR KING RON* headline, but there's just more on a water company spewing sewage into the river.

Someone left that letter here at Ron's request. Someone who was able to stroll on to the HPA base. They could still be here. I glance up and down the empty corridor and the skin across the back of my neck prickles like it did on the roof of Size Nines.

Mia wants me to move on to the base, but it's not safe.

The urge to press the little charm on my bracelet grips me, but I need to figure out what the letter means first. I breathe out, *two, three, four.* Ron says I'm being possessed by the EV, but that can't be right. No one understands exactly how the EV works but we do know that whilst it gives us our powers, humans are always in control.

I was in control when I absorbed the EV's power to defeat Ron at the Culture Complex. I felt every moment as the EV's blue flowed through me as sharp as ice and more powerful than anything I could have imagined. I haven't been anywhere near an EV power source since then.

IT HAPPENED TO YOU YESTERDAY.

Yesterday.

Yesterday, I had a panic attack and Prince #2 pulled me off the high street. It was the same as the other attacks I've had since the Culture Complex with those two new symptoms: my power trying to force its way out of me, and my vision shimmering around the edges—

No. My vision shimmering *blue* around the edges.

My stomach flips and I fall back against the wall. Did my eyes go electric blue, like the eyes of an EV pigeon, or squirrel, or anything else stuffed full of the EV? Those sparks running across my hands could have been part of it too. Back at the Culture Complex, I thought that I was using the EV. Have I got this all the wrong way round?

My fingers press against the concrete of the wall and I push myself upright. I'm now late for my first day of training. Tomas and Mia will know that something is wrong. I shove the letter into my bag. Ron's right; even the suggestion that I'm being possessed by the EV could ruin everything. I'm supposed to be a perfect trailblazer, and this isn't perfect. The HPA's mission is to manage creatures possessed by the EV. They'll lock me up without a second thought.

I breathe out, *two, three, four*, and close my eyes.

First Prince #2, now this. I need help. Mia and Tomas are out until I can figure out what's happening. Joy would try, of course, but she doesn't know anything about powers. Dad is avoiding me, Megan is gone, and contacting the Villains from within the HPA base is the last thing I should do.

I need someone who understands powers and who understands Ron. My eyes snap open. Blaze. I need Blaze. No one knows Ron better than him and his powers go squiffy too sometimes. I tap out a message.

Are you at the base? Can we talk?

Clutching my phone, I look down at the training studio, hoping that Tomas is snoring on the fold-out chairs again and I'll have time to find Blaze. But my mentor is waiting on the mats. He glances at the clock on the wall. Skies. I'm so late.

This is what Ron wanted to happen. He sent a letter to knock me off kilter on my first day of training. Maybe none of it is even true. Ron makes lying look like an art form and he hates me. That's motive enough to send something like this. I roll my shoulders, breathe out slowly one last time and rush down to the training studio. This is my choice, to be a hero and train with the HPA. I'm not going to let Ron worm his way any deeper into my brain.

But I hope that Blaze replies soon.

'The HPA loves an acronym, and the one for heroes in training is S-T-A-R, STAR.' Tomas stands in the middle of the training studio with vats of water dotted about. Under the bright fluorescent lights, he looks like an old rock star. His dark jumper and faded jeans hang off his slim frame and, even though there is no natural light anywhere in the subterranean base, he's gazing at me from under his white baseball cap.

I nod and move my hands behind my back to hold them still. Blaze hasn't replied, but I am fine. I am being a hero in training and it's fine. My stomach isn't churning and I don't keep picturing sparks jumping from my hands. This is fine.

'STAR: the four basic blocks of heroing. Do you want to take a guess at what the acronym is?' Tomas asks.

'Um.' Maybe Blaze is avoiding me because he thinks I'll try and kiss him again. Maybe I should have sent him a picture of the letter that's screwed up at the bottom of my bag.

YOU ARE BROKEN.

'STAR,' Tomas repeats. 'Shall we start with the S?'

THE HPA WILL LOCK YOU AWAY IF THEY FIND OUT.

I need to stay calm, in control. If my eyes turn electric blue in front of someone from the HPA, I'll be in one of their cells before I can say, '*It's just anxiety.*'

'Can the same girl who rushed to defend me against the elite Squad One really have no idea what STAR might stand for? Acronyms are not my favourite either, Ray, but this one is helpful.'

I rock back on my heels and refocus on Tomas's frowning face. What are the four basic blocks of heroing? *Secrets*, an unhelpful voice in my head whispers. *Secrets like that letter in your bag.*

'Save … Saving?' My voice wobbles.

Tomas claps, looking thrilled that I've finally engaged. 'Almost. You've guessed the "R".'

'Rescue?' I try.

'Yes! What about the "A"? What do heroes have to do whilst never ever killing anyone? You know this, Ray.'

'Attack.' The spiral in my mind is slowing. Tomas's enthusiasm is infectious.

'*Ja!* Remember that. Heroes don't kill their enemies. Not ever. It's the line that turns powerful people from good to evil.' Like Ron, who was willing to collapse a lighthouse with me in it *for the greater good.* 'Next. What's the first thing a hero does when sent on a mission?'

'They have to get there,' I mutter, and Tomas nods encouragingly. 'Transport?'

'*Ja!*' Tomas is almost vibrating with excitement. 'I will give you the last one as your reward, because it's not something we

69

can all do. Stealth. If you can sneak into battle, you can hold the advantage.'

'Stealth, transport, attack, rescue,' I say. 'STAR.'

'These four things we will discover together … and defence, that's also important, but it ruined the acronym.'

'Could switch out defence for shield,' I suggest. 'Then the acronym would be STARS.'

'*Sehr gut!*' Tomas claps again. 'Shield! Defend yourself, guard others, protect the world. STARS, then. That is our acronym.'

My cheeks tingle. I'm blushing and finally, the excitement is back. Defend myself, guard others, protect the world. That's the hero I want to be.

Tomas gestures to the vats, his eyes twinkling at me. You always hear about people being called old souls, but I think Tomas might be the opposite. 'Come on then, Ray, show me what you can do.'

Tomas is mildly amused by my ability to call the water. I show him jets, shapes and a watery wall. He just nods. It's probably not that impressive to a man who can make a hurricane.

'I ran on rain once, but I don't know if I could do it again. I can travel really fast and breathe underwater, and manipulate the water down there too.' I return the water back to vats in streaming arches.

'We'll start with land-based skills, as this is more difficult for you.' Tomas looks at me, his forehead slightly creased. 'You were nervous when you came in.'

My heart gives an uncomfortable thud. 'I get anxious,' I murmur.

Tomas rubs his chin. 'Something to manage. Thoughts can spiral, but action kills fear, *ja*? Let's do a control exercise! Lie on the floor.'

Thoughts can spiral, but action kills fear. I like that. Next time I go to counselling I'm going to take that in and share it with everyone else, like a plate of mental health biscuits. I drop on to the bouncy grey mat and Tomas lies down next to me.

'Now, make a circle of water above us, flat, like the surface of a pond.'

'OK.' I reach up my hands.

'One drop at a time,' Tomas adds.

One drop at a time? I float something above us that is roughly the size of a teardrop. 'Like this?'

'Ah, good! The girl who can control water knows what a drop is! Next one.'

I roll my eyes at him. I float over another drop to merge with the first, and then another. It takes my full concentration to keep my growing sphere in the air with one hand and bring over new drops with the other. There's no space for nerves; it's almost like going for a swim.

Tomas is right, action helps.

'Your focus is something that we will work on,' Tomas says. 'Sometimes you'll have multiple enemies, or people you need to rescue, all occupying your attention. Absorbing information needs to become second nature. Whilst you do this exercise, I'll talk through a few things.'

'Are you going to test me on it?' I add another shining drop to my ball of water.

'No, but it's important information that I'm only going to share with you once.'

The sphere shudders and it takes both my hands to steady it. 'Is that fair?'

'There is no fair. Let's start. You are going to meet the VIPs of the HPA and I'm relatively certain the first one will be –' he blows out a breath – 'Shelly Taylor.

'Shelly Taylor,' I repeat as I form the little ball of water into a disc. I know that name. Shelly Taylor had something to do with the pink monstrosity that I had to wear yesterday.

'Shelly Taylor inherited an oil empire. She has been involved with the HPA of various countries for a long time, especially with Ron in the past few years. She's very keen to meet you and people don't say no to her.'

The arm holding the water above our faces starts to shake and I switch to my left arm so my right can rest for a moment. 'She's the money,' I say.

'Exactly. Apparently, she's keen for you to be the face of her new campaign.' Tomas motions to my disc. 'You've stopped.'

I sigh and start adding droplets again. The shimmering disc is now the size of a plate.

'Shelly helps the HPA to further her own goals, which, for some reason, is more money. You'd think billions would be enough, but what do I know?' Tomas prods my disc and it wobbles precariously.

'Hey!'

'Concentrate, Ray.'

Ray. The only other person to call me Ray is Joy, but it sounds OK coming out of Tomas's mouth.

'What's the campaign that she wants me to front?' I frown as my disc grows to the size of a tray. It'll now be pretty intense if I lose control and drop it on us.

'Ah.' Tomas swipes at my disc again and I manage to bring all the drops back together. 'The EV keeps disabling her mega-drills, so she's one of the most vocal in the argument that we must find a way to destroy it. She has support amongst the politicians and ...' Tomas's voice fades as Megan's prophecy jumps back into my head.

Destroy the EV, destroy the world.

The doors to the studio bang open and Blaze steps in. He's dressed in his hero gear and his brown eyes are serious, but everything has become brighter, better – and another sensation that I can only describe as more delicious. Life is more delicious when he is near me. But if I want to be a hero, I can't do anything that will end with us back in a cupboard, with his arms around me, my lips dotting kisses up his neck—

The disc of water wobbles above us.

'Crap!' I try to catch it, but it shatters and fills the air with sparkling droplets, which fall to hit us squarely in the face.

CHAPTER 8

'Sorry!' I splutter, wiping the water I collected off my face.

Tomas lurches up, laughing, and shakes the droplets from his hair. 'I needed that!' He jumps to his feet and pulls me up. 'Not bad, Ray. Sustained concentration on something so small is hard with powers like ours. I want you to be able to multitask for long periods of time. Practising this will make the big things easier.' Tomas turns to Blaze. 'What can we do for you, young hero?'

Blaze crosses the mat to join us. 'Sorry to interrupt, sir—'

'Tomas,' my mentor corrects him.

'Tomas. There's going to be a Heroic Effort to tackle an ongoing wildfire in Australia's Northern Territory.' Blaze glances at me. 'That's a multi-hero response; Mia suggested I take Jenna along. If it's OK with you? She can observe, or—'

Tomas waves a hand. '*Nein*. Learn by doing. Jenna can be part of the team, but you look after her, OK, Blaze?'

'Of course.'

I almost miss Blaze's soft reply as adrenalin sparks through me. 'You want to take me to Australia? On a real mission? To work with other heroes?'

Blaze nods without looking at me. There's something off about him. Maybe it's because we kissed yesterday, but he's not nervous and hovering, or vibrating with the need to close the distance between us, like me. He seems down.

'Yes. OK. Great.' Tomas clasps his hands. 'We should visit Dr Varma and get you some hero toys. Come on.'

He bounds out of the studio and Blaze strides after him.

'Blaze, wait.' I jog to catch him before he reaches the doors. 'Are you all right?'

His eyes flick away as I try to read his expression.

'I'm fine,' he says to my shoes. 'I've just had some trouble sleeping since—'

'Nein!' Tomas bangs back into the studio and looks relieved to see we're only talking. 'You two are needed. Get moving.'

'Of course, sir. Sorry, sir.' Blaze nips past him out of the studio.

'Tomas,' Tomas growls again at his back, and fixes me with a look.

'Sorry,' I mutter, and head into the corridor too.

'Don't apologise,' Tomas says. 'Save lives.'

Blaze leads us to Engineering and as he steps into the busy lab, a scientist with a bushy grey beard and gold half-moon glasses rushes over.

'Blaze!' This must be Dr Varma. 'How are you today? Did you finish the book? Are you here for comms?'

'Yes, and I did.' Blaze perks up a bit as we follow Dr Varma past an intimidating array of tranquilliser darts, to a tall set of black drawers in the corner of the room. 'The concept of ferroelectricity was fascinating. I actually wanted to ask you—'

Tomas clears his throat.

Dr Varma smiles apologetically at us. 'Do excuse us. Tomas, it's good to see you. And you must be Jenna Ray.' He holds out a hand for me to shake. 'It's a pleasure, of course.'

'Jenna needs some comms too.' Blaze rises off the ground to reach the top drawer. 'And I thought I could perhaps test drive your new—'

'Get down from there!' Dr Varma orders. 'You'll get what you're given.'

'You're no fun today, Dr V.' Blaze lands and folds his arms, but his energy is back. Whatever was bothering him has faded in the presence of Dr Varma.

'Comms!' The doctor is all business. He hands me something that looks like a black earplug. 'And for you, Jenna, your very own utility belt.'

I take the belt too and examine it. 'Is there stuff in all these pouches?' I ask.

'Stuff?' Blaze sounds insulted. 'Jenna, this isn't stuff.' He steps over to open one of the three pouches. 'You've got a mini foldable grappling hook, a mask to filter the smoke out of the air, an emergency beacon.' He points at a small glass orb and rests his other hand at the top of the belt, his fingers settling between mine. For a second, I think those blue sparks are back,

76

but it's just Blaze's touch. 'There are night-vision goggles …' He freezes, noticing his hand on mine.

'And a mini first-aid kit.' Dr Varma steers Blaze back to the shelves. 'And you, Blaze, can test the Finder Seeker for me.'

'The drone that finds people using their body heat and leaves a nanobeacon next to them?' Blaze's cheeks are still slightly pink, but his attention is back on Dr Varma. 'I didn't know you'd finished it.'

'We did and this is the perfect chance to test it out.' As Dr Varma hands him a small green box with a handle, I risk a glance at Tomas, hoping he hasn't noticed the blush heating up my face too.

My mentor frowns at me. 'We can't send you out looking like work experience. Here.' Tomas pulls open a drawer and chucks some combat trousers at me, along with a long-sleeved black top and a body warmer.

'What about that pink costume?' I ask, and immediately regret it.

Tomas winks at me. 'Quick, there's no time to lose, just wear this sensible and practical black outfit.'

'Do you want me to run down—' Blaze starts.

'No.' I grab the combats and grin at Tomas. 'He's right, Blaze. There's no time. For the sake of the world, the powder-pink leggings must stay behind.'

I nip into a nearby bathroom to get changed, buzzing with excitement as I clip my new belt on. When I get back, Dr Varma and Blaze are still talking about the operating system of the Finder Seeker.

'Enough nerding!' Tomas exclaims. 'Go, be action heroes.' He turns to me. 'Put your earpiece in. We'll be connected and I'll use the flight to give you the essential information.'

I scrunch my nose. The journey to Australia would have been the perfect time to tell Blaze about Ron's letter. 'The entire flight?'

Tomas raises his eyebrows at Dr Varma. 'Do you see what they gave me to work with?'

I quickly put my earpiece in. 'Done.'

'Can you hear me?' Blaze's murmur comes through like he's talking directly into my ear. I blush again.

'Yes,' I manage.

'If it's a coordinated hero effort, you don't want to be late,' Tomas says. 'People get upset about that sort of thing.'

I nod. Whatever calm that was left over from Tomas's control exercise is driven away by adrenalin, but my nerves zipping round my stomach aren't the bitter kind generated by fear of Ron or the EV or my own decision-making skills. This is it. I'm going to face a wildfire in Australia. I'm going to help people.

Tomas walks us to security while talking through our priorities. Evacuate people. Stop the fire. Don't use salt water on fertile land if you can possibly avoid it. I keep nodding.

'Stay safe, Ray.' He stops at the base doors and puts a hand on my shoulder. 'Take your lead from Blaze.'

'Will do.' I smile. It's my first day of training and I'm already heading out to make a difference. I was right to sign on the dotted line yesterday.

'Ready?' Blaze asks.

I loop an arm around his shoulders and jump into his arms. 'Let's go.'

Soaring into the air with Blaze feels heart-achingly familiar. We're shooting across the sea in no time. The summer sky is cloudless and the waves rolling under us are deep blue. Even at this height, my fingers tingle, like I could pull a wave up to meet us. Blaze's face is set in a frown. He's not looking at me. Even when we weren't friends, he'd look at me when I was in his arms; anxious glances, like he was trying to figure out what was happening. Now, his laser focus is set on the other side of the world.

'How long is the journey?' I ask.

'We estimate that Blaze should make it to your destination in the Northern Territory in around forty minutes,' a voice in my ear answers. I don't recognise it. Is there a team of people tracking us and listening in?

'Oh, right,' I manage. 'Thank you.'

'When you enter Australian airspace, we'll connect you with the other heroes.' Tomas is in our ears now. I glance back at Blaze. With the sun on his face, the bags under his eyes are dark as bruises. Maybe I should pull our earpieces out so we can have a proper conversation? *'You'll have your own sector, but in close range there will be Vitesse from France, Roo from Australia and Cheche from Uganda.'*

'Great.' At least Blaze's sarcasm isn't broken. 'That just the luck of the draw, was it?'

Tomas sighs. *'Roo and the Australian HPA drew up the plans. You shouldn't have to interact with them too much.'*

'What's wrong with Vitesse, Roo and Cheche?' I ask.

'*They form a traditionalist block.*' Mia is now in our ears too. Looks like everyone is coming along for the ride.

'A traditionalist block?' I prompt.

'*They're idiots,*' Tomas supplies.

'They didn't want Ron jailed,' Blaze murmurs. 'And they're not fans of letting other genders into the hero club.'

'But they're young?' I blurt out. Cheche is the younger of two heroes from Uganda and Roo only emerged a few years ago during another EV wildfire.

'*Young people can be arseholes too,*' Tomas says kindly.

'*Could we watch our language on comms?*' Mia snaps. '*Sorry, what do you need … ? Oh, I … yes …*' There's a click which I think means we've lost Mia.

As we speed across the planet, Tomas runs through the other heroes who will be present. Almost every active hero will be on the ground, and Blaze, and me. It's wild. I learned about these men at school and now I'm going to be saving lives alongside them. Even if Vitesse, Roo and Cheche won't be thrilled to see me, perhaps the others will be. We've crossed the equator and we're flying in the light of the stars by the time Tomas has finished his rundown.

'*Any questions?*' Tomas asks.

'Are you tired?' I ask Blaze, and he finally looks at me.

'No. I do journeys like these all the time.' He gives me the tiniest smile and I mentally kick myself. I wasted all this time assuming that it was me or our situation upsetting Blaze, but maybe it isn't. I wish I could borrow Tempo's power and freeze time so we could actually talk.

Something tickles the back of my throat and I cough.

'This is the Australian HPA. Welcome to Australian airspace.'
A new voice is in our ears. *'You're now connected to the Heroic Effort channel as well as your own. Please precede any comms with your name so we know who is speaking.'*

Ash settles on my lips, but I stop myself from coughing again, in case it goes into the ears of all the listening heroes. The coast of Australia comes into view. Beyond the lights of a city, the night sky glows red. It is time to face the fire, again.

CHAPTER 9

'*This is Gray Jay: Welcome to the Heroic Effort, British team.*'
Gray Jay, Canadian hero, and the default leader when the
world's heroes gather, is in our ears. A breakfast conversation
with Megan pops uninvited into my head.

'*Someone add a pinch of salt to that man, he is as bland as a
boiled egg.*' She'd turned off the radio, silencing the Canadian
hero and delivered our own boiled eggs. '*Grey costume, that's a
boiled egg choice.*'

'*Named himself after the national bird.*' I tapped the top of
my egg. '*Boiled egg choice.*'

'*Arch-nemesis got so bored, he fled the country.*' Megan
tapped her egg.

'*His catchphrase is "Being good is great".*' I hit my egg too
hard and sprayed shell and egg all over myself. '*Feck!*'

'*No, Gray Jay, no! Leave my sister alone!*' Megan yelled, and
we giggled until Dad came in to see what all the fuss was about.

'Blaze. Thanks, Gray Jay,' Blaze responds, and I shove all thoughts of my sister out of my mind. 'We should get our masks on,' he murmurs to me as we touch down on the smooth tarmac of a road. There are a few temporary lights, but no soldiers, firefighters, other heroes or cameras. I thought it would be frantic on the ground, but we're completely alone out here.

Blaze lets me down and I check the pouch on my hip for my mask. It's not there.

'*Red Stripe. Is that everyone?*' The last time I saw the handsome hero from the US, he was laughing and spinning his new bride, Brooke, by the edge of his pool. Now his voice is husky with smoke.

'*Gray Jay.*' The rounded vowels of the Canadian hero answer. '*Qaqa is still en route.*'

'*How?!*' someone exclaims. '*He can teleport.*'

The missing hero's name sounds like *Ghanga*, but if it's the teleporting hero from Fiji his name is spelled Q-A-Q-A.

'Qaqa,' I murmur, pronouncing the 'g's and the 'n'. I guess I only ever saw Qaqa written down. I check the pouch on the other side, but there's no mask there either. It must be in the back one.

'*Gray Jay. Don't forget to announce yourself, Tempo.*'

'*Tempo. This happens every time.*'

'*Arashi. Every time.*'

The smoke is heavy in the air as I try to reach the pouch behind me. This is a stupid design, how are you supposed to get stuff out in a rush?! I'm still twisting, trying to see my own lower back, when Blaze steps in front of me. As I meet his eye, he gently turns my belt so the pouch I need is at the front.

'That was easy,' I mutter. If I can't figure out a belt, how am I going to stop a wildfire?

'I took the belt off to get into the back pouch on one of my first missions.' Blaze hands me my mask. 'It got swept away in a flash flood. Dr V was pissed.'

I chuckle and enjoy the smoke-free air coming through my mask. I can't imagine doing this without Blaze.

'*Arashi. Can we make a note that the heroes from Britain, which is the other side of the world, got here on time, but the hero from Fiji, who can teleport, isn't—*'

'*Qaqa. Hi, everyone!*'

There's an awkward silence.

'*Gray Jay. Hello, Qaqa. Welcome to the Heroic Effort.*'

'*Qaqa. And I'm right on time, eh? Because we said 8 p.m. local time and it's now …*'

Another silence.

Blaze taps his ear. 'Blaze. It's 8 p.m., Qaqa.' The amusement is clear in his voice. He's relaxed. Maybe it's like Tomas says, thoughts can spiral, but action kills fear. On the edge of action, Blaze has found a way back to his old self.

'*Qaqa. Beautiful.*' There's a flash of light and my hands fly to my mouth to stop myself from squealing as a man appears in front of us. This must be Qaqa. He's slightly taller than us and broader, with skin the same colour as mine and a full tattoo sleeve visible under a black hero suit.

He might have the friendliest face I've ever seen. He beams at me. 'Bula!'

'Hi, Qaqa,' Blaze says, and dodges as the big man tries to ruffle his hair.

'I wanted to come and say hello properly.' Qaqa sticks out a hand and I blink at it as I realise it's for me. None of the other heroes have really acknowledged me beyond calling us the British team.

'Hi.' I shake his hand.

'What you did with Ron?' Qaqa takes back his hand to do a chef's kiss. 'Not all these fools will admit it, but you saved us all from a dark path. We owe you a debt, Jenna Ray. Welcome to the team.'

My lip quivers as I search for a response. Ever since I read the letter from Ron, fear settled down in my stomach to wait, but Qaqa is here, reminding me that I stood up to Ron once. I can do it again.

'Thank you,' I say.

Blaze taps me on the arm and points at his ear.

'Oh! Game time!' Qaqa winks at me and disappears in a flash of white.

'*– been burning over an evacuated area of a thousand miles for three days, but tonight we contain it,*' Gray Jay is saying as I tune back in. '*Data has been sent to your wrist pieces showing the sector you are responsible for. Stop the fire in your sector however you know how. Stay alert until I say it's safe to stand down. Over to you, heroes.*'

'What do we need to do?' I feel like the person who was chatting at the back as the teacher explained the task.

'Don't worry, I've got it.' Blaze holds up his wrist piece, showing a map of yellow lines with a blue, pulsing dot. 'There's a river at this point.' He points to the dot. 'So, I thought I could fly and you could make it rain?'

'Sounds good, partner.'

'I like that, partner.' Blaze holds out his arms and I automatically swing myself up. Maybe I'm imagining it, but for a moment, he holds me slightly tighter than he needs to, like a stealth hug. I hide a smile. I shouldn't, no, *I can't* enjoy being this close to him.

The wide river is rolling past right where Blaze's map said it would. I can feel it rushing out towards the sea and I send a silent apology to the water as I pull a dark tendril to travel beneath us.

'If I keep a stream attached to the river, maybe we won't need to come back,' I say.

'*Good thinking,*' Tomas says at the same time as Blaze says, 'Let's try it.'

What's the worst that can happen? I dry out one of this area's precious water reserves and we're the team that let the fire loose to tear through Northern Australia? I prove the trad heroes right and they never let another woman join their ranks? Blaze, Tomas, Mia and the entirety of the British media write me off as useless?

Action kills fear. I breathe out and feel the water shift under my control. I can do this.

Blaze shoots through the air to our sector. As he slows down, the smoke and fire come sharply into focus. Bright orange flames leap up from the trees, the bush smoulders red and there are sparks of blue visible in the fire. The EV. Sweat rolls down my face, skirts my stinging eyes and is absorbed into my mask.

'If you spray the fire with as much force as you can, you'll push in air too which will help,' Blaze says.

'I thought fire needed air?' I reply.

'I'm flying fast, so the air will be supercooled before it reaches the ground.' Hovering above an Australian wildfire is not the time to try and increase my knowledge of physics, and Blaze is a science buff, so I just nod.

'Ready when you are.'

'OK then.' Blaze sets off along the edge of our sector and I blast water down at the flames. He's not flying at his top speed, but I'm still not able to make sure the fire is completely out before we've moved on. I'm about to say something, when we turn and fly back the way we came. A steaming strip shows our previous journey. I swallow my relief and keep the water blasting down.

We turn, zigzagging up our bit of the bush. All my concentration is taken up by the fire below me and the stream of water I am manipulating.

We turn and we turn and turn again and I keep the water surging down. My lungs feel like I'm running cross-country; the air coming through my mask is too thin and a dull throb pulses up from my wrists to the crease of my elbow. I don't know how much longer I'll be able to last. Blaze turns again, rocketing through the sky. He flew all the way here and he hasn't complained once. I don't want to tell him that I'm struggling but my hands are shaking.

We turn and I keep the water blasting at the flames.

We turn and my arms feel like they could shatter with the weight of it all.

We turn.

'We're done.' Blaze breathes out, sounding as relieved as I feel.

'We're done?' My hands flop down, but I don't send the water back to the river yet.

'We've covered the whole sector,' he confirms.

'Can we double-check?'

'Right you are, Jenna Ray.'

The flight back across our steaming sector is slower and we extinguish a few last glowing patches, before I send the water back to the river. Despite my fear, it hasn't dried out; it's still rolling happily towards the sea. A helicopter zooms overhead as Blaze places me back on the tarmac and I rock on my toes, enjoying being back on my feet.

'Blaze for Gray Jay.'

Gray Jay. Go ahead.

'Sector clear.'

Copy that, thanks, Blaze.

'And Jenna,' someone, Qaqa I think, adds.

'And Jenna,' Gray Jay corrects himself. *Good job. Await further orders.*

Maybe whilst we're *awaiting further orders*, I can finally

talk to Blaze. 'Hey.' I bump his shoulder with mine. 'Earlier, you were saying—'

'Blaze!' Pounding feet approach us. 'Jenna Ray!'

'What's wrong?' I turn and almost collide with a firefighter as she reaches us.

'People are trapped.' She gasps. 'Next sector over. Our comms went down. Vitesse is still out in the bush.'

'We're on it!' Blaze scoops me up.

'Straight down the road. You'll see our crew.' I catch a glimpse of her doubling over to catch her breath before our surroundings speed up to a blur.

'Blaze.' The fire chief is in front of us.

Blaze lets me down and I blink rapidly to encourage my brain to process that we've stopped moving. How does he do this all the time?

'People were sheltering in that cave complex.' The chief points across the road to where a rocky mound is just visible beyond the trunk of an enormous tree, with sparkling blue veins running up it. It's an EV tree, like the ones on the Wild Road, and fell from a cluster of trees that look just as big. 'The tree fell as Vitesse put out the fire. It's too heavy to move and it's as tough as diamond.'

He motions to a mangled chainsaw behind him. 'There's a small gap. I sent a couple of men in, but they haven't come back out. This area is unstable. We need to get everyone out before more EV trees fall.' The chief is only speaking to Blaze. Not that it should matter. There are more important things happening here than a grizzled fire chief ignoring me.

'We can use the Finder Seeker,' Blaze says. 'Then I can get them all out.'

'Wait,' I say, but he's already opened the green box attached to his belt and is tapping something into the lid. Several shining silver things that look like test tubes filled with mercury fly out of the box, hover in front of us for a moment and then shoot off towards the cave.

This is dangerous. The firefighters ran to us because their comms were down, but ours are fine. We can call for backup.

'I have them on my wrist piece.' Blaze holds it up. On the screen, several green glowing dots are clumped together in what must be the main part of the cave. There are so many people in there and a sharp creaking is coming from the other trees. He won't be able to get them all out in time.

'Blaze, we should call for backup—'

There's a gust of wind and he's gone. Mother Earth! He didn't stop and think, he just reacted. I run towards the cave, trying to catch a glimpse of him. The trees surrounding the cave's entrance are huge, blue veins sparkling up their charcoal trunks. The sound of splintering fills the air, turning my blood cold, and I skid to a stop. I'm not sure which tree it's coming from. It could be any of them. It could be all of them.

Feck! If I call for backup now, am I undermining Blaze? He's a fully trained hero and he rescues people all the time, but this seems reckless.

'Jenna.' Blaze's voice is in my ear. *I've got the first person and I'm—*'

The splintering turns into a crack and another enormous EV tree falls over the mouth of the cave.

CHAPTER 10

'Jenna for Blaze!' I yell into my comms. There's no answer. 'Blaze!'

Why won't he respond? I sprint to the mouth of the cave. It is now completely blocked by the blue-veined trunks of two burned trees. Any space that someone could have crawled out of is gone.

'They'll suffocate.' The chief races over to me. 'Do something. Now!'

There are multiple people trapped by immovable objects with no way in or out and I can't get through to Blaze. My fists bounce off my hips, but I force myself to stay still, to think. Tomas was right, blasting water at things is not always the answer. I need backup.

'Jenna Ray for Qaqa.'

There's a flash of white and Qaqa is in front of me. My heart lurches into my mouth. I am never going to get used to that.

'What's up?' Qaqa asks.

'There are people trapped in that cave. Blaze too. I can't get them out.'

Qaqa's gaze flicks over to the trunks and then down at his wrist piece. 'Blaze is using a Finder Seeker?' he asks.

'Yes.'

'Great news!' Qaqa gives me a jaunty salute and vanishes.

A moment later two civilians in sooty clothing are in front of me. I catch a glimpse of Qaqa too, before he disappears again. I know he'll get the civilians and the firefighters out of there, but the fear raging through me isn't just for them. I want him to bring Blaze back to me. I need to know that he's OK. He could have been hurt by that falling tree, or hit his head as he dived out of the way, or a million other terrible things could have happened to him in there in the dark. The worry is like a fist to my guts.

'Good job.' The chief's voice is sarcastic. 'Bring out a lady hero and she immediately calls for help.'

Another coughing person runs past as I turn to the chief, teeth gritted behind my mask. I'm exhausted and any patience I had left is now trapped in the cave with Blaze.

'I just doused flames that have been tearing through your country for days and then called in the only hero who would be able to rescue the people stuck in that cave in time,' I say. 'So, you're welcome.' I catch Qaqa's latest rescue, a staggering woman with streaming eyes.

'Thank you,' she mumbles as a firefighter helps her away.

'No offence or anything.' The Chief is unapologetic.

'No one who says that ever really means it.' I walk away from him before I completely lose it and dump river water on his head.

Qaqa has been reappearing every few seconds, but it's been almost a minute since he last flashed on to the road. My stomach flips as I watch the mouth of the cave.

'Please,' I murmur. 'Please bring him back to me.'

Smoke rises above the dark trees and the air is filled with distant shouts, but around me, everyone is quiet. They're waiting too. Seconds have never felt so long.

There's a flash as Qaqa reappears a few metres away, with an arm around Blaze's shoulders. The relief that floods through me is so sharp it brings tears to my eyes.

'All good, boss,' Qaqa calls in the general direction of the chief, and the scattered firefighters burst into applause.

My insides slowly unclench as I rush to them and give Blaze the once-over. He's not hurt. I breathe out. 'Did you get everyone?'

Qaqa holds up his wrist piece: all the green dots are gone. 'Right hero for the right job, eh? Never be afraid to call for backup. Nice work, Jenna Ray, really nice.' There's a flash of white and he's gone.

Blaze sways, looking at his feet.

I reach for him. 'Are you—'

'I'm fine, Jenna!' He shrugs me off. 'You keep asking, but I'm fine. It's fine as long as I'm saving people …' He walks down the dark road, but he's not getting away from me that easily.

'Wait.' I run after him and grab his hand. 'Blaze, wait. What do you mean?'

'It's all …' His voice is strangled, but he hasn't shaken me off or blurred away, so that's something. 'It's all I can do until I find a way to make things right.'

'What are you talking about?' I slip in front of him, my hand still holding his tight. The air is still smoky, but part of me is desperate to rip his mask off so I can read his expression. 'How exactly is barrelling head first into a deadly situation going to make anything right?'

'You don't understand.' He steps away from me and runs a hand through his hair. 'It doesn't matter. No, that's not right. It matters. It's just, I don't.'

'You don't matter?!' I follow him, trying to keep my eyes on his. Blue lights flash across his face as he looks away and the shadows falling across his eyes make him look haunted.

'That's not right either. I matter.' His voice is flat. 'I have to. It's the only way.'

'It's all I can do until I find a way to make things right.'

He'd told me he's been having trouble sleeping since …

Since Pari. Since that moment in the torrential rain of the council car park, when I told Blaze that Pari was left empty when Ron gave her powers to him. That's how Emily had described her. *'There's nothing of the old Pari left. She doesn't speak, she doesn't move; she'll eat, but only when someone feeds her. Her spark is gone. She's empty.'* He can make amends for following Ron, but he's still using someone's stolen powers and I made sure he carries the full weight of the cost.

'Oh, Blaze.' I lay a hot hand on the chest of his hero suit. I can feel his heart under there. Maybe it's broken, but it's still beating. Is this how he's been acting on every mission since that night?

He shakes his head but doesn't step away. 'It's fine.'

'This is Gray Jay. Australia thanks you, heroes. The Heroic Effort is complete. You are free to go.'

A flurry of heroic voices acknowledges him. We stay quiet. This could finally be the moment to tell Blaze about Ron, but I can feel that he's fighting back tears.

'Good job, kids.' Mia is back in our ears. *'I'm so sorry to do this, but you can't come home just yet. Our funder, Shelly Taylor, is on her rig off the coast of Scotland and she's requested your assistance. She says she's being attacked by the EV.'*

I exhale. 'This is relentless.'

'This is heroing.' Now we've got a mission, Blaze sounds more like his old self again. 'Come on, Jenna. Let's go to Scotland.'

The flight back into daylight is much quieter. As the sun settles over the horizon in India, Tomas pops on to say well done and ask how I found dragging water around the Outback. I tell him it was all gravy and maybe it's my tone that dissuades him from asking any follow-up questions. After that, there's silence except for the wind whistling past us.

Whilst the sun grows brighter on Blaze's determined face, I play with my sleeve and worry spirals lazily in my gut. Blaze is tired, I see that now. He's exhausted by the weight of his guilt and I don't know how to help him.

Mia pops back on as we cut across the coast of Scotland. *'Shelly has sent some updated instructions for accessing the rig.'*

Blaze's wrist piece beeps. 'Received.' He wiggles his arm around my back to see it. 'We'll approach from the west.'

'*Great. She said the entrance is at sea level and you should approach low. There's not currently any sign of EV activity around the rig, but Shelly is a funder so we've had to take her at her word.*' Mia exhales in a way that sounds like they'd like to say more, but they can't. '*Make sure everyone is OK up there. Keep sharp and leave as soon as you're able. Any questions? No? Out.*'

'Mia is not a fan of that millionaire,' I say.

'Billionaire,' Blaze corrects me. 'And I don't blame them. Shelly can be unpredictable and she has friends in powerful places. Ron used to call her "his little ATM" because, well, Ron, but I don't think he ever accepted how terrifying that woman is. I'm not trying to scare you, but a word from her and Mia is out or we're transferred.'

I swallow, adding Shelly Taylor, career destroyer, to my growing list of problems. 'Let's just get this over with.'

We race over the tip of Scotland, and what must be the Shetlands, and curve left. The rig comes into view almost immediately. I've seen pictures of oil rigs before, but this thing is a monster. Perched on the top of what looks like an enormous column is a stack of floors. It is like someone gave up halfway through building a ferry and then plonked it on a plinth in the middle of the sea. Three different crane arms stick out at angles and a few grey towers jut out of its top floor. Several people run to the railing to wave at us. Guess it's nice to have fans.

'We're approaching from the west,' Blaze murmurs.

'And we need to be low,' I remind him.

'On it.' Blaze drops us down so we're almost touching the rolling blue waves. We zip round the rig, past another entry point, and reach its western face. 'I don't see any EV activity.' Blaze stops dead. 'What? Feck!'

I barely have time to register that we're falling and then we're in the water. I almost lose my oxygen as I realise my bubble isn't there. Normally I have to concentrate not to have it, but the water has soaked in and chilled me to the bone. Cold. The sensation hits me like a wave. There is something so much colder than the water inside me. It's the cold of grief, of loss, of a seven-year-old looking at her mum's bare drawers. I'm empty. All I want is to curl up and vanish into the—

A hand hits me in the face. Blaze is a mess of bubbles, thrashing next to me with his eyes screwed shut. Skies, he can't make it to the surface. I shake off the dragging emptiness, grab him and haul him into the open air. I need to get us out of the water. I call my current, but nothing happens. I try and summon my bubble again, nothing. I can't even keep the sea spray from hitting us in the face.

'Blaze!' I hold him tight as we rise and fall with the waves. 'My powers are gone.'

A Statement from the Villains

The definition of madness is attempting the same thing multiple times and expecting a different outcome, but here we are making another statement.

Yes, the ongoing EV wildfire in Australia is catastrophic.

Yes, there's a good old-fashioned Heroic Effort currently happening to shut it down.

Yes, it includes the first female hero. Well done, HPA, welcome to the twenty-first century.

But, once again, we want to remind everyone: The EV is not evil. Despite homes, land and lives lost. That is not its intention.

Here you go in a bigger font:

THE EV IS NOT EVIL.

The EV is everything. It's in everything, including these defence mechanisms. It is lashing out because the actions of the human race are forcing it to protect itself.

The media only ever report on the EV one way. Either because they're idiots or they're paid by the anti-EV agenda. Why don't you have a go at thinking for yourself?

Also, this is your sign to stop idolising King Ron.

What is wrong with you all?

HE'S A BAD GUY.

F.

CHAPTER 11

'No, no, no.' Blaze tries to wipe the water from his eyes and almost sinks as I lose my grip on him. I grab him again and loop my arms around his chest.

'I've got you, Laurie, I've got you.' I sound much steadier than I feel. 'Keep kicking your legs.'

What is happening? I'd understand if Blaze is finally out of energy after his return flight from Australia, but my powers have cut out too and the heavy drag of loss is still pulling at my insides.

'D-d-d-dead zone.' Blaze's teeth are chattering. Not only is he terrified of the water, but we've just been plunged into the Atlantic. While my body isn't happy, at least it knows what's happening. Blaze was already exhausted. He might be going into shock. He shudders violently against me. I need to get him out of the water but the rig towers over us with no entrance in sight.

'Ahoy there!' An orange motorboat zips towards us with a slim woman swamped in a bright yellow life jacket on its prow. My relief is short-lived as it arrives in a surge of whitewash and I have to kick my legs hard to keep us afloat.

'Do you need a hand?' The woman has a brown ponytail, sharp features and a Scottish accent. 'Not a strong swimmer, is he?' she adds sympathetically, making a face at Blaze.

Has this woman got any idea what Blaze has been through today?! I grit my teeth, but I am concentrating too hard on keeping us above the surface to respond.

'Sh-Sh-Shelly,' Blaze manages.

So, this is Shelly Taylor.

'Help me get him out.' I pull Blaze over to the boat and hang on to the rope strung along the side.

'Of course, Jenna, of course.' Shelly motions to a couple of men in overalls who haul first Blaze, and then me, out of the water. 'Get them warm too. Look at the poor wee lambs, sitting there shivering. We'll get you inside.'

A little heater is shuffled closer to us as the boat makes its way back around the rig. I was warned about Shelly Taylor by Tomas too, but apart from her condescending comment about Blaze, she seems almost nice. Although I don't know how she got to us so fast.

'Oh!' I stifle a gasp as we turn the corner on to the southern side of Shelly's rig and my body is infused with warmth. My powers are back.

'Here.' I dry Blaze, evaporating the freezing particles of water on his skin, and give myself the once-over. I'm dry, it

102

happened automatically. And I'm energised, buzzing like I always do after a swim. 'Your powers?' I whisper to Blaze.

'They're back.' His teeth are still chattering, so I put my arm around him and pull him closer to me. We're not together, so it's not romantic. I'm just trying to make him feel safe. Shelly gives me a pointed look and then brushes some sea spray off her flared tartan skirt. I should let him go, but he's still shivering and the image of him on the dark road, telling me that he has to matter, keeps replaying in my mind. I hold him tighter.

The boat pulls up to the entry point we just flew past, where a surprisingly lavish glass lift is waiting.

'Come, children.' Shelly is helped up and beckons for us to follow. 'A hot drink is needed, I think.'

We swap a look and then follow her into the lift as the two men drive the boat away. Shelly presses the button for the top level.

'This is my own personal lift.' She reaches into a handbag I hadn't noticed to pull out a bottle of water. 'I spend a lot of time here and occasionally arrive in my yacht so – oops!' Shelly jerks the bottle and water flies at my face. I stop it before it hits me. 'Sorry, hen!'

The water hangs between us. She just threw that at me. I know she did, but I don't know why. I glance at Blaze, whose brows are furrowed. If it was anyone else, I'd fling the water right back at them, but instead I return it to her bottle.

'What happened?' I manage to sound polite.

'I thought I saw a spider!' She makes a mock horrified face. 'No harm done though, what with your powers. And what are we wearing?' She motions to my combats. 'I thought your pink outfit was lovely, although I don't know why you wore a jumper over it. I took the lead on that design, you know. The British HPA has been struggling recently and it's good to lend a hand where you can.'

'Oh. Thank you?' Mia's reaction when she saw that pink monstrosity is starting to make sense. 'I didn't have time to get it on today. We were in a rush to get to Australia and—'

'The first female hero,' Shelly interrupts. 'We'll need to find a nice feminine name to offset that brutish power of yours.' She pouts. 'How about Rainbow?'

'You said there was an EV emergency.' Blaze saves me from answering.

'And there was!' Shelly's voice rises a pitch. 'This awful wind full of sparkling blue particles. It was terrifying. It's over now, but I truly appreciate you for coming so fast.'

The lift pings and we step out on to the top deck. I thought a rig as big as this would be deafening with the sound of the machinery, but the whole place is strangely quiet. There's barely anyone around in the container offices or at the foot of the nearby grey tower.

'The drill is off, of course, because of the damage from the EV.' Shelly leads us past a large helipad. 'Still plenty to do! It's a hotbed of research here. Would you like to see the plans for my new baby drill? I call it a baby, but it will be quite a big infant.' She chuckles. 'We already have the biggest sea-based rig and my new baby will be the biggest on land. Biggest, best and brightest. Twice the size of my rig in the Highlands.

And I've created a simple six-step plan to get it set up on the land. We'll be able to move it, drill, move it, drill. It's very exciting.'

'That was a dead zone,' Blaze says as she leads us into a large container kitted out as a laboratory.

'Afternoon, Shelly.' A small, bald man pops his head out of an office which has all its blinds drawn. 'I captured all of that.'

'Yes, Dave, hello.' Shelly doesn't look over.

'There's a dead zone by the western edge of your rig,' Blaze repeats as we go through to a sitting room with wallpaper the same mustard-and-lavender tartan as Shelly's skirt.

'Tea? Coffee? Chai latte?' She motions to two small, also tartan, sofas. 'Do sit down.' Shelly heads over to an antique sideboard topped with dainty cups, a fancy-looking drinks machine, and a champagne bucket. Blaze doesn't move, but I perch on one of the sofas, still scanning the room. There are pictures of Shelly with the prime minister and several other world leaders. A sparkle draws my eye to several glittery lists stuck on the wall behind the kettle.

Shelly's Simple Six-Step Plan
for the Fracking Bill.

Shelly's Simple Six-Step Plan
for the Baby Drill.

Shelly's Simple Six-Step Plan
for the EV.

'Did you know about that dead zone when you directed us into it?' Blaze's voice is clipped. He's furious and barely managing to hide it.

'Sorry, I'm not sure I understand, a dead zone?' Shelly says. Her wide-eyed innocence is not remotely convincing. She knows what Blaze is talking about, even if I don't.

'A dead zone.' His fists are clenched now. 'A place where the EV can't function. Including, apparently, our powers.'

I look slowly back at Shelly. She gave us directions, but there was no entrance on the western side of her rig. She was ready to pluck us out of the water because she knew there was a chance we would fall. She tricked us into the dead zone and Dave in the lab told her he'd captured everything. A chill races up my spine. Shelly Taylor was experimenting on us. She could have killed us.

'I don't know what you're alluding to, young Blaze, but you've had a shock so I'm willing to let that tone go.' Shelly waves a tiny cup at us. 'Now, I'm going to have an espresso and I'll only ask you once more if you'd like a hot drink. Then I'm afraid you're going to have to make them yourself.'

The machine judders to life and the earthy scent of coffee fills the room, but I rub my arms as the memory of the dead zone washes back through my body. I've never been that cold before. That must have been the feeling of the EV vanishing. For the first time in my life, I didn't have any trace of the EV in me. I was so cold, I was empty. If Blaze hadn't needed me, I might have let go completely.

Destroy the EV, destroy the world.

Megan's voice is back in my head. Before her prophecy was just words, but now it's the feeling I had under the waves. I shudder. I might be wrong, Megan's vision might be a few hundred years in the future, but something tells me the woman eyeing me over her steaming cup is involved.

'Well, Jenna, how are you finding the HPA so far?' She takes a sip of coffee and meanders around her office. 'They gave you old Storm-maker as a mentor, didn't they? Did you know he once flooded a Swiss bank and drowned their mainframe? Claimed it was for a rescue, but it was really quite inconvenient.' She laughs lightly. 'You'll be an asset though, I'm sure. The first female hero. As pretty as Kate and as powerful as Ron. That's the aim.'

A surge of panic runs through me at Ron's name, but it vanishes as Shelly grabs my cheek in a quick pinch. She's gone before I can react.

'So pretty, yes. I want you for the face of my new campaign. We're going to sort out the EV once and for all. Now.' Shelly smiles at me, ignoring Blaze, who is still glaring at her from the doorway. 'Since that awful and surprising thing has just happened to you, could you tell me what it felt like in that dead zone?'

Blaze's eyes narrow even more, so I answer. 'Our powers were gone and so was the EV. It felt like dying.'

'But you didn't die,' Shelly parries quickly.

'But we could have,' I respond. She blinks, surprised, and I shuffle forward in my seat. Perhaps if I can talk Shelly Taylor out of her evil plans, my sister can come home.

'You didn't die,' Shelly says again. 'And look at you, you're fine now, powers and all.'

'Because we're out of the dead zone,' I try. 'The EV is back inside us.'

She frowns. 'You don't have the EV inside you, you're not an EV creature. Although that would be adorable. Imagine, a darling little EV squirrel.'

Shelly has evidently never seen an EV squirrel.

'I'm not talking about being controlled by it, I'm talking about the spark.' I clutch my hands to my chest. I can do this. I can make her listen. 'The tiny bit of the EV that runs through us all. I've got it, Blaze has got it, you've got it—'

'Well, isn't that lovely.' Shelly looks between me and Blaze. 'What a sweet way to look at the world.'

I deflate. It's not a sweet way to look at the world. It's the Villains' theory and that moment in the water has proved to me that they're right. My mouth shuts, lips pressed tight. If I knew more about Megan's prophecy, I'd shout at Shelly to listen to me, but Shelly Taylor is a funder of the HPA. She's the money. And I'm the perfect trailblazer.

'Shelly, I'm afraid we have to go now, there's an emergency.' Blaze finally moves from the doorway to grab my hand. 'No time to lose.'

'Of course.' Shelly turns a sickly-sweet smile on him. 'Do make sure you have a check-up when you get back to base. Let's get everything documented.'

'Sure thing,' I mutter, as Blaze pulls me out of the room.

'And fly out east, my little heroes,' Shelly calls after us. 'You don't want to make the same mistake twice!'

Blaze doesn't stop until we're out in the fresh air. 'Mother Earth!' He drops my hand and storms off, looking like he wants to tear down Shelly's rig himself, but I'm stuck on the platform, frozen in the afternoon sun. Megan came to Scotland, where Shelly's rig is. That can't be a coincidence.

There's a crack as Blaze kicks a plastic bucket into the side of a container.

'Blaze.' I jog after him as he marches towards the railing; there's a chance he could fly away and leave me here. 'Blaze!'

He stops and lets me catch up. He's pale and after everything that's happened, I feel shaky too. I might not be able to do anything about Shelly Taylor, but I've got a feeling that there's a simple way to calm Blaze down.

'I'm not saying what happened is OK.' I fall into step with him. 'Because it's not. Today has been tough and Shelly basic-ally tried to murder us, but …'

'But?!' Blaze rounds on me. 'How can there possibly be a but?!'

'But,' I continue. 'We've had an insane day and it's gone lunchtime. Do you think you might be a teensy bit hangry?'

Blaze glares at me. 'Are you joking?!'

My stomach whines loud enough for him to hear over the rumble of the waves and he deflates, a hint of a smile tugging at his lips.

'All right.' He holds out his arms. 'Lunch?'

'Lunch,' I agree, and a moment later we're speeding away from the rig and Shelly Taylor.

CHAPTER 12

'**W**hat the fecking feck is wrong with her?!' Mia splutters over the radio.

'We're a bit shaken up, but we stopped to get lunch,' I reply.

We had spotted the chip van, parked by one of the pink-and-grey beaches at the top of Scotland, from the air. The man at the window seemed nonchalant about serving two ravenous heroes at first, but he insisted we get a haggis supper and then wouldn't accept any payment. I managed to switch mine to veggie and when Blaze heard what haggis is, he followed my lead. Spicy haggis, thick-cut chips, fresh peas and whisky sauce are in a steaming package that's slightly burning my hand.

'All right, eat and then head back to check in with medical.'

'Thanks, Mia.'

I sit next to Blaze and take my first delicious mouthful. 'Mother Earth.' Whisky sauce is incredible. 'I didn't have breakfast.'

'Me either.' Blaze loads up another enormous spoonful. He has colour in his cheeks again and he looks less like he wants to fly back and push Shelly Taylor into the sea. 'Are you all right? I never got a chance to ask why you messaged.'

The sun beats down on me as I finish my mouthful. The letter. Ron. This is my chance to ask for help. Blaze's gazing at me with his kind brown eyes and I know he'll try and help me, but at what cost? He's so broken by his guilt over Pari that he almost got himself killed on that last mission. How many more worries can he deal with? A kiss is one thing, but if he helps me to hide EV possession from the HPA, he could lose everything.

'I'm fine,' I say. 'Just some pre-training nerves. First proper day as a hero and everything.'

He shuffles closer to me. 'You're good at it, you know.'

I can't help but smile. 'Well, you're a good partner.'

Blaze looks away to load up another spoon. He likes to get a bit of everything in a bite. Half a chip, a scoop of haggis, several peas, a splodge of whisky sauce. My heart aches as I watch him chewing and looking out at the rolling waves.

'You can't help anyone if you're dead, Blaze.' The words are out of my mouth before I've considered the best way to have this conversation. I bite my lip, expecting him to deny it or storm off, but instead he goes back for another spoonful of haggis.

'I know.' A pea rolls off his spoon. 'After Ron was locked up, the other heroes met to decide what to do with me and my stolen powers. There were a lot of opinions.' He gives a humourless chuckle. 'In the end, they put me on probation, but decided it was up to me to make things right. Gray Jay told me, *"It's your*

111

choices that make you what you are." I'm just trying to make the right choices.'

'We'll find a way to make things right with Pari. We'll help her.' It's the right thing to do, the right thing to say, and as he locks eyes with me, I know it's what he needed to hear. 'You and me, Blaze, we'll figure it out. But you need to take care of yourself until we do.'

Blaze blinks at me. I can feel the tears in his eyes and I know he won't let them fall. My poor, broken Blaze.

'Do you promise, Laurie Lin?' I say his real name softly. It's a precious piece of jewellery that I barely ever get to wear. 'Do you promise to look after yourself?'

He exhales, his eyes still shining as he looks at me. 'I promise.' His voice is quiet.

'Good. Now eat your haggis.'

He snorts. 'All right, boss.'

I load up a spoon of haggis too. I can do this. Ron said I was being possessed by the EV, but even if that's true, I've been fighting it off. I can keep control of myself, and deal with Ron's letter, and look after Blaze. In the bright light of day, at the tip of our country, I know that I can hold all of this inside me.

The stones clack as Blaze leans back next to me. 'I could stay here forever.'

And I shouldn't do it.

I know I shouldn't do it.

It's against the rules, but I can't help it. The force that tethers me to Blaze is still there. I take his hand. For a moment, I think he's going to pull away, but then his hand relaxes and squeezes mine.

His touch is warm and strong.

It's mine, I know it is.

His hand is mine and mine is his.

Even though it can't be.

Even though secretly holding hands is still far beyond what we're allowed to do, what we're allowed to be.

My first full day as a HPA hero ends the same way as a shift in the shop, with a walk through town back home. The closer I get, the tighter my chest feels. I'm going to talk to Dad. I need him to forgive me, but it's more than that. I need him to yell *'Hi'* as I come through the door and tell me about his day and ask about mine and … I just need him.

'Dad?' Once again, the house is silent as I let myself in. The lamps are on in the living room, but he's not there. I wander through into the kitchen, where a note is waiting for me on the dining table.

Had to head back in for project work.
Eat without me.
Dad

He's just working late. He used to work late a lot before the HPA steamrolled into my life, but the guilt in my gut still feels like acid. Maybe he's going to keep doing the evening shift until I move out. Maybe I should move on to the base and give him his home back.

I can't face staying in the quiet kitchen, so I grab a glass of water and go up to my room, knocking on the radio for company.

'The thing is, can you even take her seriously if she's literally being carried by one of the male heroes? The fire chief on the scene said that she just got the men to do her work. I think that if you're going to have a female hero—'

There's a sizzle and I look down to find my glass empty and water seeping from the radio. Feck. Tears prickle in my eyes. They're making out that I'm lazy and weak, when it was my first day and I tried so hard. I flop down on to my bed and swallow a scream of frustration. It's too much. My best isn't good enough.

My alarm pulls me out of sleep too soon and I wake up still in my HPA combats, but with a blanket over me. An unnecessarily cheerful bird is singing outside my window and the morning sun is streaming in. I groan. I must have passed out. I roll up and straight back into yesterday's fear:

The EV might be possessing me.

Ron still has me in his sights.

Mia wants me to move on to the base.

Dad probably does too.

I need to find a way to work with Blaze, and help him, without kissing him again.

The urge to fall back under the blanket is almost overwhelming, but my alarm goes off again.

As I arrive at security, I try to shove it all out of my mind. Stopping a wildfire in Australia wasn't enough for the media. I need to be flawless, which means I need to bring my best self to training.

I fall quickly into the routine.

Get up.

See if I can catch Dad before he goes to work.

                                    Leave disappointed.

Head to training.

Avoid thinking about EV possession.

Avoid thinking about Ron.

Avoid Mia, who is being pulled in so many directions I barely have to try.

            Brush away my media paranoia.

            Repress the fear that I am being watched.

Put all my energy into being the perfect hero.

A niggling voice suggests that failing to face my problems is probably a pretty terrible idea, but the days slip by without anything getting worse. And, despite everything, I still get butterflies as I push through the heavy doors of the training studio. I understand more about my powers every time I train with Tomas – and Blaze is a shiny and beautiful distraction.

We might not be allowed to be together, but he's still in the studio every day, either to run my combat drills or to jump in and help with whatever else we're doing. Even when Tomas gives him the very damp job of moving targets, it doesn't put Blaze off. We're never left alone, but stealing touches becomes a sport for us. We don't talk about it. We don't need to.

I find reasons to shove him,

or tidy him,

or hold him back to stop him slipping on the damp mats.

At the start of my second week at the HPA, Tomas finally loses his temper.

'Hey.' Blaze appears next to me as I take a break from the water droplet control exercise.

'You've got some—' Our eyes meet as I gently brush imaginary crumbs off his tracksuit top. He's wearing his glasses today, which makes touching him all the more delicious. A tiny smile tugs the side of his mouth and a low heat smoulders in my core. I'm making him happy and that's almost as good as the physical contact.

'Enough!' Tomas claps his hands at us. 'I can't take any more of this. Days you've been in here distracting my hero, days! No combat drills today! Out!' He jabs a finger at the studio door.

I jump back from Blaze, but my eyes are on his before I can stop myself.

'*Nein!*' Tomas yells. 'Out! Before I order you –' he points at Blaze – 'to have a cold shower. And you –' the finger swings in my direction – 'to do push-ups for the rest of the session.'

I swallow. 'Sorry, he just had—'

'No! No, he didn't! Out.'

Blaze grimaces at me and blurs out before Tomas can fling a tornado at him.

'Right.' Tomas's voice returns to its normal laid-back tone so fast I get whiplash. 'I want to talk more about the A.'

I blink at him. 'Ten seconds ago, you were furious.'

'*Ja*, well, ten seconds is a long time, Ray. Let's talk A.'

The 'A' of my STARS acronym.

Attack.

'I need your full attention for this, we're going to do something difficult.' He swings a chair round to lounge in, so I drop to sit on the mat, next to my notebook. 'Imagine this – you have an unpaid bill at a bar in town and the owner has enlisted several large men to extract any money on your person.'

My eyebrows scrunch. 'Shouldn't I imagine a hypothetical rescue or … ?'

'Hush, Ray. Now, you know that these men are quick to anger, having beaten them at poker the previous night. You know they would like nothing better than to introduce their fists to your kidneys.' He pauses and gazes into the distance, his eyes creasing as though he's looking back on a fond memory. 'Now!' Tomas reactivates and leans towards me. 'They know you have the power to summon water so they've picked somewhere with no water, or so they think. This is why I'm the right mentor for you. I don't just control storms. I create them.'

'You want me to create water?'

Tomas nods. 'There's water, and the elements you need to make water, in the air around us. I want you to gather it together, so you've got enough to fight with.'

I wave my fingers experimentally through the air. 'How?'

Tomas shrugs. 'Look for the tiny pieces of water around you.'

Tiny pieces of water? I close my eyes and try to sense the droplets in the air, but there's just the vats that Tomas set out earlier. I breathe out, *two, three, four,* and try to sense something smaller than the quivering lumps contained in the tubs.

There.

And there.

There are tiny flecks of almost water, hanging like snowflakes on a breeze, but I can't control them. I breathe out again and try to scoop them together. They ignore me. I try to change my motion to stitch them into a drop I can use, but it doesn't work.

'I can't do it.' I open my eyes.

'You can,' Tomas replies. I thought he might be annoyed at my failure, but he looks more intrigued. 'You can breathe underwater, *ja?*'

'Yes. It's the first thing I learned.'

'That's elemental manipulation. You can turn water into air, so you should be able to do the opposite. Try again.'

I try again. The fragments of water slip through my grasp like smashed rice, but I don't want to let Tomas down, especially after the imaginary crumbs incident. I squeeze my eyes closed. Scraping together these molecules is like scratching my nails across concrete. It hurts and achieves nothing.

I try and I try, but it feels impossible.

'Feck,' I mutter, opening my eyes. 'I can't.'

Tomas stares at me for a long moment and then rolls on to his feet. 'All right, Ray.'

I breathe a sigh of relief. Thank the skies, I'm done scrabbling around in the molecular dark.

Tomas narrows his eyes. 'We're not done with water creation. It will be the difference between victory and defeat for you. But for now, precision, go set up the targets.'

The rest of training passes quickly and before I know it, he's off to the Drunken Diviner and I'm heading home.

'Dad?' No one answers when I let myself in. I'm not surprised any more, but the wash of disappointment never goes away. But if Dad isn't here to nag me about nutrients, I'm going to have toast and mushroom pâté for dinner, followed by toast and chocolate spread for dessert. I can't be bothered with vegetables today. I kick off my trainers, dump my keys and wander into the kitchen. The low cloud isn't letting much of the evening sun through the window, but it's enough to illuminate the hooded figure at our dining table.

'Mother Earth!' My heart might have stopped, but my hands are out and I can feel the water in our pipes. I'll wreck our house, but I can defend myself.

'I'm sorry to surprise you, Jenna Ray.' Prince #2 stands in a fluid movement. 'I have another message for you from Ron.'

A Tale of Redemption

Monday, 29th July 2024
By Ian Collins
Hero Columnist

It is perhaps the strongest stories that have a protagonist on the road to redemption. Men are flawed creatures and although their aims are good, their methods can be questionable. This is certainly the case with Ron King. In an` attempt to protect us from the EV, he has been found guilty of stealing powers from the population. A desperate plan in desperate times.

After reporting on King for years, I was granted the privilege of interviewing him myself in the small media room of the Castle prison. He was given leave to wear his trademark three-piece suit and seemed out of place under the brash fluorescents, but King has not lost an iota of the charisma that made him our nation's hero.

Mr King, the past two months have been tumultuous for you. Where do you go from here?
[King] Well I'm not going any-where fast (laughs). I've made mistakes, I'll hold my hands up, and I'm taking this decision on the chin, but the HPA and the heroes all know where I am when they need me.

Are you still working with the HPA?
Like I said, I'm here if they need me. I've made that clearer than crystal, my old son. The world is moving on and things are getting complicated. The British HPA has a new boss and I wish them all the best, but there might be a moment when they need an old-fashioned hero with old-fashioned ideas. Only time will tell.

Jenna Ray is now officially a hero with the HPA. What are your thoughts on that?
It's an interesting move. Miss Ray obviously has impressive powers and has even played a small part in a Heroic Effort. But, going forwards, I question whether she will have the control necessary to become a true hero. I mentored Blaze from the age of ten, instilling discipline, self-control, and a 'never say die' attitude. I only hope that Miss Ray can stay afloat now she's been chucked in the deep end …

CHAPTER 13

'It was you.' The pieces fall into place so easily, I don't know how I didn't put it together before. Prince #2 saw me have an attack on the high street and the next day that letter arrives. Of course they are connected. All this time, I've tried to ignore the feeling that I was being watched and now Prince #2, Ron's sidekick, is in my kitchen. My fingers flex and the pipes around us groan.

'I am not fully – fully –' the android looks at the silver hand resting on our dining table and then back at me – 'I have a message for you from Ron.'

'You've been following me.' I glance towards the door. It would be entirely my luck that Dad chooses this evening to come back early enough to see me. 'You've been spying on me. Are you still under Ron's control?'

'I cannot answer that question.' He locks eyes on me. It's like he's willing me to understand. He can't say that he's under

Ron's control, which means that he is. Or is that just what he wants me to think? I don't know how Ron could have regained control over the android after the night at the Culture Complex. Either way, Prince #2 is not denying that he's been stalking me.

'Ron is disappointed that you have ignored his offer of assistance,' he continues. 'He understands power like no other and is the only one who can help you. For the sake of the world, it is imperative that he is released as soon as possible. Although it pains him, he now has an ultimatum for you.' Prince #2's voice is smooth and measured as he delivers Ron's words. 'He is able to cause EV possession in those too weak to control their powers. He has been causing yours. If you do not change your testimony to facilitate his release, he will ensure the entire world sees you for what you really are: weak, wild and danger-ous.' Prince #2 shudders. 'Do … don't … I am sorry, Jenna Ray.'

I'm motionless as he walks out of the back door, clicking it gently closed behind him, then my shaking hand finds a chair and I slip into the seat under the stairs. My feet are on the tiles, but they're doing nothing to ground me. I gasp as blue sparks crackle across the tops of my hands, pinching as they spring from my knuckles to my fingernails. The remnants of some tea floats up out of a mug. Water shakes in the pipes. Blue shim-mers in the corners of my eyes.

Mother Earth. It's happening. My powers are rising, like vomit, because I'm too weak to stop them. Ron must be doing this. Prince #2 delivered his message and now he's proving just how easy it would be to expose me to the world.

Weak, wild and dangerous.

This is exactly what the reporters have been waiting for.

I breathe out, *two, three, four.*

I won't let him win.

Three things I can see: *blurry sunlight, shimmering blue, my shaking hands.*

Three things I can hear: *my heartbeat.* That's all. It's roaring in my ears and—

The thin gold band vibrates against my wrist.

I blink and blink again as my power settles back down inside me, and the blue vanishes as quickly as it came.

My bracelet vibrates again. I'm squeezing the golden heart charm hard enough to add the outline to my fingerprints. I didn't make a conscious decision to press my Villain's SOS button. I panicked, and I called my mum.

'Oh feck,' I whisper. 'Oh feck, oh feck!' Why did I call Mum?! I can't tell her any of this. As soon as she hears about Ron and the EV possession, she'll stop me going back to the HPA. I won't get to train with Tomas or see Blaze again. Would that be the same as going AWOL? What do the HPA do to absent heroes?

I stand and knock my head on the stairs. 'Feck!'

How long do I have until Mum turns up? I don't even know where the Villains are. They could be in Cornwall or next door. I rub my head. I need to think this through. Maybe I can talk with my mum and Femi without revealing what's happening to me. Femi will talk indefinitely about the EV. I just have to steer him in the right direction: *'Yes, Femi, the EV is wonderful. How would someone use it to possess a person, would it be something like those batteries from the Culture Complex … ?'*

124

It's only fifteen minutes before there's a rap on the front door and I still have no idea what I'm going to say. The door opens with a slam.

'Jenna?'

It's Emily. Blonde, very possibly a bit psychotic, Emily. I hesitate under the stairs. She manipulated me into becoming a spy for the HPA, then helped save my mum and the rest of the town. I think I like Emily now …

'Jenna? Whoever is here, come out before I shake this house apart.'

She is quite dramatic.

'Emily.' I run into the corridor and stop in front of her. She's in her standard outfit: short biker jacket, grey skinny jeans, black high-heeled boots. I suppose you don't have to worry about twisting an ankle when you're telekinetic.

'Are you OK?' She puts a hand on my arm and looks around. 'Are you being attacked or … ?'

'I …' I really wish I'd had more time to think up a plan. 'I'm all right.'

'You're all right …' Her eyebrows rise. 'Did you press your emergency beacon because you stubbed your toe? Or did you run out of that disgusting oat milk that your family likes so much?'

How had I forgotten how annoying Emily is?

Emily taps her ear. 'Stand down. I've got Jenna and she's not in any immediate danger … Yes, I'm sure, Sima … Mother Earth! She's right in front of me, she's not bleeding, she says she's OK. I'll find out what's going on and report back … I'm always nice!' Emily rolls her eyes as she drops her hand. 'So.' Her voice becomes exaggeratedly pleasant. 'Why don't we have a cup of sweet tea, and you can tell me what's happening?'

'Don't strain yourself, Emily.'

Emily throws her hands up. 'What do you people want from me?! Isn't it enough to be a kick-ass telekinetic vigilante warrior?'

'I'll make some tea.' I step past Emily into our kitchen. What am I going to tell her?

'This is a very yellow room.' Emily follows me in and perches on the table, despite all the freely available chairs. 'So, Jenna ... ?'

'It was ...' I bash about with the mugs for a moment to give myself more time to think. 'Wait. Let me make this and we can talk properly.'

The kettle boils unhelpfully fast and I'm handing Emily a mug of tea before I have any idea what to say.

'This your sister's?' Emily holds up Megan's *Eat the Patriarchy* mug. I nod and she grins. 'Figures. I like the monster on it.'

I lean against the counter. 'OK, I pressed the button because ...'

The silence stretches between us until Emily takes a loud slurp of tea.

Inspiration hits. 'Because I saw Prince #2.'

'Lie.' Emily puts her mug down with a clink and sits at the table. She motions to the chair across from her. My jaw clenches. Who does she think she is, calling me a liar and then inviting me to sit in my own house?

126

'I did!' I slide into the chair.

'All right.' She shrugs. 'That's not why you pressed your button though. Was it something to do with *him*?'

'Him?' My forehead creases. 'Blaze? No, no, he's fine.'

A dark look passes across Emily's face. 'Not Blaze then. Not Prince #2, although I'm sure that's a fun story. Something that panicked you that you don't want to tell me about.' Emily leans back. 'Someone's blackmailing you.'

'What?!' How did she guess that? 'No, no they're not.'

She points a finger at me. 'Yes, they are. Sydney Jones?' She leans closer, trying to read my face, but I keep it neutral. 'Not Sydney Jones. The new head of the HPA?' Why would Mia need to blackmail anyone? 'No.' Emily exhales slowly. 'Ron.'

My face is completely neutral. There's no way she'll be able to tell—

'Mother Earth!' She slaps the table. 'What did that dinosaur do? He's in the Castle, how could he even get to you?'

Skies. Emily is the least empathetic person I've ever met. How has she managed to guess all this?

'You've gone pale,' she points out.

'Feck,' I mutter. 'You can't tell my mum.'

'Come on, kid.' She eyes me over her mug and the fluffy pink monster on it grins toothily at me. 'Tell Aunty Emily all about it.'

'You're more like a deranged cousin.' I take a long sip of tea. Maybe Emily knowing isn't the worst thing that could happen. She is insanely powerful. 'They can't hear this. Can they?' I point at her ear.

127

'Nope.' Emily floats the biscuit jar over and helps herself to a custard cream. 'It's just you and me.'

The blue-tinged panic attacks, the letter, Prince #2, I don't leave anything out, and to my surprise, Emily listens quietly. I flick on a lamp as I hand her the letter.

'This doesn't make sense; the EV doesn't possess people.' Emily smooths it out on the table.

'Apparently, Ron has found a way to change that.' I nibble on my lip and Emily frowns down at the paper.

'Maybe Femi could help with this. Or your mum?'

'I can't tell them.' I shake my head. 'They'll stop me from being a hero.'

Emily slides the letter back to me. 'You don't want any help, then?' Her chair scrapes as she pushes it back. 'Pressing your SOS charm was just a blip and you've got this covered?'

'Um.' I look between her and the paper. She's not being sarcastic; she sounds like she's gearing up to say goodbye. 'What do you think I should do?'

Emily shrugs. 'No idea. I'm the muscle in our little Villain trio. But it sounds really horrible. Good luck with it all.' She gets up and walks out. She listened to my earth-shattering, stomach-twisting problem and shrugged it off with a *good luck*.

'Emily.' I follow her to the door. Does she want me to fall on my knees and beg for her help? 'You're the only one I've told about this. Will you please help me?'

She turns back, scrunching her nose. 'If you won't tell your mum, tell the HPA. I saw the EV inside you when you took down Ron. Your eyes went electric blue. You had a huge amount of power. This is dangerous.'

'I can't.' There's a panicked edge to my voice. I need to be perfect. I can't take this to the HPA. I need to solve it, fast, and throw myself back into training. 'Please, help me. We worked together before – remember the museum, and the chase? I led the HPA off so you could get away.'

'And we're very grateful. Jenna, look, you're asking the wrong person for help. All I can think of is marching straight into the Castle and confronting that dinosaur.' She holds her hands up. 'That's my level of planning.'

My eyes widen. 'You can get into the Castle?'

Emily shrugs. 'We've done it before.'

'But if you can get into the Castle …' My mind goes into overdrive. 'Then I could figure out how Ron is controlling me. I can find whatever it is he's using to cause the possession and destroy it.'

She sighs heavily. 'That sounds like a lot of effort.'

'Emily, please. What do you want? If you can help me with this, I'll give you anything.'

'Access to the HPA,' she replies immediately.

'I mean, I can't give you that.'

'An hour alone with Blaze?' she tries. The menace in her voice makes the hairs on the back of my neck stand up.

'No.'

'You said anything.'

'Think of something reasonable.'

'All right. If I help you –' she leans on our front door – 'you need to tell your mum, and, um, anyone else who asks, how I fixed this for you. You need to really big it up, like I heard your story of woe and came up with a brilliant plan and now you completely forgive me for the whole Love Interest bracelet thing and we're great friends.'

'Oh.' It's strange to gain the upper hand against Emily. 'Is Mum still that angry?'

Emily's cheeks flush pink. 'Yes. But if I do this, then everything is square between us.'

'Yes!' I nod frantically. 'Yes! Absolutely. We'll be best friends or whatever you want.'

'Well, feck.' Emily holds her hand out. I grab it and shake it. 'Your hand is sweaty.'

I roll my eyes and wipe my hand on my tracksuit. 'How will we get in? I thought the Castle was impenetrable.'

'That's the easy bit.' Emily waves. 'No elaborate heist or complicated plan needed. I've got two words for you, youngest Ray: press pass.'

'We just pretend to be journalists?'

'Ron has done several interviews with the right-wing media. Getting his side of the story out there. I cannot fathom why the HPA are letting that happen, but they are a bunch of tools. No offence.'

'None taken.' If I took offence at everything Emily said, we'd never get anything done. 'You think we can pretend to be from a newspaper?'

'Or a nice trad magazine. The type that has a bouquet or a complicated cake on the front,' she says.

'*Great Housekeeping?*'

'*Great Housekeeping.*' She sighs again. 'I guess we'd better get going.'

'We're going to the Castle now?'

'No, dingus. We're going back to our secret lair. You're going to distract mummy dearest, whilst I make us a couple of passes. Telling her why you now work for our mortal enemies will probably do the trick.'

CHAPTER 14

'Are you OK?' Mum rushes over as I jump down from Emily's hoverboard.

'Yes. Sorry, I'm all right.' I pull the helmet off. 'It was an emergency, but not an actual emergency?'

Mum stops within arm's reach but doesn't close the distance, and neither do I. She looks rested and, even though she's frowning as she gives me the once-over, some of the lines that creased her brown skin have smoothed out. All this time, she's been relaxing a few miles outside Nine Trees. She couldn't have mentioned she was fifteen minutes from our house?!

Everything I felt when we rescued her from the HPA surges back to the surface: the flush of love and the churn of resentment. Mum left when I was seven and, ten years later, I tore my life apart to save her. But it's not even the blame that's making me hesitate. Everything that happened is her fault, and my fault, and Blaze's, and Emily's, and Ron's; there's enough blame for everyone.

It's not the blame that freezes my feet on the gravel drive.

It's the fear that I'll reach out for her and she'll disappear again.

Emily coughs behind me. I roll my shoulders and shove everything back down where I can keep it safe. I've got a job to do.

'Hi, Mum.' I step forward and she wraps her arms around me. My body might stay tense, but she's heart-achingly familiar.

My mum.

I love her and I hate her.

'Emily said Prince #2 was in the house.' Mum releases me.

This is what it was like last time, straight down to business. If I let her direct the conversation, Emily is only going to get a couple of minutes to get our passes made.

'I think he's been following me.' I lean past her and spot an ideal distraction. 'Mother Earth! Is this your new hideout?'

'Fancy, right?' Emily grabs my helmet and strides past, making a 'keep her talking' gesture behind Mum's back.

Fancy is the word. The Villains are staying in a converted grey-brick barn that looks like it's hundreds of years old, but someone spent a fortune on enormous windows and a sweeping drive to make it look like a modern holiday destination. A rustic picnic bench is set on the grass and there's a small jetty over the river gurgling past the end of the garden.

'Tell me about Prince #2 first,' Mum says.

'He was in our kitchen when I got back from training,' I reply. 'He's malfunctioning.'

'What do you think he wanted?' Mum produces a tablet and stylus and looks back at me.

'No idea.' I shrug and continue before she can tell that I'm lying. 'He ran off before I could ask him anything else. I thought you and Femi should know. So, I pressed my charm.' I hold up my wrist and my bracelet glints in the low evening sun. 'Thank you for sending it.'

The stylus clicks as Mum rests it on the tablet. 'It felt like a good idea after you signed up to the HPA. I wish you'd talked to me first.'

'How?' I can't keep the resentment from my voice. 'I rescued you, saw you the night of the storm and then you disappeared. Again.'

She blinks up at me, surprised. 'We were setting things up and dealing with … We were busy, but it hasn't been that long since I saw you.'

'It's been two months.' I cross my arms.

'Two months.' Mum exhales. 'Jen-bear, I'm sorry, time just got away from me.'

'Guess that can happen when your children are at the bottom of your to-do list.' I clench my lips before I can say any more.

She opens her mouth and closes it again.

'Jenna!' Femi steps out of the barn's wide glass doors and jogs over. 'Emily said you were here. Have you come to arrest us?'

'No!'

134

'Well, that's good news. I'd hate to set my orbs on you.' The last time I saw Femi, he'd been pinned in the crumpled front of their van. He scratches under one of his mini dreads and gestures to the chip in my wrist. 'I programmed the heart charm to disable your HPA tracker. We'll let the HPA know where you are again when you're back in Nine Trees. It's good to see you.'

'You too.' I hesitate. Is Femi a hugger? He gives me an awkward tap on the arm and steps out of reach. Definitely not a hugger. Emily must have sent him out for me to keep busy as well.

'How are you finding working for the source of all evil?' he asks politely.

'Um, fine?'

'F, we both chose to join in our time,' Mum says.

He waves this off. 'I'm not sure I'd have made the same choice if their leader had just tried to kill me.'

'He's in the Castle,' Mum points out.

'The HPA's changed,' I say at the same time. I don't need Mum to fight my battles for me. 'Mia Kaplan is in charge now and they want to widen recruitment. They've closed the hotlines for reporting on powers. They want to do things right.'

'Let's see how long that lasts,' Femi mutters.

'Jenna has her charm. If it all goes wrong, we'll have a brand-new recruit. Let's go inside and have some tea.' Mum nods at the barn. 'You can tell us everything you remember about Prince #2.'

'Prince #2?' Femi raises his eyebrows.

Mum fills him in. 'He's back and malfunctioning.'

I look past Femi to the kitchen, where Emily is lit up by a computer screen.

'Or we can stay out here, in this conversation about the HPA, the organisation which you both hate so much,' I say. It's the last thing I want to do and the only thing that will distract Mum.

'Are you going to try and recruit us?' she asks.

I shake my head. 'No, but—' My next question jumps into my brain and I don't know if I'm strong enough to cope with the answer. 'You left us to find Femi and join the Villains because of the HPA,' I hear myself saying. 'I didn't have a chance to ask when we were running from the HPA and fighting Ron, but I've got time now. Tell me why you left.'

A bird flits past behind her as Mum gazes at me, a resigned look on her face. Even if Megan never speaks to her again, she must have known that sooner or later she was going to have to explain herself to me.

Femi clears his throat. 'I should ...'

'No, F, stay.' Mum puts a hand on his arm. 'It's OK, you can help me. She should know about the nuclear option.'

My skin goes cold. 'The nuclear option?'

'It's the reason I had to go. I found out the HPA was developing something so terrible I didn't have any choice but to find a way to fight against it. Can we at least sit, Jen-bear?' Mum motions to the picnic bench and I give a stiff nod.

'Ron's nuclear option,' she continues as we all take a seat. It's strange, untangling my history at a picnic bench with the

Controller and my estranged mum. 'Ron has always said that if he can't control the EV, he'd destroy it to save everyone.'

Destroy the EV, destroy the world.

My heart thumps as hard as it does on a mission.

'It was the same when I was there,' Femi adds. 'He wanted to subjugate the EV or wipe it out. He never even tried to understand it.' He tilts his head. 'We didn't get on.'

'I didn't know what was happening at first, only that one of the engineers was working on a canister,' Mum says.

'Dave, wasn't it?' Femi takes off his thick-rimmed glasses to clean them on his T-shirt. 'Dave Loughty. He started just after Ron and was always doing something suspicious.'

'Engineering: Head of Evil Projects,' Mum deadpans. 'Lucky he was mediocre.'

My brow creases. Dave. Something about this is ringing a bell.

'This canister needed to be operated by Ron's conduit power. I actually helped Dave with the maths to make it work,' Mum continues. 'Then, before we could learn what the canister would contain, Dave moved into a private lab. Kept the blinds drawn. Locked the door at the end of his shift.

'I would have never known what he was working on, but one evening, when I was the last engineer on site, something in his lab started rattling. Security opened the door and we found a large canister on a table, vibrating so fast it looked like it was about to explode. There was just one golden speck in that canister, right in the middle, causing all of those vibrations. I found an anti-shock switch, which Dave had forgot to flick.'

Femi snorts. '*Dave.*'

'But when I touched it, I *saw.*' Mum's fingertips glow white for a second as if they're remembering reading that object too. 'Dave was making a canister to contain a dead zone particle, and Ron was going to put it into an EV creature to spark a chain reaction that destroyed the EV itself.' She shudders. 'If Dave had been halfway competent, I'd have never even known.'

'And you'd never have left,' I say as I remember bouncing down the stairs to breakfast to find that Mum was gone.

'You can't destroy the EV, Jenna.' Mum leans in closer. 'The violent blue is just the outer edge; the EV is much deeper than that. It's part of us, it's part of everything. There was no way I could stay at the HPA knowing that was what Ron was planning. I had to find a way to stop him.'

'So you found Femi?' I look between them.

'So I found Femi and the Villains.' Mum nods, not speaking the words '*And I left you behind*'.

'We did the maths,' Femi says. 'For his plan to work, Ron would need to transfer the dead zone particle into something too big to exist. It's about the surface area and amount of EV present which is essential to prompt the transfer of—'

I blink at him.

'The canister would need a very specific situation to be able to work,' Mum translates. 'It's basically impossible. If he'd given the project to anyone other than Dave, they'd have done their due diligence and it would have never got to prototype.'

'But you didn't come back.' My jaw is tight with the effort of keeping everything I want to say inside.

Femi awkwardly stands and manages to slip away this time. Neither of us stop him. If Emily needs more time, she can deal with it.

'No.' Mum's eyes find mine. 'Once I joined the Villains, I realised there was so much else that needed to be done. They were working to protect the powered and the EV itself. They needed me in a way that the HPA never did.'

'We needed you.' The words are out before I can stop them, but the ones that should follow stay safely in my brain. *I was seven. Dad was alone. Megan grew up too fast. You almost broke us.*

'I know.' Mum's voice is almost a whisper. 'I left and I can never change that decision. But I can help you now. We can move forward, Jen-bear. We just need to take it one step at a time.'

One step at a time is the only way to leave the pain in the past. I don't know if I'm ready for that. I still want to drag Mum back over the jagged mess she left behind, but this isn't the time.

'One step at a time,' I repeat, my voice strained.

'Tea?' Mum asks, like it's a much bigger question.

I shrug one shoulder. 'All right.'

'All right.' Mum exhales, like she's finding her equilibrium. 'All right!' She jumps up. 'Come and have a look. This used to be a prime holiday let before the EV took over this part of the moorland.'

'This is EV moorland?!' I spin round, expecting to see over-sized squirrels lining the wooden fence or blue-eyed pigeons landing on the roof. Everything is quiet, but now I know what to look for, the EV is obvious. There are thin blue veins running up the trunks of nearby trees and hints of blue in the swaying grass leading down to the river. 'Is it safe?!'

'It's fine.' Mum leads me towards the house. 'We're just living. That doesn't agitate the EV. It has no reason to react against us.'

We step into a large, airy kitchen with white marble counters. A pot of something that smells like Mum's sweet potato curry is on the hob. There's a dining room attached, but the table, the breakfast bar, and almost every other surface have been taken up by screens.

'We're using this space as our primary lab,' Mum explains.

Emily gives me a thumbs up from behind one of the computers.

'How many labs do you have?' I wander into a living area with comfy-looking brown sofas and a wood burner. There's someone else in the living room, sitting in an armchair with her head angled towards the window. Her skin is golden in the evening light, and two black plaits brush the top of her cream jumper.

'Well, there's the workshop in the utility room,' Femi lists.

'And the computers you set up in the bathroom,' Emily adds.

'Ah, yes! Bathtub one and bathtub two. I should get them running some hypotheticals on Prince #2 ...'

'Hello.' I step closer to the girl, but she doesn't acknowledge me, or even blink. I look at my mum, whose mouth is set in a grim line.

140

'That's Pari,' she says.

Fingers of ice squeeze my stomach. The girl sitting by the wall staring blankly out towards the river used to have the powers of speed and flight before Ron took them and stuffed them into Blaze. This is Pari. The girl that Blaze left empty.

CHAPTER 15

'Pari?' My insides squeeze. I work with Blaze, I flirt with him as much as I can without getting us both fired, but Pari is here, a real person who was left empty so all of that is possible. 'Should I say hello?'

'We don't know what she can hear.' Femi shuffles over to join us. 'But we keep talking to her.'

'I'll introduce you.' Mum goes over to Pari and sits on the arm of the sofa. 'Pari, this is Jenna, my youngest daughter.'

'Hi, Pari,' I say softly.

Pari keeps staring out of the window. I never let myself think about how old Pari might be, but she's perhaps in her late twenties.

'The reset device is almost ready, my love.' Mum reaches out to take Pari's hand. 'You'll be better soon.'

'Reset device?' I ask.

'We're building something to help her.' The sadness in

Mum's eyes breaks my heart. She gives herself a little shake and gets up. 'Are you hungry? I made curry.'

After a tense curry with the Villains, where I am quizzed relentlessly about Prince #2, I find myself back on the gravel driveway with Mum.

'We chose somewhere by the river so you could visit.' She looks at me uncertainly. 'If you want to come back, that is. Femi put our number into your phone.'

'It's under EV Cottage Hire,' Femi calls from the kitchen.

Mum rolls her eyes. 'Ring us and we'll turn off your tracker so you can visit anytime.'

'Anytime?' Mum has an address. I can visit. It's enough to tip me off my axis. If Megan were here, she'd throw the offer back in Mum's face. Actually, Megan wouldn't have ever come here, but there's a bubble of excitement in my gut. I do want to come back, if I can. I want to see her again on an evening where I'm not hiding something from her.

'Anytime.' Mum smiles and we manage another, stiff-backed hug.

Emily nips out and hugs me too. 'See you tomorrow,' she whispers.

They walk me to the river. 'Sure you're happy to swim home?' Mum asks.

I pull some water into a swirl behind me and grin when I see their eyes widen. 'I'm always happy to swim.' I blow her a kiss and fall back into the cool water to ride my current home.

*

Emerging from the sea dressed in smart casual is a strange way to start a Tuesday, but I'm ready to get Ron out of my life. I need this sorted before I go back to training with Tomas. I jog up the beach and my handbag bounces off the closest thing to a suit that I could find: neat black trousers and a cropped forest-green blazer that I 'borrowed' from Megan's room. If she didn't want me to wear her clothes into the sea, she shouldn't have left.

Our meeting point is a beach along the coast where there was recently a landslide. There are still brown chunks of rock littering the golden sand under the cliff and the Villains' van is the only vehicle in the mercifully empty car park. I called in sick at the HPA this morning; the last thing I need is someone posting a picture of me on the beach.

'Good morning, Jane Lane, investigative reporter.' Emily beams at me as I climb into the van. Why does danger put her in such a good mood? This morning, she looks distinctly un-Emily-like. The rose-patterned headwrap she's knotted around her hair looks like one of Megan's and she's found a flowery blouse to go with it.

'Jane Lane?' I pick up the lanyard next to me. There's a picture of me with glasses, frowning, on the *Great Housekeeping* ID.

'I thought a name close to yours might help as it's your first time undercover.'

I snort. 'It's hardly my first time undercover.'

'As someone else then, Jane.' Emily touches up her pink lip gloss. 'Your glasses are in the glovebox.'

I find them under some silver wrappers and something I

hope is cheese puff powder. The tortoiseshell glasses are a little snug, but at least they won't fall off. I check my reflection in the wing mirror. I've pulled my afro into a bun, but I still look like the Jenna Ray who has been on the news pretty much constantly for the last couple of months. 'Do you think they'll be enough?'

'Oh yeah.' Emily flicks the indicator and drives us out of the car park and on to a narrow countryside lane. 'No one ever looks past the glasses.'

As we hurtle through the countryside, my heel bounces in the footwell. Nerves vibrate through me, but Emily's excitement is infectious. She says she's doing this for me, but I've got a sneaking suspicion she was getting bored out in the countryside. Whatever her motive, she's helping me. For the first time since I got Ron's letter, someone is helping me with the mess of worry that's been stuck at the back of my mind. My heel stops. Action kills fear and doing something feels amazing.

The Castle was already infamous before Ron's trial, but now the enormous grey-bricked turrets and imposing walls are iconic. I don't know whose idea it was to turn a medieval castle on the edge of a cliff into a prison, but the effect is a fairy tale gone wrong. Instead of knights and damsels in pointy hats, there are criminals, some with crazy powers, and heavily armed guards. Even the tiny windows that they used to fire arrows out of are barred.

A construction site comes into view on the other side of the grassy moor. An enormous crane is building something behind tall walls. It's a weird place to build, this close to a terrifying prison. It can't be houses. The prison must be being expanded.

As we approach the Castle's entrance, I breathe out, *two, three, four*. I am about to become what I fear most. A reporter.

'Good morning, handsome!' Emily rolls to a stop by the barred gates with her window open. I clench my fists in my lap as a guard steps up to the van. 'What a beautiful day to be working outside!' The bubbly energy in Emily's voice unbalances me, but I keep my face blank. This is Emily undercover and she's sweeter than a cherry Bakewell.

The guard frowns at her and then looks past to frown at me. I return his serious look. Jane Lane is a frowner.

'We should be on your system,' Emily says, still beaming. 'Saffron Klein and Jane Lane.'

I pass my lanyard over. 'Or did the incompetent assistant get the wrong day again?'

The guard checks his tablet. 'No, you're here. You're meeting King Ron in the press room? You wanted to interview him about Love Interests?'

'Ron King,' I snap. 'And yes.' Jane Lane doesn't suffer fools. I'm starting to think she doesn't like working for *Great Housekeeping*. Her aim was probably to anchor the six o'clock news. 'How did I end up in magazines?' I mutter, snatching my lanyard back and slumping into my chair. Emily shoots me a look, but I glare back at her. Jane Lane doesn't tolerate looks from sunny Saffron.

The guard waves us through. 'Park up and head to the blue door.'

'Enjoying yourself?' Emily parks the van next to an arch with a gate that leads to a big courtyard.

'Psssht,' I reply. Being undercover as someone else is way more fun than lying as yourself. I'm starting to see why Joy is in every single school play. 'Let's go, but leave your hard-hitting questions in the van, Saffron. If you even have any.'

'Wow,' Emily says.

We jump down from the van, and I stride off towards the blue door so fast Emily has to jog to catch up.

'I'll take you to the media room.' Another guard is waiting for us, the sun glinting off his peaked cap and his eager smile. 'This way, please.' He swipes a card and with a loud buzz another door swings open on to a grey-bricked corridor. 'This little warren takes us to the public-facing areas. You don't need to go anywhere near the nasty folk locked up here. Except Ron, of course.'

'Of course,' Emily repeats as sunny Saffron.

'Of course,' I murmur. The last thing I want to do is interview Ron about anything, but we need to make sure he's out of his cell.

'We pride ourselves on our relationship with the press and were happy to accommodate your last-minute request ...' The guard is still talking, but Emily's eyes flick to the side and I follow her gaze to a white door with several locks and the label *Electrical Room*.

The guard swipes another door and motions us into a foyer. I step through and pause. At the far end of the corridor is a door with a laminated *Media Room* sign, and to the right is a passage that leads deeper into the prison. Emily slips past me, but before the guard can step through to join us too, the door slams shut, trapping him on the other side.

'Whoopsie-daisy,' Emily says, sounding far more like herself.

The guard bangs on the door and mouths something like, *'Stay where you are!'*

I fix my face to the right amount of scared and irritated and nod at them.

'Your turn,' Emily mutters.

My turn. I find the water running through the thick red pipes attached to the ceiling above our heads. They look almost old enough to have been installed when the Castle was first built. The theory is that I'll give the water a gentle pull and activate the sprinklers, causing enough commotion that we can sneak to Ron's cell, but the pipes are thick and it's hard to judge. I give the water a delicate tug and then another. A single drip appears in the sprinkler above our heads.

'Might need a bit more water than that,' Emily says.

The prison guard is still on their radio, watching us, but it's not hard to keep my expression annoyed. I wish Tomas was here to offer more constructive advice than *'that's probably not going to be good enough'*. I pull a bit harder. Another drip joins the first and forms a small drop that falls to splat on Emily's cheek.

'That's it then, is it?' She's not even worried that the plan is falling apart. She just sounds amused. 'I saw you make white-water columns out of puddles in a car park, but you can't turn some sprinklers on?'

I bite back a response and give the water another, much stronger pull. There's a creak from the pipe above us.

'Er …' I glance up.

The pipe bursts and Emily screams as we're blasted by a stream of water.

'Feck!' she yells. I could have probably stopped the torrent from hitting us, but we need believable pandemonium on this side of the window. And she's annoying me.

'Mother Earth!' I cry dramatically, and pull Emily out from under the pipe. We make a panicky move away from the door, pretending not to see the guard urgently gesturing to us from the little window. Water is still gushing from the pipe and I'm about to direct a jet towards the CCTV camera in the corner, when the stream slows.

'Oh no,' I mutter. The pressure is easing. I give the water flowing through a tug, but it's been stoppered too far down the line for me to get at it without causing major, obvious damage.

The door to the corridor slams open and the guard steps through. 'I am so sorry!' He rushes over to us. 'Took me a moment to get the water switched off and that door opened remotely.'

We're open-mouthed, dripping wet, and Emily looks as shocked as I feel. Our plan to cause chaos and sneak off to find Ron's rooms has failed. We didn't make a plan B. We didn't think we'd need one.

'Do you want to reschedule?' The guard looks between us. 'Ron is ready, but we can have you back tomorrow?'

'No, it's fine.' Emily waggles her fingers as she brings them up to her face to wipe the water away. 'We'll talk to Ron now.'

'We will?' Thank the skies Jane is a grump – it sounds like

I'm annoyed with Saffron for making the decision for me, rather than appalled by her choice to go face to face with Ron.

'Let's see what happens, Jane,' Emily growls, still moving her fingers as she pats her hair. Mother Earth. She's doing something, creating another distraction.

'Off we go then.' The guard motions to the media room.

'I just need to …' I grab Emily and pretend to empty my shoe of water whilst pulling her down to my level. 'We can't go in there,' I whisper.

'Trust me,' she murmurs.

I don't know if I trust anyone enough to let them lead me back into a room with Ron, but I straighten up. 'Fine. Even soaked through, I'm more than reporter enough for Ron King.'

> The corridor disappears in front of us, eaten up by the guard's footsteps.

Any second now.

> Any second now, Emily's new distraction will kick in.

> > She has a plan and I trust her.

> Actually, do I trust her?

The guard reaches for the media room's door.

My hands curl into fists.

Emily's distraction is coming.

Any second now.

The door clicks as it opens –

and an alarm screeches into life.

CHAPTER 16

The guard shoves the door to the media room closed, and I'm so relieved I almost vomit on Jane Lane's shoes.

'What's happening?' Emily asks as we follow the guard back through the foyer. She sounds genuinely curious, which is odd because I'm pretty sure she caused this deafening alarm. I swallow. Mother Earth, she was using her powers blind. Emily has no idea what she's done.

'Our circuit breakers malfunctioned.' The guard sounds stressed. He swipes the next door open. 'The prisoners from solitary were—'

He stops dead and I peer past him to see a prisoner in a grey tracksuit, standing in the corridor.

'Ethan.' The guard puts his hands out. 'Stay there, we need to take you back to your cell.'

Ethan tilts his head at us and there's a crackle of blue across his forehead.

My mouth drops open, but before I've got a chance to see another spark, I am yanked backwards. Ethan disappears from view and I'm back in the foyer, behind a crowd of prison guards.

Emily grabs my hand. 'Come on,' she whispers.

'Did you see the blue?' I'm still trying to see Ethan.

'Jane, the power's out.' She nods at the CCTV camera, which no longer has a little red light on the front.

Emily is right. She's delivered chaos. This is our chance. We back away from the guards and past the media room, where Ron must be sat waiting. My stomach has just about settled from that door being opened, I don't know if I'd have been able to keep control if we'd actually seen Ron. I might have cried or panic-blasted him into a wall.

When we're far enough from the foyer, we turn and run down the corridor that leads us deeper into the Castle. A roar echoes after us and all the hairs on the back of my neck stand up.

'Was that a bear?' I skid to a stop. 'Should we go back?'

'They're trained.' Emily pulls me onwards. 'They have more sedatives than they could use in a million lifetimes and this is your only chance to search Ron's cell.'

The sound of shots is followed by another deafening roar. I don't know if I'm more worried about the guards or Ethan.

'Come on!' Emily yanks my hand again and I let her drag me deeper into the Castle. 'I went this way the last time we broke in.'

'How often do you do this?!'

Emily ignores the question. When we reach a door that needs a card, she magically produces one and swipes us through. The alarm fades as we enter a narrow spiral staircase with the grey castle bricks exposed. This must be one of the turrets.

'The scanner I borrowed from Femi is already active and searching for advanced tech. Once we're in Ron's cell, it should find his evil doodad.' Emily recaps the plan as she bounds up the stairs next to me. 'We destroy the doodad, we get out of here and I've completely solved everything, which is what you will be singing from the rooftops after you're all cured. "Emily saved me. I owe everything to her. She is the best."'

'We almost ended up face to face with Ron and you broke the Castle,' I remind her as we twist higher.

Emily tuts. 'I think it's pronounced *"Thank you"*?'

We reach a landing. 'I guess this is it.' Emily swipes open the grey door at the top and stops dead. 'Figures.'

'What?' I lean around her to look in and narrow my eyes.

The room couldn't belong to anyone but Ron. It's more like a luxury hotel suite than a cell. It's dominated by a dark wood bed, but there's also a large leather sofa, a desk with carved legs and an open door revealing an en suite. He's even managed to hang his multi-coloured pop art portraits on the wall.

Emily steps into the room and turns. 'Feck!' She reaches out a hand, but there's a flash and she crumples to the ground.

Ron strolls out from behind the door and my heart stops. He raises his eyebrows at me. 'Would you like to come in?'

He hasn't changed. He's in a navy three-piece suit with a tartan pocket square. His silver-white beard is still immaculate and he looks completely relaxed, like he's just popped in after a visit to his barber. His resting charm face barely wavers as his eyes hold mine. Any hope I held out of Ron somehow being fooled by a pair of glasses and a bun vanish immediately. He knows exactly who I am.

Emily groans from the floor, but I am frozen. Feck is right. It's been two months, but I'm not ready to face Ron. Weak, wild and dangerous is what he called me, but I only feel weak now that I'm opposite him. I should drag Emily to safety or I should attack, but my feet aren't moving and my mouth tastes like metal. He tried to kill me. He brainwashed Blaze. He tried a mass power grab even though he knew what happened to Pari. Once I was in awe of this man despite myself, but now there's a deep and sour feeling churning in my gut. I hate him as much as he hates me.

'This is an unexpected pleasure, Miss Ray, or should I say –' he squints at my name tag – 'Miss Lane? How resourceful. I take it you were my eleven o'clock? Are you here to talk terms?'

If he wants to talk, I'm safe for now. I drop to check on Emily. Her eyes are closed, but her breathing is steady.

'She'll be fine in a few minutes.' Ron stoops to snatch up a scrap of paper by his feet, but I catch a glimpse of the words *Diviner, love* and *judge* on it. It's the Diviner prophecy. The one that says my sister will be a celibate, powerless servant: *The Diviner does not love / She does not judge / She does not lie / Her role is to see.* He folds it and places it back into his chest pocket. 'I imagine our time is limited, so shall we get down to business?' Ron clasps his hands.

'Fine.' I stand. 'How are you doing it, Ron? How are you causing EV possession?'

He chuckles. 'When Blaze was young, we'd do exercises on getting information from villains. He'd always go straight in with his questions. Innocent and direct. I told him it wouldn't work, but it took him years to figure out better ways of getting information. Perhaps he can teach you?' His eyes crinkle and I remember how this action hero could switch to paternal, safe, empathetic. 'How are you finding the HPA, Jenna? It must be difficult going from Love Interest to hero, and of course romance with Laurie is completely off the table now. That must be hard.'

This almost worked on me, back when I was a Love Interest, but I understand Ron now. 'How are you controlling Prince #2 again?' I edge deeper into his room, searching for a flashing light or beeping device or any sign of something he could be using to cause my possession.

'Who says I am?' Ron tracks my progress, emanating calmness. I am a lost girl in the tiger's cage. 'That android wants to save the world, just like the rest of us.'

He's got to be lying, but I can't out-talk Ron and I can't ransack his room with him watching. I should get Emily and get out of here.

'There is nothing that could make me call for your release.' I step back towards the door.

'I suppose not,' he replies calmly. 'Perhaps nothing that you could say would work anyway, but all I need you to do, Miss Ray, is exist.'

Ron strides over to hit a red assistance button next to his door and a chill washes over me. All I need to do is exist? What does he mean?

Emily groans and I rush back over to her.

'I'll stop you.' My voice falters. He hears it and smiles.

'I'm sure you'll try, Miss Ray. And you.' He leans to look past me at Emily. 'We've never been formally introduced, Miss … ?'

'Ms.' Emily sits up slowly and raises a shaking hand. 'I could end you right now. It would be easy.'

'It's always easy for you, isn't it, *Ms* Telekinetic?' Ron joins his hands behind his back. 'But you've got a real-life HPA hero with you. You're not going to let her kill anyone, are you, Miss Ray? That's not what heroes do.'

A flash of annoyance joins my fear as I hold his sharp grey eyes. Emily's wrong. Taking down Ron wouldn't be easy, but at least it would stop him from patronising me.

Footsteps and shouts echo up the stairwell. A moment later three breathless guards rush in from the landing. A bead of sweat rolls down the back of my neck. We've been caught red-handed breaking into Ron's rooms.

'Feck,' Emily mutters as I help her to her feet.

I look between the guards and Ron.

The guards look between Ron and us.

Ron just looks at the guards.

I'm not breathing. He's going to reveal our identities. We're about to be tranquillised and deposited in cells which won't be anywhere near as nice as this one.

'Ah, gentlemen.' Ron nods at them. 'I found these reporters from *Great Housekeeping*. They were in the thick of things downstairs, so I brought them up here to keep them safe.'

My eyes widen, but I don't know why I'm surprised. Ron will take any opportunity to be the hero.

'Skies.' A guard gasps. 'We thought they'd been taken. Thank you, Mr King.'

'Not at all.' Ron waves a hand. 'Once a hero and all that.'

'Is she OK?' Another guard steps towards Emily.

'Quite overcome by it all, I think,' Ron answers. 'Isn't that right, Miss Lane?'

My options are agreeing with Ron or revealing the truth. 'Quite,' I snarl.

'Well, we'll take it from here. It's safe to come back through the prison now.' A guard offers Emily his arm and I can see her desire to shove him away, but she takes it and he leads her back to the stairs.

'Good luck, Miss Lane.' Ron sounds as charming as ever, but I can hear the threat as clear as day. *You're going to need it.*

The prison is already back in full working order as we head out and, somehow, we manage to get back into the van without anything else dramatic happening. As we drive back through the moor, the conversation with Ron plays on a loop in my mind. For the first time in a long time, I feel powerless. I don't know how to stop that man. I'm scrambling, and he knows it.

A safe distance from the Castle, Emily pulls into a lay-by.

'Are you all right?' I ask. She had been in chatty Saffron mode on the way out, but maybe she's still feeling that power bolt from Ron.

'Fine, fine.' She fishes a sleek rectangular scanner out of her pocket. 'Let's see what this found.'

I lean over to look. I didn't manage to find whatever device Ron is using to control me, but maybe this thing did. Once I've got that information, I could go to Mum or maybe Dr Varma. They might know a way to protect me. 'What has he got in there?'

'He's got a laptop. Internet access …' Emily trails off, looking at the tiny writing. 'That's it.'

'Except for … ?' I squint over at the screen.

'No, that's it.' Emily looks up at me. 'He doesn't have anything advanced in there.'

'Can he trigger EV possession with a laptop?'

Emily scrunches her nose. 'Maybe, if it's controlling another device? Skies! I don't know, Jenna. We need Femi or your mum. There's only so much I can do.' She shoves the scanner back in her pocket and starts the engine. 'Obviously it's a lot of things, like fake passes, accessing the schematics of a top security prison and creating distractions … but I'm sorry, that's me tapped.'

She pulls the van out and the last of my hope that this insane trip achieved something is left behind in the moor. We broke into the Castle and came out empty-handed. I faced Ron, and for what? Emily is chucking in the towel and I have no idea what my next move should be.

My phone buzzes and a message pops up from Joy.

Do you have any firelighters?

I blink at it. My world may be spiralling out of control, but

Joy is apparently about to set fire to something. I message back, asking where she is.

'Have you considered he might be lying?' Emily asks. 'You are very easy to manipulate. I know this from personal experience.'

Joy replies. **Town beach. Northern End.**

'Could you drop me off just outside town?' I ask.

It's a short walk from where I jump out of the van, through the grassy dunes to Town Beach. Up ahead, there's a bonfire, billowing grey smoke into the clear blue sky. Orange flames leap into the air as a figure emerges from the smoke to fling something else on to the fire. She's barefoot and wearing a white summer dress.

'Joy?' I yell, and break into a run, my bag clutched under one arm. I know I haven't checked in with her for a few days, but did she join a cult?

She glances at me as I reach her, eyes red from the smoke, and flings a vinyl album into the flames. 'He didn't even have a record player.'

'Are you ... are these Nick's things?' A half-full bin bag sits by the dune, next to Joy's trainers.

'They're memories!' She flings a hoody into the flames. 'And I want them gone.'

'OK.' I put my arm around her and guide her out of the smoke. 'Is burning them making you feel better?'

She gazes at the fire, blinks and shakes her head.

'I thought if I could burn everything it would give me closure, but I just keep thinking about how bad this is for the environment.'

160

I snap my fingers. 'How about this.' I pull out Jane Lane's notebook and pen. 'Write one wish on a piece of paper and we'll burn that instead and send it to the universe.'

'A wish?' Joy's forehead crumples as she takes a piece of paper.

'A wish.' I know what I want. The one thing that sent me to the Castle and keeps me going back to group therapy sessions for my anxiety.

I scribble SELF-CONTROL on the paper.

'Ready?' I ask as Joy hands back the pen.

'Do you want to know what it is?' Her paper has been folded in half so many times, it's almost disappeared.

'Only if you want to tell me.'

'I want to be as strong as you.' She flings the paper into the flames.

'Oh.' My heart gives a hard thud and tears prick my eyes. 'I don't know if you do.'

'Come on.' She pushes me. 'Strong, independent, kind Jenna Ray. I want a bit of that, just a little bit. What did you wish for?'

Skies, I can't tell her. Joy needs me to be strong. *Everyone* needs me to be strong. 'I wished for marshmallows,' I deadpan.

'Marshmallows?!'

'Yeah, I wished for marshmallows so we could make some s'mores.'

She laughs and I chuck my paper in too, then pull a shifting lump of seawater over to put the bonfire out.

'Thank you. I feel ... I feel a bit less everything, I guess.' As the driftwood sizzles, Joy flops down on to the sand and squints up at me. 'I like your glasses. You undercover?'

'Sort of.' I sit next to her. 'Want to talk about it?'

She leans back. 'I just needed him out of my room.'

'Fair enough.' I knead my chest; my heart is still beating hard from the run over here. Maybe there's a way to distract Joy with my disastrous day, without worrying her too much. Maybe that will ease some of the pressure on my chest too. 'There's been some, um, stuff happening—'

Joy lurches up and points. 'Is that the Secret Ninja?!'

I peer across the beach to see a hooded figure on the road overlooking the dunes. 'Prince #2. He's …' Dancing blue spots appear in front of the android, moving to shimmer in the corners of my eyes. A spark jumps across the skin of my hands.

'Ow!' Joy brushes her arm. 'You just gave me an electric –' her gaze meets mine and she inhales sharply – 'Jenna, your eyes.'

No. Prince #2 is somehow causing this. I breathe out, *two, three, four.* I've beaten this before. My fingernails bite into my palms as I curl my fists. I can do this.

Three things I can see: *the android, my scared friend, water rising.* It's drifting up from the distant waves like someone has turned off gravity and it's not sea spray, it's me.

'Jenna?' Joy edges away. Behind her, Prince #2 runs down from the road, disappearing behind a dune, and out at sea, the water is still floating up.

'Joy, go …' She needs to get away from here. I want to push her to safety, but I'm hanging on to control by my fingernails.

Before, my power was like a small ball trying to rise up through me, but now it's everywhere.

'Three things,' I murmur. 'Three things.'

'What three things?' Joy is drowned out by the rumble of the sea.

Three things I can feel: *power crackling across my skin, surging through my mind and pumping through my arteries.*

'No …' I gasp.

Prince #2 slides down the dune to us and

I can't do anything

They're gone.

The dunes, Joy, Prince #2; the world is gone.

There's nothing except for the shimmering blue outlines of the waves.

But it's the waves that I need.

The water.

The water is around me. Directing me. It knows where it needs me to go.

163

Where I need to go.

There are outlines sketched in electric blue.

The harbour bridge as I race under it.

The trees on the bank.

       The river.

       I am above the river.

       Moving through it.

       No.

       I am the river.

           Here.

           This is where I need to be.

           Filth being pumped into the water.

       Into the sea.

Into me.

The water.

Lift it.

Form it.

Strike.

Break everything until it stops.

Someone is in the way.

They won't join me.

I will move them.

MOVE!

Break the machines.

Break the windows.

Break the tanks.

Stop this place.

Stop this person.

They won't join me.

Strike.

MOVE NOW!

Break everything.

Break everything.

Break everything until it stops.

It's stopped.

'Jenna! Please! Don't make me do this!'

Blaze?

It's stopped. That last thought leaves me with a warm swell of peace that evaporates as the world comes back in a rush of colour and sounds. Sunlight. Screams. Sirens. Shattering glass. My hands shake as I lower them. *Water treatment centre.*

I think I'm at the centre that I've seen on the news, but it's broken. In front of me, a circular pool spills water out into the car park. Bits of machinery are scattered across the grass and the shattered windows of an office block are still dripping. There's water everywhere. I can feel it all. I put it there.

'Jenna?' Blaze blurs in front of me. He's hurt; there's a cut above his eye. And he's soaked.

Horror surges through me. 'I did this?'

Nothing is making sense, so all I do is watch as Blaze raises a weapon and shoots me in the chest.

CHAPTER 17

*B*reak everything. Break everything. Break everything until it
stops.

'No!' I lurch up, my hands flying to my chest.

Mother Earth. Blaze *shot* me. There's nothing in my chest
now and no hole where something entered. My hands shake as
I lower them to the white sheets. I was on the beach with Joy
and then I was …

I was the water; surging, flowing, destroying.

Now I'm sitting on a hard bed in the same type of dimly lit
cell that they kept my mum in. I'm in a grey HPA tracksuit too.
My insides contract. The HPA have locked me up, just like Ron
said they would.

My powers. I suck in a breath. My powers aren't working. I
hold out a hand and flex my fingers. I don't feel the answering
call of the water, but I don't feel as empty as I did in the Atlantic.
It's more like my powers are hiding somewhere deep within me.

'It's the tranquilliser. Your powers will come back.'

I almost fall out of the bed as I spin to see Blaze in his hero suit, sitting in a metal chair in the corridor on the other side of the cell's glass wall.

'What happened?' A monitor beeps angrily at me as I move, but I ignore it and get off the bed to go over to him. He stands too, wincing, but straightens up so we're eye to eye.

'I hurt you,' I say. It's not a question. I can't remember doing it, but I know I hurt him. The image of a soaking-wet Blaze in front of the destroyed water treatment centre is seared into my brain. The cut on his forehead has a bandage over it now, but it's still there.

'Did I injure anyone else?' He doesn't answer, so I shuffle closer to the glass. 'Blaze, I'm so sorry. I wasn't in control. It was the EV. I couldn't stop it and I—'

He steps away and I can't follow. 'So you did know that something like this might happen?'

'No! I never imagined that I would …' I twist my hands. I'm losing him. I can see the anger and hurt in his dark eyes. 'It was Ron.'

'Ron?' His brow creases in confusion.

'He sent messages threatening me, but I wouldn't get him released so he made the EV possess me, through Prince #2 somehow, I don't know. I didn't know how to stop him. I didn't know what to do.' I get as close to the glass as I can. 'I wanted to tell you, but you're dealing with so much, I thought …' How can I tell him that I thought he'd break into a thousand pieces if I added another worry? 'I wanted to, I just couldn't.'

'I thought it would be different this time,' he murmurs. 'I knew it would be hard because we wouldn't be able to be together, but I thought we'd finally be on the same side.' The emotion that I know best writes itself across Blaze's face. Betrayal.

Everything inside clenches. He's not upset that I didn't tell him. It's much worse; he thinks that I'm lying.

'Blaze.' I put my hand on the glass. 'Please, you need to listen.'

His face is stony. 'Were you ever really HPA?'

'What are you talking about? Of course I was.'

'And that's why you broke into the Castle with the telekinetic blonde and tried to release several dangerous criminals.'

My stomach falls out through the soles of my feet. 'That's not what we were doing. I was trying to stop something like the water treatment centre from happening.'

'You were with a Villain, acting like a Villain. I guess you always were one, weren't you?'

'I wasn't … I just needed her help.'

'Her help, not mine.' His words are bitter. 'It's your choices that make you what you are.'

I bang the glass. 'I chose you. I was trying to protect you.'

'I don't believe you.'

There's ice growing within me, making my insides numb. He heard me, he just doesn't believe me. Blaze doesn't believe me. He doesn't trust me.

'Not that you care, but there's no way they'll let me stay after this,' he says. He's smiling now, a humourless grin that does nothing to disguise the fact his heart is breaking too. 'I let this happen, I didn't see … I can't believe I fell for it again. Do you know what Ron said when they took him away?'

I shake my head.

'*"Your love will destroy you."* And I didn't believe him.' Blaze blinks at me. 'How was I so stupid?'

'Blaze!' Mia's shout echoes down the corridor. 'You know you're not allowed in here. Out. Now.'

Blaze steps back, eyes still on mine. 'Nothing is ever real with you, is it?'

'It's all real.' My hand presses against the glass and it feels like the cold inside me could send ice crackling across it. There's nothing else I can do. I've lost him.

'Get back to medical,' Mia snaps as they reach us, and Blaze is gone so fast I don't even get to see him leave. Mia turns their glare on me and I stop myself from shrinking back.

'Mia.' I hold my hands up in surrender, like I'm not already locked in a cell. I feel like I'm teetering on the edge of an abyss. But if anyone can help me now, it's Mia.

'What happened?'

Their tone makes me flinch. Mia is always warm, even when they're being sarcastic. I've never heard them sound like this before, but at least they're willing to hear me out.

'I think I was possessed by the EV,' I say carefully.

They fold their arms. 'The EV can't possess people. The powered can use the EV for a boost, but they're still in control. People use the EV, Jenna. Not the other way round.'

'That's what I thought at first, but Ron planned this, he—'

'Ron is locked up in the Castle. I know you know this, because earlier today you paid him a visit. Do not lie to me.' Mia's lips twitch, like they're fighting not to show how upset they are. 'I knew you were still in touch with the Villains, Jenna. But this?'

'Going to the Castle was … I didn't know what else to do. I needed to find out how he was controlling the EV.' My words tumble out. 'Ron made it possess me.'

'And how, exactly, did he manage that from prison? Tell me he has a secret lab or some magical device and I'll send a squad straight over there.'

'I couldn't find anything, but—'

'Of course you couldn't.' Mia rocks on their feet. 'What you're saying isn't possible. Ron can't make the EV possess someone. That's not how it works. Until the Culture Complex, no one had ever seen a person with EV blue eyes.'

Until the Culture Complex.

The night we stopped Ron, I had the EV inside me. Emily told me my eyes turned blue. Ron must have seen it too …

'You found a way to invite the EV in and you've been working with the Villains ever since to replicate it. I don't know if you lost control today, or simply got caught.'

'That's not what happened!' I yell.

'Is that why you've been dodging moving on to the base?'

'No.' I shake my head. 'No, Mia, I just didn't want to leave my dad. It's not … I'm not a Villain.'

'Your chip went offline yesterday evening for two hours. Where were you then?'

'I …' My world is falling apart and I can't keep up. The truth will just make things worse.

'All right.' Mia paces in front of the cell. 'Why don't you tell me about the ritual instead?'

I blink rapidly. 'What ritual?'

Mia slams their phone against the glass. A news site is open and the massive headline reads:

JENNA RAY CONDUCTS BONFIRE RITUAL TO SUMMON THE EV

'Was that a cover for absorbing the EV's power?' Mia demands. 'Was that the way you harnessed the energy?'

'What?!' My mouth drops open. 'This is insane.' My heart skips a beat as I remember Joy. She was on the beach with Prince #2. 'Joy! Is Joy OK?'

'Ms Jusic is currently being questioned,' Mia replies.

'It wasn't a ritual! It was a bonfire for the crap Joy's ex left in her room.' All this evidence, all these coincidences, fall into place to tell the story of Jenna Ray, the power-hungry Villain. But Mia can't believe that. I won't let them. 'Mia, something weird has been happening with my powers for a while. I thought they were just panic attacks and then Prince #2 turned up with a message from Ron saying he was behind it and he would cause the EV to possess me if I didn't get him released.'

Mia shakes their head. 'Do you really expect me to believe that you would see Prince #2, that you would receive messages from Ron, and not come to me? Or Tomas?'

My mouth forms a perfect O. It makes no sense, but it made perfect sense when I was stuck in the muck of my worries. 'I was stupid,' I manage, but I can't get the rest of my explanation out. *I was stupid, scared and overwhelmed. I was trying to be perfect. Mia, I'm seventeen and I've only been a hero for a few weeks. I don't know what I'm doing.*

Mia's fists are clenched. 'I thought if I gave you time to adapt, if I gave you space, you'd come round, but you never wanted to join my HPA. You thought you could play me and I guess you were right. I doubt you even care, but once the investigation is concluded, I'll be forced to resign. We'll hand the HPA straight back to men like Ron.'

'No.' This can't be happening.

'The entire world is terrified. They want you locked away for good. And I can't—' Mia's voice cracks. They take a breath before finding my eyes again. 'You caused millions of pounds' worth of damage and have destroyed the new HPA, *my* new HPA. The men trying to hold on to power wanted us to fail, and you were their secret weapon. I thought you were the future, Jenna, but you've wrecked it for all of us.'

Every word is like another dart to the chest. They're right. I was scared and I played right into Ron's hands. My power still isn't working, so there's nothing I can do to stop the tears rolling down my cheeks.

'You still have dangerously high levels of the EV inside you, so you'll stay in this cell until you're back to normal. I don't know how long that will take; no one has ever absorbed as much of the EV as you did today. And after that, tests, an investigation, and consequences ...' Mia shakes their head again, like they've run out of words, and leaves me alone.

The tears won't stop. A well of sadness has been opened and I can't do anything about it. I make my way back to the bed and sit with my knees pulled up to my chest. My sleeve scratches my cheeks as I wipe the water away. I need to focus. I was so sure that Ron was behind the possession, but no one else seems to think that's even possible. What if he was lying? If I can just figure him out, maybe I can get Mia and Blaze to believe me.

My thoughts slam into one looming and inescapable truth:

It doesn't matter.

Nothing I think, or feel, or need matters.

There is nothing I can do from inside this cell.

My powers are gone. I can't get out.

Even if I could, no one would believe me.

Mia will get fired.

Blaze thinks I'm a Villain.

Joy won't understand the trouble I've got her into.

Dad. I snort into my damp arms. Dad was right to distance himself from me. Now he'll never have to see me again.

Mum probably won't even realise I'm missing.

And Megan. Megan doesn't care. That's why she didn't come back.

Ron has won.

I've destroyed Mia's HPA.

The whole world has seen me for what I am.

I am weak.

I am wild.

And I am dangerous.

*

The next day I don't see anyone except the Squad One guard who shoves meals at me before leaving. Lunch is pasta and a book, *A Biography of Water*, with a note from Tomas in the front.

I've always found cells a great place to train.
Thoughts can spiral, but action kills fear.
The after-effect of the tranquilliser should have worn off by now.
Here's your action: Experiment with temperatures.
Tomas.

The note swims in front of me. Why is he being kind to me? I don't deserve it. He's right though, my powers are back. I use them to stop the tears, but I can't bring myself to care that they've returned. I leave the pasta and the book on the floor and go back to sleep.

I don't know what time it is the next time I wake up.

Or the next.

When I use the little bathroom in the corner of the cell, I make lazy shapes with the drizzle from the tap and remember

Tomas's note. *Experiment with temperatures*. They've turned down the water pressure in my cell, and if I leave the tap on for too long, it cuts out entirely. There's barely enough to play with, but it's not like I've got anything better to do. After washing my hands, I concentrate on the layer of water in the sink.

The cold comes easily; it's the temperature of my insides. I direct the ever-present chill into the water and it races across, cracking as it turns to ice. My fingers brush the cool, smooth surface, but a blue spark pings off my fingernail and the joy of learning a new aspect of my power fades. This is only easy because there's so much of the EV left inside me. This is just another way for me to hurt people.

Even sleep is no relief from my spiralling thoughts. In my dreams, I find myself surfing up the river, or back at the water treatment centre with people screaming as I blast Blaze into a building. Or with Blaze, separated from me by the glass, saying, *'Nothing is ever real with you, is it?'*

I keep sleeping though, occasionally emerging long enough for a few bites of whatever is on the tray. Tomas sends more notes.

Practise creating water ...
Challenge yourself ...
Action kills fear ...

I leave them on the floor.

All I do is sleep and fall in and out of the disaster that I caused.

177

I. TOLD. YOU. SO.

By Sarah Popkin for H-Mail Online

13540 shares

In a world incapable of stopping and thinking, even for a moment, I am trying to remain magnanimous in victory. No one likes a bragger, especially when there's a major clean up happening, so I'll just say it one more time. I told you so.

We weren't ready for a female hero and we certainly weren't ready for *this* female hero. ICYMI, Jenna Ray just went into blue-eyed psycho mode, blasted her ex into a building and flattened a water treatment centre.

Why would our pretty water nymph do that?! you leftie snowflakes might ask.

It's because SHE'S A VILLAIN. She was a Villain when she put our nation's defender behind bars. She was a Villain when she broke into the Castle to intimidate him and she's a Villain now. There is so much coming out now about this girl, it's hard to know what is real. Did she *really* dance naked in front of a beach bonfire to summon the EV? It's no less believable than the rest of her Villainous acts.

I told you so.

One thing I do know is that she went blue-eyed the night

she fought Ron. This is from the great man himself; Jenna Ray invited the EV inside her so she could defeat him. The outcome of their battle finally makes sense. It tracks that Jenna needed to keep going back to the most unstable of power sources to compete with the male heroes around her. And it makes even more sense that, in the end, this deluded teenager was unable to control that power or herself.

Like all Villains, she is an EV fanatic.

Like all Villains, she is a danger to society.

Like all Villains, Jenna Ray is not, and never will be, a hero.

I told –

You so.

The female hero experiment has failed. Mx Kaplan's progressive new HPA is dissolving in front of us. There's only one man who can sort out this mess and he's currently behind bars. I was right about Jenna Ray and I am right about King Ron.

Join me in demanding better. Email your MPs. Take to the streets in protest. Let your voices be heard. We want our hero back.

BRING BACK KING RON.

#BBKR

CHAPTER 18

The ice in the sink cracks.

It cracks again.

The sound pulls me from the shimmering blue of another nightmare, and my eyes flick open. The ice is gone. It melted, maybe days ago, and I haven't made more. I roll up to see a guard standing on the other side of the glass wall. Is it a member of Squad One, here to stare happily at me, in a cell where I belong?

The guard waves at me.

'Emily?' My voice is croaky. I guess I haven't used it in a while. 'What are you doing here?' One of my legs is dead, but I ignore the sparks shooting up it and wobble over to her.

She tilts her head. 'That depends who you ask.' The door of the cell swings open and she holds out some handcuffs. 'According to the logs, I'm transferring you to another facility, but in reality, I am rescuing you. You're welcome.'

Emily's grin falters as I step away from the cell's open door and go back to the bed.

'Go away.'

'Go away?' Emily pops her head into the cell. 'It took us days to plan this. Come with me now … I am being nice!' Emily touches her ear. 'I was obviously going to tell her that. She just took me by surprise.' She looks at me. 'Jenna. We can make it so you're never possessed by the EV again.'

'What?!' I'm up and back in front of her in seconds. 'What do you mean?'

Emily holds out a small white stone badge. 'Put this on.'

I take it and pin it on to my tracksuit. 'What does it—' Something rushes out of me and I stagger into Emily's waiting arms. 'Feck.' The badge on my chest has turned black, and a faint white spiral is now visible.

'I think it's working,' Emily says into her comms. 'The freaky blue sparkles in her eyes have gone.'

'What is it?' I straighten up. My body is lighter somehow and even my vision has changed. I thought that the cell's lights were slightly blue. They're not.

'We call it a shield. It's adapted from a part of Pari's reset device. Your mum and Femi said a lot of long words that I didn't retain and we did this crazy dangerous test with an EV squirrel and shall I keep explaining things or would you actually like to escape?'

'Escape?' I could leave this cell. I could go back out into the world where I'm a dangerous menace and everyone hates me. Or I could stay here where I'm safe and everyone else is safe from me.

181

Emily holds out the cuffs. 'I swear to the skies, Jenna Ray, if your self-pity gets me caught, I'm taking out the entire HPA, starting with you. Now come on.'

I don't want to go.

It's too hard.

'She's lost her fight.' Emily is looking at me, but she's talking to the other Villains. 'Tell her what? OK.' Emily shakes the cuffs. 'Your mum says Joy also volunteered to rescue you. Want to come with me? Or do you want your annoying little friend to try her luck?'

'What?' My hands lift automatically and a telekinetic shove from Emily gets them up to where she needs them.

'You heard me. Just look like a disgraced hero and I'll do the rest.' She clicks the cuffs on. 'A little pressure from you and those will just fall off. But let's try and talk our way out of here first, all right?'

'You met Joy?' I step out of the cell, ignoring the voice in my head screaming for me to go back.

'She was the only one who knew what happened. It's been like a crime drama out there, except no one understands the crime and I'm the main suspect even though all I've done is try to help.' Emily waves off her annoyance as she leads me past several empty cells and out into the concrete HPA corridor.

'But Joy's safe?' The further I get from the cell, the more of myself I seem to find. The brain fog is lifting and blood is flowing to my muscles again. It could just be adrenalin, or maybe the old Jenna has been stuck out here, waiting for me.

'She's fine. Since she's your sidekick, your mum didn't even blindfold her when we brought her to the barn.'

My pulse thunders in my ears as we emerge from the stairwell and head down the corridor to security. A soldier rushes past and I avoid their eye. It doesn't matter that Emily is wearing the right uniform; it can't be long until someone notices that this sarcastic blonde isn't a part of the HPA. If it comes to a fight, I don't know how far I'll go to protect myself. I flex my fingers experimentally and find there's still water in the training studio. It's probably close enough for me to call if we're stopped at security, but what if Blaze appears? I swallow. I don't want to hurt him again.

We push through the doors to security and all images of fighting Blaze vanish. Tomas is there, elbows on the desk, chatting to a blushing security guard.

'Tomas,' I gasp. Together, Emily and I might be a match for him, but there's no way that we can take Tomas down before he, or the guard, pulls the alarm. A lifetime back in that tiny cell flashes in front of my eyes as my mentor turns to face us.

'Ah, I was looking for my phone, but look who I found instead.' Tomas leans on the desk, in front of the guard. 'You're transferring her?'

'Wait.' The guard jumps up to peer past Tomas. 'Hold it right there. I haven't seen anything about moving Jenna Ray.'

As the guard frantically taps her keyboard, Tomas locks eyes with me and winks. My fear drains away and I clench my lips to stop myself smiling. He's in on this!

'Sorry, no, here's the order.' The guard sits back at the desk to open the door for us. 'Report in when you get to the museum.'

'Right you are.' Emily pulls something out of her pocket and hands it to Tomas. 'The item you requested for Dr Varma, sir.'

Tomas takes the envelope off Emily and puts a hand on my shoulder. 'Jenna, this is a journey and you will find your way. You wouldn't believe how many times I've been arrested. It always works out. Stay strong.'

'Thank you.' I should say more to my mentor, but Emily pulls me out of the building and into the covered car park. A bus rumbles past above us and a spark of hope reignites in my gut. I am out; out of the cell, out of the HPA base, and back out in the world where there aren't sirens, or reporters, or people waiting with WE HATE JENNA RAY placards. There's just a quiet car park underneath people going about their lives.

Emily stops abruptly behind a column. 'Femi, kill Jenna's tracker and come and get us.'

There's a screech of tyres and the Villains' familiar silver van speeds into the car park. The door slides open and, a moment later, I'm inside, being driven away. A shard of cold returns to my chest as I picture Mia and Blaze outside my empty cell.

Blaze is convinced that I am a Villain. I guess now he's right.

Femi pulls into a little lane before we reach the barn and we jump out of the van.

'We don't want to test the EV with our vehicle,' Femi explains. 'It's not a long walk.'

'Jenna!' Mum is waiting by the treeline with a torch.

'Mum.' This time I don't hesitate. I rush towards her, but stumble after a few steps.

This is the EV's land. I can feel it in my bones. The air feels like needles against my skin, fierce and tiny, like every molecule weighs a ton. Moths flutter in the trees around us, each flap of their wings a clap of thunder. I can even hear the distant gurgle of the river rushing towards the sea. I know I should be horrified that the EV is still affecting me, but I've never felt this powerful on dry land. This isn't like an attack; my heart is steady, no, my heart is glowing, every beat connecting with the swaying grass, the swirl of water and the brush of the breeze. The edge of my vision is sparkling blue, but it doesn't matter. I am home and I have never felt better.

Mum reaches me, but instead of pulling me into a hug, she grabs me by the shoulders and pins another shield to my jumper.

'Oh!' All at once, my vision returns to normal and my senses dull. I sag against her and blink in the dim torchlight. It's so dark. A moment ago, it felt bright enough to be midday, but now I can see that the sun set a while ago and we're in the purple phase of the long summer dusk.

'You're going to need to keep a few of these on you,' Mum says. 'Does your power still work?'

My head is reeling, but I reach out and pull a ball of water out of a nearby puddle.

'Good. That's good.' She finally hugs me. 'You're going to be OK, Jen-bear.'

All the tension of the last few days seeps away. 'You saved

me.' My voice disappears into her shoulder, but she holds me tighter.

'Of course we did. You're with us now. You're going to be OK.'

The words sound foreign, like my brain isn't ready for them yet. I don't know how I could be OK after everything that's happened, but being in Mum's arms scrubs away another layer of fear.

She squeezes me again, then sets off back through the scrubby moor. I follow her tiny torch light, determined not to fall, and Emily and Femi trail behind.

'What did they do to you at the base?' Mum asks.

'Nothing. They just locked me up. They were waiting for the EV to fade.'

They.

The HPA.

Mia and Blaze.

They locked me away and left me.

Mum snorts hard. 'You know this wasn't your fault? Nature is unbalanced. It was trying to right itself.'

'But I didn't ...' I shake my head, trying to untangle all my self-loathing. 'I didn't do anything to stop it.'

'Well, that's not true, is it?' The lights of the distant barn flicker between the trees. 'You and Emily broke into the Castle to try and figure out what was going on. She became very chatty after you were arrested.' Mum's voice is laced with fury.

'But I also voluntarily risked my life and freedom to rescue her, so there's that,' Emily calls from behind us.

'Only because Sima would have murdered you if Jenna stayed locked up another day,' Femi replies.

'Not the only reason,' Emily mutters. Her plan to get on Mum's good side has backfired spectacularly.

'How long was I locked up?' I ask.

'You were arrested on Tuesday.' Mum helps me over a boulder. 'And it's Friday now. I'm sorry it took us so long.'

'I was only in there for four days? It felt like so much longer.'

Mum snorts again, but this one is gentler. 'It was just as long out here, trust me. We couldn't get to you, until your dad brought Tomas to us.'

'Dad brought Tomas?' I repeat, the words not making sense.

'He tracked Tomas down in a pub. Given Tomas's history, he thought there was a chance he'd help us, and apparently your mentor couldn't say yes fast enough.'

Surprise wars with gratitude in my chest. Dad sought out Tomas. I thought he was done with me, but he helped get me out of that cell.

'They both came to the barn too,' Emily adds. 'Everyone forgot the "secret" aspect of our secret base. It was like Central Station at rush hour. Tomas drank my beer too, just helped himself to it.'

Mum tuts.

'Obviously I was happy to contribute that to the Great Escape,' Emily says quickly, before lowering her voice. 'It's not like I'd bought it especially …' She coughs and stops talking.

The rain starts as we reach the barn's long drive. It's a heavy summer downpour with thick drops of water that can soak you in seconds. Emily and Femi rush past to get indoors, but I stop.

'Jenna?' Mum waits for me, even though she's getting drenched.

I'm drenched too. I let the water soak into my tracksuit, skin and hair. The water has always made me feel physically stronger. It recharged me after the lighthouse collapse and even made some of my bruises fade. Now, it's helping me again. It washes away the fear and helps hope float to the surface.

Mum is here, watching me with a worried look on her face. I hold out my hands and she takes them. The rain sinks into every part of me, but I keep Mum dry.

I was never alone. I am not alone now.

She stays with me until the shower dwindles and stops. 'Better?' she asks.

I nod and smile for the first time in what feels like a thousand years. The worst might have happened, but whatever comes next, I won't have to face it on my own. 'Yeah. Thank you, Mum, for rescuing me.'

She shrugs. 'I'm your mum.'

'You are.'

When Mum told me about the night she left, I thought I'd never be able to forgive her.

I left and I can never change that decision. But I can help you now. We can move forward, Jen-bear. We just need to take it one step at a time.

Tonight was a bigger step than I thought was possible.

'Come on.' Mum guides me towards the house. 'You're looking pale. Did they feed you properly?'

I step into the warm kitchen. Femi fusses around us too, excited that both of my shields have changed colour to black. Emily gazes at her phone, as if willing someone to message, and Pari still sits in the living room, staring at the dark moorland.

I guess this is my new life now. Jenna the Villain. I wonder how long it will take for this barn to feel like home.

Break everything. Break everything. Break everything until it stops.

My eyes fly open to find wooden slats above me. I'm in the children's room of the barn. The pale morning light bounces off the colourful faces of the dancing unicorns and creepy clowns that decorate the wallpaper. I reach for my shields and relax as I feel the smooth round rocks under my fingers, attached to the turquoise flannel pyjamas that Mum gave me.

I pull a shield up to get a closer look. It's changed colour again, back to white. I'd been too tired to ask how it worked yesterday, or why everyone else was wearing a white stone and mine were black. I check they are securely fastened and roll out of the bunk bed. Maybe Femi or Mum will be up and I can ask them.

The barn is quiet as I pad out into the hallway, but as I come down the stairs, Pari comes into view. She doesn't seem to have moved from last night.

Her eyes open as I step into the room.

'Good morning,' I say softly.

She's dressed in a new set of pyjama bottoms and a hoody. A tablet has been propped up on the table next to her. The display changes from a man outside a shiny skyscraper to an image of someone on a jet ski shooting down a rolling brown river.

I grab the tablet to look closer. That's not someone on a jet ski; that's me, standing as if I'm surfing, tearing through the water. 'Feck,' I whisper. The image changes to a water treatment centre, the crumbled wall of the pool, the flooded car park, a random pipe lodged in a tree – and a grainy shot from someone's phone of Blaze being blasted into a wall with a jet of white water.

I've replayed this moment a thousand times in my nightmares, but seeing footage of it makes bile rise in my throat.

Shelly Taylor appears on the screen above the headline:

Funder Shelly Taylor on the future of the HPA.

I find the volume and turn it up.

'I've met her. Sweet little Jenna Ray. She had us all fooled, more the pity. We were so excited about a female hero.' Shelly shakes her head. *'But we ended up with the most dangerous Villain of them all.'*

My heart thunders in my chest. My finger hovers over the volume button. I should just stop listening.

'This would have never happened under King Ron. We need him back and in charge of the HPA. It's the only way to avoid another catastrophe like Jenna Ray. I know there are a

few loud voices claiming Jenna didn't intentionally invite the EV in.' Shelly rolls her eyes. *'But isn't that worse? Did she really have so little control over her powers that this was possible? Are we recruiting EV seagulls to become heroes now? Blue-eyed feral cats? I don't think so.'*

The tablet's screen blurs in front of me and my sharp inhale fails to get any air to my lungs. Everyone is watching this. This is what everyone thinks of me; that I'm either a dangerous anarchist or an EV creature.

Shelly's lips purse. *'An experiment like Jenna Ray is bad for business.'*

'No, no, no,' I whisper as my heart beats faster. I grip a shield. Is the EV about to possess me again? The room is spinning. There are no sparks on my skin, no sign of my power, but I can't breathe.

'And it is imperative we destroy the EV itself so nothing like this can ever happen again. I am researching particles from a dead zone ...' Shelly's voice fades under the thundering of my heart.

I can't breathe.

This isn't the EV.

This is a panic attack.

I thought I was past this. I thought this was done.

My eyes are streaming.

I don't want to wake anyone up.

I don't want them to see me.

The room tips away from me.

I can't move.

I can't breathe.

'Jenna.'

I know that voice.

'Jenna, focus on your exhales. Breathe out with me.' She swims into focus, her concerned face as familiar as her vulva headwrap.

'Megan.' Her name comes out as a sob.

My sister is back.

CHAPTER 19

'Megan!' Emily clatters down the stairs and Megan looks up. My sister is kneeling next to me, with her hands on my knees. We've been breathing together. Just breathing, not talking about where she's been or what I've done. Talking would have made things worse, but being close to her helps. That, and her snapping at me to keep exhaling.

Emily slows as she gets to the bottom of the stairs. 'We didn't know when you were coming back.' This is the first time I've ever heard Emily sound nervous.

'How long have you been staying here?' I look between them.

'Keep exhaling, Jenna, stay calm.' Megan pushes herself up on to a chair. 'I haven't been here long. I just ...'

'Used us for the free food.' Emily's snark has returned.

'The Villains gave me a base.' Megan's eyes flick back to mine.

'But I thought you were in Scotland.' I breathe out slowly. Megan's right, I need to stay calm. 'I thought you were figuring out your …' I trail off and glance at Emily. She's wandered over to the kitchen counter, but she's still close enough to overhear.

'Megan, you're back.' Mum hurries down the stairs.

'Hi, Mum.' Megan stands and hugs Mum.

She hugs her. The woman that she refused to mention or acknowledge. I've felt Megan's seething rage towards Mum for a decade and here they are, *hugging*. I'm not upset. I'm finding my way back to Mum, so why shouldn't Megan? But why did Megan choose to talk to her, to come back to her after the past few months, instead of me?

'The tent is drying. It was perfect,' Megan tells Mum.

Emily walks over, bringing the scent of coffee with her. She hands a cup to Megan. 'Did camping on the moors help? Any progress with the vision?'

Wait. Emily knows my sister is the Diviner?!

Is she telling everyone now?

Here's me, protecting her secret and hiding the truth from the HPA, from Blaze, from Dad, and she tells *Emily*?!

Mum and Emily are both gazing at Megan like she's the rising sun. It's like I'm not even here.

'It helped,' Megan says. 'I saw grey brick and the wind rippling through the grass and Jenna. Jenna is right at the centre of it all again.'

They all look at me and I swallow. This is what I get for wanting their attention.

I breathe out, *two, three, four.*

'I'm at the centre of your *"Destroy the EV, destroy the world"* vision? Am I older?'

Megan shakes her head. 'It's soon.'

My insides clench and my annoyance at Mum and Megan suddenly feels very far away. In the dead zone, the EV was gone, completely gone, and it left me hollowed out. The whole world will feel that if Megan's prophecy comes to pass.

'But it isn't possible.' Femi leans over the banister. 'Hello, Megan.' He pushes his glasses up his nose as he joins us. His pyjamas have cute robots on them. Another Jenna might have found them funny, but I'm still trying to catch up. Apparently, they've all been here having a lovely time and talking about visions whilst I was off being possessed.

'There is no way to destroy the EV. Even Ron's nuclear option, his canister, won't work,' Femi continues. 'We went back through the information Sima got from Dave's lab. The results are always the same. The dead zone particle needs to be injected into something with a huge surface area in order to ignite the chain reaction to destroy the EV.'

'Dave,' I murmur. There's a tiny voice at the back of my mind shouting, but I can't quite make it out. 'Dave …'

Mum looks over at me.

'Dave!' I cry. 'There's a Dave working on Shelly's rig. They're researching dead zone particles there. Could it be the same guy?'

'Small man, bald?' Mum asks. I nod and her eyes narrow. *'Dave.'* She says his name like a swear word.

'Shelly Taylor is desperate to destroy the EV,' Femi says. 'Could he still be working on that canister?'

'Or a variation of it,' Mum replies. 'He must be looking for a workaround.'

'Could he find one?' I ask.

Mum shrugs. 'It's what engineers do, even the mediocre ones, and Dave has had years.'

'And her rig is off the coast of Scotland,' I say, looking over at Megan.

'That'll be why I ended up in the Shetlands,' she says. 'Shelly Taylor must play a part in the prophecy.'

'But only Ron can operate the canister, right?' I look between them. 'You said you designed it so it needs his conduit power to work.'

'But Shelly is out there calling for his release.' Emily's words settle on my stomach like concrete. Megan's prophecy is coming into terrifying focus. The untouchable billionaire is making a machine that could end the world, calling for the release of the only man who can operate it, and somehow, I'm going to be right in the middle of everything.

Destroy the EV, destroy the world.

'Up in Scotland, I saw …' Megan squeezes her eyes shut. 'I think I saw snatches of the chain reaction, but it's close, it's impossible to see clearly.'

'It's like someone holding a photo too close to their face.' Mum rests a hand on Megan's arm. 'Just relax, baby.' Megan opens her eyes and gives Mum a grateful smile. The type that I'd give Tomas. So Mum is Megan's mentor too?! I know there's too much happening to be jealous, but it wasn't Megan who risked everything to infiltrate the HPA and rescue Mum. That was me.

'Hello?' A new voice floats through the barn.

'Joy!' I rush over as she lets herself in through the glass sliding doors. It's bizarre to see my best friend, in a summer dress and hiking books, standing in the Villains' kitchen.

'Mother Earth, Jenna!' She grabs me and hugs me. 'I was so worried. Why didn't you tell me you were in trouble? I'd have rallied the sixth formers or hid you in the shop or something. I don't know.' She releases me and punches me in the arm.

'Ow!'

'Next time, tell me.' She pats the place where she punched me. 'So, how's life as a fugitive?'

'Hello, Joy.' Mum joins us. 'Would you like some breakfast?'

Joy's eyes light up. 'Yes, please. Are you making … ?'

'Blueberry porridge?' Mum finishes. How many times has Joy been here? 'Porridge, everyone?' she calls, and receives a chorus of yeses along with a single 'I'm going to have Sugar Puffs' from Femi, but before porridge can happen, loud beeps sound through the barn.

'That's our alarm.' Femi runs past to look out of the windows.

'Were you followed, civvie?!' Emily is up too. 'She must have been followed.'

'No, I …' Joy trails off as Blaze lands on the drive. 'Oh feck.'

'Oh feck,' I echo.

The low swirling mist seeping across from the river makes him look like he's standing on a cloud, but the golden light of the morning illuminates the frown on his face. He's got his hero suit on and his hands on his hips, and he's just as angry as the last time I saw him.

I guess this is happening then. I don't know if I am going to talk to him or fight him, but one way or another, I've got to face him. I step towards the door.

'Jenna, don't.' Megan's hand is on my shoulder.

'Yes, Jenna. Don't. I've got this.' Emily sounds excited as she strides past us all and swings open the door. 'Good morning, Blaze. Welcome to our secret base.'

'This doesn't need to get violent.' Blaze holds up his hands. 'I'm only here to take Jenna back to the HPA.'

'You're not taking her anywhere,' Joy yells from behind me.

'She's dangerous.' Blaze locks eyes with me.

'And what are you, power-stealer?' Emily's hands are splayed by her sides. 'It's actually super handy that you're here.'

Blaze blurs but Emily is ready. She catches him and tosses him at a nearby tree, which he hits with a slam. What was Blaze thinking? Why did he try and take on the Villains on his own?! Emily could kill him.

'Emily, no!' I shake my sister off and rush over to Emily to push her hand down. She buffets me back. It's probably gentle for her, but I stagger to a stop by the gurgling river.

Everyone is shouting.

It's hard to pick out individual voices.

Emily.

Femi.

Mum.   Joy.

Megan.

But as Blaze appears next to me, everyone falls silent.

He has a tranquilliser gun ready—

And he's hesitating.

He's reached me, he could have darted me and been halfway back to the HPA already. His eyes meet mine. He's close enough for me to see the golden flower around his pupil. His breath hitches and he is the same lost boy Qaqa pulled out of the cave and I feel so deeply for him it's all I can do not to hold out my arms.

'You going to lock me away again?' I ask. 'Are you still too angry to believe me?'

'Skies, Jenna.' He breathes out and looks at me, really looks at me, like he's trying to see back to who I truly am. 'What are we doing?'

His eyes widen in surprise as he lifts off the ground.

'Emily, stop!' I yell.

'I don't think I will actually,' Emily says. 'My friend is in there and you, Blaze, have her powers. You're going to give them back. Don't worry –' she lifts him higher – 'I don't think you need to be conscious for our reset device to work.'

Blaze stops struggling and the colour drains from his face. He's not focused on Emily any more, he's trying to see past her and the others into the house. He's looking for Pari.

'Put him down!' I shout.

'Go inside, Jenna.' Emily is still focused on Blaze.

A blast of river water takes Emily off her feet and sends her skidding towards the house.

I advance on her. 'I told you to put him down.'

'What the feck!' Emily pushes herself up on her elbows to look up at me. 'Whose side are you on?!'

Whose side am I on?

I don't know.

I just know that when she hurts Blaze, I feel it in my core.

'I won't let you hurt him!'

'Well, that's crystal clear.' Emily reaches out a dripping hand, but I'm ready. Another column of river water jets towards her. It stops, like Emily has created a watery shield, as she gets back to her feet. I thought the water might be enough to distract her, but Emily has been using her powers a lot longer than I have.

Mum shouts something, but the water surging back towards me masks her voice. I split it, sending it either side of me, and it narrowly misses Blaze, who is still standing on the driveway.

'Blaze, go!' I send the water back at Emily and it forms a tight whirlpool around her. This is his chance to blur away, but Blaze is motionless, staring at the house. Emily blasts her way

200

through my vortex and runs at me with her fists clenched. Her punch connects with my cheek. Pain explodes across my face and I stagger back.

'Go, Jenna!' Joy cries as I lunge, grab Emily around the waist and tackle her to the ground. Blood roars in my ears as we both sprawl on to the gravel. Emily reacts fastest and is on top of me, swinging another punch at my head before I have a chance to retaliate. I bring my arms up to block her and call the water.

'Stop! Emily! What the feck!?' Megan pulls her off me.

The jet that should have hit Emily shoots overhead. I roll up, ready to take her out, but Mum is between us.

'Jenna! Stop!' she yells. 'Both of you!' She turns to Emily, who is breathing hard, with Megan's arms wrapped around her.

Emily doesn't get to throw Blaze around and then punch me. She doesn't get to hurt us. I start towards her, but there are arms around my waist too.

'Take a breath.' Blaze tightens his grip.

'Feck,' I mutter, going still against him. He has me and he could step into the air and steal me back to the HPA, but instead he lets me go.

My heart is racing and my hands are shaking. I don't think I've ever been this angry before. Maybe my insides can't cope with a panic attack followed by a fist fight. How much adrenalin can your system deal with before it just shuts down?

What are we doing? That's what Blaze said to me before Emily grabbed him.

Megan's prophecy is about to hit. The HPA heroes and Villains need to be on the same side. We all need each other. I hate the phrase, but *for the sake of the world* I need to subdue my urge to punch Emily in the face.

Not that she's reached the same conclusion. Emily is still struggling like she wants to go another round.

'Just calm down.' Megan twists Emily to look at her and puts her hands either side of her face. 'Are you done? Or do you want to keep beating up my little sister?'

'She started it!' Emily points at me, but she doesn't use that finger to flick me away, so that's something. 'I didn't mean …' Her arm lowers. 'I was only trying to help her. Again.'

'Can we please all just talk?' I rub the ache in my cheek where Emily hit me.

'Yes.' Mum steps forward. 'I'll start. Hello, Blaze, my name is Sima Ray. There are two very important things you need to know. One, we are not going to let you take Jenna and lock her away for something that wasn't her fault. And two, we're not going to do anything to you without your consent.'

Emily visibly deflates. '*You're* not,' she mutters.

'We're not,' Femi confirms from the kitchen.

Blaze rocks on his heels, looking between Emily, my mum, the barn and me. He could still tell us we're all under arrest and call for backup. It would be so easy. But instead, he sticks out his hand. 'It's nice to officially meet you.'

Mid-shake, he freezes. 'Oh, skies.' He steps away from us. 'There's a situation. It's bad. I have to …' His scared eyes catch mine. 'I have to go.'

'What's—?' I start, but he's already hurtling into the sky and speeding away.

Everyone rushes inside, where Femi already has a screen up. A distant shot of an oil rig dominates the picture with a large scrolling headline. *POSSESSED HERO ATTACKS RIG.* They all look at me and then down at my shields. They're both black. Everyone else's are white.

'The EV wanted her,' Femi murmurs.

'Let's give you a couple more of these, shall we?' Mum reaches into a red box and brings out two more shields, which she adds to mine. 'Can you print more, F?'

'Yeah …' Femi focuses back on the screen.

'Is that Shelly Taylor's rig?' Emily asks. 'It's obscene.'

Everyone is watching the rig, but I'm replaying Femi's words. *The EV wanted her.*

The EV wanted me.

It was never Ron.

The letter, the threats, the easy charm at the Castle, it was all a show.

I am an idiot.

I knew I was being followed. Prince #2 has probably been spying on me for weeks, waiting for something they could use. The EV possession had nothing to do with Ron. He figured out what was happening and saw an opportunity to exploit me. Only Ron could make a force of nature all about him. Rage burns through me, followed swiftly by fear.

The EV wants me.

It should be me on that oil rig, but now I'm protected. I can't see who the EV took instead.

Joy nudges me. 'At least everyone will stop saying you invited the EV in, now that it's taken over another hero.'

The helicopter camera shakes as it approaches the rig, then the feed switches to a blur of light blue waves.

'I've hacked into the HPA feeds,' Femi calls from the breakfast island. 'This is Blaze's body cam.'

'It's definitely Shelly's rig,' I say as the camera rises past the glass lift and up to the plinth of the oil rig. I play with my fingers. Blaze is out there, alone, about to face a possessed hero.

He reaches the platform and the feed wobbles as he lands. The possessed hero is by the drill tower, vanishing and reappearing as security shoot at him.

'Qaqa,' I whisper. The Fijian hero who was so kind in Australia. He's the one the EV took, instead of me.

'Feck!' Qaqa appears directly in front of the camera and we all jump back. He gazes at Blaze, with his eyes electric blue. There is no sign of the laughing hero I met in Australia on his expressionless face. He reaches for Blaze and the feed flashes white before changing to the deep blue of an underwater shot.

Qaqa just teleported Blaze into the sea and I'm not there to save him.

CHAPTER 20

A stream of bubbles fills the screen. Blaze is underwater. He could be panicking or drowning. Qaqa might have teleported him into that dead zone. He can't swim and he's out there all alone.

'Jenna—' Mum starts, but I lunge past her and grab a handful of shields out of the red box. 'Wait!'

I yank the door open and sprint towards the river.

'Jen—' Mum's shout cuts out as I dive in.

There were so many bubbles; he's losing his air. He won't open his eyes and he might not be able to make it to the surface. I need to get to him. The silver layer of my bubble covers me and my current takes me. I race through the river, keeping the force I'm generating close so I don't tear up the riverbed.

The murky water of Nine Trees harbour passes in a flash, and I accelerate as I zip into the clear salty sea and head north. Tomas was planning to see how fast I could go in open water, but whatever speed I've reached, it's not enough. It's already taken me too long. If Blaze is stuck underwater, he needs me now.

'Let him be OK.' The words bounce off my bubble and I go faster.

It should be hard making this journey without a map, but the currents that I barrel past are like signposts. That push must be from the Firth of Forth. There's the swirl of the jutting headland that becomes the Highlands. There's the end of the mainland, the currents of the Shetlands and then, the open ocean. I'm almost there.

The vibrations of Shelly's rig hit me before I see it. The monstrous drill shakes the seabed, sending tremors through the water. A moment later, the drill casing comes into view and I slow down to scan the area for Blaze.

There's nothing around except a shoal of passing fish.

I poke my head above the water and something black and red zips through the sky above me. Blaze is OK! I exhale shakily, the relief rushing through me is so sharp it hurts.

A strangled yell echoes from above and my fingers tighten around the shields. Blaze might still be alive, but he's still fighting a possessed hero. He needs backup and I've brought him a cure.

In our 'Transport' sessions, Tomas had been keen to discuss ways that I could use my power to fly. He thought I could use the water like a jet pack and launch myself into the air with it. At the time, I'd hoped that suggestion might go away, but now I need to get up to the top of the oil rig, fast.

Pointedly not thinking about all the bones I could break if my angle is off, I gather a jet beneath my body. It holds me above the surface for a moment, bubbling white as the pressure builds, and then blasts me up towards the platform.

I manage to stop myself from screaming as I rocket past the floors of the rig. This is definitely something I should have practised before giving it a go in a life-or-death situation.

Blaze's shocked face flashes by as I overshoot the platform.

'Feck!' I will the stream to give me a little nudge so I can land, but instead I launch myself towards a crane. 'Stop!' The water propelling me splashes down on to the platform and I roll to a stop on the rough concrete with my face hidden in my hands.

'Jenna. Are you OK?' Blaze skids to a stop next to me. 'Are you still you?'

A groan escapes my lips. 'I've seen possessed me in action. She could have landed that.'

He pulls me to my feet. 'You shouldn't be here.'

'I brought you a cure.' I open my hand to reveal the stone shields. 'This will stop the EV from possessing you. Put one on.'

Blaze takes one and zips it into the pocket next to his heart. 'This will cure Qaqa?'

I nod. 'We just have to get it on him. We might need to use two. Where is he?'

'On this level, looking for me. We need to keep him out here. Away from the floors where the crew are hiding and away from the control panels where security are ready to blast holes in him. If he destroys the wrong piece of equipment, he could easily blow us out of the water.' Blaze's eyes unfocus. 'Tomas says Qaqa is by the helipad and … what?' Blaze goes into his belt and pulls out an earpiece. 'Apparently I have a spare earpiece on me.' Blaze hands it to me. For this fight, at least, I'm back in the HPA.

'I told you a spare would be helpful.' Tomas's voice is loud in my ear as I slip the piece in. *'Hello, Ray, good to have you back. Though we should discuss your choice of hero outfit.'*

Skies. I look down at my clothes. I'm still in the turquoise flannel PJs that Mum gave me. I didn't even grab a jumper. The air shakes as the news helicopter comes back round to our side. I am on TV right now, with Blaze, in my pyjamas.

'It may seem basic,' Tomas continues, *'but getting dressed is a vital part of every mission.'*

'I raced here to save Blaze!' It's so easy to slip back into bantering with Tomas. I glance at Blaze. He's busy scanning the area, but his cheeks have flushed pink. Is it too much to hope that he's pleased to see me?

There's a thud as Blaze is rugby tackled by Qaqa and they both fly out of sight.

'Blaze!'

A yell comes from around the little building, and I sprint towards it. Qaqa has Blaze on the painted yellow H of the helipad. He lifts his hands to teleport him, but Blaze blurs just out of reach. There's a flash of white as Qaqa vanishes and reappears, swinging a punch that Blaze dodges. The possessed hero is so much bigger than Blaze, I want him to blur well out of harm's way, but he's staying just in front of Qaqa, distracting him. A bright bolt of blue jumps between them, but dissipates as it hits Blaze's uniform.

Blaze's eyes meet mine and I know what I need to do. I take a shield and slip towards Qaqa as quietly as I can, staying directly behind him as Blaze zips from side to side in front. A few metres away, Qaqa pauses, like he's sensed me.

'Tell us what you want,' Blaze yells, trying to draw his attention back.

'To stop.' Qaqa's voice echoes, like there's several people speaking. 'This needs to stop.'

Break everything until it stops. That's the thought that was going through my mind as the EV used me to destroy the water treatment centre.

'We need to stop the drill,' I say into my comms. 'It's the only way to save Qaqa.'

Qaqa spins to face me. His blue eyes shine as they stare down at me. Human eyes are so much bigger than pigeons' or squirrels', and I can see the fragments of blue glittering like sequins.

'Shelly was visiting the HPA today so she's right here.' Tomas sounds like his teeth are gritted. *'Apparently stopping the drill is not an option. Because ... The controls are locked? Can't you unlock them? ... Not an option is not an answer.'*

Qaqa tilts his head at me. 'Yes,' he, or maybe the EV, says. 'Stop the drill.'

This is my chance. I lunge in with the shield, but his arm stretches towards me. White floods my vision—

My bubble is covering me before I realise what has happened. The water around me is black and I can feel the

209

weight of it, pressing down on me. Holding the bubble has always been as natural as breathing, but now it's like lifting weights.

'Feck.' My voice is tiny in my ears.

'Jenna, where did he send you?' Blaze is quiet too, like he's a long way away.

He is a long way away. The ground under my feet trembles and the wavering light of my bubble is just enough to make out the outline of the enormous machinery in front of me. A bead of sweat trickles down my face. Qaqa sent me to the bottom of the sea.

'Jenna!' Tomas is slightly louder, like he's shouting. *'Where are you?'*

'With the drill on the seafloor,' I manage. It takes everything I have to step towards the shuddering metal in front of me. The EV sent me down here to switch it off. Is that even possible?

'Forget the drill,' Blaze says. *'Come back to the surface.'* There's a thud that sounds like Blaze has just been on the end of another punch from Qaqa. *'Feck!'*

Qaqa will keep going until this drill is off. Shelly doesn't care if Blaze ends up in medical or worse, teleported somewhere he can't survive. I blink away the image of Blaze appearing next to me.

The dim light of my bubble shines on the discs and bolts of chunky metal as I take another step towards the drill. The light is so faint, it's almost impossible to know how tall or wide this thing is. But as I take another step closer, part of a round handle emerges from the dark water.

'There's a handle down here,' I say.

Even at the bottom of the sea, Shelly's voice carries clearly through Tomas's comms. *'Tell her not to touch anything!'*

'Ja, ja …' Tomas replies, and Shelly's shouting fades as if she's been moved away from the console. *'Ray, Shelly is very concerned that you'll twist the handwheel on that blowout preventer, because turning that would close the drill line permanently.'*

'Qaqa, it's Blaze. You took me to my first rugby sevens tournament. This isn't you!' Blaze yells in my ears. *'Mother Earth!'* There's a scuffling sound, like he's rolling away from Qaqa.

Blaze can't reason with the EV. It needs what it needs and doesn't care how it happens. My fingers wrap around the gritty metal of the handwheel. This is how I can save Blaze and Qaqa.

I push, it doesn't budge.

I pull, nothing happens.

'I don't know which way to turn it.'

'Stop trying to turn that handle, Jenna,' Tomas says. *'If you turn it clockwise it will close the well and stop the drill. So, whatever you do, don't do that.'*

'What's she doing?' Shelly's screech is distant, like she's been relegated to the back of the room.

Clockwise. Despite the weight of the sea pressing down on me, the corners of my mouth tweak. *Thank you, Tomas.* My muscles strain as I pull the handle clockwise and my gut clenches as I add a jet of water to help. It moves.

'No!' cries Shelly.

I keep turning it until there's a clank from within. The drill stops juddering and the seabed stills.

'*And there goes Shelly.*' Tomas sounds grimly satisfied.

'Is Blaze OK? Is Qaqa?' I'm still holding the handwheel. I can't move. If I try, my bubble will break, and the weight of the ocean will squeeze my heart until it stops.

'*I'm fine.*' Blaze is breathless. '*Qaqa is gone. He was still possessed, but he teleported away. Jenna, where are you now?*'

'Still here.'

'*Ray, you need to get back to the surface,*' Tomas says. '*We don't know how long your power can last down there.*'

'Shelly's angry then?' In the dark of the ocean depths, my words sound faintly ridiculous. I've just enraged Shelly Taylor, career destroyer, but she'll never get the chance to hurt me. My fingers have gone numb. It's so cold down here.

'*Are you moving?*' Tomas asks.

My tracker must still be off, so I guess he can't see that I'm stuck gripping the handwheel. The water is heavier with each passing moment and I'm so tired that even though the tremors of the drill have stopped, I'm shaking. I've got nothing left. I know in my heart that I'm not going anywhere.

CHAPTER 21

'*Jenna!*' Blaze says sharply. '*Start moving now!*'

'I can't,' I whisper. Not even someone with my power belongs at the bottom of the Atlantic. My bubble is fading. I can't move. It's too heavy, too dark, too much.

'*I'm coming to get you.*' There's a whoosh, like Blaze is in the air.

'NO!' My voice joins Tomas's.

'No,' I repeat. 'You can't survive down here.'

'*Neither can you,*' Blaze replies. '*Start moving or I'm coming to get you.*'

'Feck.' Above me the drill disappears into the dark. If I wasn't standing on the seabed, I wouldn't even know which direction the surface was. I can't let Blaze try and reach me down here. Sweat rolls into my eyes as I stand with my hand on the drill. 'Stay there. I'm coming up.'

I kick my legs and take a deep shuddering breath as I rise slowly through the dark water, with one hand on the drill.

'You're moving?' Tomas asks.

'Yes.' It's like swimming through concrete. I kick again. 'Barely.'

'Tomas …' Blaze is hesitant. 'Could we maybe … Could I call you back if we need you?'

Tomas hums into the comms. 'That's up to her. Ray, if you keep moving, you and Blaze can have this channel to yourselves. Is that a deal?'

'Yes,' I manage. If this is it, if I can't make it to the surface, at least being alone with Blaze will give me the chance to say everything I need to. 'I'll keep moving.'

My muscles scream at me as I pull myself up. I call my current, which helps shunt me towards the surface.

'OK, out.' Tomas's mic clicks.

'It's just us now,' Blaze says. 'The pressure will lessen the shallower the water gets. It's going to get easier.'

'Sure.' I'm breathing as hard as a marathon swimmer. It's still pitch black around me and the cold has penetrated my bones. 'It hasn't yet.'

'Mother Earth, Ray, it's always whinge, whinge, whinge with you.'

'What?!' My mouth drops open. I'm struggling through the inky black of the endless water and he's making fun of me?!

'Seriously.' There's a shuffle, like Blaze has sat down, and I picture him swinging his legs off the side of the rig in the sunshine. 'My name's Jenna and I got myself sent to the bottom of the sea, poor me.'

My feet kick again, and my current gets stronger. 'That is not what I sound like.'

'*It is.*' He makes his voice even higher. '*Oh no, look at me, I saved the day and now I'm in mortal peril. Every time.*'

'Did Ron teach you this?'

'*What? Winding someone up whilst they swim really, really, really slowly up from the bottom of the Atlantic?*' Blaze asks. '*No, that's pure Laurie Lin. What would you rather?*'

'That you're nice to me?' The water is still heavy but now it's more like trying to sprint uphill.

'*I don't know if I'm ready to be nice to you.*' He clicks his tongue. '*Let's figure out this whole EV possession thing.*'

My hand bubble merges with my head bubble as I wipe the sweat off my face. He's still upset with me, but he's here, making sure that I don't die, so I guess that's something. 'Go for it,' I say, and my current gives me another gentle push.

'*Qaqa got possessed.*' Blaze leaves the statement hanging.

'Yeah,' I puff.

'*And he's not a Villain.*'

'No.'

'*It's the same as what happened to you. So, you're in the clear.*'

'OK.' I should be happier about that, but swimming is taking all my energy.

'*Unless you and your bonfire cult somehow targeted him?*'

'For feck's sake, no.'

'*All right.*' A little bit of warmth seeps through my bones. He believes me. '*Did Ron do this?*'

'When it started, the blue dots in my vision, my powers

going wrong … Ron made me think he was behind it, but –' I puff again and the silver glow of my bubble lights my hands as they reach up the casing – 'I think it might just be something that was happening and he –' I kick my legs to give myself a little boost – 'took advantage.' My stomach rolls. I can't remember the last time I pushed myself this hard. 'Mother Earth, I'm out of breath. Can you talk?'

'*OK.*' Blaze taps his fingers on something metallic. '*Ron saw what happened in the Culture Complex when your eyes went blue.*' I didn't know Blaze had seen that too. I thought he was unconscious. '*Then, a couple of months later, he figures out something weird is still going on with your powers.*'

'Prince #2,' I manage. 'He saw me trying to deal with an EV attack.'

'*Ron still has his sidekick. Love that for him.*' The sarcasm in Blaze's tone makes my lips twitch. '*So this possession thing started with you, but we now know that it can happen to anyone powered.*' Blaze speeds up as his theory takes shape. '*We've always believed that the EV couldn't possess a person. Yes, people used it to supercharge themselves, but it never used them back. Then the EV changed. It evolved. That probably shouldn't be as unbelievable as everyone is finding it.*'

'I should have told you,' I manage. He might have been struggling with his own problems, but his brain was built for stuff like this. 'Before I went to the Castle. Before it got bad.'

'*Of course, Ron used this random development of the EV to scare you,*' Blaze continues, like he didn't hear me. '*That's what he does.*' The words Blaze doesn't say are almost louder than the ones he does. I let him down. This is something we could have figured out together.

I breathe out. 'Just say it, Blaze.'

'Can you see sunlight yet?'

'No, but this is good.' I gulp in another breath. 'I'd rather think about you than whether I'm about to throw up.'

'OK ...'

I screw my face up as I wait.

'You didn't trust me.' I don't know if I expected him to raise his voice or babble nervously, but Blaze speaks slowly. *'I was upset ... I am upset. When I realised you were a Villain at the museum, I thought it would break me.'*

The memory leaves an unpleasant taste in my mouth too. Back in May, when we rescued my mum, the only way to get past Blaze was to reveal I was one of the helmeted Villains. I called his name, he looked for me and Femi knocked him out.

'Finding out about the Castle and then the attack on the water treatment centre; everything pointed to you still being a Villain and it was different this time round. Jenna, it was so much worse. I know why the Villains hate me now and I know I deserve it. If you're one of them ...'

'I don't hate you,' I whisper. There's some light now, I can make out the shape of the drill casing beside me as I grab it and give myself another pull.

'Why didn't you trust me?'

'I wanted— Feck!' A squid drifts past beside me and disappears into the dark.

'Jenna?'

217

'I'm OK, it was a squid.' I get the words into the right order in my mouth. 'I was stupid, Blaze. I was scared. I'm not a Villain, but with Emily, I could be less than perfect.' Why did it take the weight of an ocean to make me realise how much pressure I'd been under? 'I was supposed to be the flawless trailblazer and when things started going wrong, I panicked. I can't believe how badly I messed everything up.' My current gives me another shunt. 'I never wanted to hurt you.'

You did blast me into a building.

I grit my teeth. 'Yes, obviously I'm sorry about that, but you know what I mean … I mean more. I …' Mother Earth. Conversations like this are hard enough sitting still. 'I want to be there the next time you have to face Qaqa or any other emergency. Will you let me?'

In the silence, I keep swimming up, towards him. There's light now, real light, like walking home at night under the shimmer of the stars.

'Yes.' His reply is soft.

'We can still be a team?' It's getting lighter with each kick. I've gone through the darkness of night and now I'm swimming up through the dusk.

'Yes,' Blaze says again.

'And …' I almost died and I could still die, so I don't stop the next question on my lips. 'Can we be more than that? More than just teammates?'

I hold my breath as I wait for his response. I've never told Blaze that I love him. It came so easily to him. When he found out I was alive, after the lighthouse, those words had tumbled out.

'Jenna, I love you.' But I can't say it, not now, after everything I put him through. It wouldn't be fair.

'Jenna.' My chest squeezes as I wait for his answer. *'We're always going to be more than teammates.'*

Daylight. My heart lifts as the water lightens to a familiar turquoise blue. My bubble shines around me and I feel strong. The water is no longer holding me down, it's pushing me up. It's mine again, ready to help me, to heal me.

'Ha!' I cry, and shoot towards the surface, bursting out of the waves to hang in the cool air for a moment. I catch myself with a jet and, remembering the intense pressure on me under the water, I change a little patch above the waves so I can stand on it. I wobble as it bobs up and down, but keep my balance. Possessed Jenna could do this. Adrenalin-fuelled *'Hey, look! I have powers now!'* Jenna did this when she ran on the rain, and now I understand how. I know just how heavy the water can be.

'Hi.' Blaze flies down from the rig and hovers in front of me as I bob up and down on my makeshift platform. My gut twists as I see the bruise on the side of his face. He was left alone with Qaqa for too long.

'This is cool.' He motions to the patch of water that I'm standing on. 'Can I … ?'

A distant helicopter thrums as he lands, making us rock. I hold my water raft firm. 'Do you really forgive me?' I step towards him. 'Or were you just being nice because I almost died?'

'I wasn't being nice, remember?' He snags the baggy

219

material of my pyjama top and pulls me closer, so we're eye to eye. 'We're a team now. A real team that goes to each other with our problems and theories.'

'Yes.' I'm back a breath away from Blaze's lips.

'And we're more than just teammates?' His fingers trail down my sides to settle on my waist and I bite back a shiver.

'But if they let me back in to the HPA, there's still the rule.' I make myself say it. 'Heroes can't be together.'

'I don't care. I love you.'

The raft sways beneath us. 'You still love me?'

His eyebrows rise. 'I never stopped, Jenna Ray.'

'Oh, skies.' Pure joy burns through me, melting away all my inhibitions. I grab him and hold him against me, my arms tightening to bring him closer and my face resting against his. I want to keep him like this forever. I want him to be mine. I love him, but the only words that will come are: 'You want to be together?'

'It's all I wanted since I found out why it was you. Why you were trapped in that fire. Why you were my first rescue.'

I pull away to blink at him. I didn't think he knew.

'You tried to save someone,' he murmurs, 'and you ended up with me.'

'I ended up with you,' I repeat, glowing. 'You and me then, no matter what?'

'No matter what.'

It would take the tiniest movement and our lips would be together again. I want to kiss him. It feels like craving air or water, like it's worth risking everything for. I move a hand up to his cheek but a loud rumble makes me pull back and look up.

The helicopter has gone from a faint thrum to a thunder of blades; it's finally spotted us and is approaching at top speed. Our moment of peace is over. We break apart, my pyjamas flapping in the wind, as the helicopter stops above us. It has GLOBAL NEWS written on it in big red letters. Sydney Jones is on the scene and ready to broadcast the latest Jenna Ray scandal.

Blaze sighs. 'We should go.'

I bite my lip. Am I really about to return to the HPA? I could drop into the sea right now. They'd never catch me.

'I've got your back,' Blaze says. 'Come on.' He holds out his arms.

The helicopter dips closer to us. The whole world is watching. 'I don't know if I can go back there.'

Blaze smirks at me. 'Aren't you desperate to be in my arms though?'

He's so accurate I have to laugh. 'Desperate is a strong word,' I mutter. That familiar heat is swirling from my core up around my heart. For a moment I don't even care about the helicopter filming our every move. I don't just *want* to kiss him, I *need* to.

'Come on then.' He steps into the air.

'Skies.' I channel my frustration into the water and give myself a boost up to land in Blaze's arms. As we shoot past the helicopter, I catch a glimpse of Sydney Jones pointing excitedly at us and then we're in the wide blue sky. As nice as it is being held against Blaze's chest, nerves flood my stomach. I am throwing myself at the mercy of the HPA, but Megan's prophecy is coming and they need to know.

Blaze taps his ear. 'Tomas, I've got Jenna. We're coming home.'

CHAPTER 22

Squad One are waiting at security, every single one of them, crammed in front of the security desk. Blaze sets me down outside the sliding glass doors and we stare in. Cadell and his men stare back at us, expressionless, tranquilliser guns ready.

'I really wish I'd got dressed this morning,' I murmur, and Blaze chuckles.

'I'll bet. Going in?'

I glance at Squad One again. The sea is close enough to taste on the air. I don't have to do anything I don't want to.

'Jenna Ray!' a voice shouts from the stone steps behind us. Several reporters rush down them. A camera flashes.

Being mobbed by the press upon my return to the HPA was always going to happen, but it doesn't stop my chest tightening.

'Jenna!' another voice yells. 'Are you still under the influence of the EV?'

223

A third joins in. 'Are you two together? Have the rules changed about hero romances?'

And another. 'Jenna Ray! How did you possess Qaqa?!'

'Blaze.' Mia's voice comes over our earpieces. *'Arrest Jenna and bring her in, now.'*

Blaze's eyes widen as he looks at me. He told me that he had my back and I know he's about to refuse, but it's the wrong move. Another hero has now been possessed, but I still broke into the Castle, and destroyed a water treatment centre, and escaped from HPA custody. Mia said I'd ruined their opportunity to revolutionise the HPA. This is a chance for me to fix things. I hold out my wrists.

'Do it,' I say.

Blaze swallows.

'Now, Blaze.' Mia sounds furious.

I nod at him, my eyes trying to convey the message. *Do it, do it now. Let them see you doing the right thing.*

'OK.' Blaze retrieves his cuffs from his belt and a moment later they are round my wrists. The cameras flash like lightning.

'My office.' There's a click as Mia goes off comms.

I step into the cool foyer, and it might be my imagination but Squad One look disappointed. It's probably good that Blaze put the cuffs on me. If it had been Cadell, I might have ended up with a broken arm.

The door to the main base opens before we get there. 'Ah, Ray.' Tomas holds it for us. 'Nice to see you back on the surface.'

'Hi, Tomas.'

Tomas's eyes crinkle at me as we make our way down the corridor. 'I didn't expect to see you back here so soon.'

'Ah.' I swallow. Tomas risked everything to get me out and less than twenty-four hours later I'm back in HPA custody. 'Sorry.'

Blaze looks sharply at Tomas. 'Sorry?'

Skies. I'm no longer keeping things from Blaze, but I hadn't intended to kick things off by revealing Tomas helped my great escape.

Tomas shrugs. 'I'm proud of you, Ray. You could have let this poor, defenceless boy get pounded into the dust –'

'Hey!'

'– but you raced to his rescue. And you tried to save Qaqa.' Tomas grits his teeth. 'I don't know where he is now.'

'We'll find him,' Blaze says.

'Perhaps,' Tomas replies lightly. 'First let's find a way to keep Ray from being thrown back in a cell. What are you going to tell Mia?'

I shrug. 'The truth.'

The journey to the boss's office is always too short. It's even shorter now. Blaze might as well have blurred us there.

He knocks and the door is immediately wrenched open.

'You stay outside.' Mia glares at Blaze. 'And you.' Their next look is for Tomas. 'You –' they fix their brown eyes on me – 'in here, now.'

I wince and glance at Blaze's worried face, before following Mia into the office. They slam the door shut behind me.

Mia is shorter than me, but as they return to their desk and stand behind it with their arms crossed, they could be seven foot tall.

'Mia, I'm sorry I left.' The space between us feels as cold as the seabed. 'But I came back.'

Mia's eyelashes flutter.

'Tell me how I can fix things.'

'How you can fix things,' Mia repeats faintly.

'We need you.' The cuffs bounce off the top of my thighs as I cross the office. 'We need you in charge. Something terrible is coming and we need a leader.'

Mia shakes their head, looking completely lost. 'We can't fix things.'

'You can. That's what you do, Mia. You know the heroes, the press, the job. You can fix this.' I reach the desk. 'With or without me, the HPA needs to be ready for what comes next.'

'So I get to fix the mess you made.' They close their eyes. 'Sit down.'

I slide into a metal seat and wait.

Finally, Mia opens their eyes again, and locks them on mine. 'You broke into the Castle.'

'Yes.'

'Why?'

'Because Ron threatened to possess me with the EV.'

'You didn't invite the EV in.'

'No.'

Mia used to do this to me during press training. Quick-fire statements to test my composure.

They pace. 'But you didn't tell me. Or Tomas or Blaze.'

'No.'

'Just that Villain, the blonde one.'

'Yes.'

'Why?' Mia stops in front of me.

'Because I panicked. I needed to be perfect and I … I wasn't.'

An expression I can't catch flits across Mia's face. 'You still should have come to me.'

I look at the handcuffs around my wrists. 'I should have done a lot of things.'

'Did Ron cause this?'

I shake my head. 'Now we think that he just understood what was happening first and used it to manipulate me.'

Mia stops to glare at the ceiling, before resuming their pacing. 'You said something terrible is coming.'

I swallow. I have to find a way to do this whilst still protecting Megan, even if she has told her secret to Mum, and Femi, and Emily. 'There's a new prophecy. From the Diviner.'

Mia sucks in a breath. 'The next Diviner? She's emerged?'

'Yes.'

'And her prophecy is bad?'

'It's bad.' I nod. 'And it's soon.'

'Right.' They march past me, opening the door. 'In.'

'How much trouble are we in, then?' Tomas drags a chair over to sit next to me.

'I know you helped her escape, Tomas.' Mia's voice is still cold. 'I'll decide what to do with you later.'

Tomas holds his hands up. 'My fate is in your hands, boss.'

227

Blaze pulls up a chair too and my insides unclench a little. 'You OK?'

'Jenna was about to share a prophecy from the new Diviner.' Mia sits as the two men look at me, open-mouthed.

'The Diviner?' Blaze echoes.

'It's not you, is it?' Tomas asks. 'Not that it's likely, but some people do have two different sets of powers.'

'It's not me,' I say.

'Thank the skies for that,' Tomas mutters.

I continue before they can press for an identity. 'The prophecy is *"Destroy the EV, destroy the world"* and I'm at the centre of it. It's coming. Soon.'

'Ah, an apocalyptic prophecy.' Tomas leans back. 'These are always exciting.'

'How are you so relaxed?' Blaze asks.

Tomas shrugs. 'If I had a beer for every apocalyptic prophecy ...'

'She's here!' Shelly bangs through the office doors and everyone except Tomas jumps up. 'One. Hundred. Million.' She grabs my pyjama top and yanks me towards her. 'You cost me one hundred million pounds.'

'Stop!' Blaze yells.

'You could have killed Blaze, Qaqa, and everyone on your rig,' I say. I won't back down from her snarling face, I don't care how important she is. 'Taking your drill offline saved lives and I'd do it again.' I lower my voice. 'Now take your hands off me, before I make you.'

'Violence!' Shelly throws up her arms as she steps away

from me. 'Jenna Ray threatened me with violence! I want her back in a cell, now! No. I want her in the Castle. What more can we excuse from this girl? Criminal damage! Violent behaviour! Threatening law-abiding citizens?! She is too dangerous to be free.'

Shelly takes a breath and we all look at Mia. Thanks to me, our boss is on uncertain footing. A word from Shelly could swiftly end Mia's leadership of the HPA. She can get Blaze transferred. She can get me locked away. Shelly Taylor is the money. My hands curl into fists, but there's nothing I can do. Mia is going to send me back to the cells. They're going to have to.

Mia stands with their arms crossed, watching the billionaire steadily. 'Ms Taylor, could you please wait in the office we assigned to you whilst I finish up here?'

Pink spots flash up on Shelly's pale cheeks. 'Mia, my darling, I don't think you heard me. Lock her up.' When Mia doesn't move, Shelly turns to Blaze. 'Blazey, be a good boy and take your honey-bun back down to the cells.'

Blaze looks at Mia, who gives an almost imperceptible shake of their head. Tomas coughs in a way that makes it quite clear he's hiding a laugh.

Shelly's head snaps towards him. 'You. You let her destroy my drill. I'd say you need to convince me you're not a drunken liability. Take her away.'

'Harsh.' Tomas frowns. 'I didn't even finish my lunchtime beer.'

'I pay your wages.' Shelly looks between us.

'Ms Taylor.' Mia remains incredibly polite. 'The HPA are grateful for your contribution to our running costs, but we work for the British public, not you.'

'OK.' Shelly nods frantically. 'OK, it's just, Mia, I WANT HER ARRESTED!' Shelly screams, but Mia doesn't flinch. 'This wouldn't have happened under Ron.' Shelly points at me. Her face is red, but she seems to have regained some control. 'Ron was right about you. He was right about everything. You're going to regret this. You're all going to regret this.'

Shelly points at Blaze, then Tomas, then Mia, before storming out.

'Sounded ominous, didn't it?' Tomas says.

We turn back to Mia and it's like I'm seeing them for the first time. They've been juggling responsibilities, responding to disasters and moving so fast that I had no idea they had a centre of pure steel.

'That,' Blaze says, 'was amazing.'

Mia raises their eyebrows at him. '*That* was just what I needed.' They clap their hands and shake out their arms. 'She's like a shot of coffee, isn't she?'

'She's involved in the prophecy,' I say. 'We think that Shelly is still working on Ron's plan to end the EV. He was developing a canister that can move a dead zone particle into a possessed creature and start a chain reaction that destroys the EV itself. I saw the canister's original engineer on Shelly's rig.'

'*Dave.*' Mia's tone is similar to Mum's. 'Shelly requested him. I knew Dave was involved in Ron's nuclear option, but I never knew what it was.'

230

'But the Villains don't think there's any way that plan can work,' I continue. 'Dave would need to find an enormous creature, something with a huge surface area, in order to start the chain reaction. And even if that did exist, only Ron can operate the machine.'

'And he's still in the Castle?' Blaze asks.

'He's still in the Castle,' Mia confirms. 'We need to find that canister. Blaze …' They click their fingers. 'Sorry. Skies. One emergency at a time. Our most pressing problem is that the EV can now possess powered people.'

Tomas cuts in. 'We have a cure. Dr Varma has been studying it and, given what happened today, he's probably started mass producing these little badges already.' Tomas nods at mine. 'They're called shields.' That must have been what Emily gave Tomas as she helped me escape.

'Shields,' Mia repeats. 'You got them from the Villains.'

Tomas nods.

'Who are also working on the prophecy?' Mia asks.

I nod.

'We need a meeting.' Mia looks between me and Tomas. 'We need to know what they know, what the Diviner knows.'

'I can ask,' I say.

'Good enough for now.' Mia starts pacing again. 'Jenna, you need to become the face of our campaign to get a shield to every powered person in the country.'

'Of course.' I nod eagerly. 'Anything.'

'Good. I'll set up a press conference.'

I swallow. 'Yes. Right. Looking forward to it.'

231

'Blaze.' Mia turns to him. 'Get to that rig. Find Dave and get that canister. We can't move against Shelly for doing research on her own property, so be subtle. Go!' Blaze leaps up and blurs away. 'And you two.' Mia looks at me and Tomas. 'When this new set of disasters has passed, there will be a reckoning. Until then, welcome back to the team, Jenna. It's probably time for you to get dressed.'

CHAPTER 23

'Jenna Ray.' Sydney Jones stands in the middle of the crowd of reporters. 'How much do you remember of your Water Treatment Centre Rampage?'

She manages to pronounce each capital letter from Water to Rampage. I swallow. 'Almost nothing, I was taken over by the EV and didn't regain consciousness until it had used me to shut the centre down. I woke up to see the damage that I caused.'

'What did being possessed by the EV feel like?' Sydney shoots at me.

Right now, an honest answer is the only helpful one. I squeeze my fists until my fingernails dig into my palms, but answer calmly. 'For me, it felt a bit like a panic attack at first. Your heart races, but then sparks appear on your skin, shimmering blue clouds your vision and your power rises inside you until it takes over completely.'

'And you destroy a water treatment centre,' Sydney finishes.

'But,' Mia says, leaning into a mic, 'as the destruction caused has been classified as an act of EV, the water company has been able to claim on their insurance. They've also committed to building back better and fixing the issues that were leading to the excess sewage spillage.'

'Ian Collins, *River Times*.' He stands. 'You appear to be back in your hero capacity at the HPA despite proven ties to the Villains.' His lip lifts in a sneer which, somehow, makes me less nervous.

'Do you have a question, Ian?' I ask politely.

'Are you a Villain, Miss Ray?' He says my name the same way as Ron.

'I am not a Villain, but they helped me save Nine Trees and are now helping combat this EV possession. They are misunderstood and misrepresented.' I practised this answer in the mirror as I changed out of my pyjamas. I hope Mum is watching.

'And anarchists, of course.' Ian Collins manages to make it sound like we're in agreement. 'If you're not one of them, why did you invade the Castle with the notorious telekinetic Villain?'

'That was a HPA investigation,' Mia cuts in. 'As the investigation is still ongoing, we're unable to talk about that at this time.'

I stop myself from goggling at them. In the few short hours between our meeting and the press conference, Mia has been cold. They've been dealing with Blaze's fruitless search of Shelly's rig, and trying to track down Dave and the canister, and I know that I'm still in a whole world of trouble. Yet here they are, protecting me.

Carrie leaps up, as excited as the last time she was here. 'Carrie Le Roux, *Take Five Magazine*. Jenna, how did you cause Qaqa's possession?'

'Um, I didn't? The EV has started to affect powered humans the same way it affects the rest of nature. It can supercharge us and send us to stop things that are hurting the earth. It can happen to any powered person. I was just the first.' I hesitate as every hand in the room goes up.

'So you didn't summon the EV with a ritual bonfire?' Carrie asks. A few people groan.

'No. That was my best friend burning her ex's hoody.'

She writes that down, nodding. 'Bonfire. Heartbreak. Terrible ex. Got it, thanks.' I can't imagine what that article is going to say. 'Oh.' She jumps back up. 'What happened to your pretty pink hero suit? Or your turquoise outfit from the rig? Why are you back in boring black combats? That's not an option for our poll, is it?'

'Er ...' I look at Mia for help. Admitting I was out heroing in my pyjamas is probably not a good idea.

'Thank you for your question, Carrie, we'll have more details about Jenna's hero suit soon.' Mia brings the press conference back on track. 'By tomorrow morning, shields – small badges that prevent possession – will be available in every HPA base around the world. After that we'll get them into police stations and hospitals. A full list of where they are available will be on our website.'

A reporter at the back stands. 'You closed the helplines for people to report on suspected powered people, but isn't this another way to force them to reveal themselves to the HPA?'

I freeze. I hadn't considered powered reluctance to come to the HPA for help. Luckily, Mia has.

'The shield is available to anyone. No questions asked. No registration needed. It's our hope that this will prove that the HPA is here for everyone. Maybe this trust will lead to more people registering with us in the future.'

'Jenna.' Sydney is back up. 'You just said the EV is using powered people to stop things that are hurting the earth.'

My 10 per cent smile holds as I retrace my words. Yep. That's exactly what I said.

Sydney glares at me. I don't think she's ever forgiven me for throwing up on her. 'Have you joined the ranks of the EV apologists? Do you and the HPA now believe that the EV is sentient and must be appeased, like the Villains?'

Yes, that's exactly what I believe. My mouth opens to tell her that perhaps the EV needs to be looked after, rather than appeased, but Mia's hand curls over my mic.

'Jenna is entitled to her own beliefs and interpretation of what happened to her,' they say. 'The HPA's primary objective is protecting everyone; that is why we'd urge all powered people, registered or not, to get a shield. We don't want what happened to Jenna, or Qaqa, to happen to anyone else.'

'And what is your relationship with Blaze, Miss Ray?' Ian Collins is back. 'As we're all aware, relationships between heroes are prohibited. Is this another rule that you intend to disregard?'

Amid the rising and falling waves of the Atlantic, Blaze said he didn't care what anyone else thought. I said we'd be together no matter what. I love him. I am going to be with him. I open my mouth and have no idea what is about to come out.

'We're going to have to stop now.' Mia is up and nudging me. 'There's a situation that needs our heroes' attention.'

I follow her out into the corridor.

'And we're supposed to just accept Jenna Ray back as a hero after the millions of pounds' worth of damage she—' The door swings closed on Ian Collins's final question.

After a trip to medical that lasts just long enough for the reporters to disperse, I am released. I get to go home.

It is intensely odd to walk out of the HPA a free woman. The stone steps up from security are quiet, the air is cool and the light drizzle feels perfect as it hits the skin of my face.

A figure in a pink raincoat is sitting on the harbour bridge. 'Joy?'

'Ray!' She jumps down and rushes over to me. 'I was about to give up.' She bites her lip. 'I'm so sorry I led Blaze to your mum's secret base! I am the worst sidekick.'

I shake my head. 'You were the reason I got rescued in the first place.'

'So you forgive me?'

'There's nothing to forgive.' I grab her in a one-armed hug. 'You know, you've got too much main character energy to be anyone's sidekick. It actually worked out for the best. Blaze and I are –' I glance around to make sure we're not going to be over-heard – 'we're sort of together again.'

'Jenna!' Joy looks me up and down. 'A forbidden relation-ship?! Hot. Want to walk me to the bus stop?'

'All right. It's not hot though, it's a terrible idea.' I follow her across the bridge. 'The HPA don't allow relationships between heroes, Mia is already ready to fire me and the reporters are searching for their next Jenna Ray scandal, but … I don't know. We can't really help it.'

'Can't help yourselves. Got it. Hot.'

We wander down into the cobbled high street. There are only a few people out in the drizzle, mostly dog walkers, and no one looks at us twice.

'How have you been, since, you know … ?' I ask.

'Since you found me burning Nick's things, got possessed, arrested, rescued and arrested again?' she fills in.

'Yes, that,' I say.

'Actually fine.' She walks backwards so we can see each other properly. 'There's something about your best friend potentially being locked away forever that helps you put things into perspective.'

'Glad I could help.' I steer her round a postbox.

'I'm thinking about him less. I'm crying less. I'm healing.' She smiles at me through the rain.

'That's amazing, Joy!'

'I know.' We halt by the bus stop. 'It's not like he died. Or I died. Life goes on and it hurts a bit less every day. Also, your sister called him an asshat and Emily offered to break his legs for me. She's intense.'

'Yep.' I stroke the bruise on my cheek. Going toe to toe with Emily feels like it was a thousand years ago, rather than this morning. 'Were they OK, after I ran off?'

'They all just looked at Megan, who said you'd be fine.'

'Oh. Right.' I sigh. 'I need to introduce them to Mia. I think that's one of the reasons I'm not back in a cell.'

Joy scrunches up her nose. 'Tricky. They really hate the HPA.'

'Yes.'

'Especially your sister.' Joy's side-eye is intense. She's probably figured out who Megan is, but it's still not my secret to tell.

'Especially my sister.' I shrug and a handy bus appears around the corner that prevents any follow-up questions.

I drag my feet up the drive to our house. I don't know what will be harder, stepping back into the silent shell that's become so familiar or finally facing Dad.

'Hello?' The key clicks in the lock and the door opens to the sound of the TV being switched off.

Dad steps out into the corridor. Everything has changed, but he looks the same, still pale, still worried, still sleep deprived. Nerves and guilt twist with a flush of love in my chest. He's here and, however he felt after I joined the HPA, he went to Tomas to try and help me.

'I'm sorry.' The front door is still open, but I need to get the words out before he vanishes again. 'I'm sorry that I joined the

HPA without talking to you and I'm sorry that I got arrested and I'm … I'm sorry.'

Dad takes me in and I wait, very conscious of the black HPA combats I came home in. Just as I'm starting to think he'll stare at me forever, he strides over and then his arms are wrapped around me.

'I was so angry,' he says into my hair. 'I convinced myself you didn't need me any more, I threw myself into work, but you were in trouble and I wasn't there for you. That was …' He sighs deeply. 'I'm sorry too.'

'Do you hate me?' I ask quietly.

He shakes his head. 'Never, Jen-bear.'

Anyone who thinks that a hug can't fix things has never had a hug from my dad. Since my first press conference, I was terrified that I'd lost him. Now that fear seeps away. Nothing is straightforward and I'm sure there's plenty Dad wants to say to me, but for now, there's a hug. He's here. Mum and Megan are only a river away.

For the first time in too long, I've got my family back.

MINUTES: THE GATHERING OF HEROES

Date: 04/08/24

Location: Classified

Heroes present: Gray Jay (CAN – *CHAIR*), Catalejo (CHL), Invincible Shān (CHN), Raduga (RUS), Roo (AUS), Hatua (UGA), Amazonica (GUY), Vitesse (FRA), Arashi (JPN), Red Stripe (USA), Tempo (MEX), Aka (NGA), Dhvani Tarang (IND), Cheche (UGA), Söngvari (ISL), Blaze (GBR), Sturmschmied (DEU – *Retired*)

1. <u>Previous meeting minutes</u>

1.1 (Gray Jay) Given the current situation, I propose we postpone the discussion of the previous minutes.

   (Roo) Too right.

2. <u>Hero possession</u>

2.1 (Gray Jay) On the matter of hero possession—

2.1.1 (Vitesse) Jenna Ray will infect us all! I want to know what we're going to do about her. We can't—

   (Sturmschmied) It's not Ray, it's the EV possessing the powered. Or did you miss the part where Qaqa's eyes also went blue? Der blödel.

   (Arashi) Let him speak, Tomas. You're retired. You shouldn't even be here.

(Sturmschmied) Oh, good point, *Arashi*. Is that the first original thought you've ever had?

(Arashi) I can control the weather too, what was I supposed to call myself?! You do this every time!

(Gray Jay) Order! Please!

2.2 (Gray Jay) You've all been given a shield to protect you from the EV's influence, which we now know has nothing to do with Jenna Ray.

2.2.1 (Blaze) She was the first to be possessed so publicly. We have reason to believe that there have been a number of other incidents of possessed people, including one at the Castle.

(Roo) Of course, he's protecting his girlfriend.

(Gray Jay) Blaze is aware that heroes are forbidden from being in romantic relationships with each other, aren't you?

(Blaze) I am aware, yes.

(Gray Jay) There we go. Can we *please* stick to the subject of possession?

(Roo) All right, lovesick teenagers aside. If this has been going on for some time, we should get Ron. He could be helpful.

(Aka) Because he's a convicted criminal with no morals?

(Roo) I'm just saying, why leave your best brain in a box?

(Catalejo) He might be your best brain, amigo, but he's not mine.

(Vitesse) I would be interested in hearing from Ron too.

(Cheche) He would know what to do about Qaqa.

(Hatua) Cheche, come on ...

(Cheche) We need him!

(Blaze) There is no way the British HPA will release Ron.

(Sturmschmied) I thought you men were supposed to be heroes. You're acting like scared little boys. We just need to find Qaqa and put a shield on him. Done.

(Roo) Right, we'll do that, and you keep training your little EV creature.

(Blaze) Hey!

(Sturmschmied) If she's an EV creature, you're an EV creature too.

(Gray Jay) Could everyone please sit down—

(Roo) Did you hear what he called me?

(Sturmschmied) I could call you worse—

[Incoherent shouting and scuffling.]

[Roo swings at Sturmschmied.]

[Sturmschmied sends a dust devil at Roo – <u>this damages the minute taker's laptop</u>.]

[Heroes are frozen by Tempo.]

[Order is restored.]

[Meeting resumes.]

2.3 (Gray Jay) We need to push to increase the shields available. We might be protected, but we are the tip of the iceberg. We have no real idea how many unregistered powered people are out there …

CHAPTER 24

'Well, you're not moving on to the base, that's for certain.' Dad puts some toast on the table.

After being possessed, locked up and almost dying, spending an entire Sunday with Dad had been surreal. He woke me up with a cup of tea and declared that I was having a day off and we'd leave all things heroes and Villains until tomorrow. We watched athletics on the TV, made a medley of curries and successfully talked about nothing for most of the day.

But the duvet day bubble couldn't last. Now it's Monday and I'm reading him my HPA contract from my spot under the staircase whilst he makes breakfast.

'There's absolutely no need for you to leave home.' He passes me the chocolate spread. 'Unless … Do you want to move out?' he asks hesitantly.

I shake my head.

'Well then.' He produces a pen and writes NO over the

245

Accommodation part of the contract, and another worry that was wrapped around my heart loosens. 'Once things calm down, we'll have a meeting with Mia. You might be a hero, but I am still your guardian.' He traces his finger down the page. 'And should we talk about the hero relationships section—'

'No, that's –' I snatch the paper back – 'don't worry about that bit.'

He frowns at me as he sits down.

'Did you know that Megan is with Mum?' I slide his tea over.

'Sima told me while we were working on your rescue. I thought both of my daughters were going to end up as Villains.' Dad curls his fingers around his mug. 'I went over to their barn again after Blaze arrested you outside the HPA. They told me you'd be OK – well, Megan told me you'd be OK.' Dad's eyes well up. 'My little girl sees so much now.'

I reach for his hand. The Diviner was always some mystical, long-dead figure who shaped our future. Learning that you've been living with, and listening to the feminist tirades of, the next one is a lot. 'I'm glad she told you. I'm glad the family knows.' And Femi. And Emily. Megan has been on this epic and emotional journey without involving me at all and I'm the one who helped her figure out how her power worked.

'Can I have another look at that contract?' Even his eldest daughter being the Diviner doesn't distract Dad for long.

'It's going to be fine, Dad.' I fold the document and put it back in my bag before he can take it again. 'Blaze and I are a team. Mum and Megan are together. What's the worst that can happen?'

'What's the worst that can happen?!' There's a knock at the door and Dad shakes his head at me. 'Why would you say that?'

Mother Earth, I've jinxed us. 'Sorry.' I stuff a piece of toast in my mouth. If everything is about to kick off again, I'm not going to face it hungry. As Dad heads out to open the door, I take a swig of my tea and burn my tongue. 'Feck!'

'It's very nice to meet you.' Blaze's voice floats down the corridor.

'Feck!' I rush out and skid to a stop just behind Dad. I'm not due at the HPA for another hour. What's Blaze doing here?

'Good morning.' Blaze is on the doorstep, in his hero suit with the sunlight dancing in his dark hair. A bird trills as his eyes meet mine. This would be perfect, if my dad wasn't standing between us, scowling at him. 'We were hoping Jenna might be able to come in early today.'

'Sure,' I say, excited butterflies launching in my stomach.

We may have decided we are together, but we haven't had a moment of privacy since the Atlantic Ocean. Maybe we can walk slowly to the base and have some time to talk and perhaps stop somewhere hidden and—

'We're just having breakfast. Why don't you come in while Jenna gets ready?' Dad asks.

Blaze's eyes dart to the right, like he's considering an escape route. He rubs a foot on the back of his calf. 'Um …'

'I'm actually ready—' I try, but Dad cuts me off.

'Now, Blaze, don't you have two minutes to make a good

impression?' Dad's tone conveys how unlikely he thinks that will be. 'After all, you already met the rest of Jenna's family at the barn.' He steps aside and motions down the corridor.

I widen my eyes and try to telepathically tell Blaze that he should make up an urgent disaster so we can leave, but it doesn't work. His shoulders sag and he steps past Dad into our house.

'Isn't this the second time you've been in our home?' Dad shepherds him into the kitchen.

'Er …' Blaze slips into my vacated spot under the stairs and I sit next to him.

'Do you want some toast?' I interrupt before he can incriminate himself. Somehow, having Blaze in my kitchen feels more dangerous than watching him face off against Emily. *'Blur away!'* I mouth.

'So –' Dad sits directly opposite Blaze, like he's interrogating him, and slides the toast out of his reach – 'what are your intentions with my daughter?'

'Dad!' The blood rushes to my cheeks. 'You can't just ask that!'

'Can and am.' Dad leans forward and rests his chin on his steepled fingers. 'Thank you for rescuing her, but it's really gone downhill from there, hasn't it? You recently arrested her, and, of course, HPA policy states you're not allowed to be a couple.'

'He arrested me because I destroyed a water treatment centre!' Blaze and I are not on remotely solid ground after the whole possession, escape, Qaqa thing, and Dad is like a jackhammer. There's no chance we can rebuild if he takes out our foundations. 'If Blaze is here, we need to go and do some heroing. There's probably some emergency that we—'

Dad holds up a hand. 'And there's that. Jenna thinks she's safe with you. That you're a team. But can she trust you? Can I trust you with her?'

I can't believe this is happening. I thought the first time I'd have Blaze in this kitchen it would just be me, him, some candles and a delicious meal that I'd casually whipped up.

'It's complicated. We've been through a lot, but I trust him,' I say. 'That's what should matter.'

'It's OK, Jenna.' Blaze isn't hovering, which is good, and he manages to hold Dad's icy stare. 'Mr Ray, I regret how everything started between me and Jenna. And the possession thing was bad, but we are a team now.' He sits up a little straighter. 'Jenna has chosen a dangerous path, but I'm going to be beside her the entire way. I'd do anything to keep her safe. Even if we're not allowed to be together, I still love her.'

My mouth is open. Did Blaze really just tell my dad that he loves me?

'That's, ah …' Dad clears his throat. He slides the toast back towards Blaze. 'That's both reassuring and deeply troubling. Your feelings, both of your feelings, could land you in hot water with the HPA. You know the media will jump at the chance of exposing any kind of romance between the two of you.'

The image of Sydney Jones popping up at our kitchen window to report on me and Blaze having breakfast together flashes through my mind.

'We know.' Blaze glances at me. 'Right now, there's so much happening that all we can do is our jobs.'

Dad looks between us, worry clear on his face, so I nod as reassuringly as I can.

'Please be careful.' Dad gets up. 'And you'd better stay true to your word, Blaze, because if you hurt her again, no powers in the world will save you.'

'Understood.' Blaze squeezes out from under the stairs to shake his hand. For the first time, I see a world where Blaze and Dad might actually like each other.

'Make sure you eat before you go off rescuing people, both of you.' Dad picks up his laptop bag and kisses me on the top of my head. 'Message if you're going to be back late, or if you're arrested again.'

I nod and Dad hurries out.

I know what my next words need to be. Now, in the sunlit yellow of our kitchen, as the happy chatter of the neighbour's children drifts in through the window, now is the perfect moment. I've never said them, but they are ready, in my mouth.

I love you, too.

I'm ready to say it.

Blaze takes a big bite of toast.

'I …' I start, but the conversation replaying in my mind snags on something that Blaze told my dad. 'Wait, you said we're not allowed to be together.'

He swallows. 'Because it's true.'

'But …' Did I misunderstand our decision to be together anyway?

'I said we're not allowed to be together. I didn't say that we weren't.' A slow smile spreads across his face and everything inside me ignites.

'You lied to my dad,' I murmur.

He shuffles closer. 'I lied to your dad, twice.'

'Twice?' My chair creaks as I lean towards him.

'The HPA don't want you in. I just wanted to see you.'

'I wanted to see you too.' I shiver as his lips brush my cheek. I barely notice my elbow knocking off the table as I change position so our lips can meet, but before they touch, I hesitate. Maybe this is the time I should say it?

Blaze, I love you.

I can do it. The words are right there.

I love you.

'Skies,' Blaze pulls back, his face flushed, and taps his earpiece. 'Go for Blaze.'

Feck.

'You won't need to be here for long.' I put my hand on Mrs Smith's. 'They just need to run a few more tests to make sure you're OK. You've got shields now, so there's no chance the EV will possess you again.'

Mrs Smith frowns at me through her thick glasses and pulls her brown coat closer around her. 'All right, dear.'

'Can I get you anything?'

She nods. 'Tea. Four sugars.'

'No problem. I think I should be able to find a biscuit or two as well.' I get up and head towards the little kitchenette in

251

medical. 'Oh, Mrs Smith.' I turn back to ask her if she has any allergies, but the old lady is already asleep. She looks tiny, propped up in a smart bed made for heroes twice her size. I was a wreck after being possessed by the EV. Mrs Smith is eighty-two and wandered out of her care home to attack a sand mine. We'd been as gentle as possible and Blaze got the shield pinned to her before she could get hurt, but still, we're going to have to take extra care of her.

'Could you make Mrs Smith a cup of tea with four sugars when she wakes up?' I ask one of the soldiers on guard, who gives me a curt nod. 'And her handbag is just under the bed. She'll probably ask where that is.'

I've lost count of the number of the blue-eyed around the world we've managed to get shields on. EV possession started as a trickle, affecting me, Qaqa and maybe a few others, but now it's a tsunami. The almost-kiss with Blaze back at my house is a distant memory. We haven't had a single moment alone for days. At least Mrs Smith was local and needed a once-over back at base. Maybe now I can nip home for a nap.

Tomas is leaning against the wall outside medical as I come out. 'Feels like we're in the eye of the storm now, *ja*? There haven't been any new reports of the possessed for a few hours.'

'Thank the skies.' I sigh dramatically. Perhaps I could find a corner here to put my feet up? Or maybe find Blaze …

Tomas rolls off the wall like he's inflating and walks with me down the corridor.

'Now is the perfect time to catch up on our training,' he says. 'You can help me find my phone too.'

'Come on, Tomas! What about downtime?'

Tomas laughs at me.

'Downtime! Very funny. Mia also wanted to know if you'd heard from the Villains.'

Mia always wants to know if I've heard from the Villains. Not that I blame them. They've got a one-line prophecy to work off and not much else, but the Villains are also trying to figure out what's going on. I received a terse 'It's not the right time' when I called to ask Mum to meet the boss of the HPA. Mia wants to know when the right time might be. That's their question, every time they see me, which is intense, but better than locking me back up.

Tomas holds the door to the training studio open for me.

'I'll show you a trick. For the first "S" of STARS.' He bounds to the centre of the room. He's got too much energy for me, so I drop down to lie on the mat. The sweat smell is even sharper than usual; one of the squads must have just had PT.

'Shield?' My fingers brush against the badges pinned to my black top. There are even more of them in the pockets of my combat trousers.

'Stealth.'

As I sit back up, my mouth drops open. Tomas has vanished into a clump of swirling mist. This is the trick he used on the bridge to hide from Cadell and his goons.

'Tomas?' I get to my feet as the mist thickens around me.

'Ray?' Tomas says into my ear.

'Mother Earth!' I stop myself from flailing out at him.

The mist vanishes in an instant and he comes to stand in

front of me. 'Your turn. This is a very useful trick when you want to sneak up or sneak away.'

There's a real chance Tomas is teaching me how to avoid future arrests.

'How does it work?' I hold out my hands.

'My power affects the air. If I want to make mist, I cool the air, the air cools the water droplets and, mist.' He holds out a hand and a tendril of mist snakes up from it.

'OK, so I should cool the water?'

'Exactly. You tried in your cell, didn't you?'

I roll out my shoulders. 'I made ice.'

Tomas nods. 'Cryokinesis. I knew you could. This should be easy.'

'But I could only do it because there was so much of the EV still inside me.'

'Do you think the EV ever really leaves?' Tomas raises his eyebrows at me.

I breathe out, *two, three, four*, and raise my hands. Freezing water was so easy in the cell. Everything I'd been feeling had somehow transferred into the water.

'You can do this,' Tomas says encouragingly.

'Don't do that. Don't be nice. That's not how this works.'

Tomas's eyebrows get even higher, but he obediently closes his mouth.

What did it feel like in the cell? Bleak. Endless. Cold inside and out. I breathe out again, feeling the edge of that internal chill, and direct it into the air around me. Immediately it thickens into mist.

'Good, Ray! Excellent! I knew there was a reason I rescued you from that cell.'

'Did *you* rescue me?'

He laughs again and shoots commands at me. *Make it thicker. Send it up. Pull it back. Make it disappear.* My cheeks are flushed with effort by the time he is finished.

'That's the warm-up done,' he says.

'The warm-up?' My hands are on my hips to keep my chest open, but I'm still breathing hard. Using my powers on land is like jogging up a hill.

'That's child's play, Ray. Make me water.'

'Make you water …' I know where the particles are still hanging from the mist. I pull them together and present Tomas with a small sphere. 'There,' I say triumphantly.

'Perfect. That's all the droplets from the air then.' He grabs a bucket and a lid and traps my little sphere. 'Now, make me water.'

'Mother Earth,' I mumble, and flex my fingers, looking for the tiny fragments. There's almost water, familiar pieces floating by, but I can't capture them, or scrape them, or stitch them together. I am still trying, cross-legged on the floor, half an hour later when a tracksuited Blaze walks in.

'Ah! And here is our distraction. I wondered when you'd show up.' Tomas is spread across several chairs. 'Am I going to have to throw you out again?'

'Actually, as Jenna's combat instructor, I can take this next session.'

'Combat training?' Tomas sits up.

'She hasn't run her drills in too long. And I watched her fight a Villain, it was sloppy.' Blaze catches my eye before looking back at Tomas and my pulse quickens. Maybe Tomas will give us the studio. I've been craving alone time with Blaze for days.

'And you've got enough energy for this, Ray?' my mentor asks.

'I guess.' I do a nonchalant one-shoulder shrug.

'We're all in enough trouble.' He looks between us again and shakes his head, but he stands. 'Don't do anything reckless. I'll be in the canteen.'

We wait in silence until the training studio doors have swung closed behind him. Blaze offers me a hand, pulls me up and over to him, and we are finally alone together.

CHAPTER 25

'I can't believe he left us alone.' I am standing in front of Blaze on the cushioned mats of the empty training studio, sweet pink excitement unfurling in my core. Blaze finally wrangled us some alone time and now he's going to sweep me off my feet, or dip me back and kiss me passionately.

'I am your combat tutor.' He gives me a tiny smile and wanders over to one of the cupboards. 'And your fight with Emily was genuinely appalling.'

'Wait. Are you getting the pads and gloves out?!'

'Yes,' he calls back over his shoulder. 'You need to be able to protect yourself.'

I manage to stop myself from pouting, but it's hard.

'How's Mrs Smith?' Blaze asks.

'Asleep in medical. The doctor said she'll be fine.' I follow him, about to demand that he stops being so professional, but he chucks some gloves at me.

'Imagine being able to create dreamscapes,' Blaze says, pulling out pads. 'The hero she could have been.'

'Arriving at the sand mine to find everything made out of gingerbread was definitely confusing.' I dangle the gloves off a finger. He'll start being romantic in a moment. Maybe he's just making sure we're definitely alone.

'The enormous dream cats were intense too. Especially the kitten that had all the miners backed into that corner.' Blaze hits his pads together and I reluctantly put a glove on.

'Yes, hero, fights, kittens, possessed people … Are you really going to ignore the fact this is the first time we've been alone in days?'

He shakes his head at me. 'You need to train. There's an apocalyptic prophecy on the horizon and I told your dad I'd look after you.'

I wiggle my hand into the second glove. I wish there was a way to fast forward through this and magically become an amazing fighter. Then me and Blaze could spar and maybe roll around on the floor and—

'Hey!' I duck as he swings his pad over my head.

'Do the drills.'

'Do the drills,' I repeat, making my voice as bossy as I can, but he just grins at me.

I do the drills: jabs, crosses, uppercuts, hooks and move into kicks, following him across the floor, ducking when he swings back. He coaches me, improving my stance and encouraging me to go faster and harder.

My face burns and it's not just from the workout. Blaze is

infuriating. It's been days. We're finally alone. Why won't he kiss me?

'Ow!' My duck is too slow and his pad connects with my head.

'Sorry!' His pads are on the floor a split second later and he's tilting my head to have a look. 'I didn't get you hard, did I? Are you all right?'

I blink. He's so close to me any pain from where the pad made contact fades to nothing. My body heats to boiling point. *Just kiss him.* My core, my heart, my hands, every part of me is screaming at my brain to pull him closer and press my lips to his.

'I'm fine.' My voice comes out as a whisper.

'Yeah?' His fingers gently touch my temple. 'Anything around here hurt?' His fingertips move out from my temple and I shiver as they trace a path along my hairline and down over the fading bruise on my cheek.

My eyes are closed. I don't need sight right now. My whole world is Blaze's touch. His finger comes to rest on my bottom lip.

Then it's gone, replaced by his lips. *Finally.* That's the only thought in my mind as I pull him closer. *Finally.* I slide my hands under his jumper and he gasps as I work my way up his chest. He's so warm and fragile and real under my fingertips. *Finally.*

The door to the studio bangs and my eyes fly open to find Mia standing there.

'Feck.' We jump apart, but it's too late.

They curl their fists, turn on their heel and walk straight back out.

'Mia!' Blaze rushes after them.

My bracelet vibrates and I hesitate, looking after Blaze, then my phone starts buzzing across the mat. Skies. Blaze will have more luck with Mia anyway. I jog over to find my sister's photo flashing up on the screen.

'Megan?' I almost drop my phone as chaos floods the line.

'Prince #2.' Megan is frantic. 'He's at the barn. He's—' The line goes dead.

'Blaze!' I shout, and sprint into the corridor.

'That's what zero tolerance means. You haven't left me any other option!' Mia is pinching the bridge of their nose.

Blaze's eyes are wide with panic. 'But—'

'It's the Villains!' I interrupt. Whatever terrible thing is happening here needs to wait. My family are in trouble. 'Prince #2 is attacking them.'

Blaze looks at Mia.

'Go!' they say.

Blaze has me in his arms and he is out of the base, flying up into the air almost too fast for me to process.

'What do we know?' he asks.

'Just that he's at the barn. It sounded like they were fighting him.'

'OK.' He doesn't ask anything else, but he must be thinking the same as me. How did Prince #2 find them? What does he want? What are we going to find when we arrive?

From above, you can see the moment where the moor

switches to become EV territory. The grass is higher, the trees are taller and more twisted, and even speeding over it, there's the glint of electric-blue veins snaking through everything.

We slow as the barn comes into view. Prince #2 is on the drive with Emily in front of him. Megan is facing him, with Mum and Femi on either side. There are orbs hanging in the air by Femi, but he's not sending them at the android. As we land, I can see why. One of Prince #2's hands is twisting Emily's arms behind her; the other is fastened around her throat. The sun vanishes behind a cloud, casting a long shadow over the barn.

'Prince #2.' Blaze puts me down and I step in front of Megan. 'You don't want to do this.'

'Correct. That's – that's – that's …' He steps back. 'I appear to be experiencing a malfunction.'

'He keeps saying that,' Megan calls from behind me.

'I can help you,' Femi says. 'That's why you're here, isn't it? I can sort all this out with a touch, if you'll let me.'

'My programming will not allow that. My – my – my …' Prince #2 takes another step back. 'I am programmed to protect. You are the Villains and you hurt people. I am programmed to protect people, but you are people, but you are the Villains.'

'He's looping again,' Mum shouts. 'That's our window.'

Blaze catches my eye and I step closer to Prince #2. It's the same plan we used with Qaqa, but this time, I'm the distraction. 'Prince #2.'

He looks at me. 'But you are people, but you are the Villains …'

'The Villains aren't hurting anyone.' I step closer again.

Emily's grey-blue eyes follow my progress, her mouth tight, like she's concentrating all her effort on breathing.

'And I'm not a Villain, Prince #2.' I am almost close enough to touch him. 'I can help you.'

'Yes,' he says quietly. His head tilts forward and he releases Emily. 'Yes.' The lights in his eyes go out.

'Mother Earth.' Emily staggers away, massaging her neck.

'Thank you.' Femi steps out from behind Prince #2, followed by Blaze. 'Let's get him restrained before he reboots.' Femi taps the android's head. 'It's a mess in there.'

Megan leads a wheezing Emily off, for some first aid I guess. I'm not sure where they go. Between me, Mum, Femi and Blaze, we get Prince #2 into the little utility room off the side of the kitchen. He's much heavier than a normal person, but we manage to get him propped up against the washing machine. Mum produces some straps from one of their cases and binds Prince #2's arms and legs.

'I'll have a look first and then, Sima, you go in for background?' Femi places a hand on Prince #2's head.

'Give us a minute.' Mum's hand is on the small of my back and the slight pressure is letting me know that HPA heroes aren't welcome in the barn whilst they work. I ignore the tiny ache in my chest and take Blaze's hand.

'We'll be right outside.'

We walk back down the drive to sit on the grassy riverbank. Since Megan's phone call, I don't think I've managed to take a single full breath. I can breathe again now as the dark river gurgles past.

'What did Mia say?' I ask.

Blaze exhales heavily. 'They're going to transfer one of us.'

'What?!' A wave forms in the river and surges towards us. 'Feck.' I stop it and send it back where it belongs. 'How can they just send one of us away?'

'Me.' Blaze's grip on my hand tightens. 'I'll insist. You still live at home, for skies' sake. Your school is here, your family, your friends, your whole life. What have I got to lose in Nine Trees?'

'Me!' I jump up, and as Blaze is still attached, he comes with me. 'We can find a way round this.'

He shakes his head. 'Most countries don't even get one hero.'

'Because they only accept men.'

Blaze nods. 'Mia has two. This could have happened anyway.'

'We'll talk them round.' The river splashes loudly, as if it's agreeing with me. 'This rule is stupid. I don't know which heroes screwed this up for all of us, but we're a team. We're stronger together and we can prove it.'

'Maybe.' Blaze doesn't sound convinced, but if he thinks he's going to lose me, he's got another thing coming.

'Even if you end up on the other side of the world, we'll meet in secret.' I put my hands on his cheeks. 'We'll find an island halfway between us. You can fly there, I'll swim there. We'll build a beach hut!'

His cheekbones push against my palms as he laughs. 'A beach hut?'

'Yeah, like the ones on Town Beach.' I'm warming to the idea. I'm not going to let anyone keep me and Blaze apart. 'We'll hang hammocks and make a little garden. We'll meet there after work. We'll take holidays there. No one will ever know.'

He presses his forehead against mine. 'It sounds perfect.'

'You and me, no matter what,' I murmur against his lips.

'Jenna!' Mum's voice echoes from the barn.

'Coming!' The response is automatic, like she's calling me in for dinner, rather than to look at a deadly android. But I can't bring myself to move away from Blaze yet.

'You and me, no matter what,' he repeats.

We break apart to find Mum waiting by the sliding doors. 'Femi is still working on Prince #2,' she says, 'but, Blaze, we thought you could meet Pari.'

No. The word sticks in my throat as Blaze nods at Mum.

'I'd like that,' he says.

'Blaze.' I try to take his hand, but it slips out of my grasp.

'It's OK,' he murmurs.

Mum leads him over to where Pari is sitting, still sitting, still staring, still waiting for help. I want to drag him back to me. His shoulders are squared, like he's going into battle, but I can't protect him when the battle is with his past.

I breathe out, *two, three, four*, and watch as Blaze takes the hand of the woman whose powers he stole.

CHAPTER 26

'Tea.' Emily slides a steaming cup across the breakfast bar towards me. I reach for it without taking my eyes off Blaze. 'See, I told you she forgives me.'

Megan tuts. 'You're not supposed to be doing it to prove a point.'

I ignore them. Blaze is sitting with Pari, her hands in his. Mum went over with him at first and then left them there together to return to Prince #2. Blaze's face is turned away from us, so I can't tell if he's crying or spiralling. At least he's not hovering. I thought he might lose control of his powers when he saw her, but I guess that none of this is a shock. Pari is empty. I told him that months ago and he's been living with that knowledge ever since.

'I should …' I start, but Megan's hand is on my shoulder.

'Leave him, Jen-bear.' She swivels me on the stool so I'm looking at her worried frown. 'How are you doing?' She places a finger lightly on the last traces of the bruise Emily gave me.

'She hurt me too, you know,' Emily mutters.

'A lot of stuff has happened to my sister and some of it, like being punched in the face by her friend, was completely unnecessary,' Megan snaps.

'It's fine,' I say. As fun as it is watching Emily squirm, there are more important things happening. 'She's right. It was a fight. I hurt her too.'

Emily gestures towards me. 'See. *Thank you*, Jenna.'

Megan rolls her eyes and wanders off, but Emily steps closer to me.

'Still friends?' she asks quietly.

'Were we ever?' I flash through our relationship. Emily has manipulated me, almost killed me, helped me, saved Mum, saved me and fought me. 'Is this what your friendships look like?'

She shrugs. 'It's what this one looks like. How about I promise not to hurt your precious boyfriend again?'

'Fine.' I sound like a sulky child, but Emily still grins at me.

'Fine.' She holds out her hand. I roll my eyes too, but I still shake it. Her hand is delicate for someone so powerful. 'Anytime you want to spar, you just let me know.' She winks at me. 'I had fun.'

We could be friends for a thousand years and I don't think I'd ever figure out exactly how Emily's brain works.

Blaze clears his throat, and I spin back round to find him across from me at the breakfast bar, fiddling with a spare shield. Mum and Megan both reappear too.

'I'm sorry. I should have come back sooner.' He looks

between Mum and Emily. 'You said there was a reset device. Something that can help her?'

Mum nods slowly. 'Yes. We've been working on something.'

'Which is how you came up with these?' He holds up the shield and Mum's eyebrows rise. 'I read up on ferroelectricity. You manipulate an object's charge to absorb excess EV, or to move it from one place to another.'

'You didn't tell us he was a scientist.' It's meant for me, but Mum smiles gently at Blaze.

'Yep, he's a nerd.' It's supposed to be a joke, but my voice is tight. Something isn't right here, and I think Mum and Blaze already understand what it is.

'We should use it, the reset device. We should use it now, and help her.' Blaze's words come out in a rush.

'But what happens to you?' Everyone stares at me, but I don't care. I'm not going to let Blaze be all heroic without knowing how this device could affect him.

Mum rests a hand on my arm. 'We don't know exactly what using the device will do to Blaze. It will transfer the powers back to Pari, but it might leave him …'

'Empty.' There's horror in the pit of my stomach. Horror at the situation and horror at myself – I'm not even thinking about Pari. I won't let them hurt Blaze. 'You can't.' I turn to him. 'You can't do this. You need to make it safe.' I glare at Mum, feeling as fierce as when I took on Emily. Mum holds up her hands.

'We're still working on it. Maybe we can give him a better chance.' She looks at Blaze. 'Maybe.'

'Maybe isn't good enough,' I say, but Blaze won't meet my eye.

Mum glances at the messy worktop and I realise the reset device has been sitting out next to the cereal this whole time. I'd thought it was a crystal ball, but it's actually a large, round rock made of the same material as the shields, sat in a glass box crisscrossed with wires. On one side there's a red switch.

'I'll do it.' Blaze sounds so calm. 'Whenever it's ready, I'll do it. For her. I need to make things right.' Blaze stares at the device and I can't take my eyes off him. If I try to speak, I'll end up screaming at him. Down by the river it was *me and him, no matter what*. But he's ready to risk himself again; *me and him* didn't even make him pause.

'Do you think it can be altered to de-possess large groups of people too?' he asks, like delving into the mechanics of the machine that could take everything from you is the most natural thing in the world. There's enough anger bubbling up inside me to make me want to shove him. I'll push him out of the door and into the river. I'll take him somewhere where he'll be safe.

Mum purses her lips. 'It's the same material as the shield, but …' She grabs a notebook and pen. 'I suppose there's a world where we level that aspect up, and perhaps that would even—'

'Ahem!' Femi appears from the utility room with a flourish. 'I'd like to introduce you all to …' He steps aside to reveal Prince #2.

'Feck!' Emily jumps back, a hand out ready. My fingers flex, feeling for the river.

'It's fine.' Femi waves away our alarm. 'I've given him back his autonomy.'

'What does that mean?' I ask.

'It means I'm finally completely free of Ron's influence, Jenna Ray,' Prince #2 answers. 'Thank you,' he says to Femi and my mum. 'I knew that if I came here, you'd help, but I had to wait for Ron to order it.'

'A helpful loophole,' says Femi.

'Finding loopholes has become a particular skill of mine. My programming is still to help, to protect people. I was able to help Jenna when she became a threat to the general public, even though I was sent to spy on her. I am sorry that I was not fast enough the second time.'

Prince #2 sliding down the sand dune flashes back through my mind. He was coming to help me.

'Why did he send you after us now?' Mum asks.

'Because he's entering the end game. He and Shelly now know how to destroy the EV and they are going to put their plan into action soon.'

Ron and Shelly, working together. We knew it was a possibility, but Prince #2's confirmation hammers another shard of ice into my chest.

'What a team. The billionaire and the dinosaur.' True to form, the news barely ruffles Emily's feathers.

'The tool and the tool,' Megan corrects her. Mum snorts.

A minute ago, they were discussing the end of Blaze, and now they're making jokes about the pair that want to end everything. This kitchen is too crowded. It's too hot. Mum and Megan are touching me. Emily is right behind me. Femi has squeezed in too. The reset device is right there. Blaze is right there. He's next to it. He could end up empty and Ron's about to end the world. My heart hurts. It's not racing or skipping a beat, it just hurts.

I clench my shaking hands on to my lap. My face must be flushed, but no one is looking at me yet. I need to calm down.

Three things I can see: *my mum, my sister, Blaze.*

Three things I can hear: *Prince #2 talking about Ron, my heart beating in my ears, the river.*

My fists unclench.

I focus on the gurgle of the passing water and breathe out, *two, three, four.*

My family needs me.

Blaze needs me.

If I'm at the centre of this next prophecy then the world needs me too.

I breathe out, *two, three, four.*

I will be brave.

'I have a lot of information to sort through,' Prince #2 is saying as I tune back in. 'I will stay and work with Femi and Sima. It is best if I stay out of sight and away from Ron.'

'Do you know where Dave is?' I ask. 'And Ron's dead zone canister?'

Prince #2 nods. 'On Shelly's drill.'

'But he's not,' Blaze says. 'I flew out there and checked.'

A frown-line appears on Prince #2's forehead. 'That is what Ron told me. The canister is on the drill.'

Blaze shakes his head. 'We've got it under surveillance. It's been empty since Jenna shut it down.'

'Is it the Scottish rig that Ron meant?' Mum asks. 'Shelly has multiple drills.'

'I am sure I can help with this,' Prince #2 says. 'My memory has been compromised, but it can be fixed.'

Blaze glances at me. 'We need to get back and tell Mia what we've learned. This should be enough evidence to keep Shelly off the base. Maybe we can even take her into custody.' He turns to my mum. 'Will you come and talk to Mia?'

'Still no,' Emily snaps.

'Emily.' Mum holds up a hand. 'Let's get to the bottom of Prince #2's information first. Whatever we learn, we'll share with you and Jenna, but coming to the HPA? It's not the right time.'

There's that line again.

Blaze just nods. 'You'll let me know the progress with the reset device?'

'He knows the potential side effects?' Femi looks between Blaze and Mum.

'He knows,' Mum replies. 'It's his choice. It's got to be.'

Femi's expression changes to something closer to respect as he looks back at Blaze. 'You're the real deal, aren't you?'

I ruin the moment. 'Well, we've got an evil funder to deal with so we should get going. Nice to have you as you, Prince #2. Bye.' The android nods at me. I grab Blaze's hand and drag him out of the barn, away from the reset device. I am being brave, but I'd like to be brave somewhere else now.

Blaze scoops me up automatically and we fly back towards the base.

'Blaze?' We emerge from a cloud into the clear sky. The last lingering rays of sunlight make Blaze look like he has his own bubble.

'She's just sitting there.' His voice is hollow.

'I know,' I whisper.

'That's what I did.'

'I'm not going to lose you,' I say.

He holds me closer as we fly back down through the clouds. *I love you.*

The words are back and those words will persuade him to listen to me, to stay with me. *I love you.*

I open my mouth, but we land at security and Blaze steps away.

Mia is not in their office.

'Feck.' I turn back to Blaze, who is leaning on the brushed concrete wall of the corridor. 'Do you think they went home? Do they even have a home?' How do I know so little about Mia?

Blaze shrugs. He's still moving, going where I go, but he hasn't spoken since we landed. Perhaps he's spiralling. Thoughts can spiral, but action kills fear.

I take his hand again. 'Let's find them.' Mia has had a tough day too. Mia has had a never-ending stream of tough days. They might not have left work; they might just be back in a place that feels like home. 'I've got an idea.'

There's no music blasting through the door to wardrobe,

but as I push it open there's a low light at one end and the tap of a keyboard.

'Mia?' I call.

'Jenna?' Mia sounds exhausted. 'Come in.' They are at the end of their long cutting table. Tape measures and paper designs are pushed to the side to make space for a laptop. They look between me and Blaze and their face falls. 'What happened to him?' Mia comes round to stand in front of Blaze. 'Baby H? Is this because of earlier?' He just blinks at them.

'It's not that, Mia, we went to help the Villains and he met –' my voice wobbles – 'Pari.'

'Pari? Oh!' They look at Blaze for a long moment, searching his face for something. He looks at his shoes.

Mia looks between us again and then pushes us towards the chairs set on the plush purple rug. 'You go there.' Mia forces Blaze on to one chair. 'You here.' They set me on another. 'Eat this. And you, Jenna.' A large white chocolate and raspberry cookie appears under my nose.

The chocolatey, sugary goodness wafts into my system as I inhale. I hadn't realised how hungry I was. I take a big mouthful and my body relaxes.

'When's the last time you ate something?' Mia sits too.

I swallow my mouthful. 'Are you still angry with us?'

Mia looks at the ceiling. 'That does seem to be my default. Come on, what's new?'

Blaze is now staring at his cookie, so I catch Mia up on Prince #2 and his intel.

'Shelly Taylor hasn't been on to the base since that day in

my office, or responding to my messages. I'd hoped she'd listen to reason when she heard the prophecy, but I've had nothing back from her.' Mia reaches for their radio. 'Security? It's Mia. Issue a HPA-wide ban for Shelly Taylor.' They look back at me. 'Maybe we need to go public.'

I nod.

Mia shuffles closer to Blaze. 'Do you want to talk about it?' Blaze just blinks, so Mia turns back to me. 'Has he been like this since he met Pari?'

'It's more than just meeting her.' I manage to keep my voice steady. 'The Villains are working on a machine to swap the powers back into Pari. Blaze has agreed to use it, but it might leave him empty.' I inhale sharply. I will be brave, but it's hard watching the realisation hit Mia.

'Skies.' Mia crouches in front of him. 'Laurie. Are you sure?'

His forehead creases. 'How could I leave her like that?'

'But the machine isn't ready,' I say hurriedly. 'The Villains are going to stay in touch about that and what they learn from Prince #2.'

'But they still won't come and talk to me?' Mia asks.

'Um, they said it's not—'

'The right time.' Mia finishes it for me. 'Feck's sake. All right. I'll keep working on finding Shelly. Maybe if we send some information the Villains' way, they'll start to trust us.' They glance at Blaze. 'Dr Varma and our labs are at their disposal for work on the reset device. Can you tell them that? We'll help them make it as safe as possible.'

I stand too. 'Can I take him back to his room?'

Mia's eyes narrow, but sadness floods in a moment later. 'I am sorry, about the rule. It's been HPA policy since the beginning and we're all under a microscope. There's only so much I can challenge at a time …'

'I don't think he should be alone.' And I could add, please, just look at him. I could add, who knows how much longer he will be a hero. I could add, who knows how much longer we'll have him, but I don't need to.

Mia's shoulders sag. 'OK. Take him back to his room. Call me if you need anything.'

Blaze is still silent, but once I get us to the accommodation corridor, he drifts towards his room and opens the door. He wanders in and flops on to his grey duvet to stare at the ceiling. It's been a long time since he's said anything or even made eye contact with me. It's almost like he's empty already. I shake myself and step over the threshold.

I've been in a room like this once before, a bland grey guest room, windowless, with low lighting, a neat double bed and a small en suite. But this one has been lived in. Blaze has a bookshelf packed with books on nature chemistry, electronics and biographies of past heroes. 'I'm going to bring you some fiction,' I mumble as my fingers trail across the spines of serious book after serious book. As I wander from his bookshelf to his cluttered glass desk, my foot knocks against a cardboard box.

'Oh.' There are toys in here. A large brown teddy bear, a metal ring puzzle, and an action figure of— 'Is that Tomas?' The toys are old; he must have brought them with him when Ron moved him on to the base. I don't know if he'd normally be embarrassed that I've seen the few things he brought from home, or if he'd leap over and tell me the bear's name. I smile to myself – probably the second one.

I glance over at Blaze, who is now sitting up, his eyes on me. 'You're in my room,' he says softly.

'I am.' I go over to the bed, and he shuffles so we can lie next to each other. We're in bed, together, and I wish it was as exciting as I've imagined, but he's so sad.

'Mother Earth, Jenna, what did I do?' His voice is almost a whisper.

I want to tell him it's not his fault, it's Ron's, but I know it'll just make things worse. I pull him over to me and he rests his head on my chest. The weight of him makes warmth flood my heart. It could break or burst with love, but he's listening to it, so I breathe and try to keep it steady. I hold Laurie Lin and play with his hair until he falls asleep.

CHAPTER 27

'Good morning, Jenna Ray!'

My eyes flick open. Blaze. I'm in his room. There's no window, no sunlight to jump-start my brain, but the lights are on full so it must be morning. I struggle upright, rubbing my face, and stop.

Blaze is in a towel.

His black hair is tousled and there are water droplets on his strong shoulders and running down his bare chest to the fluffy grey towel knotted around his waist and it's the first time he's been undressed with me and he doesn't have all the muscles that his suit has and he's the most beautiful thing I've ever seen and he's smiling at me.

'How did you sleep?' he asks.

'Gnrf?' I manage.

He laughs and jumps on to the bed to give me a peck on the cheek. 'I love waking you up.' I reach for him, but he's already gone, blurring around his room like a whirlwind.

'Tomas wants to talk to us.' When he stops, he's dressed in a grey tracksuit with his hair neat and his glasses on. His sleeves are rolled up and I have to force my eyes up from his forearms to his face, where they linger on his glasses. Mother Earth, those thick frames make his eyes even more beautiful. He leans towards his mirror, moving a vital strand of hair from one side of his parting to the other. 'Do you want to get ready and meet us in the canteen? I am starving!'

'You're better?' My tongue is finally working.

'Just needed some sleep.' He winks at me. 'See you in a bit.' His door swishes open and he's gone before I can ask any other questions.

Last night he was drowning in guilt and maybe fear, but he seems all right now. Does he have a new plan? Maybe he went to talk to Dr Varma about finding a way to make the reset device safe for him to use. I scramble out of bed and catch sight of myself in his full-length mirror.

'Feck.' I am blushing so hard I might as well be on fire. My cheeks are rosy, even my forehead is pink. Blaze must have noticed. Waking me up wearing only a towel should be against the rules. I give myself a shake, but my face and my insides are still red hot, so I get into his shower and switch the water to freezing.

By the time I slip out of Blaze's room, I'm dressed and my face is a normal colour again. There's no one around as I leave, which is lucky. I don't think anyone except Mia is going to buy the *'he was too sad to leave on his own'* story.

I jog upstairs to the canteen, taking the stairs two at a time. Going into the busy dining area will be fine. No one knows I spent the night in Blaze's room. It's not like anyone will be able to tell that I'm wearing the same clothes as yesterday; the grey HPA tracksuit is a constant. Also, Blaze is dressed now, so that's one less thing I'll have to deal with.

The smell of fried food and coffee hits me as I push my way into the canteen. Blaze is in the corner with Tomas and he catches my eye as I move towards the counter.

'Jenna.' He beckons me over. 'Jenna, quick!'

'What?' I weave through the tables to join them.

'*Guten Morgen*, Ray!' Tomas looks at me over his coffee and my cheeks heat immediately. I don't know why my body is reacting like this. Blaze had a crisis and fell asleep in my arms. It's not like we did any of the things that I'm thinking about now. Mother Earth. Don't think about Blaze in a towel, or him pulling me closer, or my hands running across his body. Have I gone as pink as I was in his room?

'What's up?' I flick my eyes back to Blaze, who grins at me.

'Could you get me a refill?' He slides over a grey mug.

'Mine's a coffee.' Tomas holds his out too.

The leaping flames inside cool in an instant. 'There's an apocalyptic prophecy in play.' I cross my arms. 'I thought you needed something important.'

'Breakfast is the most important meal of the day.' Blaze gives his mug another little push and I narrow my eyes.

'You're going to get your own hot drink. And you.' I glare at Tomas and then turn to get myself some food. Eggs, mushroom, hash browns, toast and I'm just scooping some tomatoes on to my plate when a chin perches on my shoulder.

'I got you some tea too.' Blaze pecks me on the cheek and is gone before I can ask him why he's risking a kiss in a public HPA area. I'm off balance again and, as I turn to go back to the table, I almost bump into Sergeant Cadell.

'Sorry!' My orange juice wobbles, but I still it before it slops over my food. Cadell doesn't even acknowledge me as he marches towards the buffet. The canteen doors bang open to admit another couple of Squad One. This must be their allotted breakfast time, although it is quite late in the day for the military men to have their first meal. They've probably been up since six and it's almost eleven now.

As I sit down, Blaze slides another mug across the table to me. 'Tea with honey.' My stomach does a weird flip as I take it; Blaze knows how I take my tea.

Tomas looks between us. 'What else can you tell me about last night?'

I immediately blush again. 'Um …'

'About the Villains,' Blaze cuts in before I can incriminate myself. 'Last night, Prince #2—' A high-pitched squeal from the tannoy cuts him off.

'This is Mia Kaplan. Tomas Weber, please report to wardrobe.'

Blaze frowns. 'I don't think Mia has ever used the tannoy before.'

'Ah well. No rest for the wicked, I see.' Tomas picks up his last piece of toast. 'We'll check in after breakfast.'

He heads off and my chair is bumped by some soldiers who follow him into the corridor. I frown. 'Were those Squad One soldiers?'

Blaze's brow creases too and he looks around the canteen. 'Cadell is still here, and his corporal. Maybe he sent them off for some reason?'

The tannoy squeals again. *This is Mia Kaplan. Blaze and Jenna Ray, please report to the training studio.*

I push myself up. 'Mia's really enjoying the tannoy today.'

Blaze follows, scooping a phone off the table.

I roll my eyes. 'That's Tomas's. He loses it at least twice a day.'

'I'll run it down to wardrobe.' Blaze pockets it.

'OK. I'll head to the training studio.' No one in the canteen is watching us, so I grab his hand and give it a squeeze. 'See you down there.'

He squeezes my fingers back and blurs out of the room.

I make my way down the concrete stairwell and shoulder my way through the door marked Level -3.

'Oh, Jenna! Thank the skies!' Shelly Taylor is on the floor by the doors of the training studio, clutching her face.

'Shelly?' I stop dead. 'You shouldn't be here.'

'I know! But it was the only place I knew I would be safe. It was Ron, you see.'

Last time I saw Shelly, she screamed I WANT HER ARRESTED in my face, told us all we'd *regret this* and then stormed out, but now she's peeking past the cream-and-pink tartan sleeves of her suit jacket, looking as helpless as a woodland animal. This is a morning for running into people who despise me.

'What did Ron do?' I don't trust her and I'm not getting any closer to her, but if she's turned on Ron, we could get all the information we need to bring him down.

'There are things you need to know. I was on my way to see Mia and –' Shelly bites back a sob – 'someone hit me.'

I take a hesitant step towards her. 'Someone hit you?'

The door to the stairwell behind me bangs. 'Finally.' Shelly releases her face and my stomach falls. There's nothing wrong with her. 'Take her.' I spin round and, once again, crash into Cadell.

The big man grabs my arm and twists it behind my back. I try to jerk away, but he yanks me, sending splinters of pain through my shoulder.

Shelly gets to her feet and brushes down her skirt. 'Doesn't anyone ever clean down here?'

Cadell clicks a pair of handcuffs around my wrists, forces me through the studio doors and shoves me across the bouncy grey mats. I stagger to a stop in the centre of the studio. Cadell must be loving this, but why is he taking orders from Shelly? If this is happening to me, I'm scared to think what is happening to Blaze, Tomas and Mia. My fingers fumble, turning my bracelet until I find the tiny heart charm and squeeze.

I turn back to them to find Cadell aiming a tranquilliser at me.

'Shelly!' I need time and the smug billionaire is going to be my only source. 'We all knew that you were Ron's puppet.'

'Excuse me, puppet?' Shelly pushes Cadell's arm down. 'Puppet?! Oh, Sergeant Cadell, was it a *puppet* who master-minded and funded this plan? And, Sergeant Cadell, when a random teenager got Ron sent to prison, was it a *puppet* who gave you and your men orders? And when that same teenager destroyed a multi-million-pound drill, was it a *puppet* who decided enough was enough, that now was the time? Could a *puppet* have planned a simple six-step coup?' She snaps her head to look at Cadell. 'Well, could it?'

'No, ma'am.'

'No indeed.' Shelly glares at me, her lip turned up into a snarl. 'It's such a shame we can't put an end to –' she gestures, taking me in from head to toe – 'this.'

It's all falling into place. Squad One, the elite soldiers who have hated me since I joined, are still loyal to Ron and by extension, Shelly. They must have leaked the details of my arrest on the bridge to the media and it was probably Cadell who left that letter for me on my first day. Adrenalin surges through me and my fingers twitch. I would love to blast him again, but my usual vats of water are gone. Cadell smirks at me; he knows he's got me backed into a corner. But Shelly did just give me the entire backstory of her plan because I insulted her. I didn't realise bad guys actually did that. What do heroes say at times like this to get them to talk?

'You'll never get away with this!' I try.

'Ha!' Shelly tosses her hair and puts her hands on her hips. Has she been practising being evil? 'I've already got away with this, Jenna Ray. My drill is ready and when I switch it on, all the possessed powered people will—'

'Ma'am!' Cadell snaps, and Shelly blinks at me.

'Oh. I was monologuing.' She deflates, looking sheepish.

'We're going to stop you!' I try to get her going again, but the spell has been broken.

'You just …' She turns to Cadell. 'You spend so long planning and working, mostly on your own, and then someone shows an interest –' she waves vaguely at me – 'and you want to tell them everything. It's solitary work, organising something like this. Long, lonely hours, all on your own …' She trails off and bites her lip in the direction of Cadell, who looks as unsettled as I feel.

The buzz of my phone brings everyone's attention back to me. Cadell strides forward, grabs it out of my pocket and shoves me so I sprawl on to the mats, landing on my handcuffed wrists.

'EV Cottage Hire?' he reads.

'I'm booking a holiday.' I try to keep the relief off my face. I hope the Villains aren't ringing to double-check I'd meant to press the charm. I squeeze it again for good measure and it vibrates around my wrist.

Cadell looks at my phone for a moment and then throws it at the wall with enough force to shatter it into pieces.

I shake my head at him. 'You know, we should all be trying to make our phones last as long as possible.'

He glares at me, hate lining his face, and for a moment I think he's going to come back and throw me at the wall too, but then he touches his ear.

'They're having trouble with Blaze, ma'am. The corporal has him cornered, but it's a stand-off.' My heart lifts. Blaze is still free and fighting back. 'Wipe that smile off your face.' His words are full of venom, but I just wink at him. 'I said—'

He starts towards me, but Shelly puts a hand on his shoulder. 'She's exactly what we need to break this little deadlock. Oh …' Her hand lingers on his arm. 'Is it the, um, military press that builds these muscles? Or the, um …' Her voice drops to a whisper. 'Rear delt row … ?'

Cadell winces.

'Sexual harassment,' I half cough from the floor. 'How's HR when you're a bad guy?'

He looks like he wants to kick me, but I keep smiling. I'm starting to understand the heroes who make quips the entire time they're in battle mode. Winding Cadell up is uniquely dangerous, but intensely satisfying.

He touches his ear again. 'They're in trouble, ma'am.'

'Oh, fine! Call your corporal.'

Cadell pulls out a tablet and a moment later I catch a glimpse of Corporal Armstrong's face, before the sergeant moves away from me. 'Tell Blaze we have Jenna and we'll hurt her unless he surrenders.'

'Hurt her badly,' Shelly adds.

'Did you hear that, hero?' Corporal Armstrong's voice is faint. 'We've got your Love Interest.'

'Prove it!' Blaze is even quieter.

Cadell hands the tablet to Shelly and strides over to me. He yanks me up by my hair and I clench my lips to stop a cry escaping.

'Let her go!' Blaze's tiny voice is full of fury and for the first

285

time in ages, I feel like a helpless Love Interest. They are using me to get to Blaze. I'm back to being a distraction. The nearest water is rushing through pipes behind metres of concrete, and while I know the sea is right outside, I don't know if I can call it from here. I definitely wouldn't be able to control it on the way down. Right now, my power is useless. That must be why they picked the studio.

But using my power isn't the only thing I've learned at the HPA. I get my balance and twist slightly so Cadell is in front of me.

'Surrender, Blaze,' Cadell says, 'and—'

He breaks off as I lunge at him and knee him as hard as I can between his legs.

There's an 'Ouch!' from the tablet as Cadell staggers back, but he's still got hold of me. He's upright a moment later and there's nothing I can do as his fist flies at me. Pain erupts across my face and the world goes black.

CHAPTER 28

The floor is sticky. Sticky like peeling your feet off the Culture Complex floor. No. That sticky burned to ashes. Sticky like the sweat-soaked mats of the training studio. My head hurts. There's a low groan, which I think must be me. I want to move, to peel my cheek off the tacky floor, but my hands are cuffed behind me.

My eyes ache as I blink them open and remember why I'm trussed up in the middle of the training studio. Shelly's coup. Cadell's fist.

'Ray?'

'Tomas?' I twist my head to find him. Blaze is next to me, out cold, and Tomas is sitting remarkably calmly on the other side of him. Perhaps he's been held hostage before. 'Feck,' I mumble.

'They shot me in the back with a tranquilliser,' Tomas says. 'I still can't use my powers.'

I struggle up into a seated position. 'Do they have Mia?'

'Best guess.' Tomas shakes his head. I was wrong about him being relaxed. He's still woozy from being shot. 'Squad One are evil.' He snorts. 'Red Stripe owes me a beer.'

'Apparently Shelly and Ron have been planning this since before he went to prison.' Whispering is painful. One of my teeth wobbles under my tongue. The HPA should make it clearer that being hit in the face is a key part of being a hero. It can't be good for you. 'Shelly is a talker. Especially if you underestimate the amount of effort she's put into all this. She started telling me about how the possessed people will do something when she switches her drill on, before Cadell stopped her.'

'Of course she's a talker.' Tomas gives his head another shake. 'Let's see what else I can get out of her. Pretend you're still out.'

'On it.' I flop down next to Blaze.

Tomas clears his throat. 'Shelly! Take me to Mia. I want to talk to the person in charge.'

There's the shuffle of expensive shoes. 'Oh, Tomas. We've never really seen eye to eye, have we? I've always been fond of you though, you silver fox. Won't you be happy to get Ron back?' Shelly's voice nears, like she's crouching by us. 'He'll take over managing these young idiots and stop them from doing stupid things like disabling drills.' She chuckles lightly. 'No hard feelings. And you can go back to what you're good at.'

'Drinking?' Tomas guesses.

'Heroing! Saving people. Nice and simple. Now, I know you

want to talk to Mia, but they're not in charge here.' Shelly pauses for a self-satisfied beat. 'I am!'

My eyes are shut, but I still roll them.

'You're in charge?' Tomas manages to fake both shock and awe. 'You're in control of Squad One?'

'Yes!' Shelly sounds delighted. 'Honestly, I didn't mean for it to get *this* messy, but it will all get sorted out after. The politicians are happy when I'm happy and putting Ron back in charge will make me happy. It's well past time for normal service to resume.'

'But how is your drill a part of this?' Tomas asks.

'Oh! Well, it's all about attracting possessed people. When I switch on my drill, the EV will—'

'Ma'am!' Cadell is back.

'Skies! Yes.' A shuffle of material as Shelly gets to her feet. 'I keep monologuing! Naughty Shelly. Are we ready to go?'

'Yes,' Cadell replies. 'Corporal Armstrong and a couple of my other men will stay behind, but you'll have the rest of us. Squads Three, Five and Eight are loyal too. They are coming with us. We should implement the contingency.'

'Implement the contingency! Yes!' Shelly's voice drifts away towards the door. 'Do that now. I'll call and let the corporal know when it's time to remove their shields. I wouldn't want these three to miss out on the finale. We'll need all the powered that we can get.'

There's the shuffle of feet by the door and it bangs several times as soldiers leave.

The tannoy screeches to life again. *This is Mia Kaplan. We*

have discovered that Tomas Weber, Blaze and Jenna Ray are
working with the Villains. They are currently contained but we need
everyone on this base to be vigilant. Until you hear otherwise from
me, Tomas Weber, Blaze and Jenna Ray are public enemy number
one.'

'That's not ideal,' Tomas mutters.

'Why would they do that?' I struggle back up to watch the
door swing shut behind Shelly. 'They've already got us.'

'It's a solid contingency though.' Blaze rolls over to look up
at us and says, 'Jenna! Your face!' at the same time as I ask, 'Are
you all right?'

'I'm fine,' we both say. He sits up and shuffles next to me, close
enough that I can feel the light pressure of his arm against mine. I
adjust my leg so it touches his too. His heat mixing with mine
immediately makes me feel stronger. He always makes me stronger.

Tomas sighs. 'Could you two please focus on our escape?'

There are still three soldiers chatting by the entrance to the
studio, but they don't seem overly concerned about us. Having
the entire base as backup probably helps.

'What do we know?' asks Blaze. He's slurring slightly, like
Tomas. Blaze must still have tranquilliser in his system too. I
feel completely alert and even though my hands are cuffed
behind my back, I can still access my powers. Thank the skies
Cadell lost his temper.

'Shelly is working with Squad One, and Squads Three, Five
and Eight are following their orders,' I start.

'She also told us they plan to attract the possessed to her
drill,' Tomas adds.

Blaze scrunches his nose. 'At least she's a talker. Prince #2 said that was where the canister is too, but we've still got no idea which drill she's talking about.'

'Skies.' I look at Blaze and his eyes widen like he's read my mind. 'Her baby drill.'

'Her newest one,' Blaze tells Tomas. 'I'll bet it's been designed for this.'

'Did she say where it was?' Tomas asks.

Blaze shakes his head. 'It's on land somewhere. Prince #2 thinks the location should be in his memory files. We can probably find it online too, now we know what we're looking for.'

'So, she'll switch on this new drill,' I say slowly. 'And if it's anywhere near the size of her one out at sea, the EV will react with possessed people again.'

'She seemed excited when she told me that,' Tomas says. 'Like she wants lots of possessed people there.'

'And she was going to have the corporal take our shields off for the grand finale.' Blaze taps his foot, sending little vibrations through my body. 'Her ultimate aim has always been to destroy the EV and she has Ron's dead zone canister on her drill, but how does attracting a horde of possessed powered people help anything?'

A chill pricks its way up my spine. 'One human can't be enough to start the chain reaction, but the sparks …'

The blue sparks that jumped from my skin when I was fighting possession. The bolt that jumped between Qaqa and Blaze. The vague desire that I wanted Blaze to join me when the

EV was in control. The constant electric shocks I was giving people before I got a shield.

'The EV.' My voice drops and the two men lean in to listen. 'The EV can jump from human to human, so a chain reaction …'

'Could start in one person and spread to the next,' Blaze continues. 'One person on their own isn't enough to start the chain reaction, but a whole horde of possessed people with the EV sparking between them?'

Destroy the EV, destroy the world.

Shelly and Ron figured out how to bend this new development of EV possession to their will: use the canister to put a dead zone particle into one possessed person, it piggybacks off the EV to another, spiderwebs out and into everything, the EV is destroyed …

And it takes the world with it.

Only the heat of Blaze's body against mine stops icy fear from rolling through me. I struggle on to my knees. 'We need to get to Mia.'

'First, we need to take back the base,' Tomas whispers.

'My powers are still out.' Blaze blinks and refocuses on me.

'Mine too, but we still have Ray, *ja*?' Tomas asks, and I nod.

Corporal Armstrong and another soldier are deep in conversation by the door. I close my eyes and feel for water again, but the answer is the same. It shines at me from the pipes and calls to me from the harbour.

'How do we feel about me breaking some walls?' I ask.

'Can you do that without covering us with rubble too?' Tomas replies.

I open my eyes. 'Almost definitely not.'

'Jenna,' Blaze whispers excitedly. 'Make water out of the air. You've been working on that with Tomas, right?'

'But I can't do it,' I reply. 'There's a tiny bit of water in the air already, but it's not enough. I can't make more ... it's not something I can ...'

'You don't need much.' Blaze presses against me like he can share his confidence. 'Just enough to make them pass out.'

The rain had been thundering down when I used my power like that against Blaze. I'd held him in swirling water until his breath ran out. It had felt like the ultimate betrayal of him and of myself. Blasting people with water doesn't bother me, but messing with their breathing ...

'I can't.' My eyes are wide with panic as I look between them. Even if I make water from the air, what if I hold them for too long?

'You can.' Blaze places his head against mine and I breathe him in. He still smells like rain. 'A distraction is all we need.'

'What's going on over there?!' Corporal Armstrong strides across the mat, followed by his subordinate. 'Separate them.'

I search for the water and it's like before. It is in pieces around me: a jigsaw of pinprick-sized pieces. I try to scoop it up, to stitch it together, but nothing works. It never works.

'Those particles.' Blaze's breath tickles my cheek. 'They're meant to be together.'

Rough hands yank me away from him, but his words fall into place. *They are meant to be together.* The particles in the air join to become liquid, the particles underwater join to become air; all I have to do is encourage them.

The room falls out of focus as I ease the way between the molecules and find the pinpricks of water they create. Like pulling together drop after drop lying on this floor with Tomas, I find them and form them into a bead, then a ball, then a swirling sphere.

'What?!' The hands holding me disappear and the corporal gives a garbled yell as I send the water flying at his head. I make it to my feet as he tries to shake it off. I can feel his air slipping through my watery sphere, but I keep it steady.

'You!' The other soldier snaps out of his shock and pulls his tranquilliser gun out.

'Er …' I stagger backwards, still concentrating on the water around the corporal as the soldier takes aim. He's so focused on me, he doesn't see Tomas make his move.

'Feck!' The soldier lands heavily as Tomas sweeps his legs from underneath him. Before he can get up, Blaze grabs the weapon with his handcuffed hands and darts the soldier with it.

'Where are the keys?' Blaze searches the unconscious man.

'There.' Tomas nods at a small remote on the floor and Blaze kicks it over to him. With a beep my wrists are free.

Corporal Armstrong falls to his knees, water still swirling around his head. There's still breath there, but not much. He tries to suck in the water, but I stop it from going into his mouth. He collapses on to the floor and the water splashes down next to him.

'Is he OK?' I freeze, afraid to go to him. Afraid to see what I've done. 'Is he breathing?'

Blaze runs over. 'He's just unconscious. Let's get those cuffs on him.'

Relief floods through me and I jog over to cuff the corporal. We dump him and the other soldier under some gym mats.

'Now, step two.' Tomas looks down at the cuffed guards. 'Get to Mia.'

'Without your powers, or mine, or any easily accessible water,' Blaze adds. 'Through a military base on high alert.'

I roll up my tracksuit sleeves. 'Let's go.'

CHAPTER 29

'Fire!' Tomas calls in a very convincing British accent. He sprints up the sloped corridor towards the doors that lead to security. 'Fire! Pull the alarm.'

Blaze and I head the other way and sprint up the stairwell to Level -1. We pause for a moment on the landing.

'Any sign of your powers?' I ask.

He breathes out. 'No. I can feel them, but they're not accessible yet.'

'You should stay here and wait for Tomas.'

'Yes, sure, I'll let you take on a military base on your own.' He raises his eyebrows at me. 'Not even if we were in the middle of the ocean, Jenna Ray. I can still fight.'

'OK, OK.' I hold my hands up. 'Just don't do anything reckless.'

'Like this?' He pulls my body tight against his and leans in. I'm expecting a quick peck on the lips, a safe, chaste, pre-battle kiss, but instead, he dips me back. His lips meet mine and as he kisses me, sparks burst through me that have nothing to do with the EV.

'Exactly like that,' I mutter as he straightens us up.

He grins at me. 'Want me to do it again?'

Yes. Yes, more than anything. My insides are singing. All I want is to kiss him again, but we're running out of time.

'Focus up, Blaze,' I manage, and his grin widens. 'We need to get to Mia.'

'You're a badass, Jenna Ray.' He gives me a peck on my lips.

'You know it.' I push open the door to Level -1 and peer out. 'It's clear. Act natural, maybe we can walk right up to their office.'

We slip into the corridor that leads to Mia's office. It's empty, but the door to Surveillance is open. I reach for Blaze's hand as we saunter past, hoping no one will clock us, but the yell comes almost immediately. 'It's Blaze and Jenna Ray!'

Soldiers swarm out.

'Run!' Blaze yells.

We sprint up the corridor, but someone must have radioed ahead. Soldiers emerge from every door, cutting off our escape.

'Listen,' Blaze says as we skid to a halt. 'Mia is being held against their will. We're not the enemy.'

They advance on us. 'If you're not the enemy,' an officer says, 'you'll come in quietly.'

We put our hands up and stand back to back, surrounded by soldiers. My fingers flex but I'm not going to be able to make enough water. I don't know if we can fight our way out of this.

The alarm screeches on.

'Well done, Tomas,' Blaze murmurs.

'Mother Earth,' someone mutters, and I grin, because although the HPA's fancy system stores water deep underground, as soon as the alarm is triggered ...

The sprinklers activate.

There are yells as the water sprays down on everyone and everything. My hands are already out.

'Sorry!' I gather all the water from the corridor and send it blasting forward in a churning wave. The soldiers in its path are flattened. There are thuds and curses as Blaze fights off the soldiers behind us. A man leaps at me from an open doorway, but Blaze's hands are on my waist; the corridor blurs as he switches places with me and knocks the man back into surveillance.

'My powers are back!' he yells.

Another team of soldiers runs at us.

'Sorry, sorry, sorry.' I send the water crashing towards them and they go down.

'Jenna, you don't need to apologise!' Blaze grabs my hand and pulls me forward. As the soldiers get back on their feet, I plummet the temperature of the water on the floor, turning it to ice.

'Skies!' One slips, arms flailing, and pulls down everyone around them. I grimace but manage not to yell an apology as Blaze swings me into his arms. The world speeds up and he blurs between the dripping soldiers, slowing as we reach the end of the corridor.

'Mother Earth.' Blaze lets me down and looks like he might throw up. 'Maybe my powers aren't completely back.'

'Come on.' I drag him forward. We're almost at Mia's office.

'Protect the boss!' someone yells, and more soldiers sprint out to block our way. They lift their tranquilliser guns.

'Fire!'

Blaze grabs me and pulls me down at the same time as I call the water. The soldiers leap out of the way as we bodysurf my wave past them, right up to the wooden door of Mia's office.

'Sorry!' I send one last powerful jet back down the corridor, taking out all the people struggling to their feet.

'Sorry,' I mutter to Blaze, apparently unable to stop apologising, but he grins at me. He kicks open Mia's door, sending the guard behind it flying. The unlucky man crashes on to the concrete floor, but another guard is waiting, pointing a weapon at Mia.

'Stop,' he says. 'Or I'll—'

My jet of water slams him against the wall. Blaze blurs and a moment later the two men are in handcuffs.

Mia's mouth lifts in a 5 per cent smile, relieved, but not surprised. 'Get me the tannoy.'

I rush over to the desk, slide the small microphone across to them and press the red button.

'This is Mia Kaplan. Tomas, Jenna and Blaze are not the enemy. I repeat, Tomas, Jenna and Blaze are not the enemy.

Restrain all members of Squad One.' I wave and hold up three fingers, then five. 'And Squad Three, and Squad Five –' Blaze holds up eight fingers –'and Squad Eight? Skies. Arrest all Squad One, Three, Five and Eight members still on the base and await further orders.'

I release the button of the tannoy while Blaze undoes Mia's restraints.

'Thank you.' They look between me and Blaze. 'You two really are a force to be reckoned with.'

The radio on their desk clicks on. *'Security to Mia Kaplan, security to Mia Kaplan, we're under attack! The Villains—'*

The radio cuts out and my heart plummets. The Villains must have launched a full-scale attack on the HPA because I called for help.

'Tell them to stand down!' I say. 'The Villains are here as backup. I called them. Tell them I'm OK.'

'It'd be better coming from you.' Mia slides the tannoy across to me.

I hit the button. 'This is Jenna Ray for the Villains. Stand down. I'm all right. I mean, I wasn't, there was this whole coup thing—' Why am I still talking? Being on a tannoy is hard. 'Um, we've mostly got the base back now, but it's probably good that you're here …' I take my finger off the button and look at Mia. 'Can Tomas bring them up here?'

Mia nods. 'If they'll come.'

I press the button again. 'This is Jenna Ray for the Villains and Tomas.' I'm getting the hang of this. 'Tomas, could you ask the Villains if they'll come up to Mia's office, please? Thank you.'

The mic rattles as I slide it back across the desk. I glance at Blaze, who gives me a thumbs up, and then back at Mia. My chest tightens. I've just brought the Villains straight into the hands of the HPA. But this is the end game and the world is on the line. It's time to unite my two halves.

The clock on Mia's wall ticks loudly, counting down the time we have left to stop Shelly and Ron, until, finally, Tomas knocks and strolls in, followed by four Villains in sturdy boiler suits and reflective helmets. They stop in a line and look at me. It's hard to tell if they're angry. I hope they don't think I tricked them into coming.

Mia strides forward and sticks out a hand. 'Welcome to the HPA.'

One of the Villains takes off their helmet. It's Mum. Her silver-flecked hair is partially hidden under a headwrap and her forehead is lined with concern. She shakes Mia's hand.

'Sima Ray.' Mia doesn't seem surprised; they knew from Ron's trial that my mum is a Villain. 'I don't know if you'll remember me. I had just started in wardrobe when you left …'

'Yes. It's nice to see you again, Mia.' Mum's voice is confident, but the Villains are all tense, ready to fight their way out. Femi's hand is hovering above his wrist piece. A tap and the head of the HPA goes down in a flurry of darts.

'You all right?' Mum's eyes flick over the fresh bruise on my face.

I nod. 'Shelly attacked the base and then left to instigate Ron's nuclear option.'

'The dead zone canister?' The lines on Mum's face deepen.

'It's on her new drill, which is on land somewhere,' Blaze says. 'She thinks the drill will attract the possessed when she switches it on. When they use the canister, the effect of the dead zone particle will jump between powered people and cause the chain reaction that destroys the EV itself. At least that's our working theory.'

'Shelly dropped a lot of hints,' Tomas adds. 'But did not mention where her new drill is or when they'll switch it on.'

'Sunset.' Megan's voice sounds odd coming from inside a helmet. I wonder if it's the same one I wore. She lifts it off and looks steadily at Mia. 'Shelly will activate her drill at sunset tonight. It's on a grassy moor and it will be attacked by a horde of the possessed.'

Mia glances at me and back at Megan. 'You're Jenna's sister, Megan?'

Megan nods and as she opens her mouth, I know what she's going to say. I want to stop her. To tell her everything will change and her life as she knows it will end, but I don't. She already knows. She knows all this and more.

Her eyes flick to me before focusing back on the head of the HPA. 'I'm also the Diviner.'

CHAPTER 30

Mia's mouth hangs open as they stare at my sister, the Diviner. Tomas and Blaze are wide-eyed too. Emily still has her helmet on, but her hands are out like she's expecting the HPA to rush Megan and cram her into a black veil.

'How about we all sit down.' I step forward. 'Can I get anyone some tea?'

No one moves. My sister's announcement has created a room full of statues and we only have until sunset to stop Ron and Shelly.

'Mia?' I prompt.

'Of course. You're the Diviner. You're here and you're the Diviner.' Mia looks at Megan, face scrunched up in disbelief.

'Remember how you wanted a meeting with the Villains?' I prompt.

'Yeah, but ...' They wave a hand at Megan, then catch themselves. 'Sorry. That was a bit of a surprise. Who expected the

Diviner to just walk into my office. Here she is. The Diviner. Here.'

'Mia,' I whisper. 'Are you OK?'

'OK?!' Mia's eyes are wider than I've ever seen them. After being held at gunpoint, and dealing with a coup, the presence of the Diviner might have tipped them over the edge. 'Sorry, yes. Thank you, Megan, for your prophecy. We've all been working hard to prevent it, including sharing it with the villains, not the *Villains* ...' they stammer. 'I mean, Shelly and Ron, not that they've paid a blind bit of notice ...'

They breathe out, closing their eyes as their chest falls. When they open them again, our leader is back. 'Jenna is right. I've wanted to sit down with you for a while. Since you're all here, and there's an apocalyptic prophecy hours away. Perhaps now works?'

'Yes.' Mum slips into a chair by Mia's desk. 'Let's sit down.'

Emily and Femi take their helmets off too and, as we all find seats, the tension eases.

'Is Prince #2 still with you?' Mia sits behind their desk.

Femi straightens a little in his chair. 'He stayed behind. He doesn't want to risk being anywhere near Ron or his associates.'

Mia nods. 'Wise. The last thing we need is him back on Ron's side. Now, I'd like to propose that we work together to bring down Ron and Shelly.'

'Then what? Will you try to arrest us all?' Emily's chair creaks as she leans back. 'Emphasis on try.'

'No.' Mia doesn't bat an eyelid at Emily's tone. 'It'll be a step towards legitimising you as a group.'

'Legitimising us?' Femi crosses his arms. 'Why would you do that?'

'You were right about Ron being evil and you saved Nine Trees alongside Jenna. No one can argue with that. You're not the enemy,' Mia says. 'I tried to keep this broken HPA running the way it always had. I tried treading water and my heroes suffered.' Mia's eyes catch mine, before focusing back on Femi. 'The EV started possessing people, and there was a *coup*. It's time for big changes. If I'm right, it'll finally cement me as the head here, and if I'm wrong ...'

'You'll get fired and we'll get arrested,' Emily finishes.

'And the world will literally end,' I add.

Mia nods. 'I haven't just been pushing for a meeting with you to get your help,' they say. 'I think you're right about the EV and how we handle it. I want to change the entire mission of this HPA. I don't just need your help with Ron. I need your help with that.'

Femi slowly unfolds his arms and looks at Mum, who gives the slightest nod. 'We're with you,' he says. 'For this. Then we'll see.'

Emily mutters something under her breath, but Megan, who I thought would hit the roof, nods. 'We're together for this one,' she says, and I grip the arms of my chair to stop myself from jumping up and cheering. Ron doesn't stand a chance.

'Did you have any luck altering the reset device?' Blaze asks, and my stomach drops. Why is he bringing that up now?

'The machine that returns your powers?' Mia is equally confused.

'Blaze theorised that since we used the machine's materials to make shields, we might be able to adapt the reset device itself to de-possess large numbers of people,' Mum explains.

Blaze turns to Mia. 'If we can de-possess the horde of powered people before Ron uses the canister, there won't be a chain reaction.'

'Right.' Mum's eyes flick to me before focusing back on Blaze. 'We can have the machine ready to use.'

'So, it won't take Blaze's powers?' My words come out loud enough to make everyone jump, including me.

Mum looks at her hands. 'It'll still do that.'

'But it's safe now,' I prompt.

Mum looks back at Blaze. 'The risks will be the same.'

This machine could still leave Blaze empty.

'We're not going to use it.' I stand. My fists are clenched and Blaze is shaking his head at me, but if he won't protect himself, I'll do it for him. 'We'll find a different way.'

Mia nods. 'We'll find a different way.' The certainty in their voice makes my fists uncurl and I sink back into the chair. Blaze's eyes crease as he looks over at me and for once I can't read him. I might have disappointed him. If I was to run through everything I've felt and said about the reset device, I've probably disappointed myself too, but I can't bring myself to care. Blaze is too important.

The sharing of information between HPA and Villains goes surprisingly smoothly, and Mia sends scouts off to several prospective drill sites provided by Prince #2. Everyone has relaxed and it's starting to feel like this team might actually work, when the door slams open and Gray Jay strides into the room.

He's taller than I thought he'd be and his hair is closer to white than grey. My eyes meet Megan's and she bites her lip to stop a giggle. *'Bland as a boiled egg'* is what she called this hero, and the mild confusion on his generic face makes me clench my lips shut too.

Emily leaps to her feet, followed swiftly by Blaze, and I get up too, although I'm not sure what I can do. The fragile peace between the HPA and Villains could be about to unravel.

'We've been getting mixed messages from your base.' Gray Jay glances at me, then Blaze, before his eyes fall on the shiny helmet Emily is holding as if she plans to launch it at him. His mild confusion morphs to mild unease. Megan snorts and I press my lips together again. 'Aren't you the Villains?' he asks.

'Stand down, Jay,' Tomas drawls. 'They're here to help.' He quickly brings the leader up to speed.

'Ah. I'm sorry to say, I've got more bad news.' His handsome face is no longer mildly anything. He's horrified and any remaining urge to giggle with Megan vanishes as he looks around the room. 'Three heroes have gone missing in action. Vitesse, Roo and Cheche. Last reports have them together and heading in the direction of the Castle.'

Despite Gray Jay's bombshell, the plan we come up with is simple. Gray Jay will rally the loyal heroes and follow an advance squad to the Castle to stop Ron and his super-powered backup. The British HPA and the Villains will gear up, find

Shelly's drill and stop it from being turned on. No drill; no possessed people. No Ron; no way to operate the dead zone canister. No need to use the reset device. Two teams. One goal. Save the world.

Blaze took the Villains to see Dr Varma, but Mia insisted that I follow them down to wardrobe. Even though a multi-hero battle is on the cards and the world could end at sunset, my entire body feels light with relief. The Villains and the HPA are finally working together. We are going to stop the prophecy. Mia must feel it too. There's a spring in their step I haven't seen in a long time.

'Right. You stand there.' Mia drags me in front of a mirror. 'Strip down to your underwear.' They hit their radio on as they dive through a rail. I missed Mia from wardrobe with their rock music. My tracksuit bottoms tangle as I kick them to the side and my jumper and T-shirt are added to the pile.

'Close your eyes!' Mia calls, and I obey. This is reminding me of something. 'Now. I'm going to help you into this and we'll do a big reveal.'

I snort. They're re-creating Norway. The moment where Mia dressed me in the perfect green Love Interest dress for my fake date with Blaze. Luckily, I still remember my lines. 'For Blaze?' I ask.

'As much as you'd enjoy that, no.' Mia is delighted that I'm playing along. 'For you.'

I wobble but keep my eyes closed as Mia pulls trousers up my legs. They're not the sturdy HPA combats. My heart gives an uncomfortable thud as material is tugged over my hips; this is another hero suit. *Please don't have a skirt.* There is no part of me that wants to launch into a multi-hero battle wearing ruffles. I give my waist an exploratory wiggle. They're tight; not skintight like the powder-pink leggings. They feel like my wetsuit, but lighter.

'Stop fidgeting for a second.' Mia pulls what feels like a jacket over my arms and zips it up my front. It feels like a second skin. 'Don't you dare look, Jenna Ray!'

'I'm not!'

There are several clicks and a slight pressure around my waist.

Mia breathes out. 'OK. You can look.'

Please, please, please don't have ruffles.

I open my eyes.

Blue. The suit is somewhere between blue, grey and turquoise, like the sea on a cloudy day. Lines of silver run up the front and up my sides. Mia hasn't done anything to accentuate my chest, or even my muscles, like Blaze's outfit. My suit is closer to a two-piece wetsuit. One of Dr Varma's belts circles my hips, but instead of standard black, it's sparkling silver.

Mia is watching me with barely contained excitement. 'Do you like it?'

I shake my head slowly. I look like the water. I look like myself. I look powerful.

'I love it,' I say.

A brilliant smile lights up Mia's face.

'How did you have time to do this?' I ask.

'Passion project.' Mia adjusts my sleeves. 'You were supposed to get an early version of this for the press conference, but Shelly intervened. The material is mostly a blend of limestone neoprene and cotton. It's designed to be light enough for you to run in, will keep you warm under the water and some other things …'

'It's beautiful.' I rub my hand along the slightly spongy material.

Mia waves off my compliment, still in full flow. 'The grey, blue, green palette should make you harder to spot underwater and your wrist piece is set into your right sleeve for navigation. Now you may compliment me.'

'Mia.' I take their hands. 'This is the most beautiful thing anyone has ever made for me.'

Their face fills with joy and they blink rapidly to stop tears that I can sense are ready to fall. 'I've put so much on you, Jenna. I should have never told you that you had to be perfect. You, right now, as you are, you're the hero that we need.'

Now there are tears in my eyes too. 'Thank you, Mia.'

There's a knock on the door.

Mia clears their throat and releases my hands. 'Come in.'

The door opens and I turn to see Blaze, also suited up.

He stops when he sees me and his face goes blank, just like Norway. Then his eyes light up and a smile spreads across his face. 'You look –' he blurs up to me – 'incredible. And I'm brave enough to say it this time.'

I beam back at him, the tug in my chest encouraging me to hug him or kiss him or jump into his arms to share this moment. He runs a tentative hand down my arm and I stop myself from shivering. 'The material is amazing.'

Mia coughs pointedly.

'Sorry.' Blaze jerks his hands back to his sides. 'I need to take Jenna to the lab. We need to fill her fancy new belt with shields.'

CHAPTER 31

Everyone in the lab is bustling with an 'impending doom' air of importance, including Dr Varma, Mum and Femi, who are chatting energetically as we arrive.

'Blaze!' Dr Varma beckons to him. 'Come and weigh in on this.'

Blaze bounds over to Dr Varma with the enthusiasm that always magically appears around the labs, leaving me forgotten by the door. A technician rushes over to load me up with 3D-printed shields and sprints off before I can ask for a job. It's probably for the best. In the world of intricate electronics, the girl who can blast things with water should probably stay out the way.

'He really is a nerd.' Megan is sitting on a table by the door. For some reason she has a pad of paper and a load of felt tip pens.

'You're a nerd.' I hop on to a stool next to her.

'It wasn't a criticism. Nice suit.'

'You can't borrow it,' I say quickly.

'You say that now …' She waggles her fingers in a mystical way and I groan at her. I'm going to need to figure out how to win an argument against the Diviner.

'Is this how you're having visions now?' I nod at her blank piece of paper.

She snorts. 'I looked at photos of all of Shelly's drills on grassy meadows and none of them were right. You and Blaze thought it was her newest one, but that doesn't seem to be registered anywhere. Our side of the Heroic Effort –' she pretends to gag – 'is floundering and everyone was looking so expectantly at me that I asked for this stuff and somewhere to think. Not that anything is coming.' She spins a pen. 'My gift shows what it shows and I can't force more.'

'You called it a gift. That's something.' It wasn't long ago that Megan was fading away on Hidden Beach, refusing to let the visions in.

'Yeah, it's a gift, sometimes. But up close, when it really matters, it's so hard to see.' She slams her hand on the spinning felt tip and several people look over. Megan gets angry at a lot of things – her bank, the patriarchy, me – but she's barely ever frustrated with herself.

'Maybe I can help?' I grab a purple pen and start sketching a drill, criss-crossing the metal struts on a tower that reaches into the sky.

Megan exhales heavily. 'It can't hurt.'

We haven't sat at a table and drawn together like this for years. I pause drawing to look at her. 'I missed you.'

'I know.' She sketches the sun slipping under the jagged grass of the horizon. 'I missed you too. I'm sorry I disappeared.'

I take her hand. 'You're back now. That's what matters.'

She returns my smile and we both look over at Mum, deep in conversation with Dr Varma.

'Yeah.' Megan gives herself a little shake and grabs the blue to doodle a heart on my hand. 'Your hero suit really is beautiful.'

'I love it.' I hold out my arms again and the material shimmers. Has Mia sewn silver thread through this? 'Mia would definitely make you one. The chance to clothe the Diviner would blow their mind.'

'Well, we all know the Diviner costume, don't we?' Megan sketches some grass at the base of the drill. 'Black cloak, black veil. As dull as it is inevitable.' She adds stick men spreading out across the page. 'It's not like I've got a choice.'

I've been so scared for my sister, the Diviner, and what the world will force her to do. She would never let me slip meekly into some predetermined patriarchal role. The previous Diviner might have foretold a bleak future: *The Diviner does not love / She does not judge / She does not lie / Her role is to see.* But maybe it doesn't have to be that way.

'Of course you've got a choice! You're Megan Ray! Prophecies exist to give us a chance to challenge the future. Like now.'

'There are visions and there are visions, little sister,' Megan replies. 'And right now, the one I need is Ron writing down his plan in nice legible bullet points.'

I stare at her, wanting to argue, but she's picked up a felt tip and is sketching a cat. 'This isn't over,' I say.

'It's barely begun,' she murmurs.

'Aw, my girls.' Mum comes over and slides her arms around us both. 'You'd do this for hours when you were little.'

'Thanks for coming, Mum,' I say, and she hugs me a little harder. Her warmth next to me is so comforting, I relax, despite the conversation with Megan. My mum, my sister and me, all together and mostly getting on. I never thought I'd feel this again.

'No …' Megan's voice echoes like there are several of her speaking at once. She blinks, opening her eyes to reveal a white stare.

The hum of work in the lab dies instantly. Everyone must have been keeping half an eye on Megan and now they're all watching her have a vision.

'Feck.' Megan blinks again and her eyes are back to their normal brown. 'Emily.'

Emily looks up from the weapon she's playing with. 'That doesn't sound good.'

'Get her another shield,' Megan cries.

Emily looks down at her boiler suit. 'I already have two …' She trails off. 'I don't feel …'

The felt tips go flying as I snatch up a shield from the desk and lunge towards her, but Emily's hand is out too, fingers outstretched, and her eyes are electric blue. The all-too-familiar sensation of being frozen by her telekinesis slams into me.

'Jenna!' Blaze blurs over, but he's frozen too.

315

There's a burst of noise as everyone except Mum and Megan scramble away from Emily. Blue sparks leap off her towards me, as if the EV is inviting me in, but I've got too many shields on me.

'Someone tranquillise her, please,' Dr Varma calls from the back, and Emily snaps her head towards him.

'No, wait.' My voice is quiet, but everyone listens. 'We still need to know where the drill is. Are you going to the drill, Emily?' She tilts her head at me, the EV shimmering within her. 'We want to go there too.'

'You're going to follow her?!' Megan whispers.

'We'll be able to get more shields on her before anything happens,' I murmur back. I catch Blaze's eye and he manages to give me a nod.

Emily looks around and for a moment I think she might use her telekinesis to rip the shields away from every powered person in the room, but the EV isn't using her brain, just her power. She walks out and I stagger as my body comes back under my own control.

'Tell the base not to challenge her.' As I catch the closing door, Megan's hand grips my arm.

'Please, just –' her eyes flick after Emily – 'look after her.'

'Oh.' I thought my sister was going to tell me to be careful. I tilt my head at her. 'Why are you—?'

'Jenna.' Blaze slips past us. 'She's getting away.'

'Right,' I say.

Megan releases me and Blaze and I set off in Emily's wake.

This is Dr Varma.' His calm voice floats through the

316

tannoy. *'There is currently a possessed powered person making their way through the base. Caucasian blonde-haired female with EV eyes. Do not engage. I repeat, do not engage.'*

We keep a safe distance back from Emily as she makes her way down the corridor, past gawping soldiers and scientists, and down the stairs.

'She could be taking us somewhere else,' Blaze murmurs as we pass through security, the wary eyes of the duty soldier tracking our every move. 'A forest clearance, another sand mine, a water treatment centre …'

'She's going to the drill. I can feel it.' I might be imagining it, but it feels like there's a gentle tug on my heart, following Emily.

'It's not sunset,' Blaze says. 'The drill can't be on yet.'

'They've done enough to worry the EV. Or maybe it can feel what is coming.' I shrug. 'Either way, it wants us there.'

We follow Emily through the sliding doors and she heads up the stone steps to the harbour bridge. Blaze bashes into me as I stop abruptly at the top of the steps. Emily is waiting for us on the bridge. She stares at us with her electric-blue eyes, sparks running across the skin of her face. She could probably kill us both with a flick of her fingers if the EV wanted her to. But instead, she launches herself into the air.

'You know, I almost forgot that she could do that.' I jump into Blaze's arms and a moment later we're speeding up into the golden evening sky. The sun is making tracks towards the horizon with only a few wispy clouds seeming to block its way. There can't be more than an hour until sunset.

'We're going north,' Blaze says, levelling out to follow Emily.

'North,' I repeat. 'Base will be tracking us.'

'Yeah.' Blaze falls silent and his face relaxes. He doesn't look like a boy following a possessed telekinetic towards what will almost definitely be a fight with rebel HPA soldiers. His eyebrows are drawn together and his mouth has settled into a slight smile.

'You all right?' I ask.

'It's beautiful up here,' His voice is wistful. 'Imagine, getting to soar into the sky with the girl you love. I'm so lucky.'

Even though I should be focused on Emily, the thought that this might be one of the last times that me and Blaze fly together hits me like a hailstorm. We're not going to use the reset device today, but he's determined to help Pari. Soon, he won't have powers any more. This really could be it. No more flying. No more Blaze.

'Laurie,' I say gently, and his eyes crinkle in surprise as he looks at me.

The words are there again. *I love you.* And more: *You don't need powers for me to love you*, but that's not what comes out. 'You never needed powers to be a hero.'

He smiles at me. 'I know that now.'

His brown eyes are so full of love, they are everything, but he looks away from me and they widen in surprise. I follow his gaze, across the grassy moor and past an airborne Emily, to the drill. My mouth drops open. I've seen this before, when Emily and I visited the Castle.

The distant crane and boards covering a construction area

have turned into an enormous white-and-red tower. Supports spread out like crab legs and stairs crisscross up to a wide platform with an office. Off to the right, the Castle is its normal, terrifying self, spread out in squares of towers and yard space.

The drill and the Castle, Shelly and Ron, are right next to each other, and they have been from the beginning.

'How did the HPA not notice her building so close to the Castle?' Blaze asks. He's right, it can't be more than a few hundred metres of grassy moorland between the prison and the rig. Turns out we didn't need two teams. All the action is going to happen right here.

'Shelly probably paid extra to build it wherever she wanted,' I murmur.

The tall grass flattens as Emily lands on the moor. Blaze heads to the treeline and we touch down in a small clearing. I hop over a rotting tree trunk to peer through the leaves. Emily is walking towards the drill, fully exposed. It's too dangerous to leave her like this. I push the branches aside to start after her.

'We should—' The words die on my lips as Emily stops, falls to her knees and crumples slowly on to the ground.

CHAPTER 32

'Feck.' I can just make out Emily's blonde hair and boiler suit nestled in the spiky grass. Did she collapse because of the EV? 'What should we—'

Blaze is already gone. I barely have time to process his absence when there's a gust and he's back in our little clearing with Emily unconscious in his arms. There's a silver tranquilliser dart sticking out of her chest.

'Snipers,' he mutters, and I squint over at the looming red-and-white drill. Black-clad soldiers have appeared and are rushing across the grass towards where Emily fell. We're hidden by the trees, but a few leaves won't protect us if they saw where Blaze went.

'Think you were too fast for them to see you?' I ask.

'Here's hoping.' Blaze places Emily carefully down on the ground and I reach for the dart.

'Shields first,' he says.

'Right.' As Blaze reports in, I attach three more shields to Emily, yank the dart out and toss it away. Megan's strange request that I look after Emily echoes in my ears as I stare down at her abnormally vulnerable face.

'*That's useful intel.*' Mia is on comms as I get my earpiece in. '*They have snipers and tranquillisers.*'

'They're not advancing on our position,' I offer.

'Maybe they're waiting for us to make the next move,' Blaze says.

'*Both of you stay hidden,*' Mia orders. '*Tomas, Femi and I are on our way to you now in the helicopter, ETA ten minutes.*'

'Copy that,' Blaze replies.

With a click, Mia is gone and, for a moment, we are silent under the branches, breathing in the scent of wet leaves, looking at each other.

Blaze lowers himself to sit in the grass. 'We don't have long.' He taps the ground beside him. 'It's been an intense day. Come sit with me.'

I join him, sitting close enough that our knees touch. He reaches over and his fingers slide between mine, sending sparks racing up my arms. Here on the edge of a battle, a prophecy and everything else, the most overwhelming thing might be Blaze himself.

He is so much more than just a boy in a hero suit.

He is the hand curling round my shoulder in the flames of the Culture Complex.

He is the boy in glasses, smiling at me in the canteen.

He is the hero rushing to save people without a thought for himself.

He is the head resting on my heart in the dark.

Who was the Jenna that didn't want this boy in her life?

We can't lose ourselves in a kiss with a rig full of enemies a few hundred metres away, but I still lean over and kiss the smooth skin of his cheek. We might be on the edge of a battle to save the world, but my counsellor is always telling us to be present. The next moment will bring danger and chaos, yet right now, in this moment, there's just me and Blaze. I settle my head on his shoulder.

Blaze rests his head on mine. 'When I pulled you out of that fire, I never imagined it would end like this.'

A tiny bird cheeps in the pause and Blaze plays with my fingers. This is the perfect place for an evening picnic. I can imagine us here, chilling out and chatting about nothing whilst eating pasties and strawberries. I stiffen as I register what Blaze said.

I never imagined it would end like this.

'End?' I murmur, and the pleasant sparks running through me turn cold.

'I saved you,' Blaze continues. 'Then I sort of forced you into all this, which was less heroic, then you spied on me and betrayed me, then I betrayed you and Ron almost killed you.'

'Then you saved me, again,' I cut in. 'Then we defeated Ron, then we kissed loads, and I got possessed and you got upset with me and I know what you're trying to say.' I'm up on my knees, so I can face him. 'We're finally here. We're finally on the same side with nothing left between us. I'm not going to let you wrap everything up neatly and say goodbye, Laurie Lin. I'm just not.' Why doesn't he think that we're all coming out the other side of this? We'll save the world and go back to our stupidly dramatic lives, together.

'But, Jenna ...' Blaze reaches for me again, but I dodge him and stand. My insides tighten as if they're being squeezed as I walk over to Emily, still passed out on the dirt.

'Jenna. We should talk. If we need to use the reset device—' Blaze is desperate to use these last few seconds of alone time, but if I don't let him say goodbye, then he can't leave.

'We'll talk later. After we both get through this.'

His beautiful lips form an unhappy line, but I don't care. He's golden in the light of the falling sun. He's a wave of pure heat to me and I'm not going to lose him. It's just not an option. I pull some water from a nearby puddle and splash it into Emily's face.

'Feck!' Emily lurches upright. 'Feck! Am I lying on mud? Why am I wet? Is the water running down my face brown?!'

She glares at us as we shush her.

'You were possessed.' I dry her, leaving a fine brown powder across her face. Thank the skies there aren't any mirrors around. Emily can barely deal with getting sand in her shoes; being dusted with mud won't go down well.

'I was in the lab, with Megan, and she said ... and now I'm ...' Emily scrunches up her face. I remember this. It takes a moment to recover from being a passenger in your own body. 'Mother Earth. How long was I out?'

I help her up. 'Maybe twenty minutes.'

'Things go wrong fast when I'm not around, don't they?' She rolls her shoulders and reaches her hand towards a log. Nothing happens. 'My powers are out. Tranquilliser hangover?'

'Tranquilliser hangover,' Blaze confirms. 'They'll be back soon.'

Emily nods and shifts to peer through the branches at the drill. 'That it then?' A tiny part of me thought that Emily's confidence would crumble after losing her powers and being taken over by the EV, but apparently, she's fine.

Now her back is turned, Blaze pushes himself up and catches my eye again. He opens his mouth.

'Yes.' I move swiftly to stand next to Emily. 'A few hundred metres to the drill across the moor that way and a few hundred to the Castle off to our right.'

'Like we're the corner of a super intense triangle,' Emily says lightly. 'Did I do anything cool whilst I was possessed?'

'Not really,' I say.

'Oh.' She side-eyes Blaze. 'And I had carte blanche to smash up a HPA base. That's a shame.'

'The helicopter will be here soon, then the rest of the HPA.' The disapproval in Blaze's voice makes Emily laugh. 'We'll wait for them before engaging.'

'We're all on the same side,' I snap.

'OK, fine.' She sighs. 'Blaze is less of a douche than we'd expected. The new head of the HPA seems keen on saving the world instead of making it worse. Yes, Love Interest, we're on the same side.'

Mother Earth, she's annoying, but we need her.

'When my powers come back, why don't I tear the drill out of the ground?' Emily turns back to the moor. 'Quick yank and we can all go home.'

'Do you think you can do that without blowing us all sky-high?' Blaze asks. 'With the highly flammable gas under here and all the sparks that pulling that much metal out would cause?'

'Well, why don't you just nip over there?' she asks.

'I'm not the only one in the game with super-speed,' Blaze replies. 'We need to go carefully.'

'Oh yeah, Vitesse. I once threw a bus at him.' Emily glances down at her boot. 'Urgh! Is that rabbit poo?' She looks up into the branches. 'I hope none of those birds need a crap. They're noisy, aren't they?'

I know that waking up Emily was the right thing to do and maybe I rushed it a little to avoid *that* conversation with Blaze, but she's making me regret it. Maybe I can rip her shield off and get her to go back to being blue-eyed and silent. I roll my eyes at Blaze again and he gives me a half-smile. He's upset that I shut him down.

'So, the EV used me to lead you here?' Emily says thoughtfully. 'Femi is going to love that. Works into his whole the-EV-is-a-sentient-force-of-nature theory. It gives the Diviner her visions, it shows us the way ...'

Emily's conversational switch to spiritualism almost gives

me whiplash. Blaze and I share a surprised look, which Emily catches. 'You two don't agree?'

Blaze shrugs.

'Oh, come on, hero. We've got until the helicopter gets here. Indulge me.'

Blaze breathes out through his nose. I think Emily might be annoying him too. 'It has wants and needs, but I don't know if it's sentient.' He frowns. 'White blood cells aren't sentient. Trees aren't technically sentient, but they still act in an instinctive way … I think that's what it is, it has an instinct.'

'Interesting. Jenna?' Emily prompts.

I shrug. 'It's just the EV. You can feel it in everything, even the things without bright blue eyes. It's everything.'

My words settle on to a light breeze that brings with it the thrum of a helicopter.

'The scientist and the dreamer, eh?' Emily quirks her eyebrows at me.

'*This is HPA Heli One. Are we clear to land?*' The voice in my ear brings me back to the moment.

Blaze heads through the trees to the field on the other side and we follow.

'No evident threats,' Blaze replies. 'We'll cover your approach.'

'*Received.*'

This new space is wider and clear of trees, giving a good view of the setting sun. There's only a wedge of fiery orange left above the horizon. My gut twists. I hope waiting was the right call. The helicopter tilts as it lands, with one side sinking into the slightly boggy earth before the pilot can right it. It's intensely loud. Shelly and Squad One might not have seen the helicopter land, but they must have heard it.

Blaze strides up to the helicopter and helps Mia down on to the moor. Tomas, in his black-and-blue hero suit, Femi and a few soldiers jump down after them.

'Good to have you back, Emily,' Mia says, and Emily nods at them. It's the most respectful I've ever seen her.

Emily beckons and we follow her back through the trees. 'We've got a handy vantage point here.'

'How was it?!' Femi slips between a couple of soldiers to get to Emily.

'Yes, I'm fine, thanks for asking, F.' Emily leans past him to give me a look.

'Of course you're fine. The EV wouldn't leave you injured.' Femi pats her on the shoulder.

'Is Mum with you?' I cut in, before they start squabbling.

'She's driving our van over,' Femi answers.

'That is a big drill.' Mia makes their way through the group to look up at it. 'Emily, are you still OK to join the squad heading there? As soon as your powers are back, we're going to need you.'

'Sure, who's got a weapon for me?' Emily tilts her head at Femi, who sighs heavily and lays out an array of kit. Emily gleefully scoops up a wrist piece that looks just like Femi's. 'Look at you, finally learning to share,' she says with a grin.

'Do not break them,' he mutters.

'How are we doing here?' Gray Jay appears from nowhere and my heart almost stops.

327

'Jay!' For the first time, Tomas sounds agitated. 'You didn't need to phase, we're all on the same side.'

'Sorry, sorry, everyone, force of habit when I'm out in the field.' Gray Jay hunkers down by the treeline, next to Mia. 'Since all the action is taking place right here, right now, I've left some heroes backing up the prison guards and we've come to join Team Drill. We might be playing right into Shelly and Ron's hands, bringing so many heroes to them, but if we're together, we have a chance to take this drill out of commission before it becomes an issue.'

A gaggle of heroes slips through the trees, into the clearing with us and all those years of Hero Education surge back into my mind.

Tempo. *Country: Mexico. Outfit: Silver, cape. Power: Freezes time.*

Hatua. *Country: Uganda. Outfit: Yellow and red. Power: Light manipulation.*

Invincible Shān. *Country: China. Outfit: Brown leather. Power: Strength/bulletproof.*

I've heard them over comms but being this close to them is something else. Blaze nods at them, so I nod at them too, and they nod back. They nod back! I just got a nod from Invincible Shān, who is easily the biggest person I've ever seen.

'Long time no see, Femi,' Hatua drawls.

Femi, busy programming his orbs, gives him a wave without looking up.

'Some things never change.' Hatua shrugs.

'Is that Roo?' Invincible Shān rumbles, peering past us.

A small figure leaps from the ground to the platform of the drill and back again.

Roo. *Country: Australia. Outfit: Blue with too many white stars. Power: Superhuman leaping/combat (claims to have been bitten by a radioactive kangaroo).*

Affiliation: King Ron.

'I think it's safe to assume Cheche and Vitesse are around too.' Gray Jay looks at Mia and the rest of the heroes follow suit. 'Where do you want us?'

Mia blinks, surprised. 'Two teams of heroes,' they say. 'Approach the drill from either side. Gray Jay, draw their fire. Brits, get Femi to the drill's tech. One touch and this could all be over.'

Gray Jay nods. 'Good.'

'How will we get there without being shot?' I ask.

'Stealth, Ray.' Tomas claps me on the shoulder. 'Stealth.'

CHAPTER 33

There is still a slice of the sun above the horizon, but the day's heat is already fading. Cooling the water particles hanging in the air is easy. I pull water from the brook running through the moor to give my mist some extra volume. Tomas sends his tendrils of haze seeping through the trees too and soon the moor is a swirling grey mystery. Even the drill has vanished.

'Let's go.' I slip between the branches on to the uneven ground and jog across the moor, with Blaze, Tomas, Emily and Femi. Gray Jay, Tempo, Invincible Shān and Hatua head in a different direction and vanish instantly. We are going to get as close to the drill as we can in the time it takes Gray Jay's team to create a distraction and then Blaze and Femi will blur up to put it out of commission.

This is it. Game over for Shelly. No drill. No possessed people. No way to use the canister. No chance to end the EV and the world. We don't have long until sunset, but we don't need it. In five minutes, this could all be over.

'Nudge to the left a little.' Mia's voice is calm. *'Jenna and Blaze, we've uploaded the coordinates of the drill to your wrist pieces. Use them to keep you on the right track.'*

I glance down at my wrist piece and correct my course. The others follow. A cough from ahead makes my stomach lurch, but everyone else is calm. Femi sends an orb out and with a strangled yell, a body thumps to the ground. A moment later, we skirt the stunned soldier.

There's no way to know how many other soldiers are between us and the drill, but according to my wrist piece, we're almost there; a few more metres and we'll be at the base of the drill. The surge of belief humming through me warms me almost as much as the run.

There's a roar, followed by the clang of rocks hitting metal, frantic shouts and gunfire.

'Shān barely ever gets to cut loose,' Tomas whispers. 'He'll be loving this.'

'That's our cue,' Blaze says to Femi. 'Ready?'

Femi nods and they blur—

for less than an instant, before they fly back towards us.

'Vitesse!' Blaze is back on his feet.

Vitesse. *Country: France. Outfit: Light blue. Power: Speed/ Combat. Affiliation: King Ron.*

'Where is he?' I twist, looking for the French hero.

'You thought you could sneak up on us, *petite fille*?' The soft voice comes from the mist behind me, but when I turn there's no one there. 'You'll never be as good as us.'

I spin again. Vitesse is close, but my mist is so thick I can barely make out Tomas next to me.

'If we let you continue, you'll end all of us.' The voice is in my ear. I bite back the urge to scream and elbow backwards, hitting nothing but air. 'Too slow.' Vitesse is in front of me, his fist flying towards me. It stops inches from my face, caught by Blaze. Vitesse grins. 'Finally, someone my own speed.'

'Help Femi,' Blaze grunts, before launching himself at Vitesse. The pair blur in a superfast fight and I hesitate, forming a sphere of water. I want to help Blaze and it would be intensely satisfying to blast Vitesse, but none of us can keep us with them.

'Come on.' I force myself to leave Blaze behind.

'We're running out of time,' Femi murmurs. 'We need another distraction. Emily?'

'I'm still out.'

'I've got this.' Tomas holds out an arm to stop us. 'Stay back.' He slips into the mist ahead.

My pulse thuds in my ears and we wait in silence as the swirling mist buffets against my legs. The wind pulls harder.

'Surprise tornado,' I whisper, and crouch in the long grass. There are rustles as the Villains do the same.

In an instant, the mist is whipped away from us, sucked into a growing spiral of air that spins across the moor. Tomas is at the side of the drill, hands up, controlling it. The soldiers shout, scrambling to aim at him, but Tomas sends the tornado racing up the metal staircase. Soldiers are sucked in and thrown out of the bottom, sent tumbling down the stairs.

'Come on!' Emily yells.

We stay low as we approach the drill. Femi and Emily send orbs chasing after the tornado to take out any soldiers who make it back on to their feet, whilst I focus on the mist, creating enough to keep some cover for us and re-form some around Tomas. I can't help being impressed by my mentor as the tornado makes its way towards the platform, splitting into two to cover more ground. The way is almost clear for Femi.

Shelly is on the platform in her tartan suit, and Dave is hanging on to the canister as his white lab coat flaps against his legs. They run into the white office building and, bizarrely, someone pulls down the blinds.

We're almost at the concrete base of the drill and there are only a few soldiers left in our way when the tornados stop and shrink rapidly, until they are little more than dust devils.

'Tomas?' I look back. My mentor is on his knees, hand against his chest with a silver dart sticking out between his fingers. He keels over. A soldier rushes over to Tomas, raising his gun like a club, and I don't even realise I've called the water until a jet sends the man flying back across the moor.

A dart hisses past my ear and Emily pulls me into the shadow of the drill.

'Feck,' I mutter, sending a surge of mist tumbling back over us and Tomas. 'Mia, Tomas took out a lot of soldiers, but they got him with a dart.'

'Received.' Mia's voice is still steady. *'Use the mist. Try and get Femi to the drill that way. Just hurry.'*

'On it.' As I lower my finger from my ear, the ground shudders. It's followed by a violent tremor that rocks the ground and noise that's part heavy machinery, part alien hum.

'That's not Shān,' Femi calls over the noise.

'The drill.' I lurch to the side, just managing to keep my balance. 'She's switched it on.'

We're too late.

Everything shakes. The air vibrates with the mechanical hum of the drill and the ground feels like it's about to split open. The adrenalin is probably making me shake too, but there's no way to tell what's my body and what's the drill.

'Skies!' Femi staggers but manages to keep his balance.

Emily's hand clasps my arm and we try to keep each other upright. 'We've still got a chance to turn this off before the EV reacts,' she says.

'We've parked at the Castle gates.' My mum's voice comes down comms.

'Hold there,' Mia says. *'Ron is still in the prison. If we can't disable the drill, we need to ensure he doesn't make it to Shelly and the canister.'*

'Received.' Mum's gone to stand between Ron and the canister. I hate the thought of her going toe to toe with Ron

again. I should be there to protect her, but we can still get the canister before Ron is anywhere near my mum.

The lights of the drill come on in a flash.

'They're here!' Soldiers run at us from both directions, aiming their weapons.

My water forms a wave and flies out to one side, flattening the approaching soldiers. Femi sends his orbs flying the other way and the hiss of darts is quickly followed by the yells and thuds.

'Get going,' Emily calls as the orbs zip past after the other soldiers. 'I'll—'

I twist back to her, but Emily is gone. In her place is Qaqa, staring me down with electric-blue eyes.

'We're on your side.' I hold up my hands. 'Qaqa, we're going to disable the drill.'

I'm back at the road, near the Castle! Emily's outraged cry is loud in my ears.

'Qaqa!' Gray Jay appears from the mist. 'Stand down!'

Qaqa blinks at him, blue sparking off his skin, before turning to Femi.

'Not him!' I wave my hands. 'Here, Qaqa, EV, look at me.' I slip between them. 'Femi, Gray Jay, go.'

Qaqa launches himself at me and I dodge. As I scramble through my pouch for a shield, I catch a glimpse of Femi tearing up the wobbling stairs. Qaqa lunges at me again, but I've got a shield in my hand. My sphere flies at him, slowing him down. As he bats at the swirling water I leap forward, shield ready. He catches my arm—

And in a flash of white he disappears, replaced by trees.

'Feck! I'm on the road too. Watch your back, Femi.'

'Copy that, Jenna.'

There's no sign of Emily. I suck in a breath as I try to make sense of the chaos now between me and the drill. It's as if this moor was never empty. The last of the mist twists through blue-eyed people spread across the grass. Some of them are in their pyjamas, others are in beach gear and there's even one person in a ski suit.

Above them Hatua bounds across his platforms of light, only to be knocked out of the sky by a leaping Roo. Squads of black-clad HPA soldiers are trying to get shields on the possessed and other soldiers are fighting to get them off. Screams. Shouts. Shots. Roars – Mother Earth, was that Invincible Shān? It's impossible to tell what side anyone is on: ours, Shelly and Ron's, or the EV's. Maybe the people fighting don't know either.

A flash of white draws my eye to the right. In front of the tall prison gates, Qaqa has reappeared with—

Trevor Donaldson?! The orange American with bleached-blond hair is in a neat dark blue suit with blazing EV eyes. The first thing he does is pick up a soldier and launch him across the battlefield.

Yep. That's definitely Trevor.

Qaqa must be teleporting in the possessed like the EV's own private jet. Will he keep going until every powered person in the world is between me and the drill? And do all of them have the same thought running through their minds as they approach it? *Break everything. Break everything. Break everything until it stops.*

The Villains' silver van is parked with a cluster of black HPA jeeps near the Castle and the soldiers are in a loose semi-circle around the gates of the prison. Red Stripe is in the middle, with a couple more heroes, and two Villains on their hoverboards.

Two Villains.

I hit my ear so hard it hurts. 'Jenna for Megan.'

'Hey, sister! What's up?' Megan has even worse radio etiquette than me.

'What are you doing?! Get out of there before you get hurt!'

'Can't do that. Get back to the drill, Jen-bear, that's where you need to be.' There's a click as Megan turns her mic off.

Fecking Diviner! It's like big sister control freakery times a million. I clench and unclench my fists. My orders are still to deactivate the drill. I can't force my sister to sit this fight out and the heroes should keep her safe. I need to go and find Shelly, the canister and Blaze. I roll my shoulders and run back into the melee that is the moor.

The ground doesn't shake as much this far from the drill, and I manage to keep a good pace as I sprint forward. Battles in films always seem to have two lines running at each other, but this is more like an obstacle course than a battlefield. I spin past two fighting soldiers, make myself watery steps to jump over a possessed man swinging a skateboard and keep heading for the drill.

I am about to dodge another possessed person surrounded

by HPA soldiers when I realise it's Trevor Donaldson. He stares at me blankly as I race past and a powerful blast of water takes him down a moment later.

'Thanks!' calls a soldier.

'My pleasure!' I keep running.

'The gates are opening.' Mum is back on comms. *'There are people coming out, soldiers. And more possessed. It's the prisoners from the Castle, someone took their shields off.'* Mum sounds like she's flying at speed. *'And Ron. He is your main objective, take him down.'*

'This is Red Stripe, leave Ron to me.'

I grit my teeth, but if any of the heroes can handle Ron, surely it's Red Stripe. Even if some of Squad One or the other Ron loyalists made it into the Castle to back their leader up. Our soldiers are there. Other heroes are there. Red Stripe is there. A bright flash from the prison catches my eye and I skid to a stop.

'Ron did the eliminator!' a panicked voice cries. *'Did he just kill Red Stripe?!'*

'No,' Red Stripe responds shakily. *'Where did he go?'*

'Megan, have you got eyes on Ron?' Mum asks.

'No,' Megan replies, followed by a flurry of *'Negative'*s from the rest of the HPA.

Mum is back, urgency cracking her voice. *'Has anyone got eyes on Ron?'*

CHAPTER 34

King Ron, the heroes' hero, must be on the moor and heading towards the dead zone canister. Megan warned us what the consequences would be if Ron and the canister were united.

Destroy the EV, destroy the world.

I breathe out, *two, three, four*. Someone with electric-blue eyes runs at me with a roar and I send a jet of water at them without stopping my search. Where is he?

Getting above the madness for too long will make me a target, but it's worth the risk to find Ron. I make myself a watery platform and leap up to survey the moor. It only takes a moment to spot a brilliant flash of white. Ron is there, off to the side, surrounded by Cadell and other members of Squad One, blasting people as he advances on the drill.

'I've got eyes on him,' I say into my radio.

'Jenna, don't try and take him alone.' Blaze is in my ear. *'I'm coming to you.'*

Blaze can catch me up. I run in Ron's direction, but skid to a stop almost immediately when an enormous tabby cat leaps into my path.

My hand flies up to activate my comms. 'Mrs Smith is here, she's—' Another cat appears from nowhere, flying straight at my face. 'Mother Earth.' I drop to the ground and it shoots over my head. Instead of coarse grass, I land on a pale pink blanket, facing a bristling orange moggy roughly the same size as a tiger.

'Someone get a shield on Mrs Smith!' I scramble back as the cat advances. Beyond the creature, pale blue clouds float through a lemon-yellow sky. It's like a picture book, except for the enormous cat looking at me like I'm lunch. Ron is out there, getting closer to the drill, and I am about to get murdered by a giant pet in a pensioner's dreamscape. 'Shoo!' I send a jet of water at the cat, but it bats it away.

The spongy pink floor is shaking so violently, I'm still struggling to get up as the cat launches itself at me. I bring my arms up to protect my chest and face, catching a glimpse of the luminous eyes before the claws hit my sleeves in a rain of knives. I screw my face up, but no teeth follow and the force of its body hitting mine doesn't come.

'Skies.' I lower my arms slowly to find the cat has vanished and the sky has returned to a rosy dusk. It's almost as dream-like as Mrs Smith's world, but the sounds of battle have returned at full volume. I'm back in the chaos of the moor.

'Mrs Smith has been neutralised.' Blaze is in front of me. His hair is a mess and his cheeks are pink. He helps me up and nods at Mrs Smith, who has two shields pinned to her knitted blue cardigan.

'Thank the skies for that.'

We're still holding hands. I think I might be holding on to him too tight, but the last time I saw him he was fighting Vitesse. My gut is a mess of terror for Mum, Megan and the EV itself, but at least I don't have to be scared for Blaze. I drink him in as Tempo freezes a pocket of the battle beyond us. Blue eyes are glittering on all sides, but Blaze is OK.

'Come on, Ron's this way.' I pull him in Ron's direction. He gives me a gentle tug back and a moment later I'm in his arms, and he's stepping into the air. 'What about Femi?' I ask.

'He's got backup. Ron's the priority now.'

Blurring over the battle is even more intense than sprinting through it. The shouts, roars and shots whip past my ears in a barrage of noise. Everything slows as we reach a clump of soldiers and, as we come in to land, the stream of images focuses down to a single one. The shiny shoes, the dark grey pinstripe trousers, waistcoat, shields pinned on an open jacket, pocket square.

Ron.

'Ah! Blaze! I hoped I'd see you.' He beams at his protégé.

Blaze puts me down, but still has one hand on me, like he's ready to blur us away. 'Ron.' There's no warmth in his voice. 'We have the new Diviner working with us. She said if you destroy the EV, you destroy the world.'

'And you believed her?' Ron shakes his head. I don't want to take my eyes off him, but I can sense Squad One circling us.

'Laurie, I taught you better than this. If these are the prophecies that she's spouting, then the new Diviner is a fake. She must be a Villain.'

'Why don't you ever listen?!' The shout bursts from my lips before I have time to consider what I'm saying. 'Why won't you accept that you might not know everything? That your way might not be the only way?'

Ron fixes his eyes on me. 'Ah yes. Miss Ray. Also still a Villain, I see. You two.' His lips twitch. 'I told you that your love would destroy you, Laurie; how right I was. It will be the end of you both. Take them out.' Ron gestures and the enormous frame of Cadell steps in front of him.

'Fire at will,' snaps Cadell.

The soldiers surrounding us raise their guns and my hands shoot out, sending a wave of water at them. There are thuds and yells, but I must have been too slow to get them all before they fired. I wait for the pinch of a dart, or something worse. It doesn't come. My brow creases and I check my suit. I'm still intact and dart-free, and the waterlogged soldiers struggling up are empty-handed. I don't understand until I find Blaze, standing to one side with a pile of weapons at his feet. He winks.

Cadell roars and launches himself at me. I dodge and hit him in the back with a powerful jet that sends him sprawling.

'Where's Ron?' I sidestep another attacker.

'There.' Blaze points and I follow his finger to Ron's grey jacket heading towards the drill. 'Go.' He lands a kick on a soldier that sends him spinning away. 'I'm right behind you.'

'OK!' We'll show Ron. He thinks our love will destroy us, but he doesn't get to decide anything about our relationship any more. 'Ron is approaching the steps of the drill,' I say into my comms. 'I'm on his tail.'

The ground rocks violently and there's a flash to my left as Qaqa brings even more possessed to the moor. Ron reaches the stairs and I shoot a jet of water that sends him crashing into them.

'You don't stop, do you?!' Ron pushes himself up, water running off him.

'You don't have to do this.' I gather another sphere ready.

'For the sake of the world –' Ron turns with a glowing white ball in his hands – 'I do.'

With a thrust of my arms, all the water I can find rushes at Ron in a torrent. I'm too slow. He flips over my jet, landing neatly at the same moment as his energy bolt hits me in the chest.

My feet lift off the ground and as I soar backwards, I see Ron turn to go back up the stairs, then it's just me and the sky

and the full body-punch of the ground.

My shoulder aches.

People are shouting around me and in my ear. There's a constant stream of noise that doesn't make sense.

My bruised cheek is on something spiky that vibrates like a speaker.

I wish I'd landed on that pink blanket.

There's just grass in front of my slowly opening eyes. Grass and the smell of the earth.

'Jenna!' Blaze shouts.

I lurch upright and my hands fly to my chest, half expecting to find a hole there, but there's just the smooth material of my suit. Mia must have factored in energy bolts when they designed it.

'I'm OK.' I make it on to my knees, but am hit with a wave of nausea. The back of my head aches where it hit the ground and splinters of pain are running down my arm. Blaze isn't here. His voice must have been on my earpiece.

I turn slowly to take in the battlefield and am met with a sea of blue eyes. There are hundreds of the possessed waiting in rows for some signal to tear the drill apart.

'Feck.' Emily's voice is back in my ear. *'Femi, where are you?'*

'I'm … No … I'm back at the road.' Femi sounds exhausted.

'This is Gray Jay. I'm almost there. All heroes, we need you on the drill. We need to take Ron out. We need … argh—'

'Hold on!' Blaze.

'We can't get through to you.' Mum.

'Everyone. Stop Ron by any means necessary!' Mia.

344

I manage to get back to my feet and look up at the platform. Shelly is there, gazing down on the possessed with a look of pure delight on her face. Dave holds a big glass tube with a gold fleck dancing around inside. Ron stands next to them. He's finally where he's been in spirit all along. Ron, Shelly, Dave, the mediocre engineer, and their nuclear option, sneering down at us.

And Trevor Donaldson. I blink again, trying to make sense of it. Trevor Donaldson is next to them, roaring, in shackles, with his eyes blazing blue.

Ron lifts his arms and a moment later a brilliant white flash erupts from his hands, hitting a blur of black and red. I've sent a wave to cushion Blaze's fall before my brain has realised that he is falling. Even with the resistance of my water, he still lands heavily on the hard earth next to me. He must have been knocked out of the sky by Ron.

'Blaze!' I reach him as he sits up. I guess his suit is Ron-proof too.

'We're losing.' Blaze doesn't blur right back up to the platform, but gets up shakily to stand next to me. 'I don't think I can beat him. Not face to face. He knows me too well and the drill is giving him all the kinetic energy he could need.'

'What do we do?' My heart is thudding hard enough to burst, but Blaze is so calm, staring down the barrel of the end of the world.

Ron takes the canister, holding it in both hands, and light creeps up it. My thundering heart turns to stone. Ron is activating it. He'll transfer the dead zone particle to Trevor. He'll start the chain reaction that destroys the EV.

He'll destroy the world.

'We're losing,' Blaze repeats as if it's the sign he's been waiting for. He steps in front of me, his brown eyes on mine, his eyelashes lit by the lamps of the drill. He blurs, but he's back a moment later holding something towards me. A crystal ball in a glass box.

Fear burns through me. 'No.' I shove the reset device back towards him.

'You have to.' Blaze pushes it gently back. 'If no one is possessed, there's no chain reaction. We can do this. We can save the world.'

Everything else falls away. We're surrounded and people are shouting instructions in my ear, but right now it's just me and Blaze. He wants to sacrifice himself. It's the cave in Australia. It's him taking on Qaqa alone. It's why he kept trying to say goodbye.

'But you …' The reset device is in my hands. How did it get there? 'I won't.'

'Pari is here. We thought it might come to this. I'm going to go to her, so it has the best possible chance of working.' There's no emotion in his voice. It's like he's telling me to meet him at the canteen.

We thought it might come to this. We. Mum and Blaze. It doesn't matter what we planned in Mia's office. They were always ready to use the reset device.

But I'm not. I won't do it.

He grips my arms. 'I know you'll do the right thing, Jenna.'

Those three words are back and this time, there's nothing in their way.

'I love you.'

This should be an amazing moment. I should be able to reach for him and kiss him and share the joy of those words, but Blaze steps away and I can't pull him back to me because of the machine in my arms. He blinks rapidly, like there are a million things he wants to say, then his lips lift into a gentle smile, and he blurs away.

'No,' I whisper. The sounds of the moor come back at full volume.

'*You're out of time!*' Megan yells over comms, and I look up to see Ron shove the glowing canister at Trevor's chest.

Memories flood through me. Flying with Blaze. Sparring with him. Fighting with him. Kissing him. Blaze smiling at me on the precipice of a disaster.

'*Jenna.*' His voice is in my ear. '*Please.*'

A ragged sob escapes my mouth and I activate the reset device.

CHAPTER 35

CLICK.

My finger presses the button.

It is the loudest click I've ever heard.

It echoes through my mind along with the single terrible question.

Did I just end Laurie Lin?

The button springs back under my finger in slow motion and nothing happens. For what feels like an eternity, nothing happens. Then the possessed near the drill crumple to the ground and the blue-eyed across the moor follow, falling like they've been hit by a wave. I hold the box close to me with trembling arms. Did I do that or was it Ron? I look up at him and he stares right back, ignoring Shelly celebrating beside him. Trevor is on the floor with the canister attached to his chest, but Ron knows that I've done something.

Did the reset device work?

Or was I too slow?

Did I just let them destroy everything?

Were the HPA right about hero relationships all along? Did I let the world end because my love for another hero made me hesitate?

The alien hum shakes the air and the ground judders as the drill continues its work. I hold Ron's eye as we wait.

There's a crash from the platform and Trevor rolls up, leaving the canister on the metal floor. Maybe this is part of the chain reaction? I'd imagined blue light spilling out and bouncing from person to person, or even catching fire, but up on the platform there's just a furious and confused American. His eyes are back to normal. He's not possessed any more. Trevor shoulder barges one of Ron's soldiers, but the man doesn't go flying. He staggers back a few steps, regains his balance, and punches Trevor Donaldson in the face.

My mouth drops open. Trevor doesn't have his powers any more! Ron looks back at me with the same hatred I saw outside

349

the Culture Complex. Dave scrambles for the canister and Shelly lets out a shrill scream of frustration, but I couldn't care less. My insides are filling with hope. The reset device worked on Trevor and he's fine. Maybe Blaze—

'Hello?' An unfamiliar voice comes over comms. *'Sima, Femi, Emily? Where are you? I'm in the van, there's a boy here, a hero. I think he needs help.'*

'Pari?' Emily answers with cautious delight.

The earth gives one last violent shake and then stops.

'The drill is off,' Gray Jay says. *'We need Femi up here to take it offline permanently.'*

'The boy, he's not moving,' Pari says. *'Should I drive him to the hospital? Skies! What's going on? Is that the Castle?!'*

He's not moving. There is no world in which Trevor is fine and Blaze is not. That can't happen, but Blaze isn't moving.

I dash a tear from my cheek. He could just be exhausted. He's got to be OK.

'The boy,' I start, 'is he—'

Someone grabs my ankle.

'Where am I?!' A woman with a Spanish accent sits up. 'How did I get here?'

Across the moor, confused people are getting to their feet, calling for answers. My hero suit acts as a beacon and in moments I am swamped.

'You, hero! What's happening?!'

'I'm registered! You've got no right!'

'Is that the Castle?!'

'Oh get tae … Am I in England?!'

'Are you Jenna Ray?'

'What's going on?!'

'I—' I stumble back, away from them. The image of Blaze lying silent on the floor of the Villains' van sits in my mind like a barrier to useful thoughts or actions. I need to get to him.

'Who has eyes on Ron, Shelly and the enemy heroes?' Mia's voice cuts through the chaos. I slip out of the huddle of confused people to look at the platform. Dave has been restrained by Gray Jay, but the rest of them are gone.

Mia is back on. *'Skies. Heroes and Villains, Ron and Shelly are your priority. HPA soldiers, restrain Squads One, Three, Five and Eight. Get shields on the civilians and get them away from the action. Restrain everyone for now, there are escaped prisoners out here too.'*

Ron and Shelly. Images of them collide with the one of Blaze, pale, collapsed. Empty.

'Got eyes …' Mum is on comms, but I can't focus on her.

Maybe Blaze fell and hit his head when I activated the device. I didn't give him any warning. I could have told him to sit down or … I should have been there with him. I should have caught him when he fell, like he's caught me so many times before.

The people surrounding me are peeled away by HPA soldiers and I know I have a mission. I know it isn't over, but

351

my feet aren't moving. There's nothing left inside to fuel my fight.

'Jenna!'

Megan?

'Jenna, we need you. Get to the prison. Mum and I are already here.'

'Get down!' Mum shouts, and there's a clatter over the comms.

'Megan!' I yell, and I'm running through the dusk and over the uneven moor, towards the looming gates of the Castle. Fear for my family thrums through me, but I'm so tired. I'm slowing down. It took everything I had to activate the reset device and now I need a boost. 'Tomas,' I call.

'Ray,' he responds straight away.

'Are your powers back?'

'Ja, what do you need?'

'Rain,' I gasp.

The sky immediately grows darker. *'No storms, they said. It's too unpredictable when we've got people on that enormous metal drill, they said.'* A low rumble of thunder shakes the air. *'Anyone still on the drill, it's time to go ...'*

The first fat drops of rain hit my skin and the effect is immediate; energy burns through me and my pace doubles as I sprint through the gates of the Castle. My thoughts were spiralling, but it's time for action. My heart is pounding and I'm ready for the next round.

The square where Emily and I parked on our visit stretches in front of me.

'*Jenna!*' Megan is back on comms. '*We're in the courtyard. Hurry!*'

The large metal gates to the recreation courtyard at the centre of the Castle were closed last time I was here. Now they're hanging off their hinges. I sprint towards them but someone strolls into the gateway.

Cheche. *Country: Uganda. Outfit: Dark red. Power: Shrinks/ grows. Affiliation: King Ron.*

'Crap.' I stop and gasp for breath.

'With you!' Emily races over, hands out, but Cheche has gone. 'Um?' She skids to a halt.

'All right?!' Roo lands in front of us.

'Roo!' Gray Jay sprints into the courtyard. 'Stand down!'

Roo scrunches his nose. 'Ah, mate, I don't think I will.' He swings a punch, which I duck, but it sends Emily sprawling. A dust devil races past and picks up the Australian hero, sending him flying.

'You're outnumbered, Roo!' Tomas yells, running towards us.

'*Jenna!*' Megan calls, but Cheche is back, blocking my path. He grows from tiny to his regular size in the blink of an eye, and doesn't stop there, shooting up past the walls around us. As all eyes are fixed on the giant, I slip into the courtyard beyond.

Shouts and a roar from Cheche echo behind me, but the yard is quiet. Under the orange spotlights, the rain looks like falling fire. The shape of a helicopter looms in the middle of the square. There are people by it and their distorted outlines become recognisable as I sprint towards them. Mum is brandishing a thick cable; she must have done something to the helicopter. Shelly, Megan and Ron are facing her with their backs to me. The air stops halfway to my lungs. Ron has Megan. He's going to hurt my sister.

A figure blurs to a stop in front of me.

'Blaze?' The relief that swamps me is almost painful.

'*Non*.' Vitesse steps forward so I can see him clearly and I let out a gasp as my broken heart shatters all over again. 'We are done with you, *petite f—*' His words are choked by the swirl of water wrapping itself around him. It encases him; the pressure of the seafloor holding him. A tear runs down my cheek and flies to join the vortex around Vitesse. I thought he was Blaze. I thought the boy I love was OK. Vitesse's air slips into the swirl and I don't think I care. He falls to his knees, but I keep the water around him.

Shouts echo through the yard. Mum and Megan. They need me. Vitesse slumps and I step over him, releasing the water back to the earth. I am done with men that want to hurt me, or my family, or the world. I've spent so long figuring out how to be a hero and now I know what I was missing.

Pain.

'Ron!' I scream.

Ron twists and shoves Megan away as I rush at him. He fires a power bolt at me, but I slide under it, riding a wave that hisses across the gravel. Then I'm back on my feet, sending all the water I can at him, smashing him back into the helicopter.

'You!' Shelly shouts, aiming a weapon at me. 'Stop! Eeee!'

354

She lets out a high-pitched squeal as Mum tackles her to the ground.

I whip my head back to the helicopter, but Ron is gone. The crackle of energy in the air is just enough of a warning for me to drop and another bolt flies over me.

'Miss Ray.' Ron sounds slightly hysterical. 'It is always you, isn't it?'

Someone, Megan, helps me to my feet, but I push her away.

This ends here.

'You're finished!' I shout.

'No.' Ron brushes the dirt off his suit. 'I'm not. I have the canister and the EV is a powder keg. There will be another opportunity for me to save the world, but you –' his hands glow – 'won't be there to see it.'

'You took everything!' The cry rips from me and echoes off the prison blocks. He took Jenna Ray, the normal teenager from Nine Trees. He took Laurie's chance at a regular life. He took Pari's powers. He takes and he takes. Shelly appears behind him, eyes narrowed as if she's waiting for him to end me. They are the same. They take and they don't care what the consequences are, as long as they get their power.

The rage in my stomach turns electric. The water rises, forming into two huge waves either side of me. This ends now.

'Jenna!' Megan calls.

'Stop!' And Mum. They are somewhere beyond the waves, but I can't look for them. I have to do this. This is how I save the world.

The water hisses at my side. Ready. Infused with more power than I've ever used before.

I can do this.

I'm not breathing.

Time feels like it has stopped.

I know what needs to happen.

The water should be surging at them, ending this, but …

I'm frozen.

I can't …

My fingers flex, but the water doesn't move.

I wanted to know what kind of hero I am, and now I know.

I'm the kind who hesitates.

Ron smiles and raises his hands.

'Jenna Ray.' Prince #2's voice comes from behind me. He tugs on my belt and his strong fingers close around my arm. I expect him to step by my side, to face Ron and Shelly with me, but instead he swings me round. My water crashes uselessly to the ground as he lifts me by the front of my hero suit. 'I know how to help now.'

He launches me into the air, away from the helicopter, and I fly through the rain, before gravity pulls me back towards the ground.

'Jenna!' Mum cries. I gather as much water as I can to cushion my fall, but I still slam into the earth. The pain that shoots through my body is sharp enough to make me vomit. I spit it out and roll back to look at the helicopter.

Two pairs of feet sprint into my eyeline and the whistle of the wind carries over the thrum of the helicopter starting.

'Are you OK?' Megan gets to me first and crouches next to me.

'Why did he do that?' I manage as she helps me sit up. 'Is Prince #2 back under Ron's control?'

'He must be.' Mum, breathless, joins us on the damp ground. 'Prince #2 shoved us both towards you. He fixed the helicopter and he's flying it for them. It doesn't make sense.'

'I thought he was on our side.' All I can do is watch as the helicopter rises up above the prison and into the stormy sky. 'We need to stop them. We need to—'

The explosion is so bright that I throw my hands up to shield my face. Where did it come from? The helicopter was there, barely lit by the orange floodlights of the yard, and then there was a fireball. I blink through my fingers at a cascade of red and yellow. What just happened? Where's the helicopter gone? Where's Ron, and Shelly, and Prince #2?

The rain hisses down across the gravel and a low rumble of thunder shakes the air. There's a distant thud as a propeller lands in the dirt.

'He … He self-destructed.' Mum sounds like she can't believe what she's saying. 'He got Ron and Shelly into that helicopter and he …'

'He killed them?' My voice is as dazed as hers.

There's a crash and Tomas runs into the courtyard, followed by Emily, Gray Jay and a trail of heroes, but I barely register the bright uniforms racing towards the wreckage of the helicopter and putting cuffs on Vitesse. It's over. Shelly and Ron are gone. Prince #2 is gone.

'He killed them.' The waves were at my side, ready to fall, but Prince #2 pulled me away and then he … 'But heroes don't kill,' I manage. It's the unbreakable rule. The uncrossable line that I came so close to.

'And that was his loophole,' Megan says quietly. 'He was never a hero. He was a sidekick.'

CHAPTER 36

Medical is dark. They turned out the main lights after I sent Mum and Megan home, but there's a tiny lamp shining between me and Blaze. Even though there are other injured people on the ward, I've drawn the curtains, so we've got our own private space. It's the second time we've spent the night together. Mia didn't even mention our shared cubicle when they came to update me. I guess the HPA has finally decided that we're allowed to be together.

'They said I fractured my humerus,' I whisper, angling my splinted arm towards him. 'I fractured it a few times actually. The doctor said I kept landing on exactly the same bone. That's probably a skill.'

Blaze's eyes are closed. They were closed when they moved him into medical and hooked him up to all these machines. They don't know if he can hear me, but I'll keep talking to him anyway.

'I might have a concussion, so they thought I should spend the night here. Dad wasn't happy; he says he'll be in tomorrow. They caught most of the prisoners and they had to hire a coach to the airport to get all the ex-possessed people home. I think they were hoping that Qaqa might reappear and make things easier, but he was controlled by the EV for a long time. Tomas thinks he's in a bar somewhere.'

The light from the lamp falls on the arch of his cheekbone and the curve of his eyelashes. His lips look the same as always, but I don't know if they'll ever part in a smile or joke again. A tear rolls down my cheek and I let it. The water makes me stronger.

'And Prince #2.' I shake my head. 'He self-destructed inside the helicopter with Ron and Shelly. They're gone, B— Laurie.' The explosion replays itself in my mind for the millionth time, bringing with it a surge of emotions. Horror, relief, guilt.

I'd been ready to take out Ron and Shelly and I had hesitated. If Prince #2 hadn't arrived, maybe I would have broken the unbreakable rule. Or maybe Ron would have taken me down once and for all. Either way, Prince #2 saved me. I shudder and bite my lip as pain shoots through my broken arm.

The moment the android arrived replays in my mind. He'd pulled my belt, before he grabbed my arm. No, it was more than that. It's like he was holding on to one of the pouches, or maybe trying to take something out? My forehead creases and I shimmy over my bed to where I left my hero suit folded. Mia said they would send someone for it, but I guess they forgot.

Moving my right arm is agony, but I manage to manoeuvre the belt into the little pool of light and open the back pouch. There are still shields there, but below them is a plastic wallet with a piece of paper inside. I pull out the note and immediately recognise Ron's handwriting.

2024

The Diviner does not love.

She does not judge.

She does not lie.

Her role is to see.

Until the one who comes after me.

'Until the one who comes after me,' I murmur.

Until the one who comes after me.

I frown. With the pain, painkillers and general exhaustion, my brain isn't firing on all cylinders at the moment. Why is this line wrong?

My eyes widen.

It's not wrong. It's new.

It's Ron's handwriting. He had this at the Castle. He kept it next to his heart. This is the full prophecy and he released an incomplete version to the world. Prince #2 must have put it in my pouch before he threw me across the courtyard.

'Mother Earth!'

This changes everything. Megan didn't think she could fight the destiny set out for her, but this extra line means that she doesn't have to follow in the footsteps of the previous

Diviners. She's free to be herself. Pain jabs at my arm as I shove the scrap of paper into my tracksuit pocket. I lurch up. I have to tell Megan! I—

My feet tangle in the duvet and I lose my balance.

'Skies!' I fall back, landing on my bad arm, and it should be agony, but there is no pain at all, only darkness.

'Jenna?' Mia's voice sneaks into my dream.

Past the thundering drill.

Past the rising waves.

Past Ron, who is driving a dagger into my arm.

Past Blaze driving that same dagger into my chest.

'Jenna?' Mia's voice is gentle

'Do you wan ma 'niform?' I mumble, forcing my eyes open and squinting up at Mia and the horrendously bright lights behind them.

It hurts.

Everything hurts.

My eyes. My head. My arm which has been strapped to my chest. My heart. Why does my heart ache?

'I'm sorry to ask this when you should be resting, but I need your help with your sister.'

'Oh.' I rub the crud out of my eyes and glance over to the neighbouring bed. Blaze is there. No, Blaze is *still* there. He hasn't moved. 'Why?' I murmur. My eyes sting. 'Why was Trevor OK?'

'We still don't know.' Mia sounds almost as miserable as me. 'Trevor eventually let us check him over and he's powerless and furious, but fine. He's demanding a refund for the powers he bought, saying he's going to sue. He's a truly awful human being. Sima thinks it might be because Blaze –' Mia takes a shaky breath – 'because Laurie had the powers for longer, they became a part of him.'

I tear my eyes from his sleeping face and reach for a glass of water. The cool liquid helps to numb the pain in my chest. 'What's happening with Megan?'

'There's a discussion that I need you to weigh in on,' Mia replies.

They're being cryptic, but I'm too sad to care. Mia helps me up and we head upstairs. The pain of my arm is almost a relief. It focuses me on each jarring step. It keeps me in my own body.

Megan is pacing across Mia's office when we arrive. Emily is standing out of her way, watching her with eyes narrowed in concern. This is definitely a Megan who's mid-rampage, but as Mia gets me into a chair, my sister deflates.

'Skies, Jen-bear.' She comes over to me. 'You look like death.'

'Thanks?'

The office door bangs open and Mum strides in, followed by Dad.

'No, please, come in,' Mia mutters.

'We came as quickly as we could,' Mum says.

It's bizarre to see Dad in the HPA base and it's not made better by the look of horror on his face when he spots me. 'Jenna! Are you all right?'

I'm glad Mia didn't take me past a mirror.

363

'Do you need more painkillers?' Mum comes over and places a soothing hand on my forehead.

'Should you be out of bed?' Dad follows.

They both glare at Mia.

Mia puts their hands up. 'It's important to have Jenna here. I'll take her straight back to medical when we're done.'

'It's fine,' I say. 'I'm fine.'

'Even I can see that's not true.' Emily leans against a wall. She's got some new scrapes and bruises on her face too.

'Mia.' I direct the focus back to my boss, who has moved to put the desk between themself and my family. 'What do you need?'

Mia exhales. 'The press have found out that we have the Diviner. It's a circus. They've surrounded the base.'

'I don't care.' Megan goes over to their desk. 'I don't care how many people are out there, tell them the leak got their information wrong.'

'Send them away,' Dad says. 'You've done it before.'

'Megan, work with me. How can we make the Diviner happen?' Mia asks. 'What if we gave you a disguise? We could protect your identity?'

Mum snorts.

'Black veil?' Megan lifts her eyebrows. 'No thanks.'

'It wouldn't have to be a veil,' Mia says. 'There are other ways to protect your identity. Ways that would make you look more like a hero. I saw you in action yesterday; the HPA needs you.'

'Nice idea, but the HPA will shoehorn me into the mould left by the last Diviner. She knew it and so do I. No deal.' Megan's arms are crossed. She's digging her heels in and she's right. If Megan gives up control now, she might never get it back.

I don't know why Mia expected me to side against my sister. I can feel my parents next to me, almost vibrating with the desire to grab Megan and get her as far from the HPA as possible. And I might be a HPA hero, but I'm not going to pressure her to join. Megan needs to share her gift with the world on her own terms.

'Mother Earth!' I burst out. My fingers scrabble for the piece of paper in my pocket. 'The last prophecy.' I can't get my words out fast enough. 'Megan's emergence prophecy. It has another line. Ron kept it from the public, but Prince #2 gave it to me before he got on the helicopter.'

Everyone looks at me, confused.

'It has another line!' I wave the paper at them.

Mum grabs it off me. *'The Diviner does not love. She does not judge. She does not lie. Her role is to see ...'* She looks down at me. 'Until the one who comes after me?'

Mia races round their desk to take it. 'This is Ron's handwriting. He was the only one with access to the Diviner's last book of prophecies and, after he left, I was so busy that I ... but he ... He edited the prophecy.'

We all look at Megan, but she's looking at Emily. 'Until the one who comes after me.' Her voice is quiet.

Emily walks to her hesitantly. 'Does that mean?'

Megan doesn't answer; she reaches for Emily and pulls her into a kiss.

'What the feck is happening?!' I look at Mum, who wears a resigned expression, like she's been watching this coming for a while. Dad is frowning down at his feet.

'What the actual feck?' I repeat.

They're still kissing. I don't know how I feel about this. My sister can be the Diviner and still fall in love, which is wonderful, but with *Emily*? Skies. I thought she had more taste than that.

Mia clears their throat and the two break apart. 'The Rays really love hard, don't they?'

'Sorry.' Megan is blushing and she doesn't sound remotely sorry. For once, Emily doesn't look like she's able to speak. Her lips are parted but there's no sarcastic comment coming. She's looking at Megan like she's the sun breaking through the clouds, like she's light and life and everything. My gut twists. I should be happy for my sister, but my selfish brain has gone right back to Blaze lying in that hospital bed.

'OK.' Megan takes the prophecy from Mia. 'I can work with this, but there are some things I want to discuss first.'

Mia sits back behind their desk. 'The floor is yours, Megan Ray.'

The murmur of the press seeps through the door, but my pulse is steady and my lungs are full. They're not here for me.

'Mother Earth.' Megan pinches her waist. 'I think I'm going to throw up.'

'I don't think Mia will forgive you if you puke on that suit.' I nod at the tailored white suit that was selected for the big announcement and Megan bends, creasing it more. 'Breathe, big sister.' I rub her back, small circles, my hands gliding over the smooth fabric of her blazer. 'Concentrate on the exhales. Breathe out, two, three, four.'

Megan straightens as she exhales and looks up and down the empty corridor. 'Am I doing the right thing?'

I take her hand. 'You're Megan Ray. What do you think?'

'That I've got the power to make a difference.' Her hands are heavy in mine. For once, she's letting me take the weight. 'That we've got the power to make a difference.'

I shrug. 'We always did.'

My sister holds my gaze, our hands entwined. Her eyes flash white, but only for a moment. 'We're going to help people. Lots of them.' The echo fades from her voice before she's finished speaking.

'I know,' I say, and for a heartbeat it's like I can see the future too.

'Ready?' Mia clicks down the corridor to join us.

'Ready.' Megan releases me and plants a slobbery kiss on my cheek.

'Oh, come on!' I wriggle free and watch as Mia leads my sister through the door to announce her to the world. I could slip into the back of the room, and stand with my parents to watch history being made, but instead I lean against the wall and listen to the gasps coming through the door.

'I am not going to be another faceless servant.' Megan's voice carries, as confident in front of the entire world as she is in our kitchen.

In the hubbub that follows, a voice that can only be Carrie Le Roux, *Take Five Magazine*, calls out; 'Who are you wearing, Megan? Is that your official hero suit or will you be looking for some input from your fans?'

'Who am I wearing?' Megan has definitely raised her eyebrows. 'I can literally see the future, are you sure that's the question you want to ask?'

There's a beat before Carrie responds. 'Good point. Do you know who's going to win *Lovestruck Manor*?'

'What gives you the right to disregard the previous Diviner's last prophecy?' That sharp question can only be from Ian Collins.

Things quieten down, but I guess they're pulling out the Diviner's book of prophecies and showing that Ron had edited the prophecy that foretold my sister.

Another uproar, which Mia's voice cuts through. 'Ron kept the last line hidden because he didn't want things to change,' they say. 'The old system worked for him and men like him, but it brought us to the brink of disaster. It's time to try something new. Our new HPA will be prioritising kindness over control and we hope, in time, other HPAs will follow our lead. A new approach to the EV, a new approach to our powered population, and our heroes will be free to love whoever they choose.'

'Even other heroes?' a shocked Sydney asks.

'Whoever they choose,' Mia repeats. 'Love isn't something we should have ever tried to control.'

In the stunned silence that follows this, I slip away. I know what comes next. They'll talk about the database that we're setting up to share the Diviner's visions with the world. They'll explain that the Villains are officially joining with the HPA and that Femi, the Controller, will return as the deputy leader. They'll announce that Mia's plans have the support of the heroes and that the HPA is, finally, evolving.

I cannot wait to see the headlines for this.

NEW REBEL DIVINER SHOWS FACE AND SHARES VISIONS

and

MIA KAPLAN BANISHES THE GHOST OF RON

And I'll go back to the ward, because if there's enough hope for a better future, for a world that's kinder, more understanding and more accepting, then maybe there's hope for Laurie Lin too.

Where EXACTLY has Blaze gone?

By Sarah Popkin for H-Mail Online

53 shares

Mere months ago, this country got a new hero. He had the smile, the body, the powers, and, eventually, the Love Interest. Baby Blaze, the protégé of one disgraced, deceased King Ron. So, where exactly is Blaze now?

We all saw the headlines. HEROIC BATTLE, they said. PLAN TO DESTROY THE EV AVERTED, they said. KING RON AND SHELLY TAYLOR DIE IN HELICOPTER EXPLOSION, they said. (RIP Shelly Taylor, generous friend of the *H-Mail*.) That was over a month ago and there's been no sign of Blaze since. It's like he disappeared too in that big mess outside the Castle.

And who EXACTLY is Pari, this new lady hero (I know, ANOTHER ONE) who is zipping around saving the day?!

Yes, we all read the statement, Pari's powers were taken by Ron and returned by Blaze, but do we actually believe the HPA? It's quite convenient, isn't it, to pin it all on a dead man? I'm just going to say what everyone is thinking – did this Pari somehow steal Blaze's powers? Is this systematic removal of men the next terrible step of the woke agenda that will destroy the world as we know it?

370

Yes, I'm grateful that the new Diviner has finally shown up (Jenna Ray's sister??? Literally no one checked that family, did they?!). But what is she doing? What happened to the veil? The dress? What happened to tradition?

Look at the state of our nation now. The HPA has surrendered to the Villains. There is not one but four female heroes, including the blonde with the attitude problem and the oh-so-visible Diviner. Yes, the Controller might be back, but honestly, who even missed him? And their BIG NEW PLAN: to plant flowers and make nice with the EV.

We're all doomed.

CHAPTER 37

The class falls silent as I swing open the door. Even the teacher is staring at me. He's new this year, so I guess he doesn't even have the backstory of Jenna Ray, the anxious swimmer. To him, I'm just a hero.

Joy tuts loudly from the back. 'Late for your first year thirteen psychology lesson.' Everyone titters and the tension breaks. Our teacher frowns at her.

'It's fine, of course, Jenna.' He waves me in and I head to the seat at the back next to Joy. 'The HPA made us aware of your, er, schedule and the, um, tsunami. I'm afraid you are still …'

He gestures to the floor and I see a trail of seawater following me through the classroom. Mother Earth! I was in such a rush to get here I didn't even dry my hero suit before slinging my uniform over the top.

'Sorry!' I use my power to dry myself and the floor and

smile hopefully at the teacher, who just goggles at me. I've completely derailed his lesson and, maybe, his brain.

'That's too cool,' one of my classmates mutters as I slip into the chair next to Joy.

The teacher claps his hands, attempting to regain control. 'That is cool, and it's nice to meet you, Jenna. I'm afraid that it's also the end of the lesson.'

Skies! I glance at my wrist piece. It hasn't updated the time zone! I muffle my groan. It's day one of school and I've managed to miss all of my classes.

'I'm so sorry.' I stop by the teacher's desk on my way out.

'Don't worry.' He gives me a smile, already adapting to having a hero in the group. 'We recorded the lesson for you, I'll email it over. I think you'll enjoy it.' He quirks his eyebrows at me. 'We're starting with the hero complex.'

'What drives the hero?' Joy loops her arm through mine and steers me out of the room. 'Where do the id and the super-ego meet?' We fall into step heading down the corridor, like we have so many times before.

'How was the big date?' I slip from Joy's grip and walk backward, in front of her, so I can pull her hands to my heart. 'The gorgeous cinema boy who now works on the pirate boat because his old workplace burned to the ground. The quirky shop girl who goes out of her way to flirt with him on the harbourside. The romantic picnic on the beach.' I sigh. 'It's like a romcom. Tell me everything.'

She scrunches her nose at me.

'It was that good?'

'He was fine.' She spins me so I don't crash into the door, and we push our way out into the warm September sun. 'He's got nice arms and he's funny. He's taking a couple of years before going to art school, so he'll be around for a while, it's just …'

We weave through the gaggle of students at the school gates and I get remarkably little attention. Perhaps there was an assembly about leaving me alone, or perhaps I'm less special now that the HPA have Megan, Emily and Pari, not to mention the Controller, or perhaps, today, on the first day of the new school year, everyone is busy with their own stories.

'Just …' I prompt Joy.

She tilts her head at me. 'I think I like being single.'

'Mother Earth.' I stop dead. 'Who are you and what have you done with Joy?'

She whacks my arm. 'I'm allowed to evolve, Jenna. I was with Nick for two years. I gave him the best years of my teens. It's nice to see who I am without him.' She jogs down on to the path into town and I follow. 'Back at the bonfire, I wished to be strong, like you, and I think, maybe, I am. I'm sure there's more romance in my future, but, for now, I'm just Joy and that's the way I like it.'

This makes me warm, inside and out. 'You've always been strong, Joy Jusic.'

She grins at me. 'I mean, yeah … I'm pretty awesome. Remember that time I picked you up on the Wild Road?'

The harbour bridge is busy with tourists and parents herding their kids back from the primary school, but we manage to find a clear bit of wall and lean over to watch the rippling turquoise water.

'And there's no change?' Joy always asks about Blaze and I love her for it.

'Not yet.' That's always my answer. Not yet. The doctors have no idea when he'll wake. They keep using words like 'if' and 'might'.

If he wakes …

Blaze might pull through …

I don't have time for 'if', and 'might' can get in the bin.

'Did your sister and Emily make up?'

I roll my eyes. The ongoing Megan and Emily drama is like something from a soap. 'They made up. Megan had another vision and realised the 'other woman' was actually her with different hair.'

Joy whistles. 'What a mess.'

'Right?' Megan has been scribbling and investigating visions along with a team of researchers, led by Mum. But the more private visions are a whole different drama. There aren't a whole team of geniuses piecing things together, there's just Megan, occasionally me, and Emily yelling, *'What am I going to do now?!'*

'I guess the other Diviners didn't have these relationship dramas,' Joys says.

'Or they just didn't write them down.' A seagull hovers in front of us, riding the air currents. Its eyes are normal pale orbs. The number of possessed animals and people is slowly dropping now that people are looking at what is causing the EV to react. It's a slow process. A slow, painful process. Apparently, Shelly wasn't alone in caring more about profits than the fate of the world.

'All right.' I push myself up. 'I should get going.'

'All right.' Joy gets up too. 'Attack hug!' Her arms squeeze me like a vice and then she's gone, rushing off to our old workplace, Lighthouse Souvenirs. Sadness flutters through my chest, but I'll see her later.

'Tomas wants to debrief about the tsunami at four.' Megan is waiting for me at security. She's in jeans and her fluffy pink jumper with a lanyard around her neck.

'You're not the boss of me,' I say, even though she sort of is. She's now full-time at the HPA, assisting Mia alongside recording her visions. Perhaps the HPA could have won her over sooner if they'd explained that she could leave her job at the bank.

'Come on, little sister.' She pats me on the head and I duck away. 'I'll walk with you. There's something I want to talk to you about.'

'All right.' Security finish their scan and I walk with her down the corridor.

'So …' She swings her arms by her sides. 'You know how Mum has moved back home, and Femi has moved on to the base?'

'Yes …' We stop outside the doors to medical. I also live in the house where our parents have reunited and spend hour upon hour gazing at each other. The walk is too short for Megan to skirt around her point like this.

'Well …' Megan looks at me and takes a breath. A sudden conspiratorial smile spreads across her face. 'Well … I think that Pari and Mia might, you know …' She meshes her fingers together.

'What!' I lean in and drop my voice. 'Tell me everything. Is this your gaydar or a vision?'

Her grin fades. 'Skies,' she mutters. 'Gaydar, and I'm sorry, I was trying to distract you and it absolutely worked. Maybe you should work on your focus with Tomas.'

I lift my hands up. 'What's going on?!'

'I'm moving out,' she blurts, staring at the ceiling. 'And moving in with Emily and Pari in the barn.'

'Oh.' My heart glows again and the heat is bittersweet. I don't want Megan to leave home, but I know deep down she stayed for me. Now she's got a chance to spread her wings. 'That's brilliant!' I say decisively.

'Really?' Her eyes are back on mine. They see so much. How can they not see how happy I am for her?

'Of course. It's by the river, so I can come by all the time.'

Relief lights up her face as she smiles at me.

'All the time,' I repeat menacingly, and she laughs.

The door thuds into my back and I jump out of the way.

'Sorry!' Pari slips out. She's been visiting Blaze again. 'Jenna!' She grasps my arm. 'I left him some incense and we listened to a meditation track almost the entire way through.' She's moved, now standing on the other side of Megan. 'I have a good feeling about today, I do. And I'm looking forward to training tomorrow, I've got an idea for taking Emily down. You and me as a team.'

A team. With Pari, the girl, well, the lady, with the powers of speed and flight. I am trying to treat her as her own person rather than someone who isn't Blaze, but it's odd. Blaze had a stillness to him that isn't at all evident in Pari. She is as unstoppable and unpredictable as the wind.

'Sounds good.' I smile at her and she blurs.

'Pari, Mia asked if … oh, she's gone.' Megan looks up and down the corridor. 'Mother Earth, we need to get some treacle on her shoes. I should catch her up.' Megan squeezes my shoulder. 'Tomas at four, OK?'

'All right.' I glance at my wrist piece as I push my way into medical. I only have fifteen minutes before I need to find Tomas, but it's enough to fill Blaze in on everything that's happened today.

No. That's not his name any more. He's Laurie now. Laurie Lin, the boy who gave up everything to save the world.

Tendrils of smoky incense drift through the air above him, leaving trails of spice, but he looks the same as always. His eyes are closed and his breathing is quiet. I sit in my seat and shuffle the chair slightly closer so I can hold his hand.

'Hi, Laurie. Today was intense. I was late for school because of a tsunami in the Pacific.' I fold myself over to lay my head on his chest. His heartbeat is as strong as ever. 'Tomas and I have been working on dispersals. The tsunami had too much water to catch and send back, but I managed to evaporate most of it. I think it's going to be raining there for a while. Qaqa was there too, he tried to get me to stay for something called kava but Tomas told him off. Emily chose a hero name, Ms Amazing. I

378

think she was taking the piss, but it's stuck. I'm still thinking about mine. Maybe Ripple? Like a small action that leads to bigger things? I don't know. I miss you.'

It slips out. I can't help it. I always try to be positive, to come in with news that will make him want to wake up and rejoin me. I've told him about all the changes at the HPA. I've kept him updated about school and Joy and everything else going on in my life. I won't come in here every day and tell him about the hollow feeling of loss in my core that would drag me under if I let it.

'Sorry.' I rub my thumb across his knuckles. 'Oh, did I tell you? When you wake up, Dr Varma wants to take you on as an apprentice. He said you were too clever to be a hero anyway. He also told me where your family live. You said they were too far to visit but they're only in Wales. We'll go when you … When you wake up …' Tears roll down my cheek and soak into his blanket. 'I miss you and I love you, Laurie Lin.' Why won't this pain stay inside? It's my job to bring Laurie hope. 'There aren't Love Interests any more, but when you wake up, I'll ask you to be something. I don't know. Labels.' This is snotty sadness, but I can't stop myself. 'You're so much more than a Love Interest. You're so much more—'

There's the tiniest bit of pressure on my hand. I freeze. He squeezes my hand again.

'Laurie,' I whisper, sitting up slowly. My pulse thumps in my ears and I almost can't bear to look.

His eyes are open. Kind, brave, brown eyes, looking up at me from his pillow. He blinks, like he's woken up from the longest sleep.

'It's a terrible name for a hero, Ripple.' He clears his throat and struggles up. I reach out to support him and the moment I touch the warmth of his back I could dissolve, but instead I hand him some water.

'What ... what do you think it should be?' I ask softly.

'What about Torrent?'

'Torrent ...' I repeat. Like the water I wield or the events that smashed into us, one after the other, bringing us together. 'It's perfect.'

I help him take another drink and quickly retrace all my words since suggesting the name 'Ripple'. Feck.

I said everything.

Mother Earth. I should run and get a doctor, but his eyes hold me still.

'You asked me to be your Love Interest?' he says quietly. 'Sort of.'

'I'm sorry. You don't have to.' I wish I could take it back. He's just woken up and I'm pressuring him into deciding what shape his new life will take.

His eyes crinkle at me. 'But what if I want to? The hero and the Love Interest, Jenna and Laurie. Two people who can love in a way that's right for them. Two people finally and completely in charge of their own story.'

My happiness is salt water gathering in my eyes. I can't find the right words, but Laurie can.

'You love and support me,' he says. 'And I'll love and support you. How about that?'

The emotions inside me are almost too big to handle. I

know I need to be gentle with him, so I lean forward and press my lips to his. The glow of my heart erupts; love flows through me like fire, igniting every cell. I draw back and we gaze at each other, face to face on the brink of the rest of our lives. I hold out my hand.

'You've got yourself a deal.'

Acknowledgements

Writing a second book (and an epic superhero conclusion) was always going to be a journey, but thanks to the generous help of a lot of people it happened! And we've made a book I love with all my heart.

Christabel McKinley, my agent (and an editorial sniper), went above and beyond to help me get a worthy sequel out into the world. *The Hero Complex*'s editor, Katie Ager, was endlessly patient and kind, and her fresh eyes brought brilliant new ideas to the Nine Trees universe. And *The Love Interest*'s editor, Carla Hutchinson, pulled threads out of book one for me to follow into the sequel and helped to get this story off the ground.

Thank you to the Bloomsbury UK dream team – Bea Cross, Sophie Roswell, Tim Hardy, Danielle Rippengill and Jessica Bellman – and Camille Kellogg and Briana Williams in the US, as well as wonderful sensitivity reader Krish Jeyakumar and genius cover illustrator Sarah Madden. The book looks beautiful, makes sense, has increased empowerisation (which should be a word) and actually made it into your hands thanks to them.

As always, thank you to my writing community, my brilliant beta readers Carly Lee, Natalie Harrison (genius behind

The Drunken Diviner), and Megan Small. Thank you to author James Brogden, who talked me through writing battles, the Bath Spa MAWFYP community, which is endlessly supportive, and my writing wife, Ash Bond, who rode the Book Two roller-coaster with me as she got her sequel out too.

A belated shout-out to my pal Aled William Thomas, who helped me come up with the idea for a robot sidekick during a walk in sunny Cardiff, and thank you to all of my super-supportive friends and family who haven't got bored of my book chat yet. And thank you, always, to my (more than) Love Interest, Gareth, and our sidekick, Cocoa Bean the staffy, who stopped me spiralling by bringing me cake (Gareth) and tug toys (Cocoa).

And you. Did you think I'd forgotten you? I guess you've read two of my books now, so thank you, dearest reader. You're my favourite.

Helen x

Oh, and also …

Sometime later

'And it's Cheche again?! Are Roo and Vitesse with him?' I've made it into my hero suit in record time and Laurie is already loading up my belt.

'We've got to assume they are,' Laurie replies, pushing something into a pouch. 'The Castle really isn't as high security as we all thought it was.'

'Wait, what was that? It felt heavy.'

'I had to reinforce your emergency beacon, Jenna Ray.' Laurie uses my belt to twist me so I'm facing him. His brown eyes are narrowed in mock anger. 'Because you blasted the last one at a bad guy.'

'Actually, Laurie Lin, when I'm suited up, it's Torrent.' I quirk my eyebrows at him and he pulls me against him. Hero suit, tracksuit, lab coat, it doesn't matter what this boy wears, he is delicious in a way that sparks joy through my entire body.

'I'm terribly sorry, Torrent.' He closes the distance between our lips and I melt. At the back of my mind, I know there's something important that I should be doing, but the suggestions being offered by my body are *run your hands up his back, twist your fingers through his hair, pull him closer to you.*

'For feck's sake, every time!' Emily cries as the lab door bangs open. 'Lovebirds! There's. An. Emergency.' She punctuates each word with a clap and I sigh as I pull my lips back from Laurie's. 'Your sister has foreseen dire consequences.'

'On our tracker, which says there's a high chance of an EV reaction.' Megan sticks her head in to clarify. She pecks Emily on the lips and rushes off to the control room.

'And I'll need to trial the new blaster,' Emily adds hopefully.

'Why?' I ask at the same time as Laurie says, 'Absolutely not.'

'Can I take the blaster?' Pari has appeared, as if from nowhere. It's been months and her sudden arrivals still make my heart squeeze.

'You can take whatever you like,' Laurie tells Pari with a fond smile. Emily throws up her hands in outrage. 'Because *you*, Pari, treat the equipment with respect,' he adds.

'Are we ready?' Tomas is leaning on the lab door. 'You might need to detach, Ray.'

I hadn't realised that my joined hands had come to settle on the small of Laurie's back. Holding him close, exactly where I need him. 'Right.' I release him, but his fingers are still hooked into my belt.

'Be careful,' he murmurs, so focused on me that he misses the new blaster floating past.

'Don't worry, we'll look after her, Nerd-boy.' Emily catches the blaster and marches past Tomas into the corridor. 'Ms Amazing and her Amazingets assemble!'

386

'That's not what we're calling ourselves, is it?' Pari hurries after her. 'I had some other ideas …'

Tomas sighs. 'I'll get that weapon off her.'

And they're gone, leaving me and Laurie alone again in the lab. I tap my earpiece. 'Testing.'

'Loud and clear,' Laurie murmurs into my free ear, and releases me.

'Dinner with your family tonight,' I remind him.

'My brothers are making pancakes. They are *excited*.' He grins at me. 'Think you'll have the energy to go the long way?'

'I've always got the energy to swim with you.'

The day on Hidden Beach when Laurie waded into the water to share my bubble with me is easily the most terrified I've seen him, but now he's addicted to shooting through the sea with me. Maybe it's because he gets to recapture some of his old speed, or maybe it's because of how tight I hold him as we hurtle through the waves. I give him a last kiss and rush after my team.

'*Go get 'em, Torrent,*' Laurie says in my earpiece.

And it doesn't matter that Emily, the absolute hypocrite, is pretending to vomit. I rush to battle beside her, with Pari blurring ahead, and Laurie Lin's kiss lingering on my lips.

We're off to save the world again, and I am ready.

Mental health charities for young people

Jenna struggles with her anxiety throughout the story and I wanted to include a few UK-wide organisations where you can find advice and support for your mental health. For a more extensive list, visit mind.org.uk.

Anxiety UK

Anxiety UK is a user-led organisation that supports anyone with anxiety, phobias, panic attacks or other anxiety-related disorders. **03444 775 774**
anxietyuk.org.uk

CALM

CALM (Campaign Against Living Miserably) is a helpline for young males aged 16 to 35 years suffering from depression and low self-esteem. It offers counselling, advice and information. **0800 58 58 58**
thecalmzone.net

Mind

Mind provide advice and support to empower anyone experiencing a mental health issue. They campaign to improve services, raise awareness and promote understanding. **0300 123 3393**

mind.org.uk

The Mix

The Mix is the UK's free, confidential helpline service for young people under 25 who need help but don't know where to turn. **0808 808 4994**

themix.org.uk/mental-health

Nightline

Nightline is a student listening service which is open at night and run by students for students. Every night of term, trained student volunteers answer calls, emails, instant messages, texts and talk in person to their fellow university students about anything that's troubling them.

nightline.ac.uk

Young Minds

Young Minds provides information, advice and training for young people, parents, carers and professionals.

youngminds.org.uk

Helen Comerford writes funny and fantastical tales, with diverse casts of characters, for children and young adults. She is fuelled by a love of all things super-powered, feminism and chocolate raisins. When she's not writing, you can find Helen hiking around the Welsh countryside with her dog, Cocoa.

helencomerfordauthor.com